His Dark Charms

LUCKY ME

USA TODAY BESTSELLING AUTHOR

GENEVIEVE JACK

Lucky Me: His Dark Charms, Book 1

Copyright © Genevieve Jack 2022

Published by Carpe Luna Ltd, Bloomington, IL 61704

First Edition: October 2022

Cover art by Hang Le

Paperback: 978-1-940675-87-9

v 4.0

He's lucky as sin, and we're playing for keeps.

For sixteen years, I've lived unlawfully among humans, supporting myself by playing poker. But concealing my fae identity isn't easy. When a high stakes game goes terribly wrong, only one person stands between me and lifelong servitude—Seven.

Seven Delaney runs his corner of Dragonfly Hollow with the insufferable arrogance you'd expect from someone born lucky. Not only did the sexy fae billionaire break my heart, he's responsible for the most humiliating experience of my life and is the reason I fled that fairy realm.

Returning to Dragonfly Hollow is my only way out, but there's a price. Seven requires my help, and my pixie talents, to solve a case that threatens fae society's tentative relationship with humans. I promised myself I'd never get involved with him again, but his dark charms prove hard to resist. The closer we get to solving this mystery, the harder it becomes to keep my distance. And the clearer it is that if we don't learn to trust each other again, our luck might just run out.

DEDICATION

This book is dedicated to all those striving to make the best of an unlucky start in life.

OUR AMERICAN HERITAGE

INDIGENOUS FAE IN THE AMERICAS

Fairies, or the fae, as they've come to be called, were thought to be mythical creatures for most of American history. It wasn't until 1863, when the seelie king Kieran made himself known to Union Major General George Meade, that fae existence appears in any historical documents. Meade's journals describe the fae as "... seeming entirely human but demonstrating strange and little-understood powers." At Meade's request, Kieran and his fae army assisted Union forces during the second day of the Battle of Gettysburg. The fae neutralized eleven confederate brigades without lifting a single weapon, changing the course of the Civil War. Without their intervention, General Lee might have succeeded with his offensive attack on the North.

For a short time following the end of the Civil War, the fae lived among humans and were lauded as heroes. But with their arrival came the discovery of Devashire, a region within the Appalachian Mountains on the border between North Carolina and Tennessee, previously hidden from and unknown to humans. The United States government, wishing to claim these lands for expansion, invoked the 1851 Indian Appropriations Act and attempted to move the fae to a reservation west of the Mississippi as they had done numerous other native peoples.

Kieran refused, and his army proved too much for Reconstruction-era troops to best. In a historic accord, President Andrew Johnson designated Devashire a self-contained and self-governed territory completely independent of the United States. In exchange, Kieran agreed that no fairies would be permitted to reside outside Devashire. Although it is generally acknowledged that the US federal government occasionally pays handsomely for the help of the fae under special circumstances, it is still illegal for the fae to live among humans.

Today, American citizens can visit a village in Devashire called Dragonfly Hollow where visitors can learn about the fae for a daily fee. A theme park, casino, and education center have been erected in Dragonfly and are popular with tourists. Devashire now generates revenue approximately equal to the gross national product of Germany.

Back in 1863, fae powers were never fully understood. Even the human brigades involved directly had no explanation for why their mere presence seemed to change the course of the war. Although many hypothesized fae *magic* was to thank, according to the experts at Dragonfly Hollow, fairies wield one thing and one thing only—*luck*.

ONE

There are only three times in life when everyone is equal: the moment we're born, the moment we die, and the moment we sit down at the poker table. Poker is the great equalizer. The cards don't give a shit what you look like. They don't care where you started from. All that matters is the hand you're dealt and how you play the game.

I love poker, but then you might say I'm lucky.

Luck is something I've been intimately familiar with since I was three and I learned that with a little focus I could make an ice cream cone drop from a human's hand into my own. My mother was furious that day. I licked that mint-chocolate-chip miracle so fast the human didn't want it back.

Since then, I've discovered I'm not the luckiest fae in existence or the smartest, but I know how to make the most of what I've got. I'm living proof that sometimes the hand we're dealt isn't the whole story.

Sometimes we can bluff.

Not that I prefer to lie. It would be a relief to have the

privilege to be myself if doing so didn't come with grave consequences. Out of necessity, I've been living a lie for sixteen years now, from the time I got knocked up by a human man and left my fairy homeland. Living as an undocumented fae among humans can be a bitch, but it's taught me how to make the best of a raw deal.

Today the player across the poker table fits that description. He's a vexation, a thorn in my side. For the course of this game, I've referred to him as Mr. Fidget in my head. Mr. Fidget has a name, but I keep forgetting it because until this moment I would have bet my left tit he'd run out of chips long before this.

Fidget is a newbie. None of the regulars have ever heard of him. He's young, maybe thirty, and dressed more like an accountant than a poker pro, in a pair of khakis and a checkered dress shirt straight off a clearance rack. He never stops bobbing his knee or riffling his chips. It's annoying as hell.

It's one in the afternoon, and the room I'm in reeks of billowy floral cologne, stale smoke, and the sickly sweet essence of spilled liquor. I'm experiencing a stomach-clenching, throat-constricting anxiety that flails inside me like a trapped octopus. No one would ever know. From the outside, I maintain a carefully curated impassivity, as cool and collected as one of the marble statues in front of Caesar's Palace. Nothing to see here. Just a human woman holding a few cards, ordinary as can be. I'm no threat at all. Focus on the other players.

I need this win.

The pot could finally buy my daughter the life she deserves, the life I left Devashire to give her. A normal human life, free of lies. Free of constantly looking over her shoulder.

Casually, I toy with Kiko, the shiny gold maneki-neko (aka Japanese lucky cat) who sits atop my chips. I relish the bubbly rush of luck she feeds me and direct it at the deck shuffler beside the dealer. It's a fae thing. Wielding luck is a talent each of us possesses at varying levels. As a pixie, I'm certainly not as powerful as others of my kind, but you might say I've made the most of my talents.

The machine whirs, spits out a deck, and the dealer flicks out the cards with crisp precision. I turn up the corners of my two and find that the luck I've spent on the shuffle has paid off: pocket aces.

Mr. Fidget's eyes dart wildly between his cards and my face. He swallows hard. He has the small blind, which means he was a C-note in before we even saw our cards. Action folds to me, and I raise. He calls. The big blind, not wanting to get mixed up in things, smartly folds. The dealer rakes our chips into the pot, and now it's heads-up, just him and me.

I school my features as the flop is dealt. Ace of clubs, ten of clubs, nine of spades. And just like that, my pocket aces become three of a kind. Across from me, Mr. Fidget is sweating bullets and generally looks like his heart might fail at any moment.

He mops his brow with a cocktail napkin. "All in," he mumbles.

At the moment, I have what we call in poker terms the stone-cold nuts, the strongest hand given the situation, but I know a flush and a gut-shot straight draw are possibilities. Is he all in with a draw? Any decent player knows I've got great odds... and with my luck, I call. Here we go. Let's say goodbye to Mr. Fidget.

The turn drops. Ace of clubs. Four of a kind. It takes effort not to grin like a cat with a mouse between its paws. Mr. Fidget holds his breath as the dealer flips the river.

The jack of clubs. Interesting. I've dosed the deck with a heavy amount of luck, and it's a good thing because if I didn't know better, I might be worried. The makings of a royal flush lay on the table.

It's time to show our cards. When I tip my four of a kind, I can no longer hold back a self-satisfied grin, but Mr. Fidget doesn't react as expected. He goes perfectly still, no longer moving or sweating. He's transformed into someone older, cooler, and somehow smoother. A man who belongs in a Lexus commercial. A player in nerd clothing.

Without breaking eye contact, he flips his cards and my heart stops. All the tiny hairs on my body stand on end. King and queen of clubs. Royal flush. He wins.

As the dealer rakes my chips and the crowd applauds, Mr. Fidget makes eye contact and smiles for the first time. Warning bells ring inside my head, and fear stabs an icy tendril into my heart. His teeth gleam with the slightest hint of blue.

I snatch Kiko from the table and storm for the exit, trying to look like a disappointed pro rather than a terrified illegal alien. I drain the last morsels of luck from Kiko's belly and pray this isn't what I fear it is.

People call out to me. Faces blur in my haste for the exit. As fast as my muscles will move, I weave through the crowd and out onto the Strip. I want to deny it. I want to be wrong. But there is only one thing that can turn a human's teeth that shade of indigo: blue iron. And there's only one department whose agents drink it regularly for its luck-neutralizing effects, the Fairy Immigration and Rehabilitation Enforcement agency (FIRE).

Mr. Fidget explodes out the door behind me, and I pour

on the speed, no longer even attempting to move at the same pace as the humans around me. He's gaining on me anyway. Damn, the man is in great shape for a human. I push my luck again, and a gaggle of scantily clad dancers in tall headdresses flood out of the nearest doorway and into the space between us. The distraction buys me precious distance. I duck into the Venetian, thinking I've lost him, but seconds later he's barreling through the doors, a cruel blue smile turning his lips. He's enjoying this.

I push my luck again and hear a grunt as an exceedingly large man slips on a discarded bag of chips and lands in front of him. That shot of luck was meant for Mr. Fidget, but the blue iron in his blood makes him immune. He steps over the man and relentlessly continues his pursuit.

My breath comes in huffs as I speed walk deeper into the casino and spend what remains of my luck to change my appearance. I go from brunette to blond and add a few pounds. Only I've used most of my luck on the game. I don't have enough juice to change my clothing, and I won't be able to hold the illusion for long. *Fuck*! He's drawn me down to almost nothing. I realize in full Technicolor horror that was his aim all along. Fidget's erratic play was meant to bottom me out the entire time.

I zig and zag through a dense cluster of gamblers and duck into the nearest restroom. A group of women celebrating a bachelorette party crowds the mirror. Without calling attention to myself, I rush into the last stall, lock the door, and draw my feet up so that they can't be seen from the outside.

This better work. I am dry, as is Kiko. If I push again, I'll overdraw my reserves, and for a fae, being overdrawn is deadly. Luck is a force. It's limited, like energy. A marathon runner can pour on the adrenaline and force themselves to use more than they actually have, but just like Pheidippi-des, who died when he reached his destination, fairies who overspend their luck welcome disaster. My father used to say, "An empty bucket can be filled with anything, Sophia. Never completely empty your bucket." It's one of the few ways fae can be seriously injured or killed.

I huddle, perched on the toilet, sure I've lost him, until the screams of the bachelorette party fill the bathroom.

"Get out," Fidget orders, his voice laced with malice. A few of the girls curse and threaten to call security, but their voices fade as they rush out the door. I hold perfectly still, taking slow, steady breaths.

Fidget slams the door of the first stall open.

I shiver. Out of the corner of my eye, my blond hair changes back to dark brown. My illusion fizzles like a burnt-out match. I'm out of luck. Closer, he bangs another door and then another. Only two more to go to get to mine. I have to act.

Crashing through the door, I bolt, slip past his grabbing hands, and dash back into the casino. I don't make it. He tackles me from behind, and my face slaps the floor. His boot stomps on my back before I even have a chance to register the pain.

"Stay down," he orders. Like I have a choice. He twists my arms behind my back. Blue-iron cuffs snap onto my wrists. Then Fidget pokes a needle into my arm and through a dangerous smile says, "Nighty night."

TWO

The moment I become conscious again, it's clear I'm in a world of shit. I'm naked, strapped facedown on a cold metal table in what looks like a surgical suite. Machines beep. A tray of needles rests near my head. Blue-iron cuffs clamped on my wrists and ankles keep me drained of all luck, leaving my head throbbing and my stomach nauseated.

Every part of me wants to panic. Anyone would in this situation. My heart races, and my palms sweat. But I know that how I handle the next several minutes could mean the difference between deportation and freedom. The stakes are too high for me to fuck this up, and the surest way to do that is by going on tilt—that's the poker term for when emotions cause a player to act illogically. It's something I'm practiced at avoiding, and I call on that skill now.

I don't struggle or scream. Neither will do any good anyway. Steadying my breath, I close my eyes and pretend to be asleep. A human would suffer the effects of anesthesia far longer than a fae, and my only hope right now is to introduce a sliver of doubt that I am anything but human.

"Might as well open your eyes," Fidget says. "I can tell by your heartbeat you're awake."

Fuck! I open my eyes.

"Name?" he commands.

"Soho Lane," I say immediately. "All my papers are in my purse. I am an American citizen."

He casts his gaze to the side as if my answer deeply disappoints him. "Let's try this again. I'm Agent Andrew Donovan of the Fairy Immigration and Rehabilitation Enforcement agency. You are an undocumented fae whom I've caught defrauding unsuspecting humans under the guise of being a human poker player, alias Soho Lane. We both know Soho Lane isn't real."

"It's the only name I have," I insist, and the lie comes so easily that in the moment I believe it.

"Tell me your real name now and admit what you are, or I'll have Dr. Pain prove it the hard way. Just so you know, Dr. Pain isn't his real name either, but he's earned the right to the pseudonym."

I almost wet myself when a masked man in scrubs steps into view. I've never been inside a rehabilitation facility before, but I've heard stories. Despite the name, no rehabilitation happens here. This is a place where the government uses fairies for their own ends. This is a place where fae like me disappear.

I lick my parched lips. Whatever Dr. Pain is going to do to me, nothing I'm willing to say is going to change it. Donovan is a bully, and bullies feed off getting under your skin. I refuse to give him the satisfaction. I decide then that if I'm going down, I'm going down swinging.

I reach for the only weapon at my disposal, my words. "What's *your* nickname, Agent Donovan? Does it start with tiny and end with prick? I know it's not your real name, but *you've earned it.*"

A low chuckle comes from somewhere in the room but is muffled quickly. Donovan's eyes narrow into slits. "Tell me your name," he demands again.

"What type of man has to chain a woman to a table to get what he wants?" I grind out.

Donovan's expression rearranges into a sinister tableau, and he comes closer, crouching down until our faces are level. His cold and empty eyes remind me of a crocodile's. "The type of man I am...," he mumbles, then gives a breathy laugh. "I'll tell you a secret. I'm the type of man who wants to see a woman chained naked to a steel table. I'm the type of man who gets off on hearing her scream. Really does it for me."

I can't help it. He rattles me. I blink twice. I can't keep my voice from trembling as I say, "I am an American citizen. It's against the law for you to hold me here."

A brittle laugh hits me in the face. "Time's up. Looks like we're doing this the fun way." Those reptilian eyes flick up to Dr. Pain. "Do it."

Icy metal touches my bottom rib and scrapes across the skin of my back. I realize too late what he plans to do. A metal hook jabs under my wing flap. How does he even know it's there? Wings retracted, I look exactly like a human! "No... no, no, no!" I scream.

Anatomically, I am in the wrong position to spread my wings. Terror grips me in its razor-sharp claws as I realize this is intentional. The table is designed to arch my back and force my scapulae together, a position that makes it impossible to naturally spread my wings. This isn't about Donovan proving I'm a pixie. This is about torture. It's about forcing the truth from me in the most humiliating and painful way possible.

I scream myself hoarse while Dr. Pain forces my upper left wing out from under my wing flap with his metal hook. Agony sears along my spine, causing my stomach to lurch. I force the contents back down. My scream cuts off, more because I'm out of breath than anything else. Blood splatters the stainless steel beside my face, shiny silver that I notice is already stained with someone else's blood. He unhooks his implement, and shredded gossamer droops limply over my shoulder. I'm just relieved that the wing is still attached to my body.

Agent Donovan grunts. "It always surprises me when they bleed red. You'd think it would be green or purple."

"Yeah," Pain chimes in.

My back aches. I've never experienced this kind of suffering before, this sort of *torture*. But the pain itself isn't enough to crack me; it's what that limp gossamer wing represents. There's no going back now. No lie, trick, or story will make this better. Donovan knows what I am. He has cause to investigate further. And if I don't find a way to distract him, he'll keep digging deeper into my identity.

Soho Lane has an address on her passport. That address is owned by another identity that owns another property. And if he keeps digging, he'll eventually discover my daughter's existence. That can't happen. Not until she has a chance to run. The chips are down. My options are few. The best way I know to keep him focused on me and not on my papers is to cooperate.

"Sophia Larkspur," I blurt. My real name feels strange in my mouth but then it's been sixteen years since anyone has called me by it.

Donovan lowers his ear toward me. "Hmmm? What's that?"

"My name is Sophia Larkspur. I'm a pixie," I say through gritted teeth, my face wet with snot and tears.

He rolls his lips. "Disappointing. Just when things were getting interesting, you cave. Ah well, I guess we'll have to play another day." He turns his head and commands some worker outside my field of vision, "Get her cleaned up and bring her to my office. We start tonight."

AN HOUR LATER, I'M SITTING ON A FOLDING METAL CHAIR BESIDE Agent Donovan's desk. I've never been a religious fairy, but if the goddess does exist, I pray she protects my daughter. I've done everything in my power to protect her myself. We've prepared for this event. Our home is rented under an alias, and the last name she uses for school is a different one altogether. But there are ways, undoubtedly, for them to find her. Things I've missed. I comfort myself by remembering she's a smart girl and I've taught her exactly what to do in this situation. All she has to do is follow through.

I can't take my eyes off Kiko. Donovan's set my lucky cat on top of a stack of file folders like a paperweight. Does he intend to keep her? I frown at the thought. As far as I know, she's one of a kind. The little arm that beckons you is made of blue iron, the only element on earth that can drain a fairy of their luck. But unlike Donovan's cuffs, designed of solid blue iron to both drain and neutralize a fairy's luck, the rest of Kiko is jade, a gem exceptionally suited for storing luck. Normally, I use the arm to siphon off a small amount throughout the day and store it inside Kiko for later use, when my own reserves are low.

I know she's empty at the moment, but my fingers still itch to steal her back, if only for the comfort of having something familiar in my hand. She's been with me a long time. My personal good luck charm, figuratively and literally.

"I'm going to take the cuffs off," Donovan says. "I need you to have a little juice for what we're going to do tonight. Just know that if you direct any of that luck toward anything other than the task at hand, I'll gladly put you back on that table. Every agent in this building has enough blue iron in their blood to take you down five times over. Understood?"

Poker makes you an expert at reading people. Donovan isn't bluffing. The reason I had trouble reading him at the table is precisely because he's a psychopath with zero empathy and a penchant for violence. I see now that his nervous newbie act was believable because he's a hunter who's mastered baiting his prey. He knew it would make me uncomfortable and cause me to spend my luck to try to force him out of the game. He did it on purpose to drain me. Make me easier to catch. I could respect it if he wasn't such a twisted twatwaffle.

I nod. "Understood."

He removes the heavy blue-iron manacles. As soon as they are off me, I draw a deep breath in relief as my luck bubbles in my veins again, weak but there. I close my eyes at the pleasure of it.

"Let's start with pictures. I'm going to show you a crime scene. You will answer my questions. We'll go from there."

What now? Pictures? Crime scenes? He grabs a manila

folder from under Kiko and flips through it. With the hint of luck in my veins, my thoughts race for a means of escape. My gaze lands on the gun hanging from Donovan's hip.

"Iron bullets," he says, not looking up from the contents of the folder. "Don't even think about it, Ms. Larkspur. I've been doing this a long time. It won't work."

I fold my arms over the scratchy material covering my chest. "What is this, burlap?" I squirm uncomfortably. The orange jumpsuit chafes, especially against my back. I've managed to retract my wing, but the wound hasn't healed.

"I ask for barbed wire, but they keep sending me these," Donovan says heartlessly. Goddess, he's a prick.

"Why do you hate fae so much?"

"Who says I hate fae?"

"If this is how you treat people you like, I don't want to know how you treat those you don't."

He leans back in his chair and straightens his tie. "First of all, you're not people. You're fae. A creature. Not human."

"Creatures are people too," I mumble.

"Second, you are not just fae. I happen to like fae as an occasional diversion. I've spent a few weekends at the Dragonfly."

The Dragonfly is a club in Dragonfly Hollow, the part of Devashire open to humans. Total meat market. Humans who go there are typically hoping for an exotic sexual experience with a pixie or satyr, which means Donovan likes to get freaky. Gross. "Then why the torture?"

He bobs his eyebrows. "I like the torture."

I swallow and feel the blood rush from my face.

"You know what I *do* hate? When a fae such as yourself thinks the law doesn't apply to them and takes advantage of hapless humans." He opens the file again. "I did a little research while they were cleaning you up. Soho Lane has cheated humans out of hundreds of thousands of dollars over the past decade."

More like 2.4 million over the past sixteen years. I keep that thought to myself.

"Poker is eighty percent skill," I say. "I might have used luck occasionally to gain an advantage, but most of those games I won fair and square."

He snorts. "Sure you did." He pulls a pack of gum out of his desk drawer and folds a stick into his mouth. He doesn't offer me any. "Answer me this. If you weren't intentionally preying on human vulnerabilities, why did you leave Dragonfly Hollow? It's not like you don't have a casino there."

I roll my lips together. I don't like to talk about why I ran away. It's humiliating, and I was only seventeen at the time. A lifetime ago. "Domestic issue," I say vaguely. Not a complete lie. Gambling is prohibited for fae in Dragonfly, but I keep that information to myself. I doubt it would help my case.

"Hmm." Donovan chews his gum. "Well then, you'll be happy to know I've decided not to send you back there."

"I'm not being deported?" I can't believe the luck. But I also can't believe Donovan would let me go. There isn't a sliver of kindness or compassion behind those eyes.

He gives me a long, hard look, his gaze wandering the length of my jumpsuit. When he speaks again, his voice is menacingly soft, and his smile matches his crocodile eyes. "Nope, I've decided to keep you."

His tone sends a chill through me. It's like he's picked out a puppy at a pet store—a puppy he plans to permanently chain in his yard. "Wh-why?" I hate the way my voice breaks, but I'm losing my battle to remain strong. If he finds out my real secret... If he finds Arden... *Come on, Sophia. Be brave. Stay sharp.*

Again his gaze rakes down my body. I keep my arms folded protectively across my chest. When he reaches my knees, he turns the folder around to face me. "Look at these pictures."

Huh? I furrow my brow. He shoves the folder closer, and I look down at the contents. It's an eight-by-ten photo of a bloody, twisted corpse, limbs splayed at odd angles in the middle of a crime scene. I have no idea how the person died except that it was obviously a violent death. Blood stains the pavement, splattered everywhere. "Why do you think I can help with this?"

"Because the murderer is fae."

I scoff. "Why would you think a fae did this?" Seelie fae are rarely violent. Even under extreme conditions, most seelie would avoid hurting humans outside Devashire for the simple fact of not wanting to get caught being outside Devashire.

Donovan studies me for a moment. "All his teeth are missing."

Hmm. That is strange but not necessarily fae. "Your Tooth Fairy is mythology," I say. "I'd guess this is a human-on-human crime, and the murderer didn't want his victim to be identified."

"That's what we thought too until we found his wallet in his pocket and his wife confirmed his identity. Why would a human pull the guy's teeth but then leave a big fat wallet in his pocket?"

"I have no idea."

Donovan rubs his chin. "The answer is a human wouldn't." He shuffles the picture to the bottom of the stack, revealing another. A footprint, definitely not human. "Can you tell me what creature made this?"

I study the print, wickedly uncomfortable. It looks like it was made by an eight-foot-tall skeleton. Each bone of the foot is clearly visible and is set deep in the mud. "I don't think that's a footprint, Donovan. It's much too large." The secret to a good lie is to tell a partial truth and concentrate on the true part. The footprint isn't human, but it also isn't seelie, which means that if it is fae at all, the human world has bigger problems than one dead man.

"Sophia... what made this?" he asks again through his teeth.

"I told you I don't know. Pixies and leprechauns have the same feet as humans." I stick my foot out to show him. "Satyrs also have human-looking feet most of the time. They can shift, but in their natural form, they have hooves. That's definitely not a hoofprint. Which means, whatever made that, it wasn't one of us."

"You know something more. I saw it on your face when you first looked at this picture. Tell me." He has that psycho look in his eye, the same one as in the torture room. If I'm not careful, I'm going to end up strapped to that table again. Only I can't share what trotted through my mind when I saw that footprint. There are things humans don't know about Devashire, things they can never know.

What I need is a distraction. I lean forward, allowing the vee neck of my orange jumpsuit to reveal some skin. I'm not blond or voluptuous in my natural form, but I look young and cute by human standards. My sable shoulder-length hair and large chocolate-brown eyes give me the coloring of someone who could fit in among multiple cultures under the right conditions. I'm often mistaken as Asian, although in an indistinct way. People assume my ethnicity is mixed, maybe Japanese/Italian or Korean/Irish. I've heard it all. No way can I flirt my way out of answering his questions, but I hope I can accentuate that part of me that's approachable and sweet, that thing that made human men in my past tell me I was the type of girl they wanted to take home to mama.

"What made this print?" Donovan asks again, chewing his gum more vigorously.

"I don't know," I answer sweetly, genuinely. Even I believe me, and I know I'm lying.

"Is it true that pixies can make their boobs bigger anytime they want to?" he asks abruptly.

What the fuck? Maybe I could flirt my way out of this. "If you've been to the Dragonfly Club, you know the answer to that."

He nods slowly, that crocodile smile making an appearance again. "When you're rested, you can look any way you want. You can be Megan Fox or Kim Kardashian."

Is that why he's keeping me? To make me his personal, shape-shifting sex doll? I shudder.

"I bet you can even become the monster who made this footprint." He waves the folder, and I swallow as I understand that it isn't sex he's interested in but pinning a murder on a fae. *Fuck.*

"No," I say quickly. "We can't change our overall mass by that much. And we're a nonviolent community."

He snaps his gum. "I think you're lying."

"I'm not."

He opens his drawer and withdraws a set of blue-iron cuffs. "Tell me what could have made that footprint. Or don't tell me, and we'll play the torture game again." He jingles the blue cuffs. When I instinctively jerk away, he leans toward me and whispers, "Oh, and for the record, honey, I wouldn't change a single thing about your appearance except to see you in chains."

My throat constricts and my blood runs cold. He reaches for my wrist.

That's when the fire alarm goes off.

THREE

In seconds, Donovan's office fills with thick smoke, and I use the distraction to put space between me and the blue cuffs. The chair rattles as I slip out of it, but Donovan ignores me. He's squinting at the lights blinking steadily above us as the alarm repeats a deafening blare. I cough into my hand.

He sneers and points a finger at me. "Stay right there."

The door to the hall pops open, and a panicked man appears. "Donovan, we need your help. The whole bloody place is on fire! The override system is opening cell doors."

"Fuck!" Donovan runs after him muttering something about why the sprinkler system isn't working. I hear him lock me in the office. Panicked, I search the room but there's no other exit.

The smoke thickens. My lungs sting and I cough repeatedly into my hand, hunching to keep myself low. Does he expect me to burn alive in this room? Fuck, he probably does. I try to sense my luck. I have a little, but I'm not sure it's enough. Maybe enough to get out of this room?

I snatch Kiko off Donovan's desk and rush for the door.

When I twist the knob, it's clear immediately that I don't need luck. It swings open easily. The lock is engaged, but Donovan must not have fully closed the door. It never latched. Bully for me.

The smoke is a dense cloud that blankets the ceiling as I stick my head into the hall and look both ways. Empty. At the end of the hall, an emergency exit hangs open. What a break! The override system must have popped that door too. I dash for the exit, holding my breath and crouched low.

Every part of me expects to meet Donovan outside. Where else would he go but out? But as I spill into the night, my assumptions prove incorrect. Gunshots ring out to my left, and I turn to see the rehabilitation center from the outside. I'm in the yard of a building that looks like a prison, sirens blaring behind a wall topped with barbed wire. On the far side of the yard from me, dozens of fae are flooding out of two double doors and agents are trying their best to round them up. Of course, that's what Donovan's counterpart had said—the fire caused their cell doors to open. Every agent in the vicinity is engaged in keeping the mob of fae under control.

I'm alone on my side of the yard... until suddenly I'm not. A helicopter appears above me, the thump-thump of its blades growing louder as it lands, blowing back my hair and forcing me to block my face with my arm. My mouth drops open as a familiar face leans out the side.

"Mom! Hurry!" My sixteen-year-old daughter, Arden— my heart, my reason for breathing—extends her hand from the door. I sprint toward her and dive into the helicopter's belly, scrambling into the seat beside her and strapping myself in.

"Go, go, go!" I scream to the human pilot. He nods, and

we lift off. As the chopper banks left, I see Agent Donovan running into the space where I was just standing, his face a mask of rage. He draws the gun from his holster. I turn and pull Arden into my arms, shielding her with my body, my back to Donovan. Six shots fire in rapid succession. I hold my breath but none of the bullets hit us. We're moving too fast. Too far away.

Only when the rehabilitation center is completely out of sight do I back off and look Arden in the eye. She's a beautiful, intelligent spark plug of a young woman. She's adaptable and clever as a fox. But she's human, the product of a one-night stand with a human man sixteen years ago. The fire, the door, the distraction, the helicopter, the fact that she was in exactly the right place at the right time means she had help. This is too much for a teenager to pull off on her own. Deep down I understand that some serious luck was involved in my rescue, which could mean only one thing.

"*How*, Arden?"

She tucks a strand of caramel-colored hair behind her ear and blinks wide green eyes at me. "When I found out what happened to you, I called Grandma and Grandpa."

"Noooo!" I direct my anger toward the heavens and punch the seat beside my leg. "Damn it, Arden! I gave that number to you to use only in case of emergency!"

She grimaces. "This is an emergency, Mom! FIRE had you!"

"Me, yes, but you were still safe. Why didn't you follow the protocol we talked about?"

The sigh she heaves toward me tells me exactly how she feels about my emergency plan. "No way was I going to empty your bank account and go on the run while you rotted in a rehabilitation center, Mom! It's stupid."

"You're human. You could have gone anywhere. You might have been free of this." I thump my chest. *You might have been free of me*, I think. It's too much to say it, but I'm sure she can read it in my eyes because she winces.

"I'm half fae. Just because the fae part is dormant doesn't mean FIRE wouldn't have caught up to me. There are pictures on the internet of us together. I wouldn't just have to run. I'd have to keep running. I don't want to live like that."

My brain sends me a disturbing vision of Arden strapped to a metal table, and I hold my head. I blow out a deep breath. She's right. After so many years establishing ourselves as human and living in a suburb of Las Vegas, her identity wouldn't have remained secret for long. That wasn't the life I'd wanted for her.

I nod and hug her again. It's done. The call has been made. There's nothing to do but to face the consequences. "I'm sorry," I yell over the blades. "You did the right thing."

I lean back in my seat knowing there is only one place my parents could arrange for us to be taken. Only one place where we'd both be safe from Agent Donovan and others like him: Devashire. And when we arrive, I'll have a price to pay, one that might make Donovan's table appealing.

WE LAND IN A PRIVATE AIRPORT, AND THE PILOT DIRECTS US TO transfer to a personal jet. I cringe when I notice the four-leaf clover painted on the tail of the plane. Lucky Enterprises. My parents can't afford this. I hate to think what they must have done to get the money. I'll owe them big time. Considering how long I've been gone and how little contact we've had over the years, I wouldn't blame them for leaving me to rot in that rehabilitation center. I'm both grateful and dreading what this all means.

As I exit the helicopter, Arden shoves a carry-on in my direction. My brilliant daughter had the forethought to pack me a bag. I kiss her on the cheek, thankful for an option to the smoke-scented orange jumpsuit I'm wearing. We board the plane, and a few hours later, I've changed into a pair of jeans, a cami, and a dark cardigan in time to land in Asheville, North Carolina. A human in a Jeep picks us up on the tarmac.

Forty minutes later, we wind our way into the mountains, my heart jackhammering harder with every mile closer to Dragonfly. When I recognize the route the driver is taking, I slap her shoulder. "Hey, the front gate is that direction." I point at the access road we should have taken.

"My orders are to bring you the back way," she states, never taking her eyes off the road. Her platinum hair swings just under her ears and I notice a bulge I'm sure is a gun under her vest.

"Orders?" I shake my head. Who was giving her orders? *Fuck.* Whoever was helping my parents must not know our situation. "Arden is human," I tell her. "She can't get through the moon gate. You need to take us to the front entrance."

The driver presses her finger to her earpiece and relays what I've told her. A few uh-huhs later and she addresses me again. "Someone will meet you. It's taken care of, ma'am."

"Taken care of?" I don't understand. A human can't find or enter the fairy portal to Devashire. I shake my head, panic growing and sending my stomach tumbling. "I won't leave her behind!" I warn. "I'll die before I let them separate us."

"Ma'am," the driver says sternly. "Relax. No one is leaving anyone behind, and absolutely no one is dying. If the boss says it's taken care of, it's taken care of."

"But the only one with the power to let her through is —" My breath catches in my throat. Oh no. I thought my parents might have leveraged their business to pay for my rescue. I hadn't considered they might've gone to Godmother.

My pulse accelerates, and I hyperventilate until I have no choice but to put my head between my knees to keep from being ill. This is a disaster.

"Mom? Are you okay?" Arden asks from the back seat. She pats my back and hands me her water bottle. "Drink something."

Just like Arden to be worried about me when her entire world has been turned upside down. She's always been precocious. I suppose she's had to be, considering our circumstances. I sip the water and nod to her as I hand it back. I need to stay strong... for her.

Godmother is our most powerful ruler. Humans always assume it's the king—a mistake made by creatures who've been conditioned toward patriarchy. Fae have a king, but he's a recluse. He hasn't been involved in Devashire's politics since the Civil War when he botched things royally. Godmother, on the other hand, plays an active role in leading the seelie. She's the real power. But she's not a queen or anything like it. The closest human equivalent is the Godfather, like the character from the movie. A mob boss. A power no one would ever mess with.

Godmother runs Devashire with magic and might. Unlike all other seelie, Godmother is so saturated with luck that she's capable of true magic. Some say she's a mage. Others that she learned her powers from a secret society of fae lost to time. One thing I know is that she is positively ancient. My grandmother tells me that her mother's grandmother remembered her looking exactly the same as she does today. Fae live long lives: three hundred years on average. Godmother is older—some say thousands of years old—and more powerful than any creature I've ever heard of. She can make things happen. She's also scary as fuck and deals in favors and bargains. If my parents went to her for help getting me back, I will owe a debt, one far greater than money could ever settle.

By the time the Jeep reaches the end of the dirt road and the driver parks at the edge of a dark forest, I'm a ball of nerves thinking about it.

"Where are we supposed to go?" Arden asks. She grabs the bags out of the back and jumps down from the Jeep. She hands me mine. The driver looks at me and touches the brim of her cap as she nods, then she backs up and pulls away.

"Mom?" For the first time, Arden seems genuinely afraid. The Jeep's headlights fade, and we're alone. I have a fleeting thought that we could run, but where would we go? There isn't another place on earth that's safe for us right now.

"We have to go through the woods," I say. "You'll be okay. Just follow me." I lift my suitcase and start walking. The wheels are useless where we are going. There is no path here.

"Follow you? I can't even see you!" Arden's anxiety makes her voice tremble, and it breaks my heart.

I set down my suitcase and remove my cardigan, tying the arms around my waist. It's cold, even for a fae, but it can't be helped. "I know this is scary for you. You've only ever been in the city and the desert. I'm sure the forest feels ominous. But this is where I'm from. I won't let anything happen to you." I grunt in pain as I spread my wings. My back is still sore from Donovan's torture. But with a little luck, I make myself glow.

"Oh... Mom." Her voice is full of wonder. She's seen my wings before but never at night. Never when my light was so clearly visible. The moment grabs me by the lapels and shakes. Pulling back this curtain for her, showing her what I am, it reminds me of our differences and the implications. Arden isn't fae, and where we have no choice but to go things might not be easy for her.

My voice is thick as I say, "Let's go." I lead her into the woods, thankful that she remembered her coat. We travel at a snail's pace so that she can pick her way through the underbrush at human speed. It's positively frustrating.

The forest is a pixie's natural habitat. I could fly through these trees and make it to the portal in minutes, but Arden doesn't have the benefit of my sixth sense. She has to see where she's walking before she takes a step, and the luggage slows both of us down. It takes over an hour to travel a mile.

"How much farther?" she whines, head tipped back. Arden never complains. I can count how many times we've argued about anything on one hand. She's always been a ray of sunshine and a real trooper. Not now. Now in her exhaustion, she reminds me of when she was six and would hold her hands skyward, wanting to be picked up. Only she's much too big to carry anymore, and there's nowhere to carry her to. I can see she's exhausted. I've asked too much of her tonight. But the truth is we should have been there by now. Either I've forgotten the way or the portal has been moved in my absence. The only other possibility, and this is what I'd been afraid of, is that Arden's human presence is keeping me from finding it.

"Let's rest for a moment," I say in a strained voice. I sit on my suitcase and watch her do the same. My glow flickers and burns out.

"Mom? What's wrong? What happened to your light?"

"Tired. I just need to rest." True but not the entire truth. The entire truth is I'm not sure where to go next and I need to preserve my luck. I take a few deep breaths. Worst-case scenario, we can wait here until the sun comes up, then make our way back to the main gate. At least we're in the woods. I always feel better in the woods. Well, except for the one time that changed everything. Being here again, I remember it like it was yesterday.

FOUR

16 YEARS AGO

No bigger event existed in Dragonfly Hollow than the Yule Ball. It was the event of the season, and almost every high-profile couple in Devashire had announced their engagement on the magical night. Kicked off by an enchanting parade of traditional sleighs pulled by reindeer, young fae couples dressed in formal attire rode through the Winter Wood to the town square where they danced the night away under gently falling snow and twinkling lights.

Human tourists booked tickets over a year in advance to watch the event that ushered in the holiday season at the parks. Some lined up along the parade route days before, desperate for the best view. For fae teens near the end of their school-age years, attending the ball was a rite of passage, the closest thing to prom fairies celebrated.

In sum, the Yule Ball was a big fucking deal, and I was going. Never mind that I personally couldn't have afforded the sleigh I was sitting in. My boyfriend, Seven, could. We'd dated in secret for two long years. I was as surprised as anyone when he asked me to go and tied the traditional red ribbon around my wrist marking me as his date. It shone crisp and new against my tan skin. I stared at it, repeating to myself that he wouldn't have tied it on or rented the sleigh if he hadn't meant to come.

The reindeer shook in its harness, velvety horns rocking back and forth in front of me.

"I don't think he's coming, Soph. You know... leprechauns...," Penelope Hawthorne said softly, her wings fluttering. The fact that there wasn't a hint of derision in her voice made her message all the worse. She wasn't trying to humiliate me; she was my good friend and a fellow pixie who was trying to warn me. I pivoted in my seat to see her and her boyfriend in the sleigh behind me. Her frothy pink gown was perfect for her fair skin and platinum hair. Flick, her boyfriend, sat on the bench behind their reindeer, reins in hand, right where he was supposed to be. My sleigh's driver's seat was still empty. My eyes fell on the worn red ribbon around Penelope's wrist. She and Flick had been dating forever.

"I think... I think he's just late. Something must have come up." I flashed her a wobbly smile.

She shook her head. "Sophia, I tell you this as a friend and fellow pixie. He was never coming. No leprechaun would be seen in public dating a pixie. I know you thought you two were different, but it has never happened, and it never will."

"You don't know what you're talking about," I said more firmly, although a heaviness had started in my stomach. I looked at my watch. We were scheduled to parade through Winter Wood in five minutes. If he didn't get here soon...

Penelope fluttered her wings, her expression empathetic. "I'm sorry, Sophia. Someone should have stopped this." Flick turned around and smacked her shoulder and Penelope blurted, "I'm sorry." Then she said no more.

I checked my watch again. I knew in my heart that Seven would come. This wasn't just a dance for us. This was the night we were going to go public with our long-standing relationship. We'd professed our love for each other months ago and spent countless nights in the woods or on the beach whispering sweet promises. Tonight we planned to blaze a trail and break the unspoken rule that leprechauns couldn't date pixies. Us against the world.

Maybe he got scared and decided not to come? No. I shook my head at the thought. It wasn't just about going public. We'd promised each other that we'd find a place in the woods after the dance and be each other's first. Losing our virginity to each other was something Seven would never miss out on, even if he wasn't ready for the dance and public outing. We'd waited so long. We were almost eighteen. We'd be graduating from Bailiwick's in the spring. He would have sent a message if he'd changed his mind. Something had happened. Something was wrong.

With a sigh, I took one last glance at Penelope and stood, resolved to disembark from the sleigh and take refuge in my room until Seven explained himself. But a hand blocked my path. Mrs. Harper frowned at me over her clipboard. The satyr and mother of three had organized this event, and she lowered her chin so that I was face-to-face with her horns.

"What do you think you're doing?" she said through a tight scowl.

"My date didn't come," I whispered. "Something must have happened to him. I'm going home."

Mrs. Harper shook her graying head. "Oh no, dear. I'm

sorry, but that's not possible. It's too late to remove your sleigh from the lineup. Had I known fifteen minutes ago, I might have found someone else to drive it, but I couldn't possibly in the next three minutes. You don't want to ruin the Yule Ball for everyone else, do you?"

My cheeks blazed with embarrassment. "No, but—"

"I'm very sorry. I realize this must be hard for you, my dear, but I have to ask you to be brave tonight. You are going to have to drive this sleigh yourself. Thankfully, it's just a matter of holding the reins. The reindeer are trained to follow the sleigh in front of them. Just wave and smile. I promise you can head home as soon as we park in the square." She sighed and clutched the clipboard against her chest, but there wasn't an ounce of give in her expression.

"But—" Wasn't it obvious how humiliating it would be to ride through the woods alone? The parade route was lined with fae and humans alike. Most of Dragonfly Hollow would see that I'd been stood up.

I gaped at the woman, speechless. But as I glanced at the couples behind and in front of me, I knew she was right. The sleighs were packed in tight. Mine would have to be lifted and turned to be removed from the line. True, once everyone started moving, I might be able to coax the reindeer to pull off route and let the people behind me move forward, but reindeer were very unpredictable when asked to do something they weren't trained to do. Not to mention, the sides of my sleigh were decorated to work with the others. I was the *u* in Merry Yule. Pulling out now would ruin everything.

Gods, everyone was staring. Even if I pushed past Mrs. Harper and ran for home, I wouldn't escape ridicule. I'd ruin the night for the rest of these couples, and I'd never hear the end of it.

"I can drive it if you want," a low, familiar voice said from just out of sight.

I leaned forward to see that a scrawny boy in a green apron had sidled up to Mrs. Harper. River Foxwood. I'd been friends with the young satyr I'd met in Alchemy class for years. In fact, we'd had to be separated on more than one occasion for disrupting the class with our laughter. His big brown eyes smiled up at me.

"There you go," Mrs. Harper said. "Problem solved." She sped busily away.

"I brought you this from our booth." He pointed his thumb at the Foxwood's concession stand, which was unmanned and had a lengthy line forming behind it.

My hands trembled a bit as I took the hot cocoa from him and savored a sip. It was so tempting to accept River's generous offer. I appreciated the gesture more than he'd ever know, but I was going to have to turn it down, and it was taking every ounce of bravery I had in me to do it.

"River, you can't abandon your parents' booth. Your dad would kill you."

His throat bobbed, and a flash of pity flitted through his expression. "He'd understand given the circumstances. He knows what it's like."

I realized exactly what he meant. His dad knew what it was like to be messed with by a leprechaun. In our world, there were leprechauns and then there was everyone else. Leprechauns were lucky as sin. Wealth magnets. Beautiful beyond compare. And sometimes... *often*, really... the rest of us got caught up in the gears of their empires.

I sighed. "Go back to your booth, River. I am going to drive this sleigh into the town square, and then I'm going to come back here, drink this chocolate, and cry on your shoulder, okay?" I handed him back the hot beverage.

"Deal." He took the mug and backed toward his booth. I fluffed my plum-colored skirt and climbed onto the driver's bench, lifting the reins.

"Oh my gods, is she actually going to drive?" I heard someone say. A chorus of whispers clouded the night around me.

I would not cry. No way. I was a Larkspur. We didn't have much, but we were brave, and I was raised to do the right thing. When my grandmother was my age, she'd been an archer in the Goblin Wars. She'd faced off against an unseelie uprising and seen death and destruction from the front lines. Tonight I was going to live up to the name.

The lead whip cracked, and the orchestra started to play. Mrs. Harper wasn't lying; I didn't even have to slap the reins. Without any effort on my part, my reindeer pulled me into the forest. I sat up straighter, smiling and waving, shoving all my insecurities to the back of my brain.

At first, it seemed like things would be okay. People clapped and yelled, "Happy Yule!" as we slid by. But then I noticed a few fae children pointing and laughing. Mothers whispered to each other. Humans boldly asked why I was alone in voices loud enough for me to hear, ignorant to the shame of it.

It was the longest ride of my life.

I begged the gods to make the parade go faster, but it took the entirety of an hour to reach our destination. Seeing the square decked out in yuletide splendor made my heart give a painful squeeze. Seven was supposed to jump down from the driver's seat, then help me from the sleigh before sweeping me into the center of the square. A band of the best musicians in Devashire would accompany an evening of dancing, holiday-themed cocktails, and gourmet hors d'oeuvres. Godmother's magic would make it snow all night, but no one would feel cold. There would be no wind. No slush. And sometime during the evening, Seven would lead me to the central gazebo where he would kiss me, then whisk me away to somewhere private.

My eyes blurred with tears. It wasn't going to happen, and I had no idea why.

As soon as a volunteer guided my reindeer to a halt, I moved to flee, knowing my tears had flooded the dam of my lower lids and I could no longer hold back the deluge of my grief. I had to get out of there and fast.

But there was a reason the boys always drove the sleighs. My skirts tangled around my legs as I tried to descend, and my heel caught in the hem. I tripped off the step. It happened so fast I didn't have time to use my wings to break my fall. I landed on my stomach and elbows in the frozen grass.

Two leather shoes appeared in front of me, and I stared up into a leprechaun's pitiless, laughing face. Mr. Delaney's face. Seven's father.

"Pity it came to this, but Seven did you a favor tonight," he said. "Now you know your place, pixie. You'd do well to remember it."

He left without helping me up.

FIVE

I snap out of my reverie when a firefly ignites between Arden and me, the horrific, humiliating memory fading with its phosphorescent glow. My heart leaps. All is not lost. "Keep your eyes open, Arden. You're in for a show."

"Huh?" She blinks tiredly at me.

Flash. Thousands of fireflies ignite at once, turning night into day. I pop off the suitcase and whirl. There it is! The circular stone gate was right behind me all along. How had I missed it before?

The fireflies fade, and everything goes dark again. The gate blends away into the night.

"What the hell?" Arden gasps. "Those little guys give off serious wattage! Is that normal?"

"For these fireflies it is. They're a rare synchronous variety that feed on fairy energy." I point in the direction of the circle of stones. "We're here. The portal is through the moon gate."

She sidles up to me, suitcase in hand. "Where? I don't see anything."

"I can't either. It's invisible in the darkness, but it's there. Wait for it…"

The fireflies ignite again, bathing the forest in their warm golden light. The gate appears again. "Come!" I take her hand and step forward but stop short when Arden squeezes tighter, her hand partially slipping from mine.

"I… *can't,*" she says. "It feels like there's something in front of me. I can't move forward."

The light fades into velvety midnight blue again, and I back up to her. I was afraid this would happen. Fuck that driver. I thought she said someone was coming to help us.

Flash! Like a lightning strike, the forest glows again.

We are not alone.

No, no no no. Not *him.* My breath hitches. Of all the people Godmother might have sent to meet us, why oh why did it have to be *him?*

Spotlighted by a thousand fireflies, Seven Delaney is casually leaning against the stone arch of the moon gate as if he's been waiting for us the entire time. His legs are crossed at the ankle, and the crooked grin he shoots my way is heart-stopping and oh so infuriating. How dare he smile at me after what he did? How dare he come within striking distance?

This man is as close to a nemesis as I've ever had and as much the reason for me fleeing Devashire as anything else. On the outside, he's wrapped in a scrumptious package of long, lean muscle and uncanny grace. His shoulders strain the material of his dark dress shirt, and corded forearms, scandalous in their musculature, extend beyond his pushed-up sleeves. With a hand resting lightly on abs as tight as chiseled marble beneath the material, he winks one emerald eye at me, the other twinkling in the moonlight as if he finds our circumstances amusing. His perfectly tailored trousers are a work of art, as are his handcrafted leather loafers.

In one word, Seven is stunning. I'm stunned. Arden is stunned. Likely at least half the fireflies flitting around us are stunned (at least the female ones). He is overtly sexual, undeniably handsome, and as charming as they come. In other words, a dangerous menace to all womankind.

Leprechauns have a reputation for being short and ugly in the human world. I laughed the first time I saw the University of Notre Dame's mascot. Nothing could be further from the truth. Jealous rivals and political enemies started those rumors to tarnish the reputations of the leprechaun dynasties they hated, anything to get a jab in at the luckiest fae. I can understand the sentiment. Of any of our kind, they have the most inherent luck. That translates into all aspects of their existence, including their physical forms. Leprechauns are beautiful—*always beautiful.*

Pixies like me, we're designed to blend with nature in our natural forms, but leprechauns stand out. They sparkle. And if their physical perfection weren't enough to make you hate them, they are also rich—the type of rich that's only possible through generations of wealth—a wealth that almost always leads to a power and a superiority complex.

In short, a leprechaun is a caramel-covered Adonis in couture. They're almost irresistible. Even knowing that Seven's soul is as rotten as a maggot-infested peach, his physical presence leaves me breathless.

"Seven." His name hisses through my teeth.

"Sophead," he says playfully. "I wasn't sure I'd ever see you again."

I cringe at the pet name he used to use when we were children. "Don't call me that! You have no right to call me that."

He snorts. "I didn't know rights were necessary to use a nickname."

"Mom?" Arden peers around me curiously. Without even realizing it, I've placed myself protectively between them.

"Who's this?" Seven pushes off the moon gate and approaches Arden to get a better look at her. No, he doesn't just look. He studies her like she's a specimen on a microscope slide. I move more fully in front of Arden, blocking his view.

"This is my *daughter*." I emphasize the word in a way that reminds him she's a child and off-limits. I don't trust him within an inch of her.

"I can see that," he says around a lopsided grin. "She's practically a miniature version of you."

Arden shoves around me and extends her hand before I can stop her. "I'm Arden."

I slap her hand down. "Arden, no!"

Arden flashes me an injured look.

"Never offer your hand to a fae, Arden," Seven says. "A handshake among fairies binds a magical agreement. As a human, you can't be sure the shake is just a shake. It's too dangerous for you. Keep your hands to yourself when you greet someone."

"Oh." She slides her hands into her pockets, a faint blush of embarrassment warming her cheeks.

Fury grips me in its shaking fist. "She doesn't need *you* of all people lecturing her on fairy etiquette. *I'll* teach her what she needs to know." I have taught her a thing or two about fairy culture, but who could blame her for not remembering? It's been years since we discussed it. I'd never planned for her to come back here. After sixteen successful years living among humans, I never thought she'd need to.

He ignores my tirade and smiles charmingly at Arden. "I'm Seven, by the way."

"Like the number?" she asks.

"Exactly like the number." He winks at her.

Gah! He's incorrigible. "Enough with the introductions." I slash a hand through the air between us. "Can you get her through the portal or not? You might as well know she's human."

He's still studying Arden in a way that fills me with unease. "How old are you, Arden?"

"Sixteen," she says. She'll be seventeen at the end of September. I can almost hear him doing the math. Arden came along soon after I left Dragonfly—nine months to be exact. Only my parents know the truth about my pregnancy. Did they tell anyone? If they did, I'll know soon enough. Fairies adore gossip and speculation.

It's none of his fucking business.

"Have you ever visited Dragonfly Hollow before?" he asks Arden, charismatic and steady, like he's trying to put her at ease.

"Stop it!" I grit out.

He glances uneasily in my direction. "Stop what?"

Trying to endear yourself to her, I almost say, but I halt the words before they come out of me. He's the only one with enough luck to walk us through the gate, and Arden is shivering and exhausted. I take a deep breath and blow it out, stuffing the memories of what he did to me in a dark closet at the back of my brain. I place my hand on Arden's shoulder. "We've been traveling all night. Please show us through."

His eyes crinkle at the corners. "Of course. You haven't changed a bit, Sophia. All business."

"I've changed," I snap, then narrow my eyes. "I'm far less naive."

Our eyes lock, and challenge sparks between us.

"Take my hand," he commands, holding one out to each of us. "I'll walk you through."

The last thing I want to do is to touch him, but there's no other way. *I* might be able to get through the gate without him, but I'd risk being separated from Arden. Reluctantly I slip my fingers into his. My stomach gives an annoying flutter at his touch, my internal workings betraying a lingering desire for this man. I grind my teeth and thank the stars that my will and my mind are stronger than my libido. It's times like these that having a poker face comes in handy.

Arden takes his other hand and smiles warmly up at him, her eyes filled with stars. *Fuck.* We're overdue for a long talk.

Seven faces the moon gate and takes a deep breath. The fireflies glow again, lighting up the night. I notice the strain on his face as beneath our feet, the ground begins to rumble. What is he doing? He couldn't be... My eyes widen.

Luck is different than magic. A creature with magic can create something out of nothing and command the elements to do their bidding. True magic users are rare. Seven isn't a magic user, but the luck he's wielding is more powerful than any I've known before. Luck can't create something out of nothing, but it can influence the world around it to make something that could happen on its own happen right then.

The wards protecting Dragonfly are grounded in earth. Seven is disrupting their anchor, causing slabs of rock to shift deep beneath our feet. It's a natural phenomenon, but its occurrence now, at this moment, is all his doing. The amount of luck it takes to cause a minor earthquake like this is staggering, and I can't help but gape in awe of his abilities. This level of control could stop a beating heart. It could cause a bird to fall from the sky beak first and kill an enemy.

He's stronger now than when I left. Stronger, and far more dangerous.

"Now," he says and ushers us both forward. Arden and I shuffle through the moon gate at his side. I feel the wards nipping at my heels as they close again behind me. I breathe a sigh of relief when Seven releases my fingers, and I rub the tingle from my palm that lingers after his touch.

Seven cracks his neck, then his knuckles, the tension in his body relaxing once more.

I set my bag down and orient myself. We're near the back of Wonderland, one of five theme parks that make up the Dragonfly Hollow world. My parents live two blocks from here. This subdivision is called Enchantment and is one of three residential areas within Dragonfly Hollow and the only one inside Wonderland.

"Thanks for your help," I say to Seven, anxious to leave his presence. "We can make it from here."

"I'd better escort you." He starts walking toward my old place, gesturing for us to follow.

"Really, it's not necessary," I insist.

He doesn't acknowledge my protest. I grumble as Arden falls into step behind him and I'm forced to follow along. Arden's gaze drifts to the colorful mushroom-shaped houses that line the streets. Crimson, emerald, and royal purple caps top homes with matching shutters and circular doors. It's as if we've all been shrunk down into a cartoon village, a fantastical neighborhood designed to play into human misconceptions.

"Wow, this is wild," Arden says, spinning in place to take it all in.

"Fairies don't actually live in mushrooms," I tell her. "Outside the Dragonfly theme park, our residences look exactly like human houses—better in most cases because our engineering is superior—but inside the parks, this facade sells tickets. Some of these homes are rented to humans, which is why my parents can live here inexpensively. It's convenient for them because they own a store here, and it's lucrative to play into the fantasy."

"Oh," she says. "So some fairies do live here."

"Well, yes. Quite a few actually."

"Then some fairies *do* live in mushrooms." She giggles.

I bristle. "Not naturally. Only for show."

She shrugs. "Humans didn't naturally live in two-bedroom condominiums either, but the cave got old after a while."

"Arden! You know very well what I mean."

She starts walking again, seeming to take in every detail of the street. "Yeah... it's still cool."

While she's distracted, Seven drifts to my side. "How did FIRE finally catch up to you?"

"None of your business."

"Just wondering how the feds found you after all this time. Once Arden called your parents, my people looked into your case. You supported yourself playing poker. Did you get greedy? Use too much luck?"

"The agent never said how he caught me," I mumble with a shrug. Why am I even explaining myself to him? "I still don't know."

The shallow smile he offers says it all. He suspects I

made a stupid mistake. He's probably surprised a mere pixie survived outside the wards.

"I didn't think you'd *ever* get caught," he says, and the admission surprises me enough I have to shuffle to keep from tripping over my own feet. "The FIRE agents have enough fairy prisoners working for them now that he was probably able to use their luck. I doubt he'd have been successful without help from one of us."

The connotation is that it wasn't my fault, a kind thing to say. I'm baffled by it. Why is Seven being kind to me now?

Arden chimes in from ahead of us. "She was trying to win my university tuition. My deposit is due for the fall."

"Arden, shhh."

"Aren't you a little young for college?" Seven asks.

Arden preens. "I'm a year ahead. I was admitted to an accelerated premed program at Chapel Hill."

He slants a look of admiration in her direction. "I could tell you were smart the moment I met you."

"Okay!" I say, intentionally interrupting and wedging myself between them again. We've reached my parents' place. "This is it." I usher Arden away from Seven toward the stone path that leads to the front door, rolling my eyes when he lingers in the street. Why won't he just *leave*?

As I knock on the round wooden door, I flash back to a time when I could walk in without knocking. The door was painted red then. Now it's purple. Minutes pass and no one comes. I knock again. They must know we're here. My parents had to have arranged all this.

When the door finally opens, it takes me a full minute to recognize my mother. She's aged. Her once-brown hair is now peppered with silver. Fairies aren't immortal, but their natural lives are long compared to humans, three hundred years on average. My mother isn't a day over seventy, which means her silver hair is caused by negative emotions, not trips around the sun. A pit forms in my stomach as I wonder if any of that gray hair had to do with me.

"I suppose you expect to stay here," she says by way of greeting.

"Where else would I stay?" When she says nothing, I add, "I wasn't hoping for a warm greeting, but a hello might be nice."

"Hello." She folds her arms over her white nightgown.

"Hello," I echo. A moment yawns between us. "Mom, this is your granddaughter, Arden." I move aside so she can get a better look. As soon as she sees Arden's genuine smile, my mother melts and pulls her into an embrace.

"Welcome, Arden. It's so nice to finally meet you." She oozes warmth toward her granddaughter. I thank the gods for small mercies. "You did the right thing calling us. Go ahead inside. There's a snack for you on the counter."

Arden slips past her into the warm light of the interior, and my mother turns hard gray eyes on me. She doesn't say a word but looks past me toward Seven.

"Eight o'clock sharp," he says in answer to a question that was never asked.

She nods. "She'll be there."

Seven gives me one last lingering look, then utters a hasty good night and, to my relief, finally leaves.

"What happens at eight o'clock tomorrow?" I ask.

She lifts an eyebrow. "You go to see Godmother."

SIX

On some level, I expected this. Arden and I can't stay in Devashire permanently without Godmother's permission. She controls everything here. Her word is law. Only I thought we'd have a few days to settle in before she summoned me. I assumed there'd be a honeymoon period. Guess I was wrong.

"What do you think I'll owe her?" I ask my mother, chewing my lip. I follow her into my childhood home. It hasn't changed much since I left, and memories swarm me like angry bees.

She clucks her tongue. "It's not the cost, Sophia. Rescuing you *was* expensive, but thankfully that part has been taken care of."

"What do you mean taken care of?"

She chuckles and shakes her head. "Obviously we didn't have the resources to rescue you. The money is one thing, but the luck was well beyond our means. You got yourself into quite a pickle. We thought we'd have to try to borrow it, perhaps take out a lien on the store, but honestly we don't have that kind of credit."

"Then who's responsible for getting me out?" I spread my hands. She implied the cost was taken care of. "Who else would spend that kind of money?"

She tilts her head. "He didn't tell you?"

"He who?" My stomach turns to lead. *Don't say it. Please don't say it.*

"When Arden called us, we called Godmother. We had no other options. At first she was reluctant. I think she would have left you to fend for yourself if it was her choice, but Seven insisted on leading the rescue effort. He offered to pay for the entire thing. We could hear him throwing a fit on the other end of the line. He wouldn't take no for an answer. Insisted Godmother give him permission to take action."

The punch lands squarely in my gut. "Why was he even there? How did he even know?"

Her brows rise toward her hairline. "He works for Godmother now. He's her head of security."

"Wait, Seven *works* for Godmother?" I'm utterly confused by this. It doesn't make any sense. Seven is the heir to the Delaney dynasty, aka Lucky Enterprises. His billionaire father owns the Dragonfly Casino as well as a dozen or so other businesses. Seven should be running some evil enterprise at his father's side by now, steepling his fingers in a shiny glass cubicle in the sky. While I'm sure Godmother compensates him well, I just can't fathom he'd have the time to devote to municipal service above and beyond his responsibilities to Lucky Enterprises.

My mother nods. "He splits his time. I assume there's enough overlap with what he does for Lucky Enterprises that it made sense for him to do both. He's worked for her for years." She raises a finger. "Started working for her right after you left. Anyway, Seven paid for it all. Even lent his private jet to the task and I'm sure used a fair amount of luck to make it happen. I still can't believe how quickly he brought you home—I mean, here. I suppose this isn't your home anymore." A torturous expression crosses her face.

Ugh. The guilt worms through me and weighs heavily on my heart. "I know when I left it was hard on you but—"

She holds up a hand. "Not tonight. It's too big of a conversation for the wee hours of the morning." Glancing back at Arden, she says, "Finish up and I'll show you to your rooms."

I close my eyes, dread burying me. "Wait, just tell me this: how much do you think we owe Seven?" Maybe I can pay him back anyway.

"I'm sure it cost more money than we've made in our lifetime. But we owe him nothing. He said it was his gift to us. No bargain. No expectations." She frowns. "I think he feels..."

"Guilty? Like he can make up for what he did to me by... by—"

My mother peaks one eyebrow. "Spending oodles of money and luck to rescue you from a lifetime in a rehabilitation center? Honestly, Sophia, if guilt is what made him do it, thank your lucky stars."

I groan. This is unacceptable. I cannot accept a kindness from Seven. I'm unable to reconcile it with the asshole I know him to be. He must have an angle. I place a hand on my stomach. "I think I'm going to be sick."

"I don't blame you. This is far from over. Godmother will demand a price from you tomorrow for what you did. Seven may have covered the cost of your return, but you left Dragonfly without her permission, pregnant with a human child! Pray that she finds it in her heart to forgive you and that her punishment does not include you and Arden being handed back to FIRE. I doubt the conditions of your imprisonment the second time around will be as accommodating as the first."

I flash back to the torture room and feel the hook sliding into my wing flaps. All the warmth drains from my face.

My mother's hand is on my shoulder, and for the first time she looks legitimately concerned. "Are you ill? You've blanched as white as snow."

I swallow down bile and nod. "Can we sleep now?"

Arden hears me and sets her glass and plate down before picking up her bag and joining us. My mother leads us upstairs where she sets Arden up in the guest room across from where I used to sleep. I say my goodnights, then find my room exactly how I left it. The twin-sized bed is wrapped in the same shiny purple comforter—I still love purple—and a shelf above the desk still houses a half dozen archery trophies with my name on them. When I turn around, I see the full-length mirror is still there, mounted on the wall. It catches my reflection. Haggard is the only word to describe my appearance. I hardly recognize myself.

Fucking great. Just the way a girl wants to appear in front of her stunningly attractive ex. *Sigh.*

Not that I care what he thinks anyway. *Fucker.*

Parking my suitcase at the end of the bed, I flop onto the mattress, my heart still pounding in my chest from the overflow of adrenaline.

A few minutes later, Arden appears in my doorway. "Mom?"

I scoot to the far side of the bed and hold up the comforter. She crawls in beside me. I wrap the blanket and my arms around her, rubbing her shoulder and kissing her forehead. "It's going to be okay, kid."

She presses her forehead to mine. "Do you think Grandma will let us stay? She seemed really mad."

I take a deep breath. "She will. I know what I need to do to make things right with her. I just need time to do it."

"Okay."

"Do you trust me?"

Her green eyes flash to mine. "Yeah."

"Good, because I'm going to take care of it."

She closes her eyes. Time unspools between us, and I think she's fallen asleep when she asks in a groggy voice, "Do you think I'll still be able to go to Chapel Hill in the fall?"

I stare at the ceiling, my mind racing with uncertainty. As a poker player, I'm a master at bluffing, but the line I will not cross is intentionally lying to my daughter.

"I'm not sure yet, but I'll do everything in my power to get you there."

She snuggles in closer. "Okay." Her breathing evens out, and she falls asleep in my arms. It's a long time before my swirling thoughts allow me to do the same.

*   *   *

"You've got to be kidding me!" Arden can't stop laughing as she takes in my sparkly pink gown. We're on our way to Godmother's tearoom at the center of Dragonfly theme park, and I am rocking a dress doing its best imitation of a frothy pink cupcake with glitter sprinkles.

"It's the law here," I whisper. "All pixies and satyrs must be in costume when within the boundaries of the theme park. We're all considered cast members, and it's our duty to entertain human customers."

"You said pixies and satyrs. What about leprechauns like Seven?"

I roll my eyes, bristling at the sound of his name on her lips. "Leprechauns own everything. They're the bosses, not the cast members. They wear suits."

"Doesn't seem fair," she says, her eyes narrowing. Is it possible her young mind is starting to get it? Humans might have their prejudices, bigotries, and racism, but fairies are just as awful, their stereotypes and discriminations revolving around species rather than race.

"It's not. Nothing about life here is fair. I left for a reason. You can wear your regular clothes because you're human." I crack my neck and flutter my wings. "Me? I'm a cast member. We all are when we're on Dragonfly grounds."

"That's harsh," she says. I can tell I've disappointed her. I'm sure she wants to believe in the fantasy, the veneer. We're standing in a colorful wonderland. But I'd be a terrible mother if I didn't tell her the truth.

"That's Dragonfly. It's not worse than the human world, but it's not better either. It's just different." *Different in a way that isn't beneficial to pixies.*

She nods, then giggles again. "That dress..."

I rub my stomach, not used to the way the waistband cuts into my midsection. I haven't gained weight, but after sixteen years of not using a corset, the bodice of the fairy gown is uncomfortably restricting. I try to take a deep breath to calm my nerves. "I wonder how long it will take to rearrange my internal organs to be comfortable in these styles again."

"I can't believe you can walk in those shoes!" Arden

squints at my heels, made to look like gilt vines growing around my feet. They're shiny and delicate, like everything else I'm wearing.

"They're not that bad. The cobblers here are exceptional. They can make stilettos almost feel like sneakers. Plus pixies are naturally light on their feet."

"I can't even hear them click on the pavement." Arden is truly fascinated now.

"That's a pixie thing," I explain. "It's the wings. You just haven't noticed before because I've always acted human."

"About that, you all have wings, but I haven't seen a single fairy fly anywhere since we got here. You can fly, right?"

"We can." I chuckle.

"Then why don't you fly everywhere?"

"Why don't you run everywhere? You can run, right?"

She snorts. "Because it's easier to walk, and running is exhausting."

"Exactly." I'm about to tell her how much effort is involved in flight, especially if you're out of practice like I am, when a human woman grabs me from behind by the elbow and yanks me to a stop.

"Can we get a selfie?" Although she phrases it like a question, it's actually a demand. She's wearing a Tinker Bell T-shirt that reads *I CLAP FOR FAIRIES*. Two children cling to her sides, a boy who looks about eight and a girl who might be four whose lips are stained red from the sucker in her mouth.

"Of course," I say in a falsetto that's just on the edge of singing. I turn my wrist over and hold my hands gracefully to my sides. My smile is wide enough to hurt, and I use a little luck to make myself sparkle.

"Oooh, you're so pretty," the little girl says before she

barrels into my legs, her tiny body completely lost in the layers of tulle that make up my skirt.

"Come out of there, Patty," her mother yells. "We can't see you for the picture." The woman reaches into the nest of fabric and withdraws her child. Patty no longer has her sucker, and I wonder how long it will take me to extract the candy after these people are gone.

"Oh, please hurry," I chime. "I'm afraid I have a meeting with the fairy godmother, and I don't want to be late."

"Cute," the mother says, obviously annoyed. "Frank! I need you to take a picture!"

A man wearing suction-cup satyr horns pops up from a nearby bench and draws his phone. The wife squeezes into my side, pinching my wing between our shoulders. Her children press their backs against the front of my skirt. I lift my chin and beam as if I've never had more fun. Several clicks later, they leave.

As soon as they're out of sight, I reach into my skirt and peel off the sucker. *Fuck*. That's going to leave a stain.

"Oh. My. God." Arden grimaces, joining me again from where she'd waited near the benches. "Those people treated you like you were... a celebrity!"

"Hardly. Like their idea of a fairy." I sigh. "It's like I said before, I'm a character in a theme park. Most humans don't think of us as equals or as people. We are things. Ideas. This is how Dragonfly makes its money."

"I heard what you said, but it's different seeing it." She scratches the back of her head.

I turn her toward the center of Dragonfly Hollow. "That's where we're going. Let's hurry before anyone else sees me."

Godmother's Tearoom is a cottage made of gingerbread

at the end of a cobblestone pathway. Brown slabs of cookie form the walls and roof, magically held together by swaths of white frosting and decorated with an assortment of giant candy. Gigantic green-and-white swirling peppermints neighbor mounds of gummy confections while massive bright red imperials infuse the air with hot cinnamon fragrance.

Arden pokes a gigantic gummy bear in the stomach with her finger. "Is this real?" she asks.

"Yes. But don't eat it," I whisper. "Everything in Godmother's tearoom is edible, but eat the wrong thing and you'll pay a terrible price. Humans who partake are instantly addicted. They'll come back again and again until they've spent all their money on the treats inside. If they're strong enough to deny the urge, they'll dream about this place, and the memory of it will haunt them until they die."

Arden backs away from the bear and shoves her hands into her pockets.

"Stop scaring the girl, Sophia!" Godmother appears at the gingerbread entrance, her voice a deep timbre. Physically, she fills the space of the doorway, but her imposing presence extends far beyond her skin and bones.

In the human world, an increased body size is often seen as a negative thing. Human society values thinness, sometimes to the point of celebrating a sickly physique. In my time on the outside, I often wondered if they had some bizarre fetish for vulnerability. But here, body size correlates with power. Godmother is built like the human stereotype of an opera singer, tall, wide, and thick. Every bit of her advanced size is filled with luck and overflowing with power. The stones around her neck thrum with ancient energy. Her purple-and-black feather dress sparkles with magic. Twisted off her neck and pinned elegantly behind her head, her silky black hair creates a striking frame for her ebony complexion.

Godmother is a force of nature. Ageless and frighteningly beautiful. Imposing and aloof.

I curtsy but she ignores me and addresses Arden. "It's not as bad as all that, child. Plenty of humans avoid eating my tearoom, and those who pay up front for what they eat suffer no ill consequences. Tell me, do you lick the walls of the restaurants you go to?"

Arden chuckles. "No, ma'am."

"Exactly. Anyone dumb enough to taste a building deserves what's coming to them." Godmother's gaze falls on me then, still holding my curtsy. "Oh, for the sake of Aibell! Get up and come inside. We open to the public in an hour, and we have much to discuss."

I rise to follow her, but Arden nudges my elbow and whispers, "Who is Aibell?"

"Ancient fairy goddess," I explain under my breath. "There are lots of them... gods, I mean. Fairy religion is pantheistic, and most individuals believe in multiple gods."

Her eyebrows lift. I internally chastise myself again for not teaching her more about Devashire. In my defense, I'd wanted her to have a human life, free of all this. I'd hoped she'd never need it.

At Godmother's direction, we take a seat at one of the tables inside, directly in front of a glass case filled with delectable pastries. Neither one of us had time to eat much this morning, and I watch Arden gaze at the case longingly as she sits down beside me. I'm too nervous to be hungry and too jaded to risk eating anything voluntarily in this place.

"Join us, Seven," Godmother bellows over her shoulder.

I bristle as Seven appears from the back room and strides to the table, his face locked in that permanent closed-lip smile that always makes him look like he's thinking about some lecherous secret. Gods, he's a work of art. No man has any right to be that attractive. His black T-shirt clings to an insanely etched torso, touchable soft material hugging flesh that must feel hard in all the right places. I'm appreciating his abs when my eyes catch on the gun at his hip. Since when does Seven need a gun? He's a leprechaun! He has enough luck to handle any situation without raising a finger.

"What's he doing here?" I say, my voice thick. He's stolen my breath again, left me with nothing but raspy syllables while I—oh for fuck's sake, I look like a pink meringue!

Godmother raises an eyebrow. "He's sponsoring you. He is the reason *you* are here, Sophia." Her words hold an edge that makes me sit up straighter in my chair. I do not want to piss off Godmother. Seven works for her and paid for my recovery. Of course he's here.

I fold my hands on the table and stare down at my threaded fingers.

"Better," she says. "Now you are here today because you left Devashire without my blessing or permission and have potentially created a political situation between us and the human world. Explain yourself. And I warn you, make it good, because if it wasn't for Seven, I wouldn't have recovered you. If FIRE figures out you're here, I'll have a godsdamn mess on my hands. I have half a mind to spare myself the trouble and hand you back over."

Seven winces at this pronouncement, his eyes settling

beseechingly on me. Shit luck if he paid all that money and Godmother kicks me out. It might be worth it to get myself ejected just to sock one to him.

But mine is not the only ass on the line here. I've put Arden in danger, and this is the only place in the world I can make sure she's safe right now. Her eyes are wide with nerves. Even though she has no experience with any of this, it's clear she can feel the tension and understands the danger that fills these sweet walls. The worst part is I've never told her the entire story. She knows her father was human, but not the humiliating circumstances that led to her existence. I wanted to spare her that.

"May I speak with you privately?" I implore Godmother. "I'll tell you everything you want to know about why I left the way I did, but I'd rather just share it with you alone."

"I can see this is difficult for you, Sophia, but your request isn't a private one, is it? Every person at this table has a stake in how this goes. Still, I understand it can be difficult to speak of such traumatic memories. I will help you." Godmother claps her hands and yells over her shoulder. "Bring the tea!"

A pixie whom I don't recognize rushes from the kitchen and places a tea service in front of us. There's only one cup. My skin goose bumps, and my stomach drops. Godmother pours for me. "Drink."

Arden stills and meets my eyes. She's remembering what I told her. Godmother's confections come with magical strings attached. But I have no choice. With a trembling hand, I reach for the cup. Fuck, I'm shaking so hard the tea sloshes and almost spills. Godmother gives me a warning glare, and I use my opposite hand to steady it as I bring it to my lips. I'm terrified, but worse, I feel trapped. There really is no other option. The second I stepped through the moon gate and set foot in Devashire, I made a choice. Arden and I are safer here than being hunted by FIRE. Now I need to trust that instinct.

"Tell me why you ran away." Godmother's command leaves her full, burgundy lips and plows between mine, wriggling over my tongue like a living thing and branching out into my lungs. I try to fight it, but when it slithers up again, along the back of my throat, it expands like a set of clamps that scrape up around my skull and squeeze. The pressure is intense. It's like an industrial vacuum has been hooked up to my mouth and will suck out my brains if I don't plug the hose up with words.

My lips start moving of their own volition, and the truth pours out of me in a forced jumble. "Seven... stood me up at the Yule Ball..." I try to force my lips to stop but each word gives me relief from the pressure. Holding back is agony. My sinuses throb. My ears ring. I have to give her more. "I... rode through Winter Wood... alone. Everyone laughed. I was... humiliated... After, I met a human man." I gasp at this admission, and tears start to flow. My head pounds like it might explode. The truth is pried from me by a magical crowbar. "Later... learned I was pregnant... the human way." So far, nothing I've said surprises Arden, but it's the next bit I wish I could hold back. The spell won't let me. I can't fight the compulsion. "My parents couldn't accept it... I left because... I left because..." Tears course over my cheeks and drip from my jaw. I try to hold back, but it's impossible. My skull is in a vise. Magic crushes my brain, pressure building until sweat drips down my face. I must turn bloodless, because Arden cries out. Godmother warns for her to stay in her chair. Permanent damage is highly possible if I don't relieve the pressure in my head, and in the end, I can't resist feeding the magic what it wants. "I left because... they wanted me to terminate the pregnancy. I wanted... to keep... my baby! I... wanted... Arden to live!"

As soon as the last words are out, the pain ceases. I slump over the table, my brain blissfully free of the skull-crushing suction. I close my eyes and let my thoughts float away, my mind blanking out.

"The Yule Ball, sixteen years ago...," Godmother mumbles. "Yes, I remember that night and the humiliation you sustained. And certainly this young lady was worth your sacrifice to save." I can't see her with my head buried in my arms on the table, but there's a long stretch of silence as if she's contemplating something. "Sit up, Sophia. I have made my decision."

I sit up. Only now do I notice that Arden's face is sheet white. I squeeze her hand. It must have been hard for her to watch me go through that and to learn that her grandparents weren't receptive to my pregnancy with her. I give her a small nod to let her know I'm all right. Across the table, Seven is staring at Arden too, eyes narrowed, a line between his brows. He seems genuinely concerned for her.

Gee, thanks. Not that I don't want him to worry about Arden, but I'm the one who just had a confession magically roto-rooted from my brain. Actually, I do mind. I want him to stop looking at Arden. It's weird.

"Sophia Larkspur, while I can appreciate your motives for leaving Devashire, it does not excuse your actions. You should have come to me with your problem. I hope this lesson has taught you there are no answers in the human world that can't be found in Devashire."

"Yes, Godmother. I see that now." I hope I'm convincing. The truth is, I doubt very much that Godmother would have been any more compassionate about a half-human pregnancy than my parents. "Can we stay?"

"You may stay in Devashire."

I breathe a sigh of relief.

"On one condition."

I look up, holding my breath again.

"You will assist Seven in a security matter important to our realm."

"What?" Assist Seven?

"You will serve at his beck and call until the case is closed and he delivers the answers I seek."

"B-b-but—"

"These are your terms. Do you accept?"

Godmother's magic always comes at a price. It takes me a second to get my mouth to work. Seven watches me from across the table, his expression unreadable. Beck and call. He must love this.

"Sophia?"

"Yes. Yes. Of course, Godmother." If it means keeping Arden safe, I'll do it. I'll do anything.

She hands me a small biscuit from the tea tray. "Then eat."

Hazarding a glance toward Arden, I hesitate for a moment. Once I eat this, there will be no going back until whatever this security issue I've committed to is solved. Freedom will be something I watch in my rearview mirror. I'm about to enter a prison without bars. But Arden will be free. She'll be able to go to college as we planned. I'll find a way... somehow. For her, I steel my resolve and place the biscuit into my mouth. As I chew, voices fill my head in a rush. Invisible vines jut into me, coiling and twisting in my veins. Fae chains. I am bound. I swallow down the last of it, suddenly exhausted.

"Thank you, Godmother."

She reaches across the table, and we shake hands, sealing our bargain. I move to stand.

"Sit down. We're not finished yet," Godmother says. Confused, I glance at Seven, but his expression is entirely unreadable. I sink back into my chair.

Godmother turns toward Arden. "There is still the matter of your daughter. What price shall she pay to stay among us?"

"What?" I can't help but raise my voice, although challenging Godmother isn't a wise choice. "But... but I thought you said if I helped Seven, we could stay in Devashire!"

"I said *you* could stay here."

"Exactly, a collective you." I motion between myself and Arden as Godmother chuckles in that deep rich voice of hers.

"Oh, Sophia, you have been away too long if you make such a rudimentary mistake to assume something like that."

My stomach threatens to turn itself inside out as she refocuses on Arden, and this time I can't help but shoot a pleading glance at Seven, who's gone perfectly still. But his eyes are locked on Arden, and it's clear he won't be coming to our rescue.

"How old are you, girl?"

"Sixteen."

"Old enough to pay your own price, I think. What is your name?"

"Arden."

"Your mother says you are human. We don't usually allow humans to live among us long term."

"I wouldn't be my mother's daughter if I wasn't also pixie. It's true that the pixie part of me hasn't exactly blossomed yet, but it's there." Arden stares directly and fearlessly into Godmother's eyes. Her grace under pressure is awe-inspiring.

I shift restlessly in my seat. Godmother retrieves a tiny plate from the tea tray I hadn't even noticed was there. On it sits a brownie the size of a caramel.

"Eat this, Arden. That is my price."

I shiver and desperately want to beg her not to do it. I have no idea what the brownie does, but it can't be good.

"What's it do?" Arden wisely asks.

"Aren't you a bold one," Godmother muses.

"I take after my mother," Arden says, but truthfully I've never been as brave as she's being now.

"It shows me who you truly are." Godmother studies my daughter's face.

What does that mean? Will the brownie show the balance of fairy and human in her? Or does she mean spiritually, like who she is in her heart? In tense silence, hands fisted at my sides, I watch as Arden places the brownie at the back of her tongue.

Godmother never takes her eyes off her, but what she's staring at, I don't know. Nothing happens. At least nothing I can see on the outside.

"Did you enjoy it?"

Slowly, Arden smiles. "It was delicious."

The corner of Godmother's lips twitches. "I thought you would think so."

"What was in it?" I sound desperate, but anything could have been in that brownie. Godmother once turned a man into a goat with a lemon bar. If she's hurt Arden in any way—

Godmother gives me a sharp look as if she can hear my thoughts. She stands from the table. "Go now. Both of you may stay with my blessing as long as you fulfill the terms

I've set forth for you, Sophia." She nods toward Arden and then in Seven's direction before striding toward the kitchen, leaving us sitting at the table.

Seven stares at me with a smug, half smile like he's just won a prize he wasn't expecting. Like he's feeling very, very lucky.

SEVEN

"Are you sure you're okay?" I stop Arden on the sidewalk outside Godmother's and take her face in my hands. We've just endured the most stressful situation I can imagine, but she's smiling, her eyes bright.

She giggles. "Mom, I'm fine. My God, after watching what happened to you, I was worried, but honestly, I think it was just a brownie."

"A brownie from the Godmother is never just a brownie," I say.

"You know she wouldn't hurt Arden," Seven interjects. "Godmother can be brutal, but she'd never harm an innocent." He's followed us from the tearoom and is lingering in my peripheral vision like a mosquito just out of reach of the swatter. I sneer at him.

"Arden." I take her by the shoulders. "I know this was a lot, but do you think you can go back to Grandma and Grandpa's without me? I need to talk to Seven. I promise you, whatever happened back then, they're not as horrible as you might think."

She places both hands on her stomach. "I know. I get it. I mean, it was a long time ago."

"It would be natural for you to have... feelings about Grandma and Grandpa after learning what you did today. Whatever you're feeling is fine—"

"Mom... Seriously, you were a pregnant teenager, barely older than I am now. It's not that big of a surprise that you or someone in your life considered the alternatives."

A lump forms in my throat thinking about those days. "I never considered it."

She throws her arms around me and squeezes. "I'm okay. Really."

I don't release her until I'm convinced that somehow this hasn't scarred her as much as I was expecting. "I'll meet you there then. We'll get something to eat." Neither one of us has had a proper meal since the night before my last poker game. "This won't take long."

"Take your time. I'll be fine." She gives me a half wave as she turns and strides in the direction of Enchantment. "Bye, Seven."

Seven waves cheerfully and offers her a crooked smile that makes my blood boil. As soon as she rounds the corner, I turn on him with the rage of a thousand feral wolves. "What's your angle? Why would you do this to me?"

His smile fades, his eyes wrinkling at the corners. "Do what to you? I paid to have you rescued. That's something I did *for* you, not *to* you."

"You're... up to something. Convincing Godmother to assign me to this case... thingy? Is this your way of torturing me? It wasn't enough to grind my face into the dirt in front of the entire population of Dragonfly. You have to assert your dominance the moment I return like some sort of... some sort of alpha dog. Is this a game? Is it fun for you?"

"At the moment, nothing about this situation feels fun," he grits out. "And you know as well as I do no one convinces Godmother of anything."

We both freeze and smile brightly when a human enters the square. I barely move my lips as I ask through the smile. "Can we go somewhere private to have this out properly?"

"Love to," he says through his teeth. Before I can protest, he grabs my wrist and yanks me toward a door labeled CHARACTERS ONLY. He doesn't release my hand, even when we are safely on the other side. Once the door is locked behind us, he drags me between two giant fir trees that mark the boundaries of fae territory. Humans can't come here or see or hear anything that happens back here. This isn't the Devashire fairies want them to know about. No, that would be Dragonfly Hollow with its bright colors, cheerful characters, and magical shops and restaurants.

Humans have no idea that at the edge of the woods at the back of Dragonfly Hollow is a lake, and across the lake is a wall that separates us from a dark secret. The wall looms on the horizon in all its marble glory, linking mountain to mountain, its ancient architecture radiant with even more ancient magic. It's been years since I thought of this place. How easy it has been to put it behind me.

I tear my hand from Seven's and turn on him. "How dare you? How dare you, after what you did to me! Baiting me, leading me on for months, then ghosting me in the most humiliating way. All the promises we made to each other. I trusted you, and you hung me out to dry."

"It's not what you think, Sophead."

"Stop calling me that!" I used to find the nickname endearing. Now it just feels condescending.

"Why? It happened right here." He gestures toward the lake. "Right before our first kiss."

"Fuck. You." I point a finger at his chest and charge him, teeth bared. "Fuck you for even bringing that up at a time like this." I gather myself. If this was a poker game, I might as well push my chips across the table right now. I'm an emotional mess, and emotions like this trigger poor, illogical choices. Is it his mere presence that's making me crazy or the fact that I'm exhausted and stressed to the breaking point?

"We were fifteen. I'd been teaching you to play poker. We played a game, and I won."

"Gods, your father owned the casino, and you're a leprechaun. Pretty sad how often you lost, don't you think?"

"Your bet was a dip in the lake."

"Right. Bailiwick's uniform. White blouse. You were an adolescent boy." Annoying as hell I ever let him talk me into that one.

"You weren't even knee-deep when a merman pulled you under. I was going to dive in after you, but you freed yourself before I had a chance."

"Punched him in the nose." I still remember the tug of the water as I cocked my fist.

Seven's expression softens, and he takes a step closer. "I helped you to shore, your hair sopping wet, and I kissed you."

That kiss had branded itself onto my heart. It was a rush, painfully addictive and completely consuming. How I hate to think of it now. I take a deep breath and snap on my poker face. When I speak again, my voice is cool and steady.

"The last time I saw you, Seven, you were tying a red ribbon around my wrist. You said you'd never loved anyone like you loved me and you wanted to show the world by escorting me to the Yule Ball. We would have been the first leprechaun/pixie couple to ever attend. I saved for months for my dress and waited for you in the sleigh *you* rented, smiling while the photographer took my picture, growing more and more suspicious as time trickled by. And then..." My tone hardens, even as I swallow back tears. I will not cry in front of him or give him the satisfaction of knowing how much his betrayal hurt me. "You didn't come. No call. No text. No message at all. Just the knowledge that it had all been a cruel, sick joke. So excuse me if I'd rather not remember the name you called me while you were setting me up for the fall."

"It wasn't like that," Seven says through a tight jaw.

"It was exactly like that." Getting it out like this is good for my soul. Freeing. And I've done it all without screaming or crying. Is that a look of shame on his face?

"It wasn't a joke—"

"No? I assure you everyone laughed. It's no secret that leprechauns consider themselves the superior race. I should have known better back then. I was too open and too trusting. I'm not that girl anymore."

"I liked that girl."

"Just not enough to be seen with her in public."

His face is unreadable. "There were extenuating circumstances."

"Oh, I can't wait to hear this. What extenuating circumstances? Why exactly did you leave me sitting in a sleigh for an hour only to be pulled into a dance where everyone would see you'd stood me up? Where your own father confirmed the ruse and rubbed salt in the wound?"

He hesitates, spreads his hands, and heaves an exasperated sigh. The expression that passes across his face is one I've seen before but can't immediately interpret. "I can't tell you. It's..." He seems to be searching for the right word. "Confidential."

"*Confidential?*" I gape at him. "Let me get this straight. Something happened that kept you from meeting me at the Yule Ball—the one that *you* invited me to and insisted I attend—and these same 'circumstances' meant you were unable to text, call, or send a living soul to tell me you couldn't make it? And the same 'circumstances' must have been why you didn't apologize afterward or even talk to me the next day or the next weeks, or like *ever* in the past sixteen years. That is one hell of a confidential circumstance, buddy."

He folds his arms and his eyes narrow. "I wanted to explain later, but as we established earlier today, you were busy. Very busy."

Oh no, he did not go there! My vision turns red, and my inner warrior reaches for the sharpest spear she can find and aims it right at his vulnerable underbelly. "Yes, I was. And it was *fabulous* by the way. Earth-shattering. Human men are sexual machines. Far better than it would have ever been with *you*."

He raises an eyebrow, and I can tell the barb stings. He'd wanted me then. We'd wanted to be each other's firsts. Instead, I'd lost my virginity to a human.

I got Arden out of it. What did he have?

I open my mouth to say something about the relative size of leprechaun dick, but I'm silenced when I inexplicably trip. My feet fly out from under me, and I land in his arms, flush against his chest. Our faces are close. I can see every gold fleck in his mossy green eyes.

"How do you know it wouldn't be better with me?" he asks in a voice as smooth as hot caramel. "Maybe you should give me a shot. Then you could make a fair comparison."

I shove him away. "Ew, I'm not having sex with you. If you were expecting me to pay you back for rescuing me with my body, you should have saved your money."

I try to stalk off, but a gust of gale-force wind catches my wings and blows me back into his arms.

"Two things, Sophead," he says through a crooked smile that oozes charm. "First, I paid for your rescue because I couldn't stand the thought of you being locked up in one of those FIRE dungeons they like to call a rehabilitation center. I don't expect any reimbursement."

"Yeah, right. I'm sure it was out of the goodness of your heart—"

"Second, if I wanted to have sex with you, I could." His voice drops into a husky timbre, the type that would bring most women to their knees. His words send a chill through me, and I realize what he's done.

"You made me slip just now." I glare at him and try to shove him away, but he's caged me against him.

"Yes."

"And the wind—"

The corner of his mouth tugs higher.

I plant both palms on his chest, willfully ignoring the hard blocks of muscle there as I push him away. I turn to leave, but a small tree falls behind me and splashes into the water. I have to throw myself into his arms again to keep from being struck.

"You just uprooted a perfectly healthy tree!"

"It's a sapling. I'll replant it." His gaze drifts to my lips. "Kiss me, Sophia. Let me remind you what you missed that night."

Kiss him? *Over my dead body*. Fury heats my cheeks.

His arms are around me again. Luck sparks in his emerald eyes. I can feel it, like a static charge rising in the air, a giant, powerful force, invisible but palpable. It winds around me, a hot purr against my skin. There is no doubt in my mind that if this man wanted it to happen, we would fall over, and I would somehow land on his dick. But I sense this isn't as much sexual as playful. He's trying to take me back to where we were before. The way he uses my childhood nickname. The talk of when we were kids. He's teasing me. Playing with me. Well, I don't exist for his amusement, and there is no way I plan to pick up where we left off.

"Is this what you have to do to get a date, Seven? Force women with luck?" The edge to my words is intentionally sharp.

His smirk fades, replaced by a look of disgust. It's his turn to push me away. "Fuck, Sophia, I was just teasing you back after that barb about humans."

"Teasing? Or reminding that you can take what you want when you want it?"

"I asked you to kiss me, not to fuck me."

"I'll take door number three."

He points a finger toward me. "I bought your freedom because I care about you, no other reason," he grits out, looking positively offended. "I've always cared about you."

My hands are shaking. I'm furious and frustrated. I want answers but also to never speak to him again. Worst of all, I can't deny I'd like to be back in his arms. I'm curiously horny, and the memories of our times here, when things were good, are wedging themselves into my already-confused brain. This place, the way he's looking at me, it feels like going back in time. None of it makes sense.

"Fuck it. I'm going home. Leave me and Arden alone." I start for Dragonfly.

A dark and ominous laugh bursts from him. "I *can't.* You're assigned to me, remember? Godmother's orders."

"Fuck!" I bend over and beat my fists against my thighs. This man is going to be the death of me. "Fine! What exactly is this security matter, and how the hell can I help?"

He sighs and looks out over the murky water. "Murder."

EIGHT

All my anger drains away, replaced by intense curiosity. "Murder in Dragonfly?"

"Godmother and I found the body in the square, thankfully before any of the guests did. It was brutal."

"Humans are always killing each other. It was only a matter of time before they did it in Dragonfly."

"I'm not sure a human did this."

"Why not?"

"The body was missing all its teeth and a few choice bones."

I flinch and press a hand to my stomach. "The agent at the rehabilitation center showed me a murder scene exactly like that. He wanted help finding the killer. He was convinced the perpetrator was fae."

"Where?" Seven rubs his chin, intensely interested.

"I don't know. He never told me. But there was a massive footprint beside the body. Wait, could he have been showing me pictures from here?"

"No. We found the body in the square. No mud. And no

authorities were involved. What did the footprint look like?"

"Huge. Skeletal."

"It fits." He looked toward the wall again.

"You think it's Yissevel?" I hadn't lied to Agent Donovan when I said that the human version of the Tooth Fairy did not exist. It doesn't. But there is a bone fairy, a primeval monster obsessed with the skeletons of his prey. He eats organs, but bones and teeth are his passion. What he doesn't consume, he collects.

Seven's eyes narrow thoughtfully. "I've checked with the guardians. No breach in the wall. I think someone went through a lot of trouble to make it look like it was Yissevel though."

"Why?"

"That is the question you and I have to answer. Something like this gets out, it could hurt Dragonfly's reputation as well as its bottom line."

I heave a sigh. "You mean it could hurt your pocketbook. Scare off the humans and you scare off a major revenue stream."

"Your parents too. All of us. Our entire economy relies on human guests."

"Right. What do you want me to do?"

"Come to my office. I'll show you the file on this case, and we can make a plan."

I shake my head. There's no getting out of this, but I need a break... from him, from the memories, from everything. "I just got back. I haven't even had breakfast. Arden needs me."

His lips thin. "First thing tomorrow then."

"Where's your office?"

He hesitates, just long enough for me to notice. "Drag-onfly Casino."

"Dragonfly Casino?" I scoff. "Living the dream then. Following in daddy's footsteps."

"I'm a Delaney, and my father isn't involved in the day-to-day like he used to be. I run the place for all intents and purposes."

"Bully for you. If you're waiting for my impressed face, you'll leave disappointed."

"I wasn't trying to impress you... Gods, Sophia, is this how it's going to be the entire time we work together?"

"Until we solve this murder apparently. How do you manage both running the Delaney empire *and* working for Godmother anyway?"

"We have an arrangement," he says vaguely. "A major part of my role at Lucky Enterprises is heading the security division. There's a lot of overlap."

"Busy man," I say cynically. "With all that experience, I don't see why you need my help."

Seven's smirk is back. He winks at me. "You underesti-mate yourself. I assure you, I have use for your many talents." He manages to make it sound sexual.

I groan in displeasure and scrub my face with my hands. "Fine. The sooner we find this killer, the sooner I can pay my debt to Godmother and put all this the fuck behind me."

"Do you kiss your grandmother with that mouth?"

"My grandmother is the one who taught me how to curse."

He chuckles.

I turn to leave, eyeing the trees around me tentatively and wondering if he'll allow me to go this time or if some lucky event will knock me back into his arms.

"Sophia," he says gently before I get too far. The softness in his tone surprises me, and I turn to meet his gaze. "One day you'll ask me to kiss you. I won't need luck. And when that day comes, you'll remember there's a big difference between leprechauns and human men."

"Not in this lifetime." I take off toward the gate, a shaky feeling lingering in my gut.

MY BRAIN BUZZES AS I TROMP INTO MY PARENTS' HOUSE, desperate to escape the feelings that Seven dredged up on the beach. I wish I could say I didn't want to kiss him, but I'd be lying to myself. No woman can be in Seven's presence and not feel something. I've tasted that brand of honey before, and I know how sweet it is. Kissing a leprechaun is an experience.

And that's enough of that! I shake my head, clearing it of unwanted thoughts. The punishment Godmother has doled out is one meant to open old wounds and make me feel vulnerable in ways I haven't been in years. Whether it is worse than being strapped to the torture table, I can't say. Would I rather have my wings ripped from my back or my heart ripped from my chest? The jury is still out on that one. The good news though is that this prison sentence has an end. All I have to do is solve a murder.

My mood lifts when I spot my grandmother sitting in my parents' living room, knitting what might be a gigantic Christmas stocking. It's shaped like a sock but much too big. And it's April. Typical Grandma. Sometimes her knitting projects don't make sense. One year she knitted me a pencil cozy—a tiny sweater for my pencil. It matched a sleeve for my stapler and a coat to hold a roll of tape. It's a weird habit, but her projects are always made with love.

The moment she sees me, she lights up like a halogen lamp and pops out of the recliner, sending her needles and yarn flying.

"I heard you'd come home!" she squeals with delight. Her silver hair is wound around the back of her head, and her wings flutter with her excitement. She's more than two hundred years old, but her hug is just as strong, accepting, and warm as it ever was.

"Grandma!" My heart swells at the sight of her. "I've missed you so much. But you didn't have to come all the way out here. I would have come to see you in Sunnyville." Sunnyville is a community outside the theme park in the suburbs of Devashire's capital city of Elderflame. The development is designed for more mature fairies to spend their remaining years. To come here, she's had to fit herself into a glittery blue gown. It doesn't look comfortable.

"Pish-posh. I had to see you. Godmother might have demanded any number of things from you today. When Aurora told me you'd gone to the tearoom this morning, I came right away. I wasn't going to miss a chance to see my granddaughter and great granddaughter!"

"You mean in case Godmother rejected us and ousted us from Devashire, you wanted to be here to see us on our way out."

Her blue eyes twinkle. "Well, yes." A guilt-laden look crosses her face. "I believe in you, Sophia, but you know how Godmother can be. Why, when I was about your age, I watched her enchant a satyr to strip off his own skin as a punishment for deserting his regiment. That was during the war, mind you, but still, something like that sticks with you. She can be absolutely ruthless."

I do know how Godmother can be. I once saw her tear the wings off a pixie who'd stolen from her. He didn't die, but it was a painful yearlong recovery. That was her shtick—find someone's weak spot, their vulnerability, and jab a wand into it until they did what she wanted.

"Well, considering you're not packing your bags, I take it she didn't oust you." Grandma's brows rise over her glasses.

"Arden and I can stay. I just have to do something... difficult." Grandma is far from frail, but the last thing I want to do is burden her with my problems. She is one of the few people I'd stayed in touch with when I was on the outside. One of the few people I trusted... trust.

Grandma squeals. "Whatever it is, I know you can do it, Sophia. You're the strongest fairy I know, besides me. And the smartest."

"Aside from you of course." We laugh. "Now there's just Mom and Dad to deal with."

"Ah, that will work itself out." Tears fill her eyes, and she rubs my shoulders. "I'm just so relieved you're home in one piece. When I'd heard you'd been caught..."

I squeeze her again. "I'm here now, Grandma, and I'm okay." I take a deep breath. I *am* okay. Who cares if I have to spend a few days with my teen crush? I've handled worse.

"I want to hear all about what's happened to you. Why don't you start with why you're covered in mud?" She takes in my splattered dress, worry flitting across her expression.

"Oh, uh..." I hadn't even realized that between my slip on the beach, the wind, and the falling tree, I'm splattered with dirt, water, and debris. I'm lucky no humans saw me like this. The last thing I need is another reason to face Godmother. "I visited Glaive Lake. I must have gotten dirty."

She grins widely. "Were you speaking with that leprechaun boy again? You two always loved the lake."

"He's not a boy anymore, Grandma. He's an asshole."

"They all are, honey. It's up to us to whip them into shape." She pats my hand between her own.

I cluck my tongue. "Grandpa wasn't an asshole."

"Sure he was!" she says through a laugh. "You just came along after I molded him into submission."

We both giggle, and I wonder how I ever survived without this woman's warmth. "Have you met Arden?"

"Oh yes! Bright young lady. She showed me something on her phone called a TikTok. Do you want to see the dance I learned?" Grandma bends her knees and starts rocking her hips.

"Uh, maybe later, Grandma. I should probably find her. She's got to be starving. We haven't eaten anything all morning. Do you know where she is?"

"Your parents are showing her the garden." Grandma's voice turns soft and reverent.

I lower my chin. "Not the back garden."

She nods. "Afraid so. It's time you all had this out and put it behind you. Best not to let it fester. Better to do it on an empty stomach anyway."

"I suppose." I knew this was coming. If I'm going to stay here with Arden—and we *need* to stay here—I have to make things right with my parents. In pixie world, there's only one way to do that. "Tell my story after I'm gone," I say dramatically, pressing the back of my hand to my forehead.

"Pish-posh. No pixie has ever died planting an emotion. Go, get it over with."

I kiss her on the cheek and stride toward the rear of the house and the door that leads to the pixie garden beyond. I am ready.

NINE

A pixie garden isn't simply a collection of plants but a scrapbook of memories. For my kind, it is the holy of holies. No pixie would ever invite a stranger into their garden. It would be like handing over a stack of diaries containing your most guarded secrets or opening a closet wide to expose the skeletons inside. Leprechauns and satyrs don't have gardens the way pixies do. It's one of the many ways we're different and a practice that is poorly understood outside our people.

My parents' garden waits beyond a mudroom where watering cans and gardening gloves perch on shelves above a massive utility sink and a wall array of gardening tools. I hesitate and take a deep breath, staring at the bright red door that leads to the garden with apprehension. Unlike most similar doors in human homes, this one has no window to see what waits beyond. For us, it would be like putting a window on your bathroom door. But my parents have taken Arden back there for a reason. They want to put the past behind us, and Grandma is right; it will be easier once we do.

My stomach churns. I haven't taken part in a garden ritual in almost twenty years, and this one promises to be uniquely painful. I take a deep breath and turn the brass knob, pulling the door open. The crisp, fresh scent of lily of the valley washes over me, and my eyes catch first on the carpet of white bell-shaped flowers. As I close the door behind me, I'm overwhelmed by the breathtaking beauty, exactly as I remember it yet somehow even more brilliant than my mind could reproduce. Red hibiscus the size of dinner plates bloom beside a pod of purple hydrangeas. Roses, the color of blood, vine above me, their trellis laboring from the weight of fist-sized blooms which intertwine with coral-colored clematis. Rhododendron fill in the gaps, the edges of their honey-colored flowers ending in a deep blush.

The floral fireworks welcome me forward, and I inhale the heady scent of the blooms, mingled now with the slight jasmine of the lily of the valley and a wisp of gardenia from a tree that blooms a few yards down the stone path.

"Mom?" Arden calls from around the bend. Breathless and beside herself, she gapes at me, for once looking younger than her sixteen years. "Grandpa showed me where you were born, and it's super weird."

Once I reach her, I find my father nearby, previously concealed by the lush foliage that lines the curving path. We lock eyes for a moment. I haven't seen him since I arrived, but my mother has offered no explanation for his absence.

The only word I can use to describe my dad is *formidable*. People assume that male pixies are slight, but nothing could be further from the truth. They do have wings, but just like the rest of our kind, they've adapted to look human. Matthias Larkspur looms over me, six feet tall with a thick head of hair the same color as mine except for a smattering of silver over his ears. His wings are silver too, but more steel mesh than gossamer. Today, there's steel in his blue eyes as well.

"You grew a beard," I say.

"It's a goatee."

Arden waves a hand between us. "Are we going to talk about the fact that you literally formed on a vine?" She points both hands at the plant where I was born.

"Sorry, Arden, I guess I should have explained this when we talked about sex. But honestly, it's not something you'll have to worry about, being human." I shrug.

"Half-human, half-pixie," my father insists. "And old enough to know about the birds and the bees."

Arden's eyes widen. "Are there literal birds and bees involved here? Because I'm having trouble getting my head around this."

I take a deep breath and blow it out slowly. "When a female pixie and a male pixie love each other very much, they spend time together, and when the time is right—"

Arden covers her ears with her hands. "Oh my God—"

"Both of them will cough up a seed."

She lowers her hands. "That is not what I was expecting."

"If they own land and are ready to start a family, they plant both seeds in their garden. There must be two, and if both pixies don't plant their seeds, nothing happens. When the seeds sprout, their roots tangle together and only one plant grows from the two seeds. That plant can bear zero to three children. I was an only child."

Arden's eye twitches. "You grew... in like a pod or something?"

"It's more like a glass ball. You might as well know that

genetics works differently here as well. Pixies of multiple colors and shapes can grow on the same vine. Never assume that someone isn't part of a family because their skin color or the bones of their face are different. It doesn't work that way among pixies."

"Holy crap." Arden marvels at my birthplant, her fingers coming to rest on her parted lips.

"The mother and father fairy tend the birthplant, and when their child is the size of a normal human baby, they ritualistically shatter the glass and bring their baby into the world," I explain. "And that's how pixie babies are born. After that, our development mirrors human development."

"*Normally*, that's how babies are born," my father says, staring at Arden. "Except for you. You were born the human way."

"The normal way," Arden says, her eyebrows shooting up with her nervous giggle.

"*Not* the normal way for pixies," he says, and there's an edge to his tone that I don't like him using around Arden.

I place a hand on her shoulder. "Don't listen to Grandpa. Leprechauns and satyrs have children the same as humans. Pixies are the exception, not the other way around. And our bodies... well, obviously I was *capable* of having you the human way, just like I was capable of living the past sixteen years without a pixie garden."

My father purses his lips and gives a reluctant nod, conceding that what I said is true. A muscle jumps in his jaw. This is no longer about educating Arden. It's about me and the tip of an iceberg of pain we've all been hauling around with us for over a decade.

"Arden..." I swallow hard and rub her shoulder support-ively. "I bet Great-Grandma Betty would love to get to know you better. Why don't you go inside and sit with her until Grandpa and I are finished here?"

"I thought we were getting lunch?" she asks, but then glances between me and her grandfather and changes her tune. "Um, right, I'd like to talk to Great-Grandma, and I'm sure I can find something in the kitchen."

"We'll get lunch. I just need to talk to Grandpa about something first."

She nods, seeming to understand far more than I expect her to. She strides quickly toward the door and disappears inside the house.

"Dad, I—"

"Your mother's waiting in the back. Let's go." He gestures with his head, and we continue along the garden path.

The deeper we advance into the garden, the more the plants change. While the front is a pristine, blossoming rainbow of flowers and shrubs, the landscape changes to typical green hedges halfway back. Eventually, the path is lined with succulents and cacti, prickly but still beautiful. But it's the very back where we are going, to a place hidden in the deepest recesses of the garden, a place where my parents have relegated their deepest, darkest emotions.

We stop in front of a massive black thornbush that rises like a behemoth against an eight-foot privacy wall it's almost overgrown. Its thorns are as long as my hand, and its branches are a tangled nightmare to behold. This is where my parents have planted their feelings about me, and this is what those seeds have grown into.

My mother joins us, stepping out from a small shed at the back of the property with a trowel and gloves. I glance between my mother and father and then back at the monstrosity in front of me. This thornbush is the physical manifestation of their anger, disappointment, resentment, and worry for me. Placed at the back of their garden, it's shameful to them, a manifestation of their deepest secret and most negative thoughts and feelings. I am daunted by how it's spread, choking out some of the green that used to be here.

"It's too big," I say softly. "I'm not sure anything I can say can undo this."

My mother makes a harsh throaty noise. "Not with that attitude."

I take a deep breath. The thing about fairy gardens is that we plant in them the seeds we care about. Negative emotions can be dealt with. Hate is a villain that can be fought. Disappointment can be weeded out and appeased. The only seed that will not grow in a fairy garden is contempt. Those die, if the pixie coughs them up at all. As foreboding as this thornbush is, it proves my parents don't feel contempt for me. They have loved me enough to foster this tangled monster of thorns all these years, waiting and hoping that one day I'd be here to face it down.

This can be undone.

"I'm willing to try." I take another deep breath and turn to face them.

"Start with why you left." My mother folds her arms and pops out one leg.

"You know why. You wanted me to end my pregnancy." My stomach twists, and my muscles tense with the accusation.

My father shakes his head. "We wanted you to go to Godmother and ask for help."

"Do you think you were the first fairy with an unwanted pregnancy?" my mother rattles off. "Godmother has a tea that could have fixed everything."

"By making me not pregnant anymore," I grit out.

"No. Not like that. It was early in the pregnancy. A simple time-travel spell and she could've given your past self something to undo the damage."

"Arden isn't damage," I say through my teeth. "She's beautiful and exceptional and half-human. Maybe I didn't grow her on a vine, but believe me, the human way isn't any less miraculous. And here she is, the fruit of my labor. I love her as much as I love myself. Would you have Godmother undo her now?"

My mother rolls her eyes. "You know that's not what I meant." She coughs into her hand. "Making something as if it never happened is far different than ending something that's already begun."

"We accept Arden," my father chimes in, his voice lined with grit. "She's a lovely, exceptional young woman. Reminds me of you. How dare you suggest we would hurt her in any way? No one would have forced you to Godmother's back then. Sure, we thought it was best, but it was your decision, and if you would have stayed and trusted us, we would have supported you either way."

"Maybe I should have trusted you. I admit that. But I couldn't stay, not after what happened. Not after the stares, the judgment. How could I have raised Arden in that? You know what? If I had it to do over again, I'd do it exactly the same way." Tears slip down my face and pick up speed. I've been holding them back all day, and I just can't anymore. "You don't know what it was like for me. What Seven and his father did to me, humiliating me in public like that, I was the laughingstock of Devashire."

My mother's voice is almost a scream when she responds, "You'd do it again? Abandon us? The embarrassment you experienced at the ball was a shadow of what we felt after you left. You were abandoned by a leprechaun, Sophia. Everyone knows they think they're better than us. But to be abandoned by your own daughter? One who was pregnant with your grandchild!"

"You didn't want her. I did." The words catch in my throat and come out as a croak. I shake my head.

"We wanted her," my father says. "Maybe we didn't admit it right away, but we would have come around if given a chance. I was just so angry that a human had taken advantage of you. I swear if I'd have found him, I'd have—"

"No! Dad, he was *kind* to me. The kindest person I've ever met. That human male kept me from slitting my wrists that night. Part of the reason I left was to look for him."

"Oh, Sophia, you can't be serious. A crush on a human over one night?" My father's disappointment is palpable.

"I thought I loved him. I know it's crazy, but I did." I sob openly.

"We loved you," my mother says.

My father's gaze settles on my tears. "We *love* you." His voice is choked. He turns to my mother. "We knew she was hurting, Aurora. We'd heard what the Delaneys did to her, and we didn't defend her. We didn't go to Godmother and demand justice."

"What would she have done, Matthias? The Delaneys are untouchable! Both of us hoped if we stopped talking about it, it would blow over."

I give a pained laugh. "It will never blow over. Everyone in this town knows I was the butt of his joke. I'm older now. I understand he was a bully, and I'm a survivor. But the pain is still there." I touch my chest. "And all I felt from you was a desire to hide it. You wanted to sweep it under the rug, just like my pregnancy. I couldn't do it. I couldn't swallow it down. And I couldn't give up Arden. She was... she felt magical, like a cosmic blessing."

My mother squeaked and sobbed behind her hand. "I'm sorry, but for the love of light, Sophia, if you'd given us a chance, we'd have come around."

A growl comes from my father's direction. His eyes are wild with emotion, and his lips peel back from his teeth as he says, "No, Aurora. That's a lie. I remember what it was like back then. She was seventeen, and you know damn well we would have pressured her until she caved. No, we wouldn't have forced her, but we'd have made it hell for her before we accepted it. She was months from graduation. Would we have cherished the idea of her walking across the stage with a human in her belly? Had we accepted it, we would have been cut off by every small-minded fairy in Devashire. You think it was bad when she ran away? Think of what it would have been like if she stayed. Raising a human child here? Endless scorn."

"So you think she did the right thing by leaving?" My mother spreads her hands, her face drenched with tears. Everyone is crying now, even my father.

"I'm saying we're culpable!" he bellows. "We all should have pulled together. We should have rallied the troops and forced Delaney to admit what he'd done to her. The other pixies would have supported us if we took a stand and went public. But we were cowards. How can we blame Sophia for wanting better for herself?" A deep cough racks his body.

Magic stirs in the air around us, pixie magic, fueled by luck and blending with the heady, close scent of the blossoms that make up our family garden. Every one, every plant in here started as an emotion, and there are far more beautiful ones than thornbushes. The air is shifting. With my father's admissions and understanding comes my own.

"I'm so sorry," I say, my face awash in fresh tears. "I see now what it did to you when I left. You would have loved me through it had I stayed. You would have supported my choices." I sob. "I still feel like I did what I had to do, but I should have written to you. I should have called. I should have…" My voice chokes off in a loud, barking cough before I can admit that I should have told them what I was doing and why. We'd always looked out for each other. My parents are good people, we are a strong family, and disappearing as I did didn't give them a chance to be the best versions of themselves.

"I should have defended you," my mother blurts. "I didn't. I was too scared and too traumatized by what had happened. The panic… the social isolation… I didn't want to admit it, but part of me was relieved." She doubles over in a fit of coughing.

I know what she means. In the deepest parts of her soul, she was as relieved as I was that I left. My parents would have risen to the occasion, but part of them must have been glad they didn't have to.

"I forgive you," I scream, my hair and wings blowing back in the garden wind.

"I forgive you," my father echoes, his eyes locking on mine and then on my mother's.

"I forgive you," my mother cries out, her red eyes still weeping even as a smile turns her lips.

We double over, coughing. My father is the first to spit out his seed, a prickly, walnut-sized pit that represents all the hurt we caused each other. There's a smear of blood on his palm. There was nothing easy about bringing that one up.

I'm next. Mine is smaller, dark blue, and twisted. It represents my youth, my regret, and the mistakes that were meant to be. My love for my daughter is in there too. It's both a misshapen reminder of the agony I've caused all of us and a beautiful work of nature, infinite potential wrapped in a thin organic shell. It hurt coming out but, seeing it in my hand fills me with warm, healing power.

My mother is the last to produce her seed. She raises her hand to her mouth and ejects a misshapen purple one the size of a pecan. Jagged-edged with a smooth, opaque outer dome, it holds all her shame, regret, and a tinge of betrayal.

Three seeds, each with the kernel of forgiveness inside, the magic of a pixie family bond we will never leave behind. The wind bites into us now, and my mother must bend her knees and throw her back into it to spear the ground with her trowel. She digs out earth at the base of the thornbush. Each of us drops our seed into the hole, watering it with the tears that still drip from our faces. Once she's filled in the hole and smoothed it over, the wind dies down and the sun seems to shine brighter. Panting from exertion, we hug each other, my parents kissing my cheeks and helping me to stand.

A shoot breaks ground, rising out of the place we planted our seeds. Before our eyes, a bright green vine wraps around the base of the thornbush, weaving itself along the central stalk of the plant. Squeezing, choking, ending.

"Do you think it will be enough to kill it?" I ask.

My parents both look at me and smile. "I know it will be," my mother says softly.

On the other side of me, my father laughs. "If it's not, I'll get a backhoe in here and rip it out the human way."

"Daddy!" My eyes flash at the sacrilege.

"It will be enough," he promises. We watch the green

shoot spiral around and around, tightening its stranglehold on the thornbush, until my stomach growls loud enough for all to hear.

"You haven't eaten yet?" my mother asks.

I shake my head. "I was going to take Arden to Foxwood's."

"Good idea. We'll all go. But it's not Foxwood's anymore," Mother says.

"No?" I turn to her in surprise.

"No. It's River's." She leads the way back toward the house.

"River's?" my mind flashes to River Foxwood, the satyr who showed me such kindness the night of the Yule Ball. A true friend, I'd often wondered what happened to him over the years.

"Took the restaurant over when his mother died and his father retired," she explains.

"Let's all go," my father suggests. "I'm sure Grandma is hungry too."

TEN

R iver's Tavern, previously known as Foxwood's Tavern, isn't anything to look at from the outside. It's built from roughhewn logs and mud with a moss roof and a sign that desperately needs a coat of paint. I used to come here all the time as a kid. It's on the outskirts of Dragonfly Hollow, technically part of the theme park but not a location frequented by humans. That's because the human menu is vegan. The food is delicious, but there just aren't a ton of parkgoers clamoring to the farthest corner of Wonderland for a portabella mushroom burger or bee pollen wrap with sprouts. Which means it's the preferred place for "characters" to hang out—someplace they can be themselves.

The fae menu is far less limited than the human one, and I can't wait to sink my teeth into Foxwood's famous burger. I'm curious if the menu has changed now that River runs the place. I'm drowning in memories as I pull open the heavy wooden door. But my nostalgia is soon tempered by apprehension when I experience a prickly reception.

All conversation stops and dozens of fairy eyes stare in

our direction. At first brows lift when they see me, but it's when their gazes lock onto Arden that the whispers start. My parents told me they'd kept my pregnancy a secret. This is the first time most of these people are learning I have a daughter. Well, well, well, back one day and already making an impression.

My father loops his arm into Arden's. "Come help me find a table."

I'm about to follow after them when a voice to my left calls out, "Sophia?"

I glance down at a face I haven't seen in over a decade but that I recognize instantly. "Penelope?"

Penelope Hawthorne has aged well. Her hair is still the color of snow, her skin as smooth and fair as the last time I saw her in the sleigh behind me at the Yule Ball. She's not quite as put together today. She's wearing leggings and a long sweater. There are shadows under her eyes.

She rises and pulls me into a firm hug. It's a strange gesture considering we haven't spoken in sixteen years. We were friends once, and my heart gives a little squeeze thinking about those days. My life outside Dragonfly was necessarily lonely, constantly burdened with the fear of getting caught, and I'm sad our friendship was a victim of that fear. I wouldn't blame her for keeping her distance, but she's hanging on like we saw each other yesterday.

Slowly my arms rise, and I hug her back. In a sea of unfriendly stares, her offered kindness is a lifeline. Only when she releases me do I see Flick and two small pixies at the same table. Both children have her nose and Flick's eyes. My heart warms. They've stayed together all these years. "You have kids!"

"Oh, you remember Flick, and this is Caramel and Witsy." She points at the two kids.

I smile and greet them all, then start to excuse myself to join my family, but she grabs me by the elbow.

"It wasn't because of me, was it?" she blurts guiltily. Behind her, Flick slaps his forehead as if he can't believe she's said what she's said.

"What are we talking about?" I ask, totally confused.

Tears fill her eyes. "Did you leave Dragonfly because of what I said to you before the Yule Ball?"

I balk. "No!" It's clear that this answer isn't as common sense to her as it is to me.

"It's just... It's just..." Her tears are flowing now, and I pat her awkwardly on the back because I have no idea what else to do. "I told you Seven wasn't coming, but I didn't mean for it to happen like it did. And then... And then a few weeks later you were gone!" She clutches her chest. Behind her Flick is rubbing his head like it aches.

I give her another hug, then give a little shake. "Penelope... Penelope, listen to me."

She sniffs, her wings hanging limp from her back.

"My leaving had nothing to do with you. You were right about Seven. I should have listened to you. I left for other reasons."

She wipes under her eyes. Her eyes dart in the direction my father took Arden. "Do you have a daughter?" she whispers.

I shrug. "I do. And I don't think you have to whisper. It's not a secret. If there is anyone left in Dragonfly who hasn't heard I've returned with a daughter, I'm pretty sure they will know by the end of the day." I gesture toward the crowd of patrons openly staring at me.

For the first time, Penelope notices all the gawking faces around us and her jaw drops in outrage. Pivoting in my arms, she flips them all the bird with both hands and in a voice I'd never expect her petite body to be capable of yells, "Oh, fuck all the way off, you nosy bastards. Go back to your meals!"

To my surprise, many of the fairies do. I turn wide eyes toward Flick, who's trying his best to cover the ears of their children. "She's a bit emotional right now," he says to me. "We have a third on the vine." He tips his head toward the kids.

Penelope lowers her fingers and turns a smile back in my direction. "Do you want to have lunch sometime?"

"Um, sure."

"Great! I work at the bank. Stop in whenever you get settled." She hugs me again, almost violently, and sinks back into her chair.

My heart warms at the thought. I didn't expect her to welcome me back with open arms, but I'll take it. I plod past the whispering crowd to the table my father nabbed in the back and sink into an open chair beside Arden.

"What's a raindrop?" she asks me, not looking up from her menu. Apparently, the little drama that just happened behind her wasn't enough to distract her from the promise of food.

"Dessert. It's fruity, like raspberry Jell-O, but more of a foam that dissolves on your tongue," I explain. "You should definitely get one."

"What about the forest barbecue?" she asks next. "Will I like it?"

I giggle. "I do. But it's nothing you'll get in the human world. It's a mixture of meats from local forest creatures, usually whatever the Foxwoods hunted the night before."

"What kind of forest creatures?"

"You know, rabbit, raccoon, squirrel. It's a special blend."

"I love it," my father chimes in. "I'm getting one with a side of fried okra."

Arden places her menu down. "Don't you find it weird that you guys eat forest creatures when you basically are forest creatures?"

I shrug. "I can get you the human menu if you'd like."

She frowns. "No. I want the squirrel burger."

"Forest barbecue," I correct.

"You won't regret it," Grandma calls across the table.

A throat clears behind me, and I glance over my shoulder. A handsome satyr stares down at me, golden-skinned with caramel-colored waves surrounding two curling ram-like horns that sweep along the sides of his head above his ears. A bright smile spreads across his face when his eyes connect with mine, and he stomps one of his hooves.

I pop out of my chair and throw my arms around him in a hug. "River? Oh my stars, it's so good to see you!"

He gives me a firm squeeze. "You too, Sophia. You're a sight for sore eyes." He kisses the side of my cheek. I pull away, smiling.

"Damn, River. Look at you, all grown up!" I raise my eyebrows. Although it shouldn't be any surprise that the boy who was once a scrawny young faun has bloomed into a strapping adult satyr, I am blown away by the change. By human standards, satyrs are naturally ripped to shreds. Human women who go to the Dragonfly Club all want to meet a satyr. They're built tall and broad, are naturally fit, and have a reputation for being free spirits who make generous lovers. I wouldn't know. River and I were friends, nothing more. I can appreciate that he's physically beautiful, but I've never thought of him in that way.

River greets everyone else at the table, and I introduce

him to Arden. He bows at the waist. "As lovely as your mother. Welcome to River's."

I let out a held breath. As stressful as the morning has been, at the moment, I actually feel... welcome.

"How is your father doing?" Grandma asks. My brow furrows as her cheeks pink. Did she just flutter her wings at him?

"Just fine, Betty. I'm sure he'd enjoy seeing you again at his new place." He looks at me. "He's retired out to Mermaid Bay. Sometimes your grandma goes to see him."

Oh, I mouth, brows shooting up. Grandma shrugs.

"As much as I'd love to catch up, let's get your order in. The kitchen is busy, and you must be starving this late in the day." He pulls a pad from his back pocket.

River has servers working at the tavern. I think it's sweet that he thinks so highly of my family that he's taking special care of us, taking the order himself. But then he's always been sweet and caring. It's his nature.

When everyone is done giving their order, I place a hand on his arm. "After, do you have time to talk?"

"Come to my office." He tilts his head toward the back of the tavern.

I owe him an explanation for why I never tried to contact him while I was away. "I'll stop in as soon as I'm finished."

He smiles and heads for the kitchen.

***

IF A HUNTING CABIN AND A MAN CAVE HAD A BABY, IT WOULD LOOK like River's office. After a meal that's as fabulous as I remember, I send Arden home with my family and find the satyr there, sitting in a leather chair with a rip in the side he's repaired with a piece of camouflage duct tape. The desk itself is covered in an orgy of papers. My fingers itch to form a neat stack out of them, but I don't want to be rude. The walls are equally in disarray, with lists, posters, and flyers tacked over almost every square inch.

I laugh. "No computer? Still a technophobe?"

He grins. "Hate it. Not my thing, Sophia. You know me. My idea of modern refinement is sleeping inside on a summer's night. Although I did finally break down and get a cell phone to appease my employees."

That makes me laugh. He is the outdoorsy type, far happier huddled beside an open fire than inside an office building. *So different from Seven,* I think, and then chastise myself for thinking about Seven.

"So... you're back." River gestures at a chair across the desk from him. I move the pile of papers there to the desk and take a seat. "You look exactly the same. It's almost like we were sitting next to each other in class a few days ago. And your daughter... she's beautiful, Sophia. I can't believe how much I've missed."

Same old River. I leave without a word, and when I come back unexpectedly, he's not angry, just mourns our time apart. "Listen, River, I need to tell you something."

"Start at the Yule Ball and end at today. I want to know all of it." He leans back in his chair.

"Actually, that's why I asked to see you. I feel terrible about what happened. You were so kind to me the night of the Yule Ball. What you did for me was incredibly brave and noble, and if I were a better person, I would have written you to tell you so. I would have found a way to keep in touch. You were my friend, and I disappeared on you. I'm sorry about that."

He scoffs. "All I did was bring you some hot chocolate."

"It was far more than that, and you know it." After Chance Delaney had delivered his "Seven did you a favor" speech, it was River who showed up in his truck to drive me home. I hadn't had the strength to walk or fly, and calling my parents would have added insult to injury.

His brown eyes flare. "Oh, come on, Sophia. You must know I had a crush on you back then. I just wanted time in that sleigh with you and to revel in you finally realizing that Seven was an arrogant fuckstain."

I snort. "Truth." Even as I say it though, a little voice in my head tries to tell me that he can't be that much of an asshole if he arranged to have me rescued. I push the thought aside.

Flashing a grin, I say, "Besides, I seem to recall you had something going with Crimson Everleigh at the time?"

"Crimson Never-laid? Yeah, we dated for a while. It never went anywhere."

We both giggle childishly. "You've never wanted for company, River."

He lowers his voice. "You know satyrs aren't really into the whole monogamy thing, right? We love broadly and with open hearts. And we're always fair and honest about it."

I chuckle darkly. "So I've heard." Satyrs are horny, in every sense of the word, and are notoriously caring and generous lovers. But they don't regularly practice monogamy like pixies and leprechauns do. Affairs and multiple partners are culturally accepted among their kind even after marriage. I've always admired the freedom of it, but also wondered at how no one gets hurt. I've never heard of a jealous satyr.

His face grows serious. "One thing I can say for Seven though, I think he did look for you after you left. He seemed almost remorseful."

"Hmm? Why would you think that?"

"When school started back, we had it out over what happened. I took an imprint of his face with my fist." River waves his hand in the air and smiles.

"You did not."

"I did. Fuck, he had it coming."

I snort. "He did."

"Anyway, I thought that was the end of it, but after you left, he kept coming around to ask if I'd heard from you. Over and over." He narrows his eyes. "And I started think-ing… With all that luck, I shouldn't have been able to get a hit in. You know, I get the feeling he let me punch him."

I tuck my chin in and gape at him. "Why would he do that?"

River shrugs. "I'll never understand leprechauns. I just thought you should know."

I squirm in my chair. I don't know what to do with that information. Why would he care where I was? Guilt? Fear that he'd be blamed for my leaving? But then I realize it couldn't be true.

"Whatever he was trying to do, his goal wasn't to find me. With the amount of luck at his disposal, if Seven had actually wanted to find me, he would have. Fuck, he *did* find me when my parents asked Godmother for help."

He nods. "True. So he's well and truly an insufferable asshat then."

"As far as I can tell."

River knocks on the desk twice. "I heard you've already gone to see Godmother."

"Just this morning. Did you know Seven is working for her?"

"Yeah. Has been since right after you left."

"Do you know why? He told me he's practically running the casino. He has more money than the gods. Why would he work for her too?"

River gives me a sideways glance. "You know how Godmother works. It's never about money. He must have either made a deal with her for something he wanted or done something fitting of her punishment. But if you're asking me what it was, I don't know, and neither does anyone else in this town. If they did, I'd have heard it. You know this place is a rumor mill. I knew you were back the moment you left your parents' house this morning."

I fold my arms. "Godmother says I have to work with Seven on a security-related case in order to stay."

The grunt he gives holds more than an ounce of pity. "She does know how to dole out a punishment, doesn't she? Analyzes you to find the open wound and then prescribes the thing that pokes a salted blade into it."

"I guess that's why she's in charge. She knows how to pull people's strings. Knows exactly what they can't resist and what fills them with fear. That particular talent gives her power." I look around his office, trying to think of something to say to change the subject. I don't want to talk about Seven anymore or my sentence.

He studies me, suddenly serious. "Let me guess. You have to solve whatever this is or you remain in her employ, working with Seven for free, indefinitely."

I tuck my hair behind my ears. "Sounds about right."

He taps his chin. "Let me know if there's anything I can do."

I take a deep breath. I was hoping he'd say that. "Thing is, River, I imagine one of the benefits of running this place is that you see and hear everything."

His eyes crinkle at the corners. "Very few things happen in Dragonfly without my hearing about them."

"I don't know enough about this case yet, but when I do, will you help me? Having someone like you keep an ear to the ground could give me the advantage I need to meet Godmother's terms."

"Of course I'll help you. Anything you need."

"Thank you—"

"On one condition..."

There's always a condition with the fae. I should have expected this. I raise my eyebrows. "Don't keep me in suspense."

His dazzling smile is back with an impish tilt. "Come to my firepit on the beach tomorrow night. After everything you've been through, you deserve music, ale, and a warm heart to listen to your woes. You can bring Arden if it suits." He turns over a hand in a gesture of welcome.

Bringing Arden is out of the question. A satyr's fire is an adult situation if ever there was one, and although no one would hurt her, she might see things she could never unsee. She's far too young to attend. Still, I find myself longing to go. I didn't socialize much in the human world. Too risky. Always worried about getting caught. The idea of being myself around good friends with music and laughter sounds like heaven.

"I'd love to," I say. "I mean, if that's your price."

ELEVEN

The next morning, I leave Wonderland on a crowded character shuttle for Dragonfly After Dark, the adult playground of the Dragonfly theme park world, for my meeting with Seven. Dragonfly Casino is a diamond on the horizon, all glass windows and steel girders plated gold. It's a fishbowl, intentionally designed to invite voyeurism, a playland for the see-and-be-seen crowd. The rich love to be watched doing rich people things. Here, those on the outside can witness the glitz and glamor and dream of one day being part of it.

At least *humans* can dream. Fae gambling is prohibited. Too dangerous, with our propensity to bargain and our competing access to luck.

A heavy weight forms in my gut thinking about that. I may have played my last poker game. Gods, I loved it while it lasted. Poker isn't the only thing I was ever good at, but it's the career I built and loved more than anything. What other career combines psychology, game theory, and the thrill of a big win? I've never found any other work as remotely challenging and exhilarating. Losing my ability to be a poker pro is like experiencing a small death. It's losing a part of who I am.

I shake off the thought and soldier on. This isn't about me. It's about Arden. I need to solve this case and earn my freedom. As long as I'm beholden to Godmother, I have nothing to bargain with, and my job prospects are limited due to my obligation to her. Only by solving this case can I help Arden and give her choices and a path back to the human world.

As I pass through the glass entryway, I notice humans already hugging the craps table at the front of the building. It's eight in the morning. Either they got an early start or more likely they were at it all night. I snort. Just like Vegas, Dragonfly Casino is open twenty-four seven. Humans can play until they drop from exhaustion or run out of money. Most of the time they run out of money. The house is run by leprechauns after all. Leprechauns always come out on top.

"I have a meeting with Seven Delaney," I tell the security guard who stops me at the entrance. The leprechaun is wearing a dark suit and an earpiece and scans me from the tips of my wings to my gold shoes, scowling.

The urge to smack that scowl right off his face is almost overwhelming. Getting here required a thirty-minute ride on a shuttle with subpar ventilation. I'm rumpled and annoyed. It doesn't help that I've had to borrow a dress of my mother's and it hangs on me like a sack, not to mention the pastel color is completely wrong for my complexion. Then again, it wouldn't matter if I was wearing couture. I don't belong, not because of what I'm wearing but because of what I am. I'm a pixie, and along with satyrs, we're not welcome in this casino unless we're working here, and even then, our roles are predetermined by our species. This casino has never hired a satyr for a human-facing position.

Pixies can be servers or dealers. Any position above that goes to a leprechaun.

I ignore the man's snub. I'm not here to impress, and I don't care what he thinks of me or my dress. I'm here to do what I have to do to unbind myself from my deal with Godmother.

"I have an appointment," I say again, clutching my bag in front of my hips.

He checks a clipboard on his podium. "I'm not showing any pixie appointments today. Nice try, honey. If you want to apply for a job, I can give you an application, but either way you've got to leave. No pixies at the tables. You want to meet a sugar daddy, try the club."

Utterly irritated now, I enunciate each word as if the man is hard of hearing. "I have a scheduled meeting with Seven Delaney. We're working together."

He chuckles. "Sure you do. I'm sure Mr. Delaney has all sorts of uses for a pixie that would require a private meeting, but he's busy right now."

I scoff and peer at his name tag. "Brandon, could you just call up to Seven's office and tell him Sophia is here to see him?"

Brandon stares down his nose at me and shakes his head dismissively.

"That won't be necessary." Seven appears behind Brandon, eyes dark, mouth bent into a furious grimace.

"My apologies, Mr. Delaney. I was just showing her out," Brandon says.

"Why would you do that when she has an appointment with me? One that we are late to begin because you've delayed her?"

"I... I... It's not on my..." He flips papers on his clipboard.

"Get your things, Brandon. You're fired." Seven has a

few inches of height on Brandon, but the energy he's putting off makes him appear much bigger. He's livid. The testosterone-charged, big-boss intensity focused on Brandon would make anyone's stomach clench. I take a step back, and it isn't even directed at me.

"But... I...," Brandon blubbers, pointing at his clipboard as if an excuse might spring off the pages there.

Seven snaps his fingers and a woman in a suit appears by his side. Where did she come from? Her lashes flutter when she looks at him like she's staring into the sun. Gods, the Seven I once knew is gone, replaced by leviathan in a dark suit. Is he always this intimidating at work? "Claire, please escort Brandon to the back room to gather his things and then accompany him off the premises. Find someone else to man the door."

"Yes, sir," she says, taking Brandon's upper arm. He's still gaping at Seven and then at me even as he's ushered away.

The severe edges of Seven's expression soften when he turns to me, morphing into that crooked smirk I know so well. He places a hand in the center of my back and guides me toward the elevators. "Shall we?"

Momentarily stunned, I shuffle into the compartment. His hand fills the space between my hips and my ribs, and for a second, I feel small and insignificant beside him. Only for a second. The sound of the doors closing snaps me out of it.

"I can't believe you just fired that guy!" I step away from him and cross my arms over my chest.

"His actions display a level of incompetence we don't tolerate at Lucky Enterprises."

I laugh. "The fuck you don't. Your family has been treating pixies exactly like that for decades."

He grimaces. "I have a meeting with you. It's on my calendar. He didn't even look. It's blatant ineptitude. We pride ourselves on top-notch service—"

The snort I give is laden with derision. "Right. So you didn't fire him because he was a bigot who accused me of trying to sneak into the casino to find a sugar daddy, just for not double-checking your schedule. Makes sense."

His features tighten, and he shakes his head. "He disrespected you. It was wrong. Gods, Sophia, I fired the man. What more do you expect from me?"

"How long has Brandon worked here?" I tap my foot.

He slants me a sideways glance. "I have no idea."

I shift, putting myself in front of him. "How badly did he need this job? Does he have a wife? A family?"

Seven pinches the bridge of his nose. "What do you want from me, Sophia?"

"I don't know. Your heartlessness just surprises me, that's all. It shouldn't, but it does."

Our eyes lock. "Heartlessness."

"Yeah. Heartlessness," I drawl.

He holds my gaze as he pulls his phone from his pocket. "Claire, retrieve Brandon and offer him his job back, with a warning. Yes. Thank you." He hangs up and stares at me. "Problem solved."

If I roll my eyes any harder, I'm going to see my own brain.

The elevator doors slide open, and his hand is on my back again, ushering me through a shiny marble reception area. I don't shrug it off. I should, but I don't.

A lanky redhead in an elegant black sheath dress reaches us right outside his office door. "The report you asked for," she says, shoving a stack of papers into his hands.

He thanks her with a shallow smile. They exchange pleasantries before Seven specifies we're not to be disturbed. She directs a wink in our direction before clopping off in her stilettos. Seven removes his hand from my back and leads me into his office where he closes the door behind us. He squares the papers on his desk.

"I think she has eyes for you, Seven," I say, loading on maximum snark. "Did you take her measurements before hiring her as your assistant?"

He grunts in disgust. "That's Eva, Sophia!"

I try to remember who Eva is and it comes to me in a flash. Instantly I feel like a humongous jackass. "Eva as in Evangeline? Your little sister?"

"That's the one."

"She's changed since I last saw her."

He heaves a sigh. "Tell me about it. My dad moved her office up here because she was too much of a distraction downstairs. Eva's in charge of our social media presence and public relations—constantly in the public eye. It's a full-time job trying to protect her from overzealous suitors."

A flood of memories comes back to me of how we used to take Eva for honey and lavender ice cream at Twinkleberries. His family once accepted me, when they thought we were just friends. Well, everyone but his father, Chance. A lead ball forms in the pit of my chest just thinking about the man and how cruel he was to me.

I distract myself by taking in my surroundings. Other than a wall of windows with a bird's-eye view of Dragonfly, Seven's office is a much-needed sanctuary from the fishbowl effect of the rest of the casino. He has walls and a desk of warm mahogany that matches the bookshelves that line one entire wall. A muted blue Persian carpet anchors the decor. It looks expensive and imported, just like the furniture. If I had to describe Seven's interior design style, it would be "things I can't afford."

Seven fits in here in his charcoal-gray suit that skims his body as if it was made for him and most certainly was. Gold clover cuff links glint at his cuffs, and a watch that's probably worth as much as my parents' house ticks on his wrist. He doesn't walk back around the desk as I expect him to but returns to stand in front of me so that we're toe-to-toe. He's taller than me by almost a foot, and when he slants a wolfish smile in my direction, I hate the way my stomach flips.

"This dress is..." He takes the material between his fingers and pulls. Two inches of extra fabric come off my body.

"My mother's," I say. "I haven't had a chance to buy more dresses. I had one that still fit me, but a five-year-old planted a sucker in it yesterday, so it's at the cleaners."

Amusement twinkles in his eyes. "How is Aurora doing? I trust that since you're wearing her dress you've reconciled?" He knows about pixie garden rituals. I shared with him while we were dating, although he's never actually been in my family's garden.

"Yes. All is well. I won't be sleeping in the street."

His expression turns serious. "I'd never leave you to sleep in the street."

"No, just alone in a sleigh surrounded by a pack of ravenous wolves," I mumble. I wasn't sleeping, and the wolves included his father and the rest of town, but he knows what I mean.

He scoffs, then moves around to his side of the desk. He opens his mouth as if he wants to say something else but closes it again and squares his shoulders. A professional persona chases away any remnants of the boy I once knew. "As much as I'd love to once again be berated by you about something that happened sixteen years ago, we have a job to do."

Biting my tongue, I take a seat across from him. He opens a file folder on the desk in front of me. "It happened March 20."

"The spring equinox?" I look down at the picture in the file in front of me. It looks a lot like the one Donovan showed me.

"Yes."

"I can't even tell if this is a man or a woman." The body is a bloody, maimed mess.

"It's a man, although the genitals were ripped out along with the teeth and a selection of bones."

I glance up and meet Seven's emerald eyes, thankful that the grisly picture in front of me is enough to make me temporarily immune to his charms. "I don't understand. You found this in the square the night of the equinox? There's always a huge party there to celebrate the coming spring. There would have been revelers until the wee hours of the morning."

"It happened before the party. Godmother arrived at her tearoom around five a.m. to prepare for the day's festivities. The body was already cold. She cast a concealment charm until we could remove it. Estimated time of death was three a.m."

"Who was the human?" I page through the contents of the file, looking for details.

"Michael Murphy. Just a trucker who enjoyed visiting the Dragonfly Club. Had a thing for pixies. Other than that, nothing special about him."

Included in the photos is one of Michael Murphy

smiling at the photographer in front of the dragonfly topiary at the park entrance. He's potbellied and mustached, dressed in a T-shirt that says I Brake For Fairies. I flip to the next photo and have to swallow down bile at the sight of his mangled corpse.

"The similarity of this picture to the one Agent Donovan showed me in the rehabilitation center is uncanny," I say. "I think what you said yesterday on the beach is right. Someone has gone through a lot of trouble to pin this on Yissevel. What I can't figure out is who or why. The fact that one of the murders took place on US soil points to human involvement."

"Humans don't know about Yissevel."

"No, they don't."

Seven studies me. "When you were on the outside, did you meet others like you?"

His question surprises me. "No," I answer honestly. "I'd heard rumors… a friend of a human acquaintance was arrested by FIRE. But in sixteen years, I never met another fae. To be fair, I wasn't looking for them and I avoided anything related to our kind. I was too scared it might draw suspicion." I try not to think of how terribly lonely it was living in Vegas. My human relationships were better than nothing but necessarily shallow.

"Understandable."

"If a human did this, it's not like they could come and go. Everyone who passes through the front gate is screened, and the only other way in is through the moon gate, which is only open to the fae. A fae living in the US like I was might have crossed into Devashire to commit the crime, but in that case, Godmother would have their magical signature in the wards. And neither of the scenarios explains why the murderer would try to blame a human murder on US soil on a creature unknown to humans."

He rolls his pen back and forth under his fingertips. "Godmother doesn't know about the murder Donovan told you about. Are you going to tell her, or should I?"

"You," I say immediately.

He gives a brisk nod.

The office grows quiet. He's staring at me again, and my stomach flutters in response. Stupid stomach. "So who was Michael Murphy last seen with?"

"We don't know. There was a planned power outage in that sector of the park the night of the murder. No security footage."

I blink at him. "Who knew about the outage?"

"No one who isn't accounted for. We've checked."

"Nothing on Michael's social? Facebook, Instagram, TikTok?" Humans tend to post pictures of their pixie dates.

"Michael was disappointingly discreet about his endeavors here in Dragonfly."

I ponder that for a minute while I stare at a sterling silver sculpture on the corner of his desk. It's one of those pieces of art that's both ostentatious and purposeless. He probably paid thousands of dollars for it and it doesn't even hold pencils. What is it even supposed to be? A wing, maybe? A lightbulb goes off in my head. "What about Flutter?"

He stares at me blankly.

The corner of my mouth twitches, and then my smile spreads. "You don't know what Flutter is, do you?"

"Don't be smug, Sophia. It's very unattractive."

"Ha! I bet your sister knows. I bet your company advertises on their website."

He leans back in his chair and threads his fingers across

his stomach. "Are you going to explain to me what Flutter is or should I go find Evangeline to ask her?"

I get comfortable in my chair and rub my hands together. "Oh no, I'll tell you. Flutter is a dating site like Grindr or Tinder but specifically for humans who want to be matched with pixies and satyrs."

His eyes narrow. "Do users post pictures?"

"Sometimes, but even if they don't, the site tracks who's matched with whom. I bet Michael had an account." I bound out of my chair and charge behind the desk to Seven's laptop. He rolls his chair out of the way, scowling at me like I've broken some kind of unwritten rule. Scowl away. I'm driving.

Gods, this thing is sleek. It looks like it was manufactured by aliens in some high-tech chamber that uses microscopic beams of light to assemble it. The thing is so thin if I turned it on its side, I could probably floss my teeth with it. "Password?"

He rolls to my side and presses his finger to the fingerprint reader to unlock it. I navigate to Flutter. Illustrated fairies flit across the screen, landing on giant flowers where they arch their backs and spread their knees. Nice. I search for a profile under Michael Murphy. Nothing comes up.

"Damn," Seven says.

I search for Michael. Three hundred profiles come up. I start scrolling. On the second page, Michael Murphy's mustached face stares back at me. I click his photo. "There he is. MichaelLovesWings69." *Ick.*

His profile doesn't give us any answers other than his favorite music—country—and his membership in a gun club in Alabama. There's a picture of Michael on the back of a Harley-Davidson motorcycle and another firing a handgun at a shooting range.

"Nothing here about who he hooked up with," Seven says. "I'll get someone from security to see if he can bypass the login and take a look at his profile." He reaches for the phone.

"Gods, that will take too long." I hang up the phone and navigate to a new window. I set up a new email account. MichaelLovesWings69 is taken but I get MichaelLovesWings95. Once I've validated it using Seven's system, I navigate back to Flutter and scroll down to the contact number at the bottom of the page. I start to dial but then realize the flaw in my plan.

"You're going to have to do this. My voice is too high. I could use illusion, but you make a more convincing man than me." I hand him the phone.

He looks at it like I'm handing him a scorpion. "What do you want me to say?"

I grab a pen and a legal pad off his desk and jot down a script. "This."

He scans it, then looks at me skeptically. "No way is this going to work."

Quirking an eyebrow at him, I dial the phone and hand it over. "Trust me."

Seven watches me, phone to his ear. "Hello, yes, my name is Michael Murphy and I need to change the email address on my account, only I can't do it online because my wife found my profile and closed my other email account and phone number. Yes. Uh-huh."

For fuck's sake, he sounds too formal and uppity to be a Flutter regular. I pick up the legal pad again and write in giant letters LIE BETTER!! I underline it three times.

"Yeah, I'm in hot water here," Seven says, this time sounding far more like an American trucker. "Just need you to update the email. Yeah. Sure, I can verify my identity." He glares at me in alarm.

I shift the folder in front of him and point at Michael's home address and social security number. He had to provide them to get into Dragonfly since we are a sovereign government. Seven rattles it off along with the new email. I hear the person on the other end of the line say a few words, and then he simply says, "Thank you."

He hangs up.

I smile wider. "Told ya."

Seven looks absolutely baffled. "No security questions. No two-factor authentication."

I sigh. "Flutter doesn't make its money from keeping people from using its site. They try to make it easy for their customers." I click the link to reset Michael's password, navigate to my new email account for the reset link, change it to something I'll remember, and voilà, we're in.

"Gods, you did it," Seven says, perusing Michael's profile.

Michael is what Flutter calls a *Frequent Flyer*. An icon in the corner of his profile sports an FF inside a silver set of wings. There are dozens of hookups. I grab the mouse from Seven and click on his last match. A picture of a blond, blue-eyed pixie with the handle Wing_Gurl pops up.

"Do you recognize her?" Seven asks.

I glance toward the color printer on Seven's credenza and press print. Laser. Nice. "No, but that doesn't mean anything. A pixie like her would use illusion."

Seven grunts.

"The thing about pixies though is that we often use the same illusions again and again. It's exhausting coming up with new faces. I bet if I ask around town, someone will know who this is."

"Great idea," he says. He blinks at me, and then points a finger in my direction. "And the best place to start is with a visit to the Dragonfly Club. Ask around. See if anyone has anything to say about Michael Murphy."

"I would have thought you'd already tried that," I say incredulously. If he knew Michael Murphy frequented the club, why wouldn't he have accessed the security tapes and interviewed his regulars?

Seven flashes that crooked smile. "We've tried, but you know as well as I do that pixies clam up around leprechauns, and everyone clams up around Godmother. I need someone who can change their appearance and blend in, get the other pixies to trust them."

Many of the pixies that frequent the club work in the sex trade. Prostitution isn't illegal in Devashire, and their ability to look like anyone makes them particularly desirable by humans. But a pixie wouldn't admit to it openly, especially not to someone outside their kind. Even among other pixies, it's considered immoral and reprehensible.

"That's why Godmother assigned me to this case, isn't it?" It finally clicks in my brain. If anyone has a chance of getting the pixies at the club to talk, it's me. I know how they think. My punishment isn't just a punishment. Godmother needs me.

Seven nods his head. "Yup."

I plant my hands on my hips. "Couldn't you just use luck? I mean, walk into the club and flex a little juice, and the person you're looking for will fall into your arms. Be a lot faster than me trying to pry information out of some poor pixie about this guy." I wave the printout of Wing_Gurl's face.

Leaning back in his chair, Seven tries to remain impassive, but I see a hint of frustration twitch a muscle in his jaw. If I didn't know him as well as I do, I might not have noticed.

"Oh my gods!" I grip the arms of my chair. "You've already tried, and it's not working."

He rolls his pen back and forth on the desk again. "Luck has to be directed toward something. There has to be focus and intention. I've tried various things, but nothing has worked. Godmother has tried magic. Whoever did this... they covered their tracks."

"And you're hoping I can uncover them the old-fashioned way."

"Yes. Turn on that friendly charm of yours and see what you can find out." He smirks.

There's nothing friendly or charming about me and never has been. I was born snarky and have fully embraced my sarcastic superpowers as an adult. "Right. I'm a people person."

"We go tonight."

I think for a moment and then shake my head. "Tomorrow night. There will be more people there on a Friday. More pixies. The club culture is tight. If I'm going to do this, I need to look the part of a Dragonfly Club regular. That won't be as hard as it seems considering most of them change their appearance regularly. Only by gaining their trust will I learn anything about this guy."

He nods. "Smart. Tomorrow then. I'll pick you up at eight."

My mouth drops open. "You're going too? I thought the entire point of this was for me to get these pixies to trust me."

"You might need me there for luck or a distraction. Don't worry, I'll stay out of your way."

I consider arguing with him, but I don't have the

energy. His jaw is set, and the expression he's sending my way is resolute.

"Fine. Do you have a smaller version of that picture of Michael? It might help if I can show it around." I could print his profile picture, but the guest photo is clearer and more recent.

"Snap a picture with your phone."

My cheeks heat. "Don't have one. FIRE took it. How about a scanner?"

"Unacceptable," he says around a frown. He opens a drawer on his right and pulls out a smartphone, tossing it in my direction. "I'll have my assistant reassign this one to you."

"You keep extra phones in your drawer? Who keeps extra phones?"

"In case of emergencies. I've been known to lose mine a time or two."

What? "I can't afford it!" I wave the phone between us. "Even if you gave me the phone itself, I'm not sure I can pay the bill anymore."

He levels a stare at me, looking totally exasperated. "The phone is yours, and I'll have the bill sent here. It won't cost you a thing." He grabs the phone and sets up facial recognition using my face, then puts it in my hand. "Take a picture of Michael."

Slowly, I shuffle the photos to the one where he's not dead and snap a picture. I guess I have a new cell phone. One more drop in the bucket of debt I owe Seven. No, I tell myself that this is needed for the job I'm doing for Godmother. As soon as we're done, I'll give it back. "Fine," I say. "We done then?"

"No." He stands and rounds to my side of the desk, leaning his hip against the edge tantalizingly close to my face. Something low within me clenches when our eyes meet. "Have dinner with me."

"Why?"

He pauses, licking his lips in a way that sends my heart racing. "To catch up. Get to know each other again. Talk about old times."

I lean toward him, pulled by some unseen force. I wish I could say it was his luck, but not this time. It's him, the charm, the confidence, the intense way he's looking at me like he wants me more than any of the expensive things in this room. "I don't want to know you," I say, thankful I'm a skilled liar.

He sighs. "It would make things easier if you'd just let me explain."

"Does this dinner have anything to do with the case?" I ask, standing to put more space between us.

"No."

"Then I'm not interested."

"Sophia..." He tips his head like he doesn't believe me.

Suddenly I'm exhausted, and my shoulders sag as I say, "The answer is no, Seven." Before he can use his luck on me or I do something stupid like change my mind, I stride from his office.

I move through Seven's door so quickly I almost slam into Chance Delaney. Seven's father is standing outside Seven's office, looking as pretentious as I remember, an older version of his son with shorter graying hair and sharper features that give his face an almost ratlike appearance. His green eyes are narrower, and his cheeks more sunken as well. He straightens in his perfectly tailored suit as his gaze slides down his nose at me.

"What are *you* doing here?" His tone is laced with revulsion.

For a second, I'm caught in his disapproving gaze. The night of the Yule Ball comes back to me—the physical pain of falling from the carriage followed by the emotional agony of Chance cruelly revealing Seven's intentions. *Now you know your place, pixie. You'd do well to remember it.* How it would have sickened him to know I'd had a secret romantic relationship with his son.

I'm tempted to say nothing and flee, just like I did that night. But then I remember I'm not that little girl anymore. I lift my chin and flash him a wicked grin. "Who, me? I was just meeting your son for a quick fuck."

I take my time striding into the elevator as Chance's face turns red with fury. Just before the doors close, I catch a glimpse of Seven behind him.

To my surprise, he's laughing.

TWELVE

I'm still cursing the Delaneys and mumbling to myself about arrogant leprechauns when I stumble off the shuttle at the Wonderland stop. I'm halfway to my parents' place when the phone Seven issued me rings. I roll my eyes. Gods, he's a pain in the ass. What could he possibly need so soon?

"What now?" I answer, loading my voice with annoyance.

"For one, you could cross the border so that I could punish you as nature intended." Agent Donovan's voice is eerily quiet with an undercurrent of malice.

"How did you get this number?" My words are thready with panic.

He scoffs. "Question is, who's helping you? I have your cell phone. That phone is under your alias, Soho Lane. But the thing about doing what I do, Ms. Larkspur, is I have friends in high places. One of them runs the cellular provider you used in America, one that owns towers all over the world. He was able to link Soho Lane to Sophia Lark-spur for me and put a flag on the account. That friend called me moments ago to alert me that a new phone had been set up with your real name and, wouldn't you know it, a Drag-onfly address."

Fuck! I take a deep breath. *Think, Sophia.* I picture myself at the poker table. My gambler's brain kicks into gear, and I analyze every word I've said and everything he's said. What cards have already been played? What's in my hand, and what's on the table? *Admit to nothing,* I tell myself. "I think there's been some kind of mistake, sir. You've reached a number in Dragonfly Hollow. I'm a pixie, and I've never left Devashire."

He chuckles darkly. "Hmm. I'm overdue for a visit to Dragonfly. Maybe we'll run into each other and you can tell me about your little secret." The line goes dead.

A fit of coughing overcomes me, and a prickly orange seed scrapes up my throat. Anxiety. I spit it into my hand along with a spatter of blood. It's been a long time since I let an emotion manifest like this. Maybe it's my proximity to my family's garden and the redemptive power of our reunion there that has revived the ability in me. Maybe it's the sheer terror Donovan stirs within me. Or it could just be my return to Devashire and the overwhelming intensity of the emotions I'm experiencing daily. *Damn*, I need a hot bath and a serenity candle.

I stare at the seed, a strong, innate desire to plant it squeezing my gut. Instead, I toss it to the sidewalk and grind it under my heel. I don't intend to foster this emotion. Donovan isn't worth it.

By the time I walk through my parents' front door, I'm exhausted and feeling tremendously sorry for myself again. I'm thirty-four years old and living in my parents' house. I'm being forced to follow the orders of an arrogant, preten-tious leprechaun who's responsible for the most humiliating moment of my life. A federal agent has it out for me. Could things get any worse?

"We have to talk about signing Arden up for school," my mother says when I walk in the door.

Yes, yes, it can definitely get worse.

"What brought this up?" I join her in the kitchen where Arden is helping her bake moon-shaped cookies. She greets me with a peck on the cheek.

My mother raises an eyebrow. "Well, *she* did! She hasn't graduated high school yet, Sophia. You're here to stay, and she said she's halfway through her semester. We need to get her enrolled so that she graduates on time. Arden was telling me she's already been accepted at a college in North Carolina."

I brush the hair back from Arden's face. "She has. She's brilliant."

Arden smiles proudly. "I haven't missed much school yet. Just a few days. But I only have six weeks left, and if we have to stay here, well... I don't care about walking in the ceremony, but I have to graduate."

I rub her back. "Right. Absolutely. We do need to figure something out. We will figure something out." Gods, I'm exhausted. "I'll call your old school and see if you can finish online."

My mom and Arden exchange knowing looks.

"You two look like you're conspiring. What's going on?"

Arden gives me an exaggerated, toothy grin. "It's just... I'm going to be here for months, and you're going to be here for... maybe forever. I thought it would be nice to go to school here, maybe make some friends in an actual classroom."

I shake my head, shocked my mother didn't put this to rest immediately. "The schools here have an entirely different curriculum, Arden. It's impossible. Mom, didn't you tell her?"

I look expectantly at my mother but she just shrugs.

"We can always ask, Sophia. Arden has Godmother's blessing to stay. That goes a long way."

Threading her fingers under her chin, Arden smiles wider. She bounces on her toes. I can't tell her no when she's like this.

"I'll talk to the headmistress," I say. "Maybe something can be done."

"Cool! I'm going to text Jayden!" Arden leaves the kitchen and heads for her room. Jayden is her best friend from school. Another pang of guilt hits me that I've taken her from her support system. I am, however, relieved that she has her phone and can continue the relationship. Her *phone*.

Grasping the bridge of my nose, I groan. I hear Donovan's voice in my head ...*your little secret.*

"What's wrong? You look like your brain is going to explode." Mom pulls a finished batch of cookies from the oven and slides in another sheet.

"It might. FIRE knows about Arden. Donovan linked me back to the cell phone account under my previous alias."

Mom raises a hand to her mouth. "What?"

I hold up the phone. "Seven gave me this phone and put it in my real name. Donovan called me on it not thirty minutes after. Arden's phone was on that same account under an alias. I have to assume he knows about her, maybe not her real name, but he knows she exists. And if he knows she exists, he's likely already suspended her passport."

"Oh dear."

"If Arden leaves Dragonfly, and Donovan has suspended or flagged her papers, he'll find her. He'll try to use her to get to me. I'm not sure it's even going to be safe for her to go to college unless I can get Godmother to pull some political strings."

Mom wipes her hands aggressively on a kitchen towel. "Let's think about this. Arden is human passing, and she was born there. She's a citizen. They can't do anything to her."

I shake my head. "They can do a lot. She aided and abetted me. They know now that she's part fae."

Mom frowns in my direction. Her gaze darts toward the stairs before she says in a low voice. "Devashire has a highly rated medical school. Maybe she could stay here."

I sigh. "It would break her heart. Honestly, I'm not sure how I'm going to pay for it no matter where she goes. I need to go to the bank. I had a half dozen accounts under aliases in the human world. Maybe there's one Donovan hasn't found yet."

"You know you're welcome to what we have, but I'm afraid it's not much," she offers. "The store is as successful as ever, but Mr. Jinx has raised our rent."

My parents run a gift shop in Dragonfly. Because they live here and are characters, their residence is inexpensive, but they have to rent the space to run their shop from a greedy leprechaun. The margins are thin.

"I couldn't take your money."

She holds her head. "Sophia, I'm so sorry. What a mess. I shouldn't have raised Arden's hopes by talking to her about college without checking with you first. I just assumed she belonged in school."

"It's okay, Mom. You didn't know, and it has to be addressed."

She presses her lips together and plants her hands on her hips. "You know, Bailiwick's Academy might be the answer regardless. The fae curriculum is different, but she's certainly capable of catching up."

"Without luck? She'll be at a disadvantage."

She scoffs. "You know half those kids aren't as smart as her using all the luck in their bodies."

"True."

Mom pulls me into a tight hug. "It's going to be all right. You've survived much worse than this. Kids are resilient. Arden will adapt no matter what happens. Plus, you don't know *for sure* that Donovan knows about her."

I MELT INTO HER EMBRACE, HOPING WITH EVERYTHING IN ME THAT she's right. We're interrupted when Arden calls down the stairs. "Mom, my phone isn't working!"

Pulling back, I meet my mother's empathetic gaze. "He knows."

✦ ✦ ✦

"IT'S EMPTY TOO." PENELOPE HAWTHORNE GIVES ME A sympathetic look. I'm at Wingtrust Bank of Dragonfly, and she's painstakingly helped me verify that each and every one of the accounts I'd had in the human world has been seized by FIRE.

"Even the one in the Caymans?"

She nods. "Emptied and closed. There's a note on the account that it was confiscated by the US government."

I shake my head. "Looks like Donovan has left no stone unturned."

"I'm sorry, Sophia. Is there anything else you'd like me to try?" She looks at me hopefully.

The list in my hand grows blurry. "Nope. That was the last one."

"Fuck."

"Yeah."

"I can help you apply for a loan, but they're going to want two weeks of paystubs."

I sigh. "No job yet."

She twirls her hair around her finger. "I can recommend you for a position here," she whispers, "but the boss is a leprechaun, and he hasn't hired anyone new in ages. Rumor is we're on the verge of a restructuring."

"Don't worry about me. I've got something lined up." I have nothing lined up, but the idea of working at a bank for a stingy leprechaun turns my stomach.

"So..." She tips her head from side to side. "You want to grab lunch?"

I laugh. "You've just learned I don't have a dime to my name."

"My treat. Please, Sophia. There's something I want to do, and I need a friend to do it."

I look at my watch. It's noon. All I want to do is go home and sleep until an idea of what to do next pops into my head, but the hopeful look on Pen's face is impossible to deny. I don't have the heart to tell her no. And let's be honest, I need all the friends I can get. "Sure."

Twenty minutes later, I'm sitting on the back of a giant bumblebee, eating a cucumber sandwich at a glass table twenty feet in the air. Penelope is beaming, face turned toward the sunshine. "Interesting choice," I say.

"I never get to come here. Flick is afraid of heights, and the kids are too wiggly. I always worry they'll jump. I mean they both can fly, but I don't trust that they won't get caught up in the gears." Pen is sitting atop a purple butterfly with a golden saddle, sipping champagne.

The place *is* charming. It's called Garden Party and consists of two dozen such tables revolving around a giant mechanical rabbit wearing a top hat. "Glad I could be your excuse to come then." I clink my glass against hers.

"It's just..." She shifts in her saddle. "I love Flick, but life can get so... *dull*. And all the pixies here are the same. If I listen to Swallow Everlane talk about her rosewater cookies one more time, I think my head is going to explode. I mean they're not even good! It's all the same people, Sophia. We're all older, but it's just like high school."

"You mean they're still all talking about me behind my back?" I sip my drink.

"They never stopped talking about you. You're the most exciting thing to ever happen to Bailiwick's." We both laugh at the truth in it.

"What was it like out there anyway?" she asks me. "You must have felt so free! To do anything you wanted, whenever you wanted... It must have been amazing." Her eyes twinkle with excitement.

Crap on a cracker, she's completely romanticized my life journey. I'm tempted to just nod my head and let her go on thinking I'm some sort of adventurer, but in the end, I can't bring myself to do it. What if she does something stupid, like leave Flick and try to follow in my footsteps?

"It wasn't like that," I say. "It wasn't what I wanted. It was what I had to do to survive."

Her smile fades. "In what way? It couldn't have been all bad or you wouldn't have stayed gone."

Gah, here we go. At least we're in the air. It would take

effort for her to fly away. "I was pregnant with Arden. Pregnant the human way by a human man."

She inhales sharply. "I'd wondered."

"I knew if I stayed things would be difficult."

Her face falls. "You'd be lucky if Godmother allowed you to carry the pregnancy," she says boldly.

"I find it refreshing to hear someone else acknowledge that out loud."

"I'm sure everyone denies it, but you know if you'd stayed that's how it would be."

I nod, beyond grateful for Penelope's company. She actually looks like she might understand. "I think everyone should make their own choices when it comes to motherhood, and I'm sure that another pixie might have stayed and happily allowed Godmother to undo her pregnancy."

"But?"

"But for me, I knew her. Even before the doctor confirmed I was pregnant the human way, I felt Arden. She was this other presence... *becoming* inside me, like a candle burning in the window of my soul. I couldn't risk that they might blow her out."

Pen places a hand over her mouth, then lowers it slowly. "I think you did the right thing, Soph."

I give her a nod, and she reaches across the table to squeeze my hand. "But it wasn't easy. I was homeless for a while. I had to use illusion to survive."

The space between her brows puckers, but she remains silent.

"I ended up playing poker to support us. I survived sixteen years by pushing my luck. Always running. Changing our names. I tried my best to give Arden a normal American life, but never think it was better than what you have here, Pen. You have love. You have a family. Who wouldn't want that?"

She reaches for the bottle at the end of our table and refills our glasses. "Well then, I'd like to propose a toast." I raise my glass and return her smile. "To being happy with what we have but open to new beginnings."

We both drink.

"Maybe now that you've returned, the promise of love and family is back on the table for you," she says through a smile.

I chuckle. "I think that ship has sailed."

"Bull pucky. There are plenty of single pixies in this town who would sell their best shirt for a chance at a gorgeous woman like you."

"Along with the chance to raise a half-human daughter?"

Her smile fades a little. "If they're worth their salt."

"Meh, I've already found my one true love."

"Oh?" She raises her eyebrows and leans in as if I'm about to share some luscious gossip. "Please don't tell me it's a leprechaun. I've never trusted them, not for a day. The looks, the charm, the wealth? Can you imagine being married to that?"

I laugh. "Not that I disagree, but you're not making a great case against them."

"Oh yes I am. It would be all about them. You'd be a moon in their orbit. Who would ever see *you*, lost in the shadow of their shiny existence?"

"Yeah, I guess it would be like being with a Hollywood celebrity or something."

"So reassure me that the center of your affection isn't a leprechaun." She holds up a finger. "And, fair warning, if you tell me it's Seven, I'm hauling you straight to the psych ward."

I shake my head. "No, not a leprechaun and definitely not Seven." I hate the way I have to look away when I say that. "It's Arden." I smile. "She takes up every inch of space in my heart. I don't think there's room for anyone else."

Penelope sighs. "Makes sense. For now." She grins. "Speaking of Arden, I don't suppose she'd consider babysitting for a pixie mom who badly needs a date night?"

I play with my hair and sip my wine. "I'll ask her. I think she'd like that."

"Sophia?"

"Yeah?"

"I'm glad you're back," Pen says. "You are a breath of fresh air."

I look at her, really look at her atop her butterfly, and I get it. She needs a friend as much as I do. "Me too."

[illegible]

[illegible]

[illegible]
[illegible]
[illegible]
[illegible]
[illegible]
[illegible]
[illegible]
[illegible]

[illegible]
[illegible]

[illegible]

[illegible]
[illegible]

THIRTEEN

After sunset, I make my way down to the beach where River already has a bonfire blazing. A group of satyrs and pixies have gathered on logs around the fire. I wonder if I'll recognize more of them once I'm closer. It's been a long time. People change. I wonder how much I've changed and if they'll recognize me.

A shirtless satyr with a neatly trimmed rack of antlers and low-slung cargo shorts stands and lifts a ukulele into his arms. Voices call out song requests, and soon cheerful music fills the night. By the time I sit down on a log beside River, I'm already smiling.

"Is that Patrick?" I ask, remembering the class clown who used to keep us all in stitches.

"The one and only." He wraps an arm around my shoulders and pulls me into a one-armed hug. "He's on the Dragonfly building crew now but never lost his talent for music." River gives me a smile that lights up the night, then goes on to introduce me to the others. I remember five of the seven, although I wasn't close to any of them. Still, they smile warmly—some of them drunkenly—and I feel more accepted than I ever thought possible.

"Thank you for inviting me," I tell him. "I needed this."

His hand lands on my thigh and squeezes. "No one holds any of that crap against you, Sophia. Well, none of us anyway. Just stay away from the fuckhead leprechauns."

River's smile is infectious, and I turn my attention back to Patrick's song. River pops off the log and retrieves a goblet of wine for me from a cart parked near the woods. It's elderberry. Delicious.

"Speaking of fuckheads, how did it go with Seven?" He lowers his voice slightly. I look around the fire. No one else is paying the least bit of attention to us, so I tell him the truth. If anyone can help with this case, it's River. He sees and hears everything.

"Happened March 20. A man was killed," I whisper.

His brows rise, and he turns his full attention on me. "On the equinox? That is big. How did they manage to keep that a secret?"

I shrug. "Godmother spent a fair bit of magic hiding it. Apparently the victim had a thing for pixies and frequented the Dragonfly Club." I pull Wing_Gurl's picture from my back pocket and hand it to him. "Do you know who this is under all that illusion? We think she was the last one to see him alive."

River takes the paper from me and whistles. "Interesting. The plot thickens."

I take another sip of my wine. "What do you know, River?"

He sobers as he stares at the photo. "I've seen that illusion before, on a pixie named Phoebe Willowbark."

"Do you know where I can find her? I just want to ask her a few questions."

The corner of his mouth tugs downward when he looks back at me, and I realize it's one of the few times I've ever seen River frown. "That's the thing. Phoebe went missing on March 20."

I start, open my mouth, and close it again. "Missing? Like missing as in no one knows where she is at all? No contact with anyone?" He knows what I mean. Sometimes pixies go on trips with their human boyfriends, but in those cases they usually let their families know they are okay.

He shakes his head. "Missing as in dropped off the face of the earth."

I furrow my brow. "Does Godmother know about this? Is someone looking into it?"

He chuckles darkly. "You have been gone a long time if you think the powers that be care about a missing pixie, especially one who was last seen in the Dragonfly Club."

"Was she, uh, in the sex trade?" I ask uncomfortably.

"People assume she left Devashire to be a high-end escort for her human john. It's not unheard of, but I call bullshit. I think it's an excuse for the powers that be not to look into the matter."

"The March 20 timing is suspect. It could be a coincidence, but it's definitely something to look into. What did she look like without her illusion?"

He pulls his phone from his pocket and navigates to a webpage with multiple pictures of the beautiful dark-haired pixie smiling with friends. "Her family set this up to get her face out there, help spread the word that she's missing. Special person. Loved it when she came into the restaurant."

I study Phoebe's face on the screen. I don't recognize her, but she looks younger than me. "Thanks, I'll let you know what I find out."

He groans. "I don't think Phoebe's disappearance is related to the murder you're investigating."

"How come?"

"Phoebe wasn't the first pixie to go missing the way she did."

"Huh?"

"Over the years, I've heard whispers of a predator who targets pixies at that club. There are five others, vanished without a trace, the first going back to before you left. No one has done a thing to try to find them or the one responsible. Their families have tried to pool their resources to hire a private investigator, but no one will take their case."

The idea that crimes against multiple pixies have been reported but no one has taken them seriously makes me sick. Unfortunately though, it doesn't surprise me. "I'm not an investigator, but I'll do what I can to look into Phoebe's disappearance, even if it's not related to Michael's murder. I'm going to the Dragonfly Club tomorrow night to ask around. I'll ask about Phoebe as well."

He gives me a nod of gratitude and polishes off his wine. "Just be careful what you tell fuckstain. He's head of security, and he's not going to take kindly to being called out about this."

I think about that and flash back to Seven firing Brandon for his ineptitude. Seven runs a tight ship. He would definitely take offense at the accusation that his people didn't investigate six missing persons cases due to prejudice. "I'll keep it to myself until I know more."

River's brown eyes twinkle in the moonlight. We watch Patrick sing while we drink our wine. Several minutes pass, and I see a couple of satyrs at the edge of the firelight start to kiss. The man's hand drops between the woman's legs. I snap my attention back to the fire.

"So now that you're back..." River's smile has returned, and he turns it on me. "...would you care to take a lover?"

I almost fall off the log. With widened eyes, I ask, "Why? Are you volunteering for the position?"

He grins. "We were good friends, you and me. It could be fun. Friends with benefits as the humans say."

The proposition isn't exactly surprising. River's never hidden his attraction to me, and he's not the type to be ashamed or uncomfortable about sex. But the feeling isn't reciprocated. I do find River objectively attractive, but I'm not attracted to him. Chemistry is one of those things that's either there for me or it isn't. In this case it isn't. When I'm with River, all I feel is kinship, like he's my brother or something. I try not to compare it to the fireworks that go off in my body when I'm around Seven, but I can't help but think of that now. I don't want Seven either, but I hope to have that type of chemistry with someone who deserves it one day.

Besides, as much as I like to think of myself as a modern woman, I'm not into casual sex. My cheeks grow warm, and it's not from the fire. "I'm afraid we'll have to stay benefit-free. My crazy heart just doesn't work like yours, River. I know myself, and deep down, I want love and monogamy. I care for you too much to ruin our friendship with sex."

He laughs darkly. "Have we met?" he jokes.

"Seriously," I say. "Your heart is much too large for one person, and I'm a one-person girl. It would never work."

"Got it. It's important to be honest with oneself about these things, although I can't say I'm not disappointed." Another satyr comes by with a pitcher and refills our glasses. "Friends then!" He clinks his goblet against mine.

We continue watching Patrick sing and play. I'm amazed how comfortable I feel considering the conversation we just had. The wine flows, and we chat about everything from the moon to my experience working as a poker pro. I'm feeling a little tipsy by the time I remember the other thing I planned to ask him.

"Uh, River, do you have any jobs open at the tavern? I need to find work. It seems that FIRE has confiscated all my assets."

"Aww, I'm sorry Sophia. I'm all staffed up," he says regretfully. "I'll make room on the schedule for you if you need it, but it won't be full time. Seems like a waste of talent though."

"What do you mean?"

"You should apply to be a dealer at the casino. You're more than qualified, and the pay there is stellar, far better than a server at a tavern. I'm sure fuckhead would put in a good word for ya. He owes you as much."

I groan. Everything he suggests is true, but the idea of having to potentially see Seven—or worse, his father—every day turns my stomach. "Ugh, working for leprechauns? I think I'd rather poke myself in the eye repeatedly with broken glass."

His smile tells me he understands. "Ask me again if you want me to take a shoehorn to the schedule."

"Thanks, Riv. I'm going to try to find something else, but I'll be in touch if I'm desperate."

"Nothing I like better than a desperate woman asking for my assistance." He gives a deep chuckle and sips from his wine. We stare toward the fire.

The night unfolds around us until there are so many writhing bodies in the darkness that I start to feel awkward pressure to join in. I hug River good night and slip back into the theme park through the CHARACTER'S ONLY door near River's Tavern. A streetlamp casts an ochre glow over a red cobblestone walkway. I jump when I see Seven standing in the shadows just beyond.

"What are you doing here?" I blurt.

He steps into the brightness, and in my inebriated state, I forget to guard myself against the impact of his presence. It's late, and he's traded his suit for a black T-shirt and distressed jeans. His eyes crinkle at the corners as he takes me in, but his smile is too shallow to have caused them. The smile is a ruse to hide something more. He studies me with intense interest.

"Following up on a noise complaint," he says, but I detect a lie in his voice, and I call him on it.

"Bullshit. You're following me."

He steps in closer, his gaze almost predatory. I sense his luck rise around him. It slithers by me, raw, feral energy, and I can't hold back a shiver. His hand lifts to cradle my jaw and run his thumb across my bottom lip. "Fine. Then let's just say I came because I wanted to make sure you were safe."

"I'm a big girl, Seven. I can take care of myself."

He looks at me through impossibly long lashes. "Yes you can. I've always known that about you, from the day we met."

"I was six when you met me."

"You were a very precocious and wise six-year-old."

I'd heard someone crying in the woods behind our school. Seven was there, alone and miserable. I told him funny stories, and we took him back to my house where Mom fed him cookies and eventually escorted him home. I had no idea at the time that it was odd for a leprechaun to cry or that a pixie with any sense wouldn't befriend a leprechaun. I just saw a sad person and wanted to make him happy. My parents must have approved of that plan because they welcomed him in with open arms.

"What were you crying about that day anyway?" I ask, realizing my child's mind had never thought to ask.

"I don't remember." I sense he's lying. "I was using luck to keep people away. It didn't work on you."

I giggle, the effects of the wine making me sway on my feet. "How *did* I do that?"

"I've always had a blind spot for you, Sophia." A ghost of a smile flits across his face. "Also, I was young and had focused my luck on distracting anyone who wasn't a true friend. I didn't expect a true friend would find me. I definitely didn't expect she'd be a pixie."

A lump forms in my throat. "I *was* your friend, and you were mine. Best friends back then, although I suppose you'd never admit it now."

"I admit it. Even my father would. We were together all the time."

"That's right." An early memory of his house in Elderberry Hills comes back to me. His father was indifferent then, and his mother was cool but friendly enough. "The problem didn't start until later, when we became more than friends, did it? That's when you chickened out and pushed me away." I swallow down the lump.

"He'll never be what you need," Seven murmurs, his gaze drifting toward the door I've just come through. "River is too mundane for you. You've always been a thrill seeker. You want the excitement of the big win. It's why you love poker. You've never wanted anything that came easy."

I sneer at him, angry that his words hit a little too close to home. "You don't know shit about me."

He shakes his head. "Then give me a chance to know you again..." His face is close to mine, and my inner Teenage

Sophia, what's left of her, thinks it would be a great idea to kiss him, maybe fool around a little in the shadowy grove of trees behind River's. It would feel so good. All that luck would rush into me, a hot and effervescent jet stream. I remember how addictive it felt, being the center of Seven's attention, the focus of all that power. It would be a heady thing. I step in closer until we are chest to chest and there's a flare of heat in his emerald eyes. Teenage Sophia is reveling in the growing erection pressing into her hip.

Thank the gods Adult Sophia is in control and she knows better. I clutch my proverbial cards to my chest and snap my poker face back into place, shaking off his touch and backing out of reach.

"Go home, Seven. Use all that luck on something more important than following me around, like dealing with that erection." I pantomime him tossing off, turn, and stride for home. He doesn't follow me.

FOURTEEN

"Mom? Are you still asleep?"

I prop one eyelid open to see Arden hovering over me. She's grimacing and holding a very large box with a giant black silk bow tied around it. I roll my eyeball in its sandy socket toward the clock.

"Is that right?" I mumble.

"It's *noon*! Are you sick? Why are you still in bed?" Arden sets the box on my desk and reaches for my forehead like she's going to test my temperature. Instead, she stops about a foot from me and sniffs the air. "Oh my God, you're drunk!"

"I'm not drunk." I pop open both eyes and do a self-assessment. Am I still drunk? No. Definitely not. I hold up my hand, my thumb and forefinger a few centimeters apart. "I'm a teensy bit hungover. Totally different."

"Mom!" Arden's eyes widen.

I blink a few times and sit up with a groan. "Honestly, Arden. After all that's happened the past few days and all you've learned, the thing that surprises you the most is that for the first time in sixteen years, I drank a little too much last night?"

She folds her arms and pops her hip out. "You'd never let me get away with this."

"I'll make you a deal. When you're thirty-four like I am now, I will definitely let you get away with it. I'll even watch your little rug rats while you do it, if you have any."

A giggle bursts from her lips. "You are not a normal mom."

"Never." I stand and pull her into an obnoxious hug. "By the way, I'm still working on that school thing. I'm going to call the headmistress Monday, as soon as the school opens. I had to visit the bank yesterday." I stop short of telling her there was nothing left in our accounts. I don't want to worry her. "I doubt I'd catch anyone this afternoon, and there's something I have to do for Godmother."

"I'm not missing anything this weekend anyway," she says, although I can see she's disappointed.

"We're going to get you back in school. I promise." I have no idea how I'll accomplish this promise, but for Arden, I'll find a way. "Now what have you brought me?" I move to the box. My mouth feels lined with cotton, and I desperately need a coffee, but this gift looks important.

"It's not from me!" she says. "A satyr delivered it for you this morning. Cutest guy I've seen since we arrived and my age too. I *definitely* want to go to school here."

Part of me wants to warn her off all fae men, but that's not really fair. Arden's always had a good head on her shoulders. No man will ever be good enough for her, but I hope someday she finds someone who's worth her time, either fairy or human. Someone who thinks the sun rises because of her.

"We'll work on it," I say, then turn my attention to the

box and tug at the ends of the ribbon. The bow unravels, the dark strip of silk falling away. Lifting the top off, at first all I see is elaborately patterned tissue paper. Intrigued, I unfold it.

"Wow," Arden says. "Is that a dress?"

Pinching the plum fabric between my fingers, I lift it from the packaging. "Part of one," I mumble. I hold it up to my body and turn toward the mirror. It's off the shoulder and backless with a lace-covered bodice adorned in beads and sequins. Below the waist, plum silk flares out in flirty scallops that hit well above my knee.

"There's jewelry in here too. And shoes!" Arden holds up a delicate necklace of ornately crafted diamonds and amethyst flowers, matching earrings, and a diamond cuff bracelet. In her other hand is a slinky stiletto. "I thought you had to wear Cinderella dresses. Is this allowed?"

"Any gown is allowed as long as it covers the important parts," I say, although in practice there is only one place a pixie would wear a dress like this. I dig in the box and find a card at the bottom. In Seven's even scrawl it reads, *Look the part. I'll pick you up at eight.*

* * *

MY MOTHER GIVES A LONG, LOW WHISTLE AS SHE ASSESSES MY appearance. "Gods above, Sophia. You are a beautiful woman, and that is one fabulous dress."

I smooth my hand over the waist and release a deep breath. "Thanks. I just wish there was a little more of it."

"Seven sent it?" She admires it appreciatively when I nod my head. "He knows what he's doing. This is how the pixies who frequent the Dragonfly Club dress. You'll fit in... have a better chance of getting them to talk. And you won't need as much illusion."

"Right." I tug at the hem, but it's not getting any closer to my knees. I'm just relieved that my father took Arden into town to go shopping and she's not here to heckle me.

"How is Seven?" Mom asks, her fingers tangling in front of her stomach.

"Still an asshole."

She snorts. "I know what he did to you was terrible, but it's hard for my mother's heart not to picture him as that sweet boy who first walked through my door."

I pause, remembering something I'd wanted to ask her. "Do you remember what happened that day to him? Why was he crying?"

She sighs. "I'm not surprised you don't know. You were too young to understand." She smooths her hair. "His parents forgot about him."

"Huh?"

"It was the end of the day, and I was volunteering at Bailiwick's. I'd offered to clean up your grade one classroom, so we were the last ones out of the school. You heard him crying in the woods behind the playground and ran to him as if he were a lost kitten in need of rescue. Maybe he was. The boy was a puddle of tears by the time you brought him to me. His parents simply forgot about him, left him at school. Do you know, when I dropped him off at that fancy house of theirs, his mother didn't even apologize? Just wrangled him inside and shut the door."

I close my eyes for a second, trying to reconcile my adult mind with my child's experience. "Wait... they forgot about him? But they're leprechauns! That doesn't sound very lucky."

Mom runs her hand along the misshapen knitted blanket on the back of our couch. "Luck only works when you focus on something. That woman never focused on Seven or Evangeline. Her eyes... it was like she was dead inside. That family might be made of luck and swim in pools of money, but they've never spent an ounce of it on learning to love each other, Sophia. Frankly, I've always thought the lot of them seemed a bit miserable."

I think back to the early days. Seven and Evangeline were always warm to each other and to me, but their parents were largely absent and always indifferent until the end when Chase Delaney was openly hostile to me. Mom is right. Something was missing in their family.

For some reason, the realization that Seven had a troubled family life weighs heavily on my heart. I tell myself that I don't care, that it's been long over between us and what happened back then doesn't matter, but my heart aches of its own accord. I think what bothers me most is that I never noticed. Even my seventeen-year-old self never thought to ask Seven if he was treated well at home. I'd just assumed that because he was a leprechaun—rich and gorgeous—that he couldn't have any problems as common as a poor home life.

I glance at my watch. "I'm going to be late."

Mom follows me to the foyer. "Better hurry then. Wise if you're out of here before your father sees you anyway." She chuckles. "Good luck tonight."

With a peck to her cheek, I'm out the door.

The thing about living in a theme park is that when someone says they'll pick you up, they don't mean at your front door. Dragonfly Hollow consists of five separate but connected parks. Wonderland, Dragonfly After Dark, Sunrise Kingdom, Thrilldare Island, and a water park called

Mermaid Cove. My parents live in Wonderland, which includes the Enchantment subdivision, Godmother's tearoom, Bailiwick's Academy, and River's Tavern, as well as a main street full of shops like my parents', a fae learning center, and a selection of rides and entertainment. It's a family park that is appropriate for all ages.

Where I'm going tonight is not. Dragonfly After Dark is home to a world-class hotel and spa, the Dragonfly Casino, as well as a variety of taverns and adult-entertainment venues—improv comedy clubs, sexy magic acts, and darkly lit and intimate music venues. But the cornerstone of the After Dark theme park is the Dragonfly Club.

The entrance to After Dark is about ten miles from the entrance to Wonderland, which means we have to drive there. Only no cars are allowed inside the theme parks themselves. When I visited Seven at the casino yesterday, I got there by riding a character shuttle that runs during the day from the circle drive outside the front of Wonderland to the one outside After Dark. That's as close as Seven can get to pick me up.

My stilettos click on the sidewalk, and anxiety worms its way into my brain again. I'm going to meet Seven. I'm going to have to ride in his car with all that masculine energy and tightly coiled power. Anticipation zings through me. Damn it, why am I still attracted to this man? It's like he's a sore tooth I can't keep from poking with my tongue. I wish I could take the shuttle, but it's done running for the day.

When I reach the circle drive, it doesn't take any detective work to know which car is his. A sleek black Mercedes roadster is parked by the curb, and the man himself is leaning up against it, looking annoyed. His eyes rake over me, from my hair that I've left down in loose curls to the shoes he bought me and then back up again. His expression is pained.

"What's up your ass?" I ask.

"You're late."

"You try walking a half mile in these things," I say, pointing at my feet.

His eyes catch on the hem of my dress. If anything, it's even shorter on than it looked when I held it up to myself. It barely covers my ass. The corner of his mouth turns down slightly, and it makes me smile. He bought this thing for me and insisted I wear it. If he doesn't like it, there's only one person to blame, and it's not me.

He opens the car door. "Get in."

I do, careful to tuck my skirt beneath me. He rounds the car and climbs in the driver's side, but he doesn't start the engine right away. Instead, he just stares at my bodice.

"Do you have a problem with this dress?" I snap.

His gaze lifts to meet mine, and I see heat there. Desire. In my mind, I'm thrown back to an earlier time when he was mine. Fire rushes to my core, and I can feel myself grow wet. I hate that he does this to me. I hate that he can make my stomach flutter with a single glance.

Slowly, he shakes his head, never breaking eye contact. "I don't have a problem with the dress." His voice is lower, gritty. "I have a problem with why you're wearing it. This was a bad idea. Have dinner with me, and we'll come up with a new strategy."

"Dinner?" I ask quizzically. "You want to completely blow off this plan?" I'm flabbergasted. I don't know what he's playing at, but I'm getting whiplash from his mood swings.

"Yes."

"Why?"

"You're not bait." His eyes flick down my dress again.

I swallow. "Seven?"

"Forget it. We'll find another way."

As flattered as I am that he wants to protect me from exploitation, I can't let him pull the plug on tonight. "No," I say firmly. "This is a good idea and our best bet to find a clue to who killed Michael Murphy. I need this." My voice rises in pitch. "FIRE drained my accounts, Seven. I have a kid who needs her tuition paid. As long as I'm working for Godmother, I can't devote myself to working for anyone else. I need to solve this case, and I need to do it quickly. We're doing this." I lean back in the seat and cross my arms.

He focuses all his attention on me, and I battle against a warm, melty feeling that starts in my torso despite my mounting anger. "If this is about money, I'll give you anything you need."

"I'm not taking any more of your money."

"Why not?"

"Because you're a leprechaun from one of the most powerful families in Devashire. Owing someone like you a debt will most certainly come back to haunt me. Maybe not at first. You might have good intentions at the moment. But someday you'll want something, and you won't hesitate to hold it over me. It's in your nature."

He scowls. "I can't deny that it's in my nature to make deals—I am fae after all—but this would be a gift, Sophia, just like when I rescued you from FIRE."

I scoff. "Yes, we can't forget about that, can we? Fae are so good about giving gifts without strings attached."

He runs a hand down his face, looking utterly frustrated. "You know I wouldn't hold it over you."

"I don't know you at all."

That draws a flinch as if I've hit him. "I *wouldn't* hold it over you."

I close my eyes and take a deep breath, blowing it out slowly. "You bought me this dress, Seven. This is our plan, and it's a good one. Now do your fucking job and drive us to After Dark."

He turns to stare out the windshield, a muscle in his jaw twitching. I think he's grinding his teeth. With a shake of his head, he starts the engine. "You're too smart to be used like this."

"Yeah, and sometimes smart people have to do things they'd rather not do."

A dark look overtakes his features, but he doesn't say anything else.

I lean back against the leather seat and stare out the window as he drives toward After Dark, trying to keep my breathing shallow so that I don't sniff the crisp cedar-and-grapefruit scent that wafts off his skin. It's light, clean, and elegant, and it clings to him like the silky fabric of his black shirt. *Oof.*

"So did you have a good time with River last night?" he says, a hint of displeasure in his voice.

My head whips around. Is now really the time to revisit last night? "Yes."

He growls low in his throat.

"Why were you there last night anyway?"

"We'd had a noise complaint."

I shake my head. "You were waiting for me."

"I told you, I wanted to make sure you were safe."

"But how did you even know I was there?"

"I'm head of security here. There are eyes everywhere, Sophia."

I scoff. "But why would those eyes care what *I* was

doing? Do you sit alone in your room at night and watch security videos? Seems depraved even for you."

A muscle in his jaw jerks. "In case you've forgotten, there's a FIRE agent with a major hard-on for you out there. Frankly, I'm afraid you'll get caught in his net or, worse, you might run again. I pulled a lot of strings to get you this arrangement with Godmother. I can't have River screwing it up by exposing you."

The high-pitched sound that comes out of my throat is offense made audible. "You can fuck the hell off, Seven. I don't recall Godmother charging you with being my babysitter. Find someone else to toss off to while you sit home alone watching surveillance videos."

His face remains impassive, but a tiny muscle in his eye twitches. He drives faster. After a minute or so, I say, "If you must know, I had the best time until I ran into you on the street. Elderberry wine flowed. The fire raged. Music filled the star-scattered sky..."

"And what about River?" he asks through his teeth.

I smooth my skirt. "River was a perfect gentleman."

Seven pulls into After Dark and parks in a spot near the front reserved for security vehicles. Must be nice.

"You're honestly telling me that the satyr didn't try to get up your skirt?" All this time, he's been focused on the road. Now his clover-colored eyes flash as he turns his head to face me.

I snort. I can't help it. It's just so ridiculous. Is Seven actually jealous? After the way he and his father treated me? "No," I say simply. "I didn't say that at all. I just said he was a *perfect* gentleman." I open the door and stagger out of the car before he can ruin the moment with his own barb.

He's out and after me in a heartbeat. "Did he take you

right there on the beach with the others watching? Is that how you like it now?"

Poker face. That's all he gets from me. "I thought your security cameras saw everything?"

"Not the beach," he mumbles.

I stop short, and something clicks. Growing up, Seven would often take me to that beach. I always thought it was to get away from the human guests. Now I realize he was hiding. No one could see us there, maybe especially not leprechaun-run security. The revelation doesn't sit well. "Too bad for you. You'll just have to use your imagination."

He makes a very un-leprechaun-like sound. There's nothing smooth or elegant about it. It's all male and completely feral.

"What do you care anyway, Seven? It's none of your business who's been up my skirt."

I'm a little ahead of him when suddenly his arm shoots around my waist and scoops me behind the hedgerow near the front gates. My breath leaves my lungs as I'm smashed against his chest. With the added height of my stilettos, we're face-to-face, and a flock of butterflies takes flight within me, their wings fluttering against the walls of my stomach and stirring up fizzy bubbles in my blood.

"What if I want it to be my business?" he says, his warm hand pressing into the arch of my back.

"You gave up that right when you abandoned and humiliated me." I have to say this aloud and repeat it in my head to counteract my body's exuberance at being in his arms again. Stupid body. I thought it had been the alcohol last night, but I'm completely sober now and it's all I can do not to be drawn in.

"I didn't—" He cuts himself off with a shake of his

head. "What happened to you was wrong... awful and unforgivable. But I hope you will forgive me one day."

He releases me, leaving me standing before him, completely speechless. Did Seven Delaney just apologize to me? I'm gaping, trying to decide how to respond, when he straightens, filling every corner of his suit with confidence.

"Change your appearance," he commands. His shift from apologetic to alpha boss man gives me whiplash. "You're going to walk in on my arm, and you need to look like my escort. For this to work, no one can recognize you."

I balk at his bossiness but am too flustered to argue about it. He's probably right. The rumors traveled far and wide about what happened between us. If people remember, they may avoid me. My goal tonight is to be one of them, to put them at ease.

I use a little luck and make my skin and hair lighter, my eyes and lips larger, and change the shape of my face from an oval to a heart shape. I don't need a mirror to know I look completely different.

He frowns but holds out his arm. "Let's go."

As we walk into the park and head for the club, I realize that not a single human in the dozens entering seemed to notice Seven pulling me behind the bushes or the two of us bounding out of them now. Then I remember I'm with a leprechaun. No one noticed because he's lucky. One flex of his power and every mind within range was distracted with something else at the precise time he needed them to be. Damn. It's a reminder of the position I'm in.

Seven is even more powerful now than I remember. He can have anything he wants. He's a deadly, fire-breathing beast of a man with almost unlimited resources, and I'm over here poking him with a stick and reminding him of that time he hurt my feelings when I was a kid. I seriously need to learn to keep my mouth shut.

At the door to the club, we walk right past the long line of humans waiting to get inside. Seven's hand rests in the small of my back again in that possessive way that's becoming an annoying habit. My dress is backless, and his fingers are warm against my bare skin, his thumb dusting over my spine. He escorts me past a man in a black suit at the VIP entrance. The bouncer's gaze passes right over me as he nods at Seven and opens the door for him.

The thump of the bass reverberates in my chest, and I'm transported back to the last time I was here, the night of the Yule Ball.

FIFTEEN

16 YEARS AGO

Cruel. The word echoed in my mind as I lay in bed the night of the Yule Ball. Chance Delaney confirmed that Seven had stood me up, that the ribbon, the invitation, everything was a painful, humiliating joke. "Seven did you a favor…"

Hurt and mortification seeped like rot to my bones, flooding my face with new tears. Images of people laughing at me flashed through my head. Was I any better than a worm caught under a shoe? I was a joke, the laughingstock of Devashire. And the most humiliating part was realizing how naive I'd been. Why had I assumed the social order wouldn't apply to me? I was a pixie. He was a leprechaun. Any relationship we'd had was destined to fail.

How many people had warned me? No leprechaun would be caught in public with a pixie on his arm. Oh, leprechaun men might enjoy a tryst with a pixie. They might do things in private for their own pleasure, but they did not date, and they did not marry, anyone but other leprechauns. It had always been this way. Why would I think we'd be different?

The problem was I'd taken to heart all the lectures in school about ending bigotry between species. I'd thought modern fae society was ready for change. I dreamed Seven and I would be the first leprechaun/pixie couple to publicly marry. The first but not the last. We'd be boundary breakers. After all, it wasn't so long ago that pixies and satyrs didn't share interspecies relationships, but now mixed couples were common. No one thought anything of it.

But leprechauns were different. Everyone had tried to tell me as much, and I'd ignored them. And the worst part was I'd *saved* myself for him. Almost every girl in my class had lost their virginity. But there I was, still a child at almost eighteen years old.

Miserable, I stared up at the ceiling. I couldn't sleep. There was too much pain. Everything hurt. My humiliation seemed to fill the room from floor to ceiling, pressing against the walls. All at once, I couldn't catch my breath. I ran to the window and threw it open, gasping at the cool night as if I'd been drowning.

I had to get out of that room. I had to blow off steam, or I'd never survive this. It would break me. Either I walked down to the kitchen and found a knife to slit my wrists, or I crawled out that window and found a way to numb the pain. There was really no other option.

Before I could chicken out, I got up, got dressed, and snuck out my window. The shuttle didn't run that late, and it was too far to fly, but I hitched a ride with some human tourists. The bouncer let me in the moment he saw me. I was cute and young, the type of pixie human men loved, plus I'd enhanced my features to make the most of my best attributes. And I must have looked vulnerable. Vulnerability made me catnip to human men, a limping gazelle through a savannah of hungry lions.

I hadn't even made it to the bar before men started buying me drinks. There's no drinking age in Dragonfly, but my parents had one. Had my mother known I was in a club, drinking alcohol with humans, she would have grounded me for the next decade. But I drank every fruity cocktail those men bought for me, and I flirted with every man who would pay me any bit of attention.

Anything to soothe the ache in my heart and the humiliation Seven and his father had doled out. They'd made me feel like nothing. Less than nothing. Worthless. The compliments and flirtation temporarily filled a gaping hole in my heart. I was smart enough to know their words weren't genuine, but I didn't care. Bathing in their attentiveness was the balm I needed that night.

And then *he* walked in. I'd always had a thing for American movie stars, and this man could have passed for one. Dark-haired and blue-eyed, he was tall and unbelievably broad shouldered, with a torso that tapered to a narrow waist. Women—human, pixie, and satyr alike—watched him cross the room. I couldn't tear my eyes away, and when he walked straight up to me, my breath caught in my throat.

"You look like a woman in need of some fun," Dark Stranger said, loud enough to be heard over the throb of the music. "Hard day?"

I loved that he called me a woman and not a pixie, although my wings were out. Humans often made the delineation. "The worst," I said. "My date stood me up. Just ghosted me."

He stepped in closer and leaned one elbow against the bar beside me. Gods, he smelled good, like expensive cologne but with a whiff of the outdoors, like he'd just chopped wood or something. I became temporarily speechless as I fantasized about the man wielding an axe, shirtless. I took a deep breath through my nose.

"Couldn't have been an intelligent man if he stood you up," he said.

"I thought he was," I said truthfully.

"You knew him well then."

"I thought I did."

"Now you're not sure."

I shook my head. When I met his gaze, there were tears blurring mine. "I think... maybe I was a game to him. We were playing a game I didn't even know we were playing, and so I lost."

He wiped a tear from under my eye with his thumb. "How could you ever think that? You're not a game. This man, I have a feeling he'll come crawling back to you with his tail between his legs."

The bartender slid a drink into his hand, the dark amber liquid sloshing as he raised it to his lips. The faint tinge of liquor reached my nose as I leaned forward and said, "Maybe I don't want him to. Sometimes it's just all too hard, you know?" I rested a hand on his forearm.

Those fathomless blue eyes stared right into me. "Tell me something, what did you like about this guy who ghosted you—I mean... before?"

I sipped my drink. All I wanted to do was trash Seven. I didn't want to think about why I'd loved him. I'd rather think about how I was going to wreak vengeance on him. But I found the question impossible to resist.

I stirred my drink with my straw. "I guess it was how he saw me."

"How he looked at you. So it was the attention."

"No, it was how he *saw* me. He's from a different world than I am. It would be easy for him to look down his nose at me. You probably don't realize this as a human, but pixies aren't always taken seriously."

"I've heard." Dark Stranger smiled at me, but there was nothing condescending in his tone. He seemed legitimately empathetic with my situation.

"When he looked at me, it was like he saw me, beyond the wings, beyond the labels. Like straight into my soul."

He scratched the side of his jaw and chewed on his straw. "I bet I can guess what he saw."

I giggled. He'd known me less than fifteen minutes. This should be good. "Okay. Let's hear it." I straightened and squared my shoulders.

"You are... someone who doesn't settle for what's handed to them. You're a fighter. I bet you'd rather try something ten times and fail over and over, rather than not try at all."

Snorting, I turned on my barstool so that my knees were facing him. "How could you possibly guess that?"

His eyes flicked up to the ceiling. "Well, you've just had your heart torn to shreds, and you're here in this meat market offering it up again. Either you're a glutton for punishment or you truly believe only those who take risks reap the rewards."

"Ah, but that's where you're wrong. I'm not offering up my heart. After tonight, I'm not even sure I have one."

"Then why are you here?" He had to lean toward me as another song started and the music seemed to grow louder.

"To forget. I want to lose myself. I don't want to care anymore. I'm tired of it. I'm tired of it all."

"You say you want to lose yourself, but you're beautiful and young. There's a lot about you worth keeping."

"You don't know what it's like here."

He ran his pinky along my arm from my wrist toward my elbow. "I know something special when I see it. You pixies, you're known for your illusions, but you, you're as genuine as they come. Whatever happened tonight, you'll survive. You'll come out on top."

"You're surprisingly deep for a human," I said, *and achingly attractive.* For the first time that night, I didn't feel like something scraped from the bottom of Seven's shoe. The way Dark Stranger was looking at me, I felt beautiful and *wanted.*

"Take me somewhere and make me forget," I said, loading my eyes with heat and desire. I was a virgin, but Seven and I had done other things. Everything but sex. I was ready for more. I wanted more, wanted to wipe Seven and our pact from my mind.

He licked his lips and swirled the ice in his empty glass. "What exactly do you have in mind?"

The alcohol and rhythm of the music mingled, turning me brazen. Before I could lose my nerve, I wrapped a hand around the back of his neck and met the stranger's mouth with my own in a wicked, shameless kiss. His mouth was as dark as the rest of him, lusciously warm and soft. But it was a human kiss. There was no rush of luck to curl my toes. Still, a delicious weight formed low within me.

When I pulled back, he looked crestfallen. "No," he said.

I jolted as if the word hit me on the chin. First Seven rejected me, and now this stranger in a hookup bar was turning me down? It was too much. "No? After that kiss?"

"You've been hurt. You've had a few drinks. I'm not the type of guy who takes advantage of women." He swiveled away from me and leaned his back against the bar.

I huffed my frustration. "I'm not drunk. All I want is to

have some fun and make this night not so... hellish. But listen, if you're not interested, I'm sure I can find someone else." I hopped off the barstool and turned toward the crowded dance floor, sweeping the scene for anyone who looked interested. My gaze locked with another human's, this one in a flannel and a ball cap.

Dark Stranger's hand landed on my elbow.

"What's your name?" he asked.

"No names," I said. "It will just complicate things."

He nodded his agreement. "Come upstairs with me. We can... talk."

He took my hand and led me to the adjacent hotel. I'd never been there before and had to stop myself from gaping as we rode the shiny mirror-and-brass elevator to the top floor. I wanted him to kiss me again, like before, but he just stared at the doors. Was he truly planning to bring me back to his room just to talk? Honorable *and* achingly sexy. There was something about him I just *wanted.*

We reached the penthouse and he placed a hand in the center of my back to usher me inside. I paused in the foyer to take in the shiny surfaces, the fireplace, the sitting area. He left my side and moved to a wet bar against the far wall.

"Now tell me more about yourself. What's your favorite book?" He grabbed two glasses and a decanter of amber liquid.

"You took me back to your room to ask me about my favorite book?"

His back was to me as he poured. "I bet it's something like *Jane Eyre*. Some down-on-her-luck heroine makes her way through a vicious world against all odds to find exactly where she belongs."

In fact it was *Jane Eyre*, but I didn't want to talk about books. My brain swam with thoughts of Seven, of the humiliation I'd endured, of my small pixie life and how this might be the only time I'd ever be in the penthouse of this hotel. I didn't say another word. I simply stripped out of my dress and stood naked in front of the fire.

He turned from the cart, drinks in hand, and froze at the sight of me. For a second, I wondered if I'd be rejected for the second time in less than a day. But then his eyes grew dark and a muscle in his jaw twitched. I watched his resolve melt under blazing heat and desire. He set the drinks down.

When he approached me again, we collided. His mouth on mine was a brand. It took no time at all for his clothes to hit the floor, some of them stripped off by his hands, some of them by mine. He lowered me to the floor and slid into me on the rug in front of the fire. He was a generous lover who made me feel cherished, alive, and wanted. And he delivered more pleasure than I ever expected for my first time. In his arms, I pushed all thoughts of that lying, cheating Seven from my mind.

I didn't regret a moment of it. I'd wanted my first time to be with Seven, but now, after everything, losing myself to the feeling of this man's touch was... a relief.

When I woke, Dark Stranger had gone but Kiko rested on the nightstand. A note under her read, *I want you to have her. She's supposed to bring luck. Worked for me. Luckiest night of my life.*

No signature. No name. Just how I'd wanted it.

I gave that human stranger my virginity, and in return he gave me Arden.

SIXTEEN

"Hey." Seven nudges me from my reverie, and I shake off the memory, mentally brushing away spiderwebs. "You okay?"

We've reached the VIP lounge, a quiet corner of the second level overlooking the dance floor. I nod. "Just remembering the last time I was here."

He sneers. "That's right, your human *tryst*."

I lift my chin a little and raise an eyebrow. I'm not ashamed of what happened. Honestly, everything about it felt right at the time, and even now the memory of Dark Stranger comes to me in a rosy hue. "I have no regrets. Not only was it a night to remember, I got Arden out of it. One of the best nights of my life actually."

"I bet you're tempted to search the crowd for his face," Seven snips.

In answer, I lift up on my toes to get a better view of the dance floor.

"Gods, will you just..." He hooks a hand through my elbow and tugs me toward the blue velvet sofa behind us. I sit. He sinks onto the cushion beside me, managing to convey both grace and displeasure in the descent. The way he looks at me, I sense he's going to say more about his disapproval of my personal choices, but we're interrupted when a server pops out of nowhere.

"Your usual, Seven?" she asks, her smile directed only at him.

His eyes flick over her. Clearly he has no idea who she is, and his expression remains serious as he rattles off, "Yes, and she'll have a blackberry martini." Without a glance in my direction, the server prances off to retrieve our drinks.

"I'm capable of ordering for myself," I snap. Just like Seven to take it upon himself to order for me.

He narrows his gaze on me. "You don't want a blackberry martini?"

Actually I do, but he doesn't need to know that. "No."

He tilts his head. "Yes, you do."

I scoff. "Now you think you know what I want better than I do?"

"I don't have to know. I'm lucky, and the luck says that's what you want." He flips a hand in the air derisively.

"Well, you're wrong. Next time ask me."

"Fine. I'll call her back and order something else." He raises his hand, searching the floor for our server.

I pull his arm down between us. "Never mind. I'll drink it. We're here to work anyway."

The withering look he gives me relays that he knows I've lied about not wanting it. Luck is rarely wrong, especially when someone like Seven is wielding it.

"That's right," he says. "We have work to do." He throws one arm around my shoulder and runs his opposite hand up my leg to squeeze my inner thigh. His firm grip on my skin, the scent of his cologne filling my nose—honestly, what is that magic?—and the closeness of his body are all so overwhelming. Something low within me clenches. I try to shift away, but between his hold on me and the dip of the couch, I'm not going anywhere.

"What are you doing?" I rasp breathlessly.

"Playing the part." His lips brush the shell of my ear as he says, "You're a pixie on a leprechaun's arm. My date."

I cross and uncross my legs as blood rushes to my core. I'm suddenly very aware just how long it's been since I've had sex, and despite myself, I melt into his side. "Did you just use luck on me?" I whisper.

His smile goes all the way to his eyes with his laugh. "Not even a little bit. Why?"

"No reason," I squeak. With all the strength I can muster, I push myself up off the sofa. "I'm going to use the restroom." I need to put distance between us before I burst into flames.

He grabs my hand as I pass him and gets a faraway look in his eyes. "Do you have that phone I gave you?"

"Yeah, it's in my purse." I glance at the small beaded bag hanging over my shoulder.

"Good. I have a feeling you're going to need it." Our eyes meet and hold. He releases my hand.

Seven's got a gut feeling about the case. I don't trust Seven, but I trust his lucky-ass gut.

Striding away from him, I suck in a shaky breath and reach into my bag, allowing my fingers to graze Kiko. Holding this illusion requires plenty of luck, and I need an extra hit. Luck flows into me in a rush as my mind focuses on finding a clue to Michael Murphy's murder. Not two seconds later a pixie cuts me off and darts into the bathroom ahead of me. *Bingo.*

Instead of heading for a stall, I wait at the mirror, fixing my lipstick. The toilet flushes, and then the pixie appears beside me and starts washing her hands. I'm about to ask her about Michael Murphy when she blurts, "You're the one who came in with Seven. Damn. I don't think I've ever seen him with a pixie before."

My brow furrows. How did this become about Seven, again? "Thanks, but I'm sure he has a different woman on his arm every night."

"We all look like different women." She laughs pointing at her face which is obviously masked in illusion. "Don't worry, I won't ask you who you are. Any pixie on that man's arm needs to hide her identity if she values her life and reputation. The jealousy must be real."

"Yeah. It's important to be discreet."

"But to answer your question, no, I've never seen him with anyone." She shakes her head. "Believe me, many have tried; many have failed. I assumed he was like his father."

"What about his father?"

"You know, a pixaphobe." The pixie raises her eyebrows like I must be from another world if I don't know this. "Before Seven took over, his father tried several times to impose the casino rules on the club. Wanted pixies and satyrs banned from this place unless we were working. Thinks we're fae garbage."

I snort. "That couldn't have been a popular opinion. The humans come here for the pixies."

She laughs. "Right? Anyway, things are better now that Seven's in charge. Took it over from his father a few years ago. Before that he was a major reason his father didn't get his way. He even got Godmother involved. Everyone knows it would be terrible for business if pixies didn't frequent this club."

"Leprechauns." I groan.

She laughs.

"Hey, I wonder if you might help me with something." I pull my phone from my purse and show her the picture of Michael Murphy. "Have you seen this guy around?"

"Why do you ask?"

"I met him a while ago. Lost his number. Just wondering if he's been in recently."

"He's not Seven, but he pays well. I'll give you that." She leans toward the mirror to fix her makeup. "Haven't seen him in weeks though. Sorry. He sort of dropped off the face of the earth recently, but you know how humans are. They party until they run out of money, and then you never see them again."

I nod. "Right."

She tosses her lipstick into her purse and turns to leave. "What about Phoebe Willowbark?" I blurt. "Do you know her?"

She stops and turns around to face me again, a deep vee wrinkling her forehead. "How did you know Phoebe?"

I shrug. "Around. Haven't seen her in a while."

"That's because she's missing," the pixie says through tight lips. "It's been weeks. Her family has been worried sick."

"Maybe she ran off with Michael," I say lightly.

The other pixie doesn't laugh. "You must not have known Phoebe well if you think so."

"No?" I try to keep my voice light, but my luck is sending a chill through me.

She shakes her head. "No. She hated humans. Wouldn't have been seen dead with one. Just wasn't her thing. She came here for the other fae."

"Oh." My mind races trying to process that information as the other pixie tells me to stay safe and hurries from the restroom.

Phoebe didn't care for humans, and now she's missing, but she arranged a date with Michael Murphy. She went missing around the same time as Michael's murder. I see three possible scenarios here. One, the two aren't related at all. Two, Phoebe tried something new, but when Michael came on too strong, she killed him, then tried to frame an unseelie for it and vamoosed before she could get caught. Or three, someone Phoebe was with committed the murder. Perhaps another fae that didn't appreciate the attention Michael was showing her.

Hmm. I need to talk to Seven. Phoebe hated humans, was the last to be seen with Michael, and Michael is dead. That's officially enough to be suspect in my mind. He needs to know.

I finish in the bathroom before heading back to the lounge to tell him what I've learned. I stop short when I almost collide with a dark figure coming from Seven's direction. "Excuse me," I say, automatically. Then I lift my gaze and stop breathing.

Agent Donovan! My heart pounds, and panic pumps through my veins until I realize he doesn't recognize me. I reinforce my illusion. What the fuck is he doing here? Then I remember his call and that he said he'd come. Is he looking for me?

His dark perusal skims over me. "You're new."

I give a curt nod. I try to walk around him but he steps in front of me. "How about a ride?" He reaches out and strokes my wing. I tug it from his grasp before the blue iron in his system can threaten my illusion. My stomach wants to turn inside out at his touch. The way he's looking at me makes my skin want to crawl off my body.

"I'm taken," I say in a voice that is not my own. I point my chin in Seven's direction. Donovan turns to the side and glances that way too. I'm surprised to see Seven's not alone. He's standing in front of the couch with his back to us, and his father of all people is ripping into him. For a second, I worry about catching Chance's eye—the last thing I want is to run into that man again—then I remember I don't look like me. Fuck, they're really going at it. Chance has Seven by the collar, and he's shaking him. I can't hear what he's saying, but it looks like it's escalating.

Donovan takes a step away from me when he spots the two men, seemingly put off by the idea that I'm with the leprechauns. *Good*.

"Maybe next time," he says, raking me over with a lecherous gaze. I press a hand into my churning stomach. He strides past me toward the back stairs and descends to the dance floor where humans and fairies alike gyrate to the music below, and I breathe a sigh of relief. Over the railing, I watch him disappear into the sea of bodies. Everywhere patrons grind against each other, or do their best to pick up fae at the bar. Pixies, wrapped in illusion, attempt to make themselves more desirable to lure in the best humans.

None of them realize there's a FIRE agent in their midst who dreams about making them scream.

I jump when a hand wraps around my upper arm. Seven. He plants his hand on my waist and starts guiding me toward the back of the club, moving fast. "Where are we going?"

"I need to talk to you, *now*." He looks furious. He moves faster toward the exit.

"Seven, I can't run in this dress!"

Luck bubbles in my veins. Suddenly the skirt of the dress gives, and I increase my stride to match his. We're down the back stairway and out an emergency exit before I can say another word. He opens the car door for me.

"What's going on?" I stop short of getting in and fold my arms.

But Seven isn't paying any attention to me. His expression is dark, menacing. I've never seen him so angry. "Can't do this to me. Not a kid anymore," he mumbles.

"Seven, what the hell is going on!"

Emerald eyes flash, and the intensity almost makes me stumble. "Get in the car. There's something I have to tell you."

SEVENTEEN

Reluctantly, I slide into the leather seat, feeling painfully uncomfortable about everything that's happened. All I want to do is go home and have a hot cup of tea, but as soon as I close the door Seven starts the engine and races in the opposite direction of Wonderland.

"I thought you had something to tell me," I say, buckling my seat belt. It would be highly unlikely that a leprechaun would get into a car accident, but call it a habit from living among humans.

"I do. But first we need to get somewhere safe. Somewhere he doesn't have people watching."

"Who? Your father?"

"Who else, Sophia?" He glances toward me, and his lip curls in displeasure. "Drop your illusion. It's unsettling."

I shake off the disguise. "It was your idea!"

He glances back at me, and it might be my imagination, but his eyes seem to spark when he sees me this time. "Better. You're a work of art in that dress."

"I'm a..." Did he just call me a work of art? I hold on to

the door as he takes a sharp corner. "Where are you taking me?"

"Home."

"Wonderland is that way." I point over my shoulder.

"My home. It's the only place he doesn't have access to the security footage. He owns fucking everything else."

The night grows thicker as we break from Dragonfly and enter Elderflame, the capital city of Devashire. Before I can even process that Seven is actually taking me to his inner sanctum, we're parking in a private garage under a skyscraper.

"Seven, I don't think—"

He's out and around the car, opening my door and pulling me from my seat. Still intensely angry about whatever he fought about with his dad, his steps are quick and I almost have to jog to keep up. With his fingers entwined with mine, he ushers me toward the elevator, the heat from his hand making me oddly flustered. Why does his touch do this to me after everything?

There are a dozen reasons why I should protest going home with him, not the least of which is that I'll be completely vulnerable there. Seven can overpower me in a heartbeat. Even if I use Kiko, he has more luck than I'll ever have. I shouldn't trust him.

But I can't bring myself to say anything, and despite myself, I can't move away when he clings to my hand in the elevator. I feel his touch deep within me. There's so much sexual tension in the small, enclosed space I can feel it pressing against my skin like moisture on a humid day. It ricochets off the walls. I'm carnally aware of every square inch of him beside me. It's so quiet, I can hear myself swallow.

And then he moves. His hand slides from mine as the

doors open and he walks into a sparsely decorated but elegant foyer.

"This is a bad idea," I mumble as I follow after him. He ignores me.

Another leprechaun in a dark suit waits at a desk beside a beautifully crafted door. Seven nods to him. "If anyone asks, I'm not here. No one goes in or out. Understood?"

The man nods. Before I know it, Seven has unlocked the door and swept me inside.

What have I gotten myself into? This is a far more intimate scenario than what I wanted to experience with this man tonight. I'm not sure that I'm strong enough for this. His presence ignites too many memories. Too many feelings. They're all tangled up in me in a confusing knot that weighs heavily at the pit of my stomach and has the blood rushing lower. It's a thrill, and Seven was telling the truth when he said I was a thrill seeker. My desire to self-protect wars with my need to dive headfirst into the excitement of the moment.

I fold my arms, a barrier between us. "What the hell is going on, Seven?"

He doesn't answer right away. Instead, he moves through the foyer—oh my gods, this apartment has a massive foyer—and into a main room with a wall of windows overlooking the city. *Fuck*, who lives like this? If I thought Seven's office was decorated in a style called things-I-can't-afford, this condo is things-so-out-of-my-price-range-I-didn't-know-they-existed!

I glance down to watch three koi fish swim through the center of his living room. A custom fish tank winds like a river through the pale marble floor under a thick pane of glass. I've never seen anything like it.

"Nice fish."

He glances at me. "The river ends at a pool on the balcony. You can feed them if you'd like."

Is he really asking if I want to feed his penthouse fish? Now? "Maybe later."

He nods, then crosses to a bar in the corner of the room. Across the glass river with the fish is a seating area anchored by an ecru carpet with a subtle geometric pattern of interlocking rings. Atop it a stone coffee table that's big enough to accommodate a human sacrifice is neighbored by a sofa the color of fresh whipped cream and two chairs that belong in a museum. Everything faces the windows and the balcony beyond. There's no TV or magazines or clutter of any kind. If there is a single grain of dust anywhere in this room, it's well hidden. There is, however, a shiny black baby grand piano in the corner.

Does he even play?

"Would you like something to drink?" Seven pours himself a glass of amber liquid from a decanter.

"Who even fills that thing? Why can't rich people pour from the bottle like everyone else?" I ask.

The corner of his mouth twitches. "My housekeeper, and it oxygenates the whiskey. Any other questions?"

"Yes," I say immediately. "Why the fuck am I here? And why the clash-of-the-titans action in the Dragonfly Club? I thought the glasses were going to shatter from the luck coming off you two."

He snorts and walks to the windows, taking his glass with him. He leans an arm against the pane and rests his forehead against it.

"This thing between us, Sophia, it's a mess. A big, fucking mess."

I bristle. "There is no *thing* between us, Seven. There hasn't been for a long time."

He just keeps staring out across the city.

"Tell me what you remember about that night. Hit me with it."

"You know what happened. We talked about this on the beach."

"I want to hear it again, from your perspective."

"My perspective?" I stiffen. What the hell is his game? But then something inside me decides it might be fun to lash out. He's asking, and I have a lot of rage to air. "Fine. Here's what happened. I arrived at the staging point exactly on time. My dress was the same color plum as this one. You probably didn't know that considering you never saw it. It was strapless and full, and my mother had rented a tiara. I looked and felt like a princess. But the only thing that really mattered to me was the red ribbon tied around my wrist. As excited as I was for the ball, I was more excited about you. We'd dated in secret for two years and had been friends since first grade. That night we were going to make every-thing public."

"We were going to do more than that," he mutters.

"I thought I was telling this story."

He tips his head. "Please."

"None of my friends believed I was actually dating you. A pixie dating a leprechaun was unheard of in Devashire. Dating a Delaney was impossible. But I was sure you loved me. We'd spent so much time together. For fuck's sake, we'd made a pact to lose our virginity to each other."

I study his reaction as he shifts uncomfortably and takes another drink. When he doesn't turn from the window, I continue. It's easier, talking to his back.

"The sleigh was blood red, and a thick blanket of gray fur was draped across the seat. My shoulders were cold, and I wanted to wrap that blanket around me. But since you were late, Mrs. Harper—do you remember Mrs. Harper?—told me I'd have to sit in the driver's seat and hold the reins because it was too late to get out of line by the time I admitted to myself you weren't coming. So I lifted my massive skirt and somehow situated myself on the bench to drive the sleigh. That put me up high enough that all the other couples could easily see me. Giggles and whispers exploded around me. Everyone knew you'd set me up."

He closes his eyes and gives his head a shake. His voice is gritty as he says, "Go on."

"I didn't believe them of course. I thought you loved me." I curse my voice for cracking. "You'd never do that to me, I told myself. But you *had* done it to me, and for the entire journey through the Winter Wood, every fairy we knew, and plenty of humans we didn't, pointed and laughed. Why was that girl driving her own sleigh? Who was that? Was she going to the ball *alone*? Was that even allowed? I heard it all, Seven. Can you imagine the humiliation? No, I don't suppose you can. How can I paint you a picture? Every word was a paper cut, and by the time I reached the square, I was hemorrhaging."

"Sophia..."

"Not done." My voice is stronger now, my emotions tilting toward anger. I cough into my hand but force down the prickly emotion that threatens to come up. "As soon as we were given the okay to leave our sleighs, I attempted to disembark, but with no one there to help me down, I tripped. I landed face-first in the snow."

Seven makes a sound deep in his throat and takes another drink. I'm glad he's still not looking at me because a stupid, fucking tear has squeezed out of the corner of my eye. I wipe it away quickly and continue. I need to get this out. It's cathartic.

"So I'm on the ground, my heels hopelessly tangled in my skirt, tears streaming down my face, and suddenly *your father* appears in front of me. I think he's going to help me up and explain what's happened to you. I mean, I was over at your house a lot as a kid. He'd known me since I was six. But he doesn't reach out his hand. Instead, he looks down his nose at me and says, 'Pity it came to this, but Seven did you a favor tonight. Now you know your place. You'd do well to remember it.'"

I cough harder into my hand, feeling that seed of resentment and mortification climb my esophagus. I swallow it down again.

"Then what?" Seven asks.

"Then he walked away, leaving me inside a ring of staring, pointing, whispering people," I say incredulously. "I couldn't get my feet under me. Not until River appeared, unhooked my skirt from my heel, and helped me stand. He walked me to his truck, where he used his hunting knife to cut that fucking ribbon from my wrist. And then he drove me home."

Seven winces. Gods, he looks like he might be sick. He walks to the bar and pours himself another. "But you didn't stay home, did you?"

"No."

"And then there was Arden, and you were gone."

"Yes."

"A matter of weeks."

"I left at the end of winter break. I'd done a fabulous job avoiding people until then. I couldn't face going back to school, given the circumstances."

He turns to me. Only then do I see that his eyes are rimmed red and the look he gives me is dark, murderous. It's so unsettling I have to take a step back.

"Have you ever wondered where I was when this was going on?"

I jolt. "Of course I have! But based on your father's comments, I had a pretty good idea you were home, having a good laugh at my expense." I scratch my jaw.

"Oh, I was home." He shakes his head as the words open a wound in my heart I thought had healed long ago. "That afternoon, my mother told my father that I was taking you to the ball as a date, not as a friend. He pitched a fit. See, up until then, he'd tolerated the fact we were friends because he never thought his son would dare slum it with a pixie romantically. The very idea was beyond his comprehension."

My breath flows out of me as if he's punched me in the gut.

"I stood up to him. Told him that not only was I going to the Yule Ball as your date but that I loved you."

Now my breath catches, and I'm just confused. If that's true, then—

"He poisoned me with blue iron, Sophia. I didn't come to the ball because I couldn't. I was locked in a room, completely drained of luck."

EIGHTEEN

Icy tendrils crawl along my skin and make the tiny hairs at the base of my scalp stand on end. "W-what?" I ask, unable to keep my voice from trembling. Blue iron is prohibited inside Devashire. If anyone knew about the small amount inside Kiko, I could get in big trouble. Poisoning another fae with it is grounds for imprisonment.

His jaw works and his eyes meet mine. "My father poisoned me and locked me up. In his words, he was keeping me from tarnishing the Delaney family name. I was so fucking sick. He drained me of so much luck I went negative and puked for hours. It was so bad, my mother couldn't take it. Eventually, she packed her bags and left. Ended up divorcing him over it. That and other reasons."

"Your parents are divorced?" I had no idea. All the luck in the world and they couldn't fix their family or their marriage. I shake my head. "Wait, this doesn't add up. I didn't leave immediately. It was... weeks. Why didn't you come tell me? Why didn't you try to explain?"

His jaw is so tight, I think he might snap a muscle. A shadow moves behind his eyes. "Several reasons. First, we were out of school, on winter break. I had no excuse to leave the house and my father forbade it—forbade it in the sense I was watched twenty-four hours a day. He wouldn't let me speak to anyone, so I couldn't get a message to you. He took my phone. When I finally got it back, you wouldn't answer my texts. You wouldn't take my calls."

"I left without my phone. Too easy to track."

"Your mom eventually told me as much. Soon after, my mother moved out and left me behind ... left me with him. My home life was in tatters."

"Wait... your mom left without you? Knowing he'd poisoned you?" After what I learned about how she purposefully forgot him as a child, this doesn't surprise me as much as it should, but still seems exceptionally cruel.

He brushes a hand over the sleeve of his suit, a disgusted expression twisting his lips. "She didn't have a choice. My father is the most powerful leprechaun in Devashire. I don't blame her, not really. She was trying to make it out alive. And that's the second reason, Sophia. He's too strong. What do you think would have happened if I'd found a way to get to you? What do you think he might have done to you if I'd tried to make things right back then? He'd poisoned his own son. He's above the law. Even if I could have found my way out of his grasp, I couldn't put you at risk by being seen with you again."

For a second, I'm tempted to doubt what he's saying to me. For years I've convinced myself that Seven was the villain of my life. Except I can see the pain etched into his face, and it's real. He's many things, but unlike me, he's a horrible liar. Besides, what he says about Chance being above the law rings true. Chance isn't just lucky, he's rich and well-connected politically. A sick feeling swells inside me, and I cough again.

His gaze narrows on me. "After you left, I looked for you. I was barely eighteen when I got involved with the security division of Lucky Enterprises to have access to the systems I needed to search for you. When I became an adult, I amped up the search. I've got to hand it to you Sophia. You vanished. I started to think you'd died."

"I was careful. I changed my appearance and used luck to secure a passport. Still, with all the luck at your disposal, I don't know why you didn't find me. I was good, but not that good." It's so weird. Donovan was able to find me, after all, and he's human. "What does this have to do with what happened with your father tonight?"

"He saw me at the club with a pixie. You, but not you. He doesn't usually come in, but he said he was there to meet a colleague. He laid into me. Threatened to cut me out of the Delaney Empire and leave everything to Evangeline if I didn't check myself."

I can't curb my sharp intake of breath. I knew Chance was an asshole, but hearing it from Seven's lips is still shocking. "Can he do that?"

"Unfortunately, yes. He owns a controlling interest in everything under the Lucky Enterprises brand. I might be CEO of the club and COO of the casino and hotel, but he can still have me ousted. My father is a greedy son of a bitch, Sophia. My mother got precious little in the divorce. Enough to keep her comfortable for the rest of her life, but nowhere near what she deserved. But it's not the money that worries me. I don't care about the money. I never did. What worries me is the man himself. If he wanted to hurt you..."

"He's not going to hurt me." I shake my head. "You said yourself he didn't even know it was me there today."

He rubs a hand over his face. "He saw you at the casino

yesterday... Tonight, he blamed you being back for reviving my interest in pixies. He said he was disappointed that he hadn't gotten rid of you back then for good."

"Gods, he's a dick." I want to vomit. Never did I realize how deep Chance's hatred ran for me and my kind. "Don't worry about it, Seven. When we meet about the case, we'll just be careful to meet where it won't be an issue. I'll stay on my side of Dragonfly, and he can stay on his."

Seven closes his eyes and gives his head a hard shake. My words seem to have enraged him rather than comforted him. He strides toward me, sending the koi darting off as he stomps over their river to reach me. "What if I don't want to stay away from you?"

I take a step back. "What do you mean?"

"Please say you forgive me, Sophia." His voice cracks. "You have no idea what this has done to me over the years. Once I heard what happened to you, what he said to you, I tortured myself thinking about it. I couldn't apologize then, but I can now. I'm sorry. I'm so sorry."

"So you knew... before this. You knew what he'd said to me?"

He grunts. "River told me. Popped me one too." He rubs his stubbled jaw as if he can still feel it. "I couldn't explain to him what my dad had done. I was too embarrassed and afraid of what would happen next. This can't get out. You know that, right? Not ever."

I scoff. "You were a kid, and he was abusive. You should have been removed from his care. Your mother should have protected you. She should have taken you with her. People need to know what kind of awful man he is."

He waves a hand dismissively. "My mother didn't stand a chance against him. I admire her for saving herself."

I swallow and try to look at the situation objectively.

He's right. There is no version of reality where Seven would have been removed from his father's home.

"Even now, this can't get out," he says firmly. "You can't tell anyone. I brought you here because it's the only place I know he doesn't have eyes or ears. He's too powerful, and if he feels threatened, he'll strike in ways you can only imagine. You understand that, right? It's why I couldn't tell you at the lake. I've been trying to get you back here for days."

All those invitations for dinner. He wanted to bring me here. He wanted to tell me.

I'd say that no one would care about a leprechaun poisoning his own son with blue iron, but it would be a lie. No matter how many years had passed, the *Daily Hatter* would lap it up. Poisoning another fairy with a prohibited substance, especially a child, is scandalous. The patriarch of the Delaney family doing it is media fodder. And he's right that Chance would likely not suffer any consequences. Seven wouldn't have any proof of what his father had done back then, and the fallout from a story like that would be devastating for Seven. His father would cut him off, and the tabloids would rake him across the coals. He'd be disgraced. He could lose everything.

And so could I.

If my name were dragged into the mix, my future and that of my family would be in jeopardy. My parents run a store they rent from a leprechaun. One word from Chance Delaney and that leprechaun could choose to raise their rent or force them out some other way.

"Please," Seven begs. His tortured expression is incongruent with the demanding and arrogant man I know him to be. The man is made of suits, ties, and expensive scotch. I never thought I'd see the day he had a conscience. "Say you forgive me."

There it is. The demand. His eyes hold me in their intense embrace, and his mouth forms a straight line, his jaw tight. I expect to feel his luck like I did on the beach, but my skin doesn't tingle, and I don't feel compelled in any way. Which means he's left it up to me. He wants my uncoerced forgiveness.

Maybe that's what does it. Suddenly my mental construct of him cracks, and all I see is the boy I knew, the one I liked and then later loved. I believe him. And I am floored by the vulnerability he's showing. The pain his father caused might as well be an exposed wound over his heart. The entire situation is messed up.

I can't carry my hatred for him anymore. Not now, knowing what I know. It's too heavy. But my brain is reeling trying to process everything, and I can't put into words what I'm feeling, so I simply blurt, "Yes, I forgive you."

It's as if I've dropped an invisible shield. He reaches out to cup my jaw, his fingers wrapping around the base of my head in an astonishingly possessive fashion. I barely get a breath in before his lips crash down on mine and my back and wings bump the wall behind me. Gods, the kiss takes me by surprise. It hits me like a force of nature, fierce and wild as a hurricane. If there's any part of me that questions if this is a good idea, it sails away before I can examine it closely.

I tip my head and let him in, his tongue stroking mine in a dance that stirs up long-forgotten memories. Inside, that flock of butterflies takes flight, and then the warm rush of his luck stirs my blood.

Here's the thing about kissing a leprechaun. When he wants to, when his focus is on me, all that power that saturates his body becomes a firebrand of pleasure. It feels like someone has popped the cork on a bottle of champagne inside my torso. My insides turn light and bubbly. My body feels effervescent. Everything comes alive. If kissing a man is like being lowered into a warm bath, kissing a leprechaun is like a warm bath full of Pop Rocks. This kiss is an *event*.

It's fireworks.

Among fairies, luck isn't something we can see, but we can feel it. We can sense it. It's as unique for each of us as a fingerprint. I've encountered Seven's luck before but it never registered what exactly I was dealing with. Now, an image pops into my mind, formed from the size, the power, the temperature of the *beast* in the room with me. Seven's luck rises like a giant, hot-blooded dragon whose purr vibrates against my skin where it brushes me. Heat rushes to my core. I'm throbbing between my legs instantly as his fingers work themselves into my hair. His kisses trail to my ear, down my neck. Gods, his thumb feathering across my jaw almost makes me moan.

Seven tastes of forbidden fruit and interrupted destiny. I *want* him. I crave him like a drug.

Luck purrs around the back of my neck and sinks, warm and intoxicating between my shoulder blades. It travels lower, tingling along each vertebra with firm but achingly effervescent pressure. I'm breathless as that hum shifts over my hip and down my lower abdomen to tease the tangle of nerves at the apex of my thighs. I moan into his mouth.

I'm playing with fire. This feels too good. I could lose myself in this kiss and then lose myself in him. What happened tonight is confusing enough. I forgave Seven. That's a play I wasn't expecting to make. Anything more is risking too much.

His fingers trace along the top of my bodice, a soft caress over the mound of my breast as his hips grind against mine, the hard length of him enticingly close to the ache between my legs.

Before I can lose my nerve, I plant both hands on his chest and push. "Seven, stop."

He pulls back, panting. "What's wrong?"

"We need to stop."

"Why? You want me, I can feel it." He moves closer again, and I push harder to keep space between us.

I close my eyes and try to put it into words, even as my blood sings in my veins and my core throbs with need for him. "I forgive you, okay, but that doesn't mean we can go back to the way it was."

He backs up a step. "No, but we sure as hell can create something new."

I shake my head. "It's been sixteen years. We don't know each other anymore. Not really. When you kiss me, you're kissing a memory."

"Then let's get to know each other."

I'm speechless. It's too much to take in. I hated the man only days ago, and I can't sort out my emotions in the moment to respond. I want him, undeniably, but I haven't had time to digest what a new relationship with him would mean for me. So I say nothing.

Silence stretches between us.

I'm saved from his intense scrutiny when his phone rings. "This better be important," he barks, and I can picture the person on the other end of the call cringing. No one would interrupt him now if it wasn't important. That security guard in the hall could barely make eye contact. "Fine. Yeah... Mmm-hmm."

Seven's jaw hardens. "We'll be right there. Yeah, she's here with me."

He slides his phone back into his pocket. "That was Godmother. There's been another murder."

NINETEEN

There was a time in my life when Seven was the center of my world. I loved him in a way that's only possible when one's heart is new, unbroken, and unjaded. The pedestal I put him on was tall, and I would have changed anything and everything about myself to make him mine forever. All that has changed now. My heart isn't new. It's been broken before... by him. And although I realize it wasn't exactly his fault, a cracked vase pasted back together never holds water the way it did before it was damaged.

So why am I tempted to allow myself back into his arms?

It's clear he wants me, and hell, I want him. I'd be lying to myself if I said I didn't. But the difference between teenage me and thirty-four-year-old me, is that now I know my worth. I deserve better than to be treated like a pet, a lesser being meant to be happy with clandestine moments behind closed doors. I've survived things Seven couldn't imagine. I'm perfectly fine alone; I'm resourceful and smart. More importantly, I'm a mother, and I know Arden is always watching. I'm not ever going to exist for the pleasure of a man, any man, no matter how lucky or rich. No way. Not even for a little while.

It's just after ten when Seven and I arrive at the scene of the crime, tension still painfully thick between us. "I thought you said it was supposed to be right here." I scan the cobblestone near the back of the park, not far from River's Tavern.

"It is." Godmother's voice comes from in front of me. There's a snap, and I see her standing beyond a shimmering wave of purple. I step forward, through the concealment spell, and she snaps her fingers again. The murder scene appears where before there was nothing.

When I see the body, I can't help but gag and turn away. The victim isn't human—she's a pixie—and the state of her corpse turns my stomach. There's so much blood. The stench of death hangs thick in the air around us.

Everything about the scene repels me. Unlike Arden, I never wanted to be a doctor or an investigator or any other career that involved bodies, blood, or bodily fluids. My dreams were of running my own business, far away from anything like this. I never had the stomach for horror movies or hospitals. I cover my mouth with my hand and try to think happy thoughts.

Seven appears in front of me. His voice is low and soft as he asks, "You okay? If this is too much, you can go. I can show you pictures later. It might be easier."

I open my mouth to tell him I'm okay, but I never get the chance.

"She's staying," Godmother says in her deep, resonating voice.

"I guess I'm staying." I flash him a half smile, then take a deep breath before turning around again.

It's not like I'm some delicate flower. I left Dragonfly at

only seventeen and lived on the street, pregnant, until I could luck my way into a job and then a closet that called itself an apartment. I saw things out there, drug users who fell asleep under the same underpass as I did and never woke up, prostitutes beaten by their pimps and left for dead. This brutality seems harsher here though. Blood seeps into cobblestone under a flickering gas lamp crafted to look like a mason jar filled with fireflies. The dichotomy catches me off guard. Gods, just behind us is a neighborhood of pastel mushrooms.

Whoever did this has shattered some last vestige of my childhood I didn't even know I was clinging to. There should be no safer place than Dragonfly Hollow. But evil is here, death is real, and no one is safe.

"Her teeth are gone," Seven says. "And half her rib cage."

I swallow down bile and really look at the victim. It's the left side that's missing and something else. "Her heart's gone too."

Godmother grunts and reaches for a red box that looks like it should hold an assortment of chocolates. She selects a brightly colored paper tube that reminds me of the sugar candy humans call Pixie Stix, tears off one end, and scatters the contents in the air. The yellow powder swells like a cloud and then settles over the scene. Footprints appear on the concrete that were not there before. Gigantic footprints. Both Seven and I inhale sharply. They're weirdly shaped, skeletal, and they end at the eight-foot privacy fence that forms the boundary of Wonderland. On the other side of that wall is forest, beach, the lake, and the wall.

"Yissevel," Godmother says through her teeth, her fists clenching.

"It can't be." My gaze darts between them. "Can it?"

The unseelie have been locked away for centuries. If they'd found a way through the wall, there would be a hell of a lot more death and destruction than just one human and one pixie. Yissevel isn't just any unseelie. No one could miss this monster.

Seven tips his head back and looks from streetlight to streetlight. He points toward one with a black glass dome embedded in the design. I wouldn't have noticed it if he wasn't pointing at it. "There's a camera. I'll have to go to the security office to see what it captured."

Godmother waves a hand dismissively. "Go. I'll determine time of death and try to identify the victim." She pulls a vial of silver liquid from her box.

At Godmother's words, I realize that I've been avoiding the victim's face. I'd taken in the scene, but a part of me hadn't wanted to see this pixie as a once living, breathing person. I might be able to identify her. Her head is rolled to the side, and I step around the body to get a straight look at her face. I grab my stomach, instantly chilled through. I know who this is.

"That's Phoebe Willowbark." I feel breathless as I look between Seven and Godmother. "She went missing the same day Michael Murphy was murdered."

No one says anything for what feels like a full minute. "How do you know this?" Godmother's normally large dark eyes become slits.

"A pixie I met at the Dragonfly tonight told me about her when I asked her about Michael." No need to get River involved in this mess. I pull up the family's page on my phone and show it to them.

Godmother darts a glance toward Seven. "Why did I not know that a pixie went missing on the same day Michael Murphy was murdered?"

Seven straightens, looking livid. "This is the first I'm hearing of it."

"Let me know what you find out." The tone of her voice has the hair on my arms standing at attention. Something ancient has crept in. Ancient and deadly.

The nod Seven gives her is the most deferential I've ever seen him give anyone. He extends his hand and gestures for me to come. I do, relieved when we are through the concealment spell and I can no longer smell the blood. "That was intense," I say.

He says nothing, doesn't even look at me. His entire demeanor has turned icy.

"What the hell is wrong with you?" I ask in my usual irreverent way. I'm not going to bend to this man's moods.

He continues to ignore me, until we're around the corner and out of sight of the crime scene. When he finally does turn, his expression is hard, his spine stiff, and his lip is curled in disapproval. "Is there any other information about this case you'd like to share with me? Now would be a good time. Now rather than later, when we're with Godmother."

I recoil. Fuck. His poker face is gone, and the full force of his anger plows into me. I force myself to stand a little straighter. "I just found out myself! It was important information."

"So you thought it would be a good idea to make a fool of me in front of Godmother? I'm head of security, Sophia, and a Delaney leprechaun. How exactly did you think your reveal was going to go over?"

The turn of events shakes me. Not an hour ago, this man had his tongue down my throat, and now my skin buzzes with his anger. His luck coils around him like a defensive, pissed-off dragon.

I try to take a step toward him and find that my heel is caught in the cobblestones. I glance down at my shoe, but it refuses to give. My nostrils flare. "Real mature."

He scowls like someone kicked his kitten.

Stepping out of my shoes, I flex my own luck and she rises like a tiger at my side. It's all bravado. His dragon could eat my tiger in one bite.

"My reveal? I didn't *reveal* anything. I recognized the victim and told both of you in the moment. It's not my fault no one had informed Godmother about Phoebe. How was I even supposed to know that?"

"Bullshit, Sophia. You kept this to yourself. You said the pixie at Dragonfly Club told you about her. You've known for hours and didn't share it?"

I raise a hand. "I didn't have a chance! I was too busy being whisked away to your apartment to revisit the past. Besides, since when do you care what anyone else thinks?" My poker face snaps into place to conceal how shaken I am by the emotional whiplash of the night. "Gods, Seven, you just finished telling me that you didn't care what your father thought about pixies, but suddenly you're swelling with some hypermasculine need to know everything first and be in total control?"

Emerald eyes blazing, he juts a finger in my direction. "Wanting to appear competent in front of the most powerful creature in both our lives isn't hypermasculine, Sophia, but thanks for letting me know exactly how you feel about me."

He turns to continue toward his car. I bend over and use both hands to pry my shoe from the sidewalk, then follow after him.

Whirling on me, he makes a sound like a laugh. "Go home, Sophia."

"What? Why? I thought we were going to go look at the security recording."

His eyes turn cold as ice. "Oh, I see. You don't get it because you've never managed anything but yourself." That barb slides between my ribs and almost breaks the impassive expression I've been holding in place. "Here's what happens now. I have to go back to the office and start the process of figuring out why my people didn't flag Phoebe Willowbark as a missing person. If there's some sort of bias involved, I'll have to fire the people responsible on the spot, people with families, who need their jobs."

He slams me with a disdainful look, and I realize he's echoing what I asked him when he fired Brandon. Ouch. "While that's all happening, I'll have to spend a gods-awful amount of luck to gain access to the recording of Phoebe's murder without drawing attention to it. No one else can see it. No one else can know what happened here tonight. If any of my guys have already seen it, I'll need to make damn sure they don't say a word, one way or another, because if this got out to the human population, Dragonfly could lose millions in lost park revenue until PR got things under control."

"Don't forget the Delaney empire," I say flatly. "Your bank account might shrink from the size of Jupiter to the size of Uranus, and that's also exactly where you can shove this guilt trip." Beside me, my luck tiger growls. "I know these murders are high stakes for us, but don't act like I don't have just as much on the line. My freedom hangs in the balance—my life if Godmother kicks me out of here. There's a reason she put me on this case, and it's not just to feed you information so that you can play the hero and take credit for every chip of progress that comes our way."

He recoils at that, a scowl marring his face.

"But since we're on the topic, six pixies who frequented the Dragonfly Club have gone missing over the past decade, and none of them have been investigated as potential victims. Phoebe was just the most recent one. Your people always assume they left for the human world like I did, but their families disagree. I sent word to my family. Most people would if they weren't in trouble. When an otherwise normal person vanishes without a trace, there's probably foul play involved. So maybe it's time you talked to that team of yours, and maybe it's right that a few of them are fired. I'm not going to apologize for telling the truth or for doing exactly what you brought me on this case to do."

He grunts. "Fine. But I'm still leading this investigation, and you're officially off duty." He slashes a hand through the air dismissively and turns coolly away from me. I watch him stride toward the parking lot, the press of his luck going with him. The tingle of his power slides from my skin and then vanishes.

I head for home feeling oddly cold.

TWENTY

"Mom, what do you think of my new uniform?" Arden rushes into my room the following morning wearing the plaid skirt, emblemed blazer, blouse, and tights that I recognize as the uniform for Bailiwick's Academy. I blink at the clock, wondering if I've overslept again, even though I was home at a reasonable hour and I hadn't had anything to drink. It's only seven fifteen. My alarm was set for seven thirty.

"Where'd you get that?" I ask her. "I promise I'll call the school on Monday. I just haven't had a chance."

She grins and starts jumping up and down. "I'm already in!"

I stare at her until it's clear she's not joking. "Explain."

"I went down there yesterday with Grandpa while you were getting ready for your mission and asked to speak to Headmistress Sullivan."

I shake my head. "It was late Friday afternoon. Wasn't the school already closed?"

"Yes, but I took a chance, and she was still there! I explained everything that happened, and we had a conference call with my old high school's principal. Everything just fell into place! I start Monday." Her voice is a little breathless, and excitement is rolling off her in waves.

"But... what about the tuition deposit?" I have no idea how I'm going to pay it, but Bailiwick's is expensive. Usually, they'd hold off on admission until the financing was nailed down, but if they gave her a uniform, she must have already been admitted.

She squeals. "That's the best part. It turns out you overpaid my tuition in Nevada and they've agreed to send the balance to Bailiwick's. We won't owe anything!"

My stomach clenches. I'm happy for Arden, but warning bells are going off in my head. This is one positive coincidence too many to give credit to fate. I sense luck was involved, and a serious amount of it. Overpaid tuition? That's never happened before. Instantly, I think of Seven. Last night, before things went sour, he'd tipped his hand that he still had feelings for me. He'd apologized and kissed me. Is it possible that he is behind this?

If he is behind it, I hope to hell he doesn't renege after last night. I've never seen him so angry, and I guess I can understand why, now that there's some distance between me and the situation. Yes, it would be important to anyone in his position to be perceived as competent. I get that he wants the best for his employees, and this puts him in a tight spot where he might be forced to let someone go. But I was right too. Had I withheld that information from Godmother and she found out, I might be in more trouble than I already am. And Seven did need to do something about the bias against pixies in his shop. I don't regret what I said, but I also understand where Seven was coming from last night. It's unsettling. Between knowing the truth about his abusive family life and understanding his point of view,

I can practically feel my heart making room for him, maybe even expecting the best from him. It was so much easier to just hate him.

"Congratulations," I say to Arden. "I'm glad you got what you wanted, and I'm proud of you for going after it on your own."

"This is going to be amazing!" She claps her hands and bounces out of the room.

Gods, I hope she's right. It scares me to think that she might be bullied for being human or that this might all come apart. I need to talk to Seven, see if he's behind this. If so, I'll eat crow if I have to. Arden has been through too much for me not to do everything I can to make this better for her.

I dress and descend to the smell of toast and eggs. My mother is waiting in a silver ball gown that would be at home in a Cinderella movie. My dad sports dark breeches, boots, and a flowing white shirt reminiscent of a fairy-tale prince. They both give me an exaggerated smile when they see me.

"You didn't have to make me breakfast," I say, plugging my mouth with a piece of toast.

"Yes, I did," my mother says, her smile widening. "We just got a shipment in at the store, and we could really use an extra set of hands today."

Dad clears his throat. "What do you think, sweetheart? Want to take a trip down memory lane and contribute to the family business?"

When he puts it that way, how can I say no?

* * *

AN HOUR LATER, I'M DRESSED IN MY DRY-CLEANED PINK BALL gown and designing a display of Dragonfly snow globes at my parents' gift shop, the Silver Ember. Each glass ball depicts a different street in Wonderland with a pixie stretching her arms toward the sun. When you shake them, purple and silver glitter swirls around her and her wings flap. All of them are inscribed with the Dragonfly Hollow logo and the tagline WHERE MAGIC LIVES AND DREAMS COME TRUE.

Humans buy the weirdest shit.

"Are acorns really lucky?" a man in shorts and a Dragonfly Casino polo asks me. I stop what I'm doing to give him my full attention. The polo he's wearing isn't for sale. It's a gift for VIPs. This guy has money burning up his pockets.

"Very lucky," I say. I pick one up and hold it between my thumb and forefinger. "This one acorn has all the potential to become a mighty oak tree. It's concentrated luck. Very powerful."

"Good. I'm registered for the poker tournament tonight and need all the luck I can get." He rubs his hands together.

My chest constricts. How I wish I had a poker game to look forward to.

He lifts one of the acorns and turns it in his fingers. "It's so... common. Do you have them in gold?"

I repress a laugh and flutter my lashes at him. "Sir, there is nothing common about these acorns. Each one is hand selected from our Winter Wood, the luckiest forest in all

America. And we at the Silver Ember are very careful to limit the amount that they are handled to preserve the greatest concentration of luck the acorn can hold. Why, the only thing luckier in this entire store is the goldfish, and if you are interested in one of those, I'd be happy to show you. They're in the back."

Shifting uneasily, he says, "No, no. They always die on me."

I hold my smile while inside I judge the man harshly for his inability to keep a goldfish alive.

"How much are they?"

"$25.99 each," I say. Right now they are. We don't label the bin for a reason.

"All right, I'll take four." He reaches for his wallet.

"Very good, sir. Would you like me to throw in a four-leaf clover preserved in resin? They're 10 percent off since you've spent over a hundred dollars." I flash him my most charming smile and hit him with a bit of luck.

"Oh, why the hell not? Can't be too lucky, can you?" He chuckles, his eyes dropping to my boobs.

"Never," I say with a wink. I gather his goods and deliver them all to the counter where my mother starts ringing him up.

I've turned back to the snow globes when he taps me on the shoulder, bag in hand. "Are you free later for a drink?"

I shake my head and point to a sign above the cash register: Employees are Prohibited from Fraternizing with Guests. "Thank you for visiting Silver Ember."

He stumbles out the door mumbling something about stupid theme park policies. Once he's gone, my mother rounds the counter and hugs me. "$25.99? Last week I sold a dozen for five dollars!"

I huff dramatically. "For these gorgeous hand-selected specimens?"

She peers at me over her glasses. "Your father literally rakes them off the forest floor."

We share a good laugh, and she returns to the back room and the inventory. When the front bell chimes again, I don't even look up. "Welcome to the Silver Ember."

"Is that you in those snow globes or another pixie who can't hold her liquor?"

"River!" I embrace the satyr. His brown eyes are dancing with mirth, and he's actually wearing a shirt for a change. This is as dressed up as River gets. "What are you doing here?"

"I have a date on this side of the park and thought I'd bring you a sandwich and some chips for lunch."

"A date, huh? What's your date think about you bringing me lunch?"

He chuckles. "Presumably that you must be hungry. What else would she think?"

I laugh. Must be a satyr. I'll never understand the lack of jealousy. "Who's the lucky lady, gentleman or gentleperson?"

"Lady. Katy from the education center."

"Ah." I try to remember if Katy is the redheaded satyr or the one who never smiles. I decide it must be the redhead. River's too friendly to be dating a downer.

I take the bag from his hand and set it on the counter. "Thank you. I'll put this to good use."

He rocks back on his heels, staring at me.

"Is there something else?"

He sighs. "As your friend, I feel you should see this." He reaches behind his back and pulls something from his waistband to hand to me. It's a newspaper. THE DAILY HATTER, SPILLING THE TEA IN DRAGONFLY HOLLOW SINCE 1845.

"What exactly am I supposed to be looking at here?"

River's shoulders droop. "Page six."

My eyes flick to him and back to the paper as I flip to the location of the gossip section and zero in on Fairly Goodweather's neighborhood news column. "Prodigal daughter Sophia Larkspur returned to Dragonfly Hollow this week after her life of crime was thwarted by the Fairy Immigration and Rehabilitation Enforcement agency. Although her inappropriate and illegal actions brought pain and suffering on this community (her poor parents!), it appears she will suffer no punishment or penalty. I have it on good authority that she visited Godmother the day after arrival and left with skin and wallet intact!

"Although this reporter was as disappointed as you that justice wasn't served, she is more concerned with the company Ms. Larkspur keeps. A sixteen-year-old daughter, seemingly half-human, enrolled in Bailiwick's Academy just yesterday. Lock up your sons, Dragonfly families! If this acorn didn't roll far enough from the tree, we are surely in store for more heartbreak and drama from the youngest Larkspur descendant."

My mouth falls open, and I stare at River in disbelief. "Did she? Was that? Pain and suffering! Life of crime! Acorn and tree!" My throat squeezes until my voice is high and tight.

"It's going to be okay," River says, holding up his hands. I just thought you should know.

"No! It's not okay. Where does Fairly Goodweather live, River? You know everyone in this town. Tell me. I'm going to *kill* her."

River chuckles and turns over one hand. "While you

and I know the best way for you to win over the love and support of Dragonfly Hollow is to commit murder, perhaps that particular action will be confusing to others."

"Pfft!"

He places a hand on my shoulder. "It will blow over, Sophia. Six months from now, no one will even be talking about you anymore."

"People are talking about me? What are they saying? What have you heard?"

River sighs and scratches behind one of his horns. "Do you want to come by River's for a free beer later?"

I offer a tight grin. "I'll take that to mean 'yes, people are talking about you, Sophia.'"

"Drink more beer and it won't bother you."

I laugh. "Got it." I hand him back the copy of the *Hatter*. "Thanks for lunch, River. You're a good friend."

He pulls me into a hug and kisses me on the cheek, just as the bell above the door chimes and Seven walks into the Silver Ember.

TWENTY-ONE

"This is cozy." Seven wears the same face he wore when he fired Brandon at the casino, like he owns the world and gods help anyone who gets in his way. Damn, he's larger than life. His suit hangs like it's in love with him, hugging muscle and draping elegantly in all the right places. He's broad shouldered and narrow waisted with just enough ass to make things interesting. Plus he's obviously jealous which makes my heart do a happy tap dance in my chest. Damn stupid heart. After the way he dismissed me last night, I should be making some excuse to leave the room right now.

Focusing all my attention on River, I release him with a warm smile. "Thanks again for stopping by... and for the sandwich."

"Anytime." He turns to leave. As he passes by Seven to get to the door, the two men lock stares. I feel luck rise in the air like static electricity. Seven's is a fiery dragon, an energy that's become so familiar the past few days. River's has the presence of a great horned stag. River towers over Seven physically, taller by four inches at least and with the broader shoulders and defined muscles satyrs are known for. But Seven's power dwarfs what River is putting off. It's so big it steals the air from the room.

I watch River's hand ball into a fist before he slips out the door. Absently, Seven rubs his cheek as the door chimes and closes behind the satyr.

"That was fun," I say. "For a second there I thought one of you might get piss on my shoes."

"Is he why you won't be with me?" Seven's gaze drills into me.

My mother chooses that moment to poke her head out from the back room. "Oh, Seven! I thought I felt..." She furrows her brow. "Well, I thought I felt something. What brings you in today?"

"Always a pleasure to see you Aurora." All anger has drained from Seven's expression, replaced by good-natured charm. He reaches her in three long strides, takes the heavy box she's carrying from her hands and sets it on the counter.

"Oh, thank you." She smooths her dress.

"Would it be all right if I borrowed Sophia for a few moments? It's Godmother business. I'm afraid it's important."

My mother smiles warmly. "Of course."

What? She looks like if he stayed she'd offer him coffee. Gods!

Seven holds open the front door, and I follow him out onto Main Street where we begin to stroll toward Godmother's. "Why are you here, Seven? I thought you said I was off duty."

"I owe you an apology."

My breath catches. Seven Delaney is apologizing to

me… again? That's twice in twenty-four hours. Someone send heaters to hell; it's officially frozen over.

He rolls his eyes. "Don't look so surprised. I can admit when I'm wrong."

"Leprechauns aren't well known for admitting wrong-doing or apologizing for that matter."

He shrugs. "When are you going to learn, Sophia? I'm a different sort of leprechaun."

"Hmm." Up close now, I see shadows under his eyes as if he hasn't slept well. He's still sexy as hell, but clearly something is bothering him.

"It would have been risky for you to hold back Phoebe's identity last night. I realize that now."

I release a heavy sigh. Hell if I'm going to allow him to be the bigger person about this. "I'm sorry too. I didn't mean to embarrass you. I'd meant to tell you earlier, but we were… distracted."

"Did Sophia Larkspur just admit she was wrong?" His lip quirks and eyes flash.

"When are you going to learn, I'm a different sort of pixie?"

Our eyes meet. Now there's something else in his expression, the same wolfish, masculine heat I'd seen last night. The tug of his luck slides over my skin, and I picture that dragon wrapping around me again.

I turn away and walk on. "You may wish to mark this day on your calendar and commemorate it annually in the future, preferably with cake and sparklers. I doubt it will happen often."

He chuckles and moves closer to my side. "It's not your job to preserve my reputation. Besides, you were right. I'm embarrassed to admit that the cases of those six pixies were completely mishandled by my team. In every instance, their files were closed as assumed runaways despite evidence to the contrary from their families. We have six missing pixies and one dead human, all with links back to *my* club."

The stress in his voice is obvious now, and he's lost some of his charming demeanor. I'm surprised he's admitting this in public. Until I notice we are very much alone. The nearest guests are across the street. I take in the emptiness of the usually busy street and clear my throat. "Um, are you doing this? Because if so, we should walk faster. My parents really need the midday business."

He grunts. "Sorry."

The tingle of his luck shifts like a rush of bubbles against my skin, and then a flock of families seem to see the Silver Ember for the first time and flood into the store.

"Thanks."

"Don't mention it."

I walk faster until we put additional space between us and the crowd again. Lowering my voice, I ask, "Was there anything on the security footage?"

"Yup." He heaves a sigh. "But you'll never believe it unless you see it with your own eyes."

The Wonderland security office is a single-story circular building intentionally designed to blend into the background. Its indistinct white brick walls give no clues to what goes on under the ordinary shingled roof. The only indication of the purpose the building serves is silver lettering on the glass front door that reads SECURITY.

Seven keys us in and tells a blue-uniformed satyr behind the reception desk that he's going to be in the monitoring room for a few minutes and is not to be disturbed. He leads me into an office filled with screens showing every aspect of public life in Wonderland. There's no one in here, although there's a steaming cup of coffee on the counter and a Dragonfly security jacket on the back of one of the chairs.

Seven locks the door behind us.

"Someone's going to miss their coffee," I say.

Seven types feverishly on the keyboard. "Ye of little faith. Ravi is in the restroom, and we are going to get very lucky and be out of here before he's finished."

"Of course we are," I say flatly.

A few more keystrokes and the location of the murder pops up on-screen. It's dark, but I can make out the patch of sidewalk at the back of the park in the circle from the streetlight. The time ticks along the bottom of the screen. Seconds roll by. And then the body appears in the arms of a monster.

"Yissevel," I say. "Oh my gods! He's out."

Seven nods. "Keep watching."

The monster is at least eight feet tall and looks like a skeleton aside from a thin layer of stretched pale skin that seems to barely hold bone, tendon, and muscle together. He drops the mutilated body, then takes off, bounding back over the security fence in the direction of the wall.

"That's weird," I say. "It's almost as if he's sneaking back into Shadowvale."

Seven laughs. "What else is weird, Sophia?" He rewinds the recording again. I watch.

I press my fingers against my lips. "The teeth and bones were missing before he ditched the body. She was already dead!"

"Exactly."

"This just gets weirder and weirder. Did Yissevel kill her in the unseelie realm and then dump the body here? Why? How would she even get to Shadowvale? And if she was killed here, why would he move her body?"

"All great questions. What we know for sure is that Phoebe was already dead. Did Yissevel kill her or just scavenge her bones and dump her? And if he didn't kill her, who did?"

"Who else would though? Just because he dumped and ran doesn't mean he didn't do it. But I understand what you're saying. It's so odd. How did he even run into Phoebe? And if she went missing the same day as Michael showed up dead, did he somehow lure her back to Shadowvale, kill her, and then return to dump her? Why?"

Seven shakes his head. "That's what we have to find out. None of this makes sense."

"But how do we find out? Yissevel had to have returned to Shadowvale. He's... giant. Someone would have noticed him. You would have caught him on camera."

"Yep."

"And how is he getting past the wall? We need to talk to the guardians about this."

"They will never admit that a creature made it through without their knowledge."

"We can show them this." I gesture toward the footage.

He steps in closer and looks me in the eye. "I have a better idea."

I cross my arms and wait expectantly. "Why are you hesitating?"

"Because you're not going to like it." At the impatient look I give him he says, "You and I are going to go through the wall and pay Yissevel a visit. We're going to ask the beast himself what happened."

"Go into Shadowvale?" My voice rises around a nervous laugh. The idea is senseless. Shadowvale is brimming with unseelie monsters, things without a conscience that would eat our throats out as readily as talk to us. "Are you insane? It's suicide."

He pinches my chin. "It's not suicide because you'll be with me and we will get very, very lucky. Between my luck and your illusion, we'll be fine."

I stare at him incredulously. "Are you sure about that? I have a daughter, Seven. I can't take unnecessary risks with myself."

He chuckles and slants me a crooked smile. "Nothing will happen to you, Sophia, and from what I hear, Arden is doing just fine on her own."

My breath hitches. "What have you heard about Arden?"

He narrows his eyes on the screens as he logs out and returns everything to the way Ravi left it. "Heard she made it into Bailiwick's, our old alma mater. Betsy Sullivan said she was quite charming in her interview."

"Seven... Did you have something to do with her admission?"

He gently guides me toward the door and keys us out. "I'm on the school board. I'm involved with all admissions." He winks at me.

I follow him past the front desk and out the doors just as a young leprechaun in uniform comes out of the bathroom and strides toward the room we were in. So Seven *is* to thank for Arden's admission to Bailiwick's. I knew luck was involved. It was the only explanation.

"Thank you," I say.

"For what?" He leads me down the street a few yards and then pauses on the sidewalk.

"For helping Arden get into Bailiwick's."

He scoffs. "I didn't need to help her. Everyone who meets her *loves* her, Sophia. She's just like you."

His words knock the air out of me. I had friends, sure, but I wasn't universally popular. "No one here ever loved me like that."

His green eyes flash. "I did."

I shake my head, my cheeks warming at his admission.

"You seriously don't remember? You were the darling of every teacher, a sweet pixie girl from a salt-of-the-earth pixie family."

I scoff. "If that were ever true, they don't think that now. According to the *Hatter* and Fairly Goodweather's social column, I'm a criminal who needs to be punished, and my daughter is a half-human temptress whom people should hide their children from."

Seven scowls. "This is why I never read those columns. Fairly Goodweather is an idiot."

"Yeah."

"Would you like a coffee?" He gestures to a cart nearby with an espresso machine and a selection of pastries.

I shake my head. "I have to get back to the store."

"What are you doing there anyway? You always hated working at your parents' store. You once told me working retail was a torture that would be illegal if forced on animals."

"It isn't my favorite thing to do, but I need the money."

He swaggers closer to me. "Why haven't you applied at the casino? You'd make an excellent dealer. I assure you the compensation package is the best in Dragonfly."

I heave a sigh of frustration. "I'll think about it."

"What's there to think about?"

I circle my gaze toward the sky. "Um, working for and with your abusive, dickhead father, for one. Two, watching other people play my favorite game in the world and not being able to join in. That's its own torture."

His smile fades slightly. "You can play me."

"Not the same." My brain fills with images of playing poker with him. I miss it more than I'll ever admit.

"If I could change the rules for you, I would. Even if I wanted to make an exception, I couldn't. The law comes straight from Godmother. Poker with fae isn't fair to the humans, and the last fae-only tournament we tried ended badly. There was so much luck swirling in that room, a satyr's chair broke, and he fell into the player next to him, sending the pixie crashing through the second-floor window. Thank gods he could fly."

Even as a kid I remember what a disaster those yearly tournaments were. All fae have varying levels of control over their luck, just like humans have varying levels of control over their emotions. The difference is, in a gambling situation, a typical fae combats more than just their need to control the cards. Fairies in general find it difficult to turn down a direct invitation to wager. We learn early on not to say things to each other like, "I'll bet you five dollars you can't climb the flagpole." It's not that we can't deny the urge to take those bets. It is possible, and more emotionally mature fairies will have no problem saying no to such a wager. But it creates a hunger in us, an impulse.

If you're at the poker table and someone goads you with words like, "You can't fold! Can't you see he's bluffing? You're not going to let him get away with that, are you? I'll bet you a chip he doesn't have the hand he says he does." It's difficult for us to resist. And while I've learned to suppress this impulse playing among goading humans, most fae would give in to the temptation, especially if they were tired after long hours of play. It would be an absolute mess.

"I'll think about the dealer job." I need work. There's no

getting around it. The Delaney family owns half the busi-nesses in Dragonfly, so it would be hard for me to avoid working for them in some capacity anyway, and he's right about the pay and benefits being the best I could get.

We stand there staring at each other for a moment, Seven taking me in like I'm a painting hanging in an art gallery. He's studying me.

"About Shadowvale…," he starts.

I groan. "Fine. When do we leave?"

"Tomorrow. You'll need something more appropriate for the terrain." He eyes my gown with distaste. "I'll send over some hiking gear."

The last thing I want to do is to take anything else from him, but there's no way I can afford proper clothing and equipment for a trip like this. "Fine, but seriously Seven, you've been far too generous. You know I can't repay you, right? Like ever."

"It's necessary for the job Godmother charged us to do. It's covered."

I nod, still feeling awkward about not paying my own way. "I should get back to the Silver Ember. My parents need the help today."

He cups my elbow and steps in closer. "About last night. I meant every word of what I said in my apartment."

"So did I. I forgive you."

"About what happened afterward too." His gaze settles on my lips. "We'd be good together. We *belong* together."

I look him in the eye and shake my head. After hours going over everything last night, I finally know my feelings on the subject and I boil them down into one word. "Why?"

The corner of his mouth pulls back in confusion. "What do you mean why?"

"Why do you think we belong together?" I ask. "Why

not find someone more suitable? Someone of your own kind."

He gets a faraway look in his eye. "I tried that. It hasn't worked out."

Hmmm. I'm going to have to ask my grandmother who Seven was seeing while I was gone. Internally, I slap my own face. Why do I care who Seven was seeing? Ugh.

"You want me. You kissed me last night. I didn't imagine that."

I glance away toward the safety of a bird soaring across the sky. "I did kiss you, and if I'm being honest, I do want you. But we're not kids anymore. Sexual attraction isn't enough."

"It's not just about sex."

"Isn't it? It's like I said before, we don't know each other anymore, not like we used to."

"I know you, better than you think." He brushes invisible lint from the sleeve of his suit jacket.

"Right now, I'm the fish who got away. You're intrigued. But once you had me and got me out of your system, what would be left? You'd move on to the next woman who caught your attention. A woman who most likely would fit better into your lifestyle."

He shakes his head. "That's not how it would be."

"It wouldn't? What's changed, Seven. Are you telling me you'd risk your father's wrath and fae society's scorn to have a real relationship with me? You still work for your father. You're an adult now. You have more wealth, power, and influence than anyone I know, but as far as I can tell you haven't done a thing to break his hold over you. You're still that little boy under his thumb, drinking his poison. And if I was with you, it would be back to hiding and secrets, like two horny teenagers."

He runs both hands through his hair, leaving it uncharacteristically in disarray. "I can't change the way the world works."

"So then, I ask you again, why?"

"Because I can't stop thinking about you," he says, fisting his hands. "Because there's no one else I'd rather spend time with."

"I have Arden to think about now. I can't be your dirty little secret. I don't want to lie to her or model unhealthy behaviors. If I'm going to date again, I want a real relationship. A public relationship."

"It could turn into something more, Sophia. My father won't be around forever."

"No, he won't." I heave a sigh. "But you won't do anything to upset the applecart. Even after he's gone, you have to steer the ship, right?"

His gaze drops to the sidewalk, and I know I'm right.

"You would never risk going public with our relationship because it would threaten your position in Lucky Enterprises. You have to live up to the family name. A relationship with a pixie would be scandalous, and your father would likely find a way to have you ousted from the company. Even after he's gone, going public with our relationship would be a PR nightmare. You'll never do that...."

"You're wrong." He looks at me through his lashes.

"I'm not. There's something between us, Seven. There always has been since the day I was drawn to you in the woods as a child. But we're bad for each other. The only thing that can come out of pursuing this relationship is pain. Right now, we've been apart long enough we can both move on without falling to pieces. But if we date, if we fall in love? What then?" I back up a step. "I could be wrong about this, but if I am, I'm prepared to live with the consequences. They're safer than starting something with nowhere to go."

"You done?"

"Yeah."

"This thing between us, Sophia, it's not something that comes along every day, and it promises a lot more than pain. Give me a chance and I'll prove it to you."

There's nothing else I can say. Lifting onto my toes, I kiss his cheek. "See you tomorrow, Seven."

I stride back to the store. At the door, I glance behind me to find him staring, unmoving, in the same place I left him. Slipping inside, I let the door close between us.

TWENTY-TWO

That night I sleep fitfully. I tell myself it's because we'll be crossing into Shadowvale in the morning and it's the likelihood of imminent death keeping me awake. But a tiny niggle at the back of my brain replays my conversation with Seven over and over again until I drift into dreams in the wee hours of the morning.

Seven and I sit on the beach—our beach—cross-legged in the sand before a flat stone that's serving as a table. He's shirtless, his skin glinting in the sun as if he was knitted by the gods from flesh and gold. Hard muscle cords his arms, his torso a terrain of peaks and valleys I desperately want to map with my fingers. The corners of his lips, almost too full for a man, turn up when he notices me watching him, framed within a square jaw under a direct, unyielding nose. He's a luscious specimen of a man, fueled by an intimidating, tightly coiled, almost-regal strength. I picture him with a crown on his head and a scepter in his hands, sparkling from his gods-anointed throne. Seven would be a powerful ruler, but not one who exercised brute force with an iron fist. No, he'd be the type of king defended by nature itself, a tsunami that wore down his enemies, unlimited in his persistence as any mountain.

"It's your move," he says.

Only then do I notice the cards in his hand, the art on the back a picture of Kiko nestled in a field of clover. I glance down to find I'm fully dressed. There are five cards in my hands. Five-card draw. We must be playing strip poker, and I'm winning.

Power brushes past my ribs, his luck coiling around us, the purr of a contented dragon. The energy licks my skin, threatens to consume me. His eyes glow a brilliant emerald green—keen, insightful eyes that hold the promise of pleasure and something I want far more. My breath comes in pants as my body heats, the desire to strip off my dress almost unbearable.

I force myself to concentrate on my cards. Two kings, two queens, and a ten. I toss the ten into the discard pile and draw. But the card I select isn't from a poker deck at all. It's a tarot card. A picture of a man and a woman in a garden, the Lovers. My brow furrows. Confused, I drop the card in the center of the stone table.

Seven's smile fades. "You win again."

He stands, and I realize he's already completely naked. A dark storm moves in overhead. He thrusts his hand into his chest, pulls out his heart, and drops it, still beating, into my hands.

BUZZZZZZZ. My alarm screams at me from the side table. I sit bolt upright and slap the Off button, then stare at my palms. There's no blood.

Of course there's no blood. What the hell is wrong with me? I massage my temples. All the talk of playing poker with Seven yesterday must have worked its way into my subconscious. Weird.

I shake the memory of the dream from my head and go in search of coffee.

*

"I don't like this, Sophia," my father says in that deep, commanding voice dads everywhere use on their daughters when their safety is at risk. "Going into Shadowvale? It's foolish. When was the last time you heard of any seelie going through the wall? If anyone has done it in the past century, I haven't heard. And what about Godmother? It seems as though she would be the best candidate for this task given her relative power."

It's before sunrise, and I stand in front of my father decked out in the equipment Seven had delivered to our address the afternoon before. I'm wearing high-tech clothing made from insect-repellant fabric, specially designed to work with my wings, and boots that make me feel like I'm walking on clouds. The pack on my back is filled with more wing-friendly clothing, designed for any weather, as well as a hat and other sun-protective gear. A plastic bladder in the lining holds plenty of water, strategically positioned to fit between dual compartments containing dried food and a survival kit. Kiko's back there too. I've filled her jade belly with as much siphoned luck as she can hold.

"Seven is one of the most powerful seelie fae in existence, and he's working with Godmother. He won't let anything happen to me. It will be a short trip, in and out. Everything will be okay." It's a good thing I can bluff with the best of them because I have no idea if what I just shared is true. Will Seven be lucky enough to avoid hostile unseelie? Who knows? Will it be an in-and-out mission? No idea. It certainly isn't safe.

"I think Seven just wants to have you to himself in the mountains for a day or two," Grandma says slyly. She came by again to see me off and holds a purple mass of knitted yarn in her hands. She thrusts it at me. "I made you a hat, dear."

I hold up the purple bowl-shaped project. It's a hat for a giant. If I poked my head through a hole in the center, it would easily cover my shoulders like a stole.

"Thanks, Grandma."

I kiss my dad on the cheek and tell him to try not to worry, then hug my mother. I save Arden for last.

"I'll miss you," she says.

"Are you sure you'll be okay?"

She rolls her eyes. "I'll be fine, Mom. More than fine. Everyone here has been incredibly nice to me, and I have Grandma and Grandpa. Don't worry about me."

I squeeze her tight and kiss the side of her head unnecessarily hard, hoping it will stick. "You're the best kid, Arden. I'm not sure any other teenager would have survived being completely uprooted as well as you."

She shrugs. "Honestly, it's a dream come true."

My brows shoot up in surprise. "Really?"

She smiles sheepishly, her green gaze darting away from mine. "I'd been thinking a lot about this, actually, before everything went down. All my school friends had another year and planned to apply to different colleges. Everyone seemed distant once I told them I was graduating early. And I'd always wanted to meet Grandma and Grandpa and see what this place was like. Plus it bothered me how you never connected with anyone because you always had to hide who you were. I just wanted us to be a family before I had to go away and everything changed. A real family without secret identities. I'm sorry you got caught by FIRE, but to be honest, I'm happy how things turned out. I wished for this. Does that make me a terrible person?" Arden blinks at me as I realize that what started out as a lighthearted confession has taken on a note of heavy guilt.

"No, it doesn't make you a bad person. I'm glad you're focusing on the positives and making the best of the situation." I hug her again. "Now I told Seven I'd meet him at Godmother's in fifteen minutes. I better get a move on before the park opens and I have to explain to some human family why I'm dressed like this.

"Wait," my father says. "You're forgetting something." He hands me my old bow and quiver from when I was on the archery team at Bailiwick's.

"Oh my gods! I can't believe you kept this all this time!" I graze a hand over the items like they're long-lost friends. "And you made me living arrows!"

"Just three to get you started. We used wood from our new birch tree out back."

A tear forms in my eye. The birch is the plant that crowded out the thornbush at the back of their garden, the one born of the three seeds we planted the day we forgave each other and became a family again. Living arrows are a pixie thing. We are the only creatures who can carve the wood in such a way that the branch remains alive. Bright green leaves form the arrow's fletching. They can last days if watered properly and fly as if they are guided by the wind itself.

"We?" My voice cracks.

"Mom, Grandma, and me. One from each of us." I look

toward Grandma, who's smiling lovingly, then at Mom, who steals another hug, and then to Dad, who gives me one last peck on the cheek.

"I'll be home soon." My eyes blur with unshed tears. I stroke a hand over Arden's hair. My heart swells with love for each of them. And then I really do have to go because I'm definitely going to be late. To a chorus of goodbyes, I charge out the door and hope to the gods that I'm doing the right thing.

✽✽✽

WE ARE NOT THE ONLY FAE ON THIS PLANET.

On the other side of the wall, the unseelie rule.

The seelie are the only thing keeping the unseelie from devastating the human population.

Humans don't know about the unseelie. While pixies, satyrs, and leprechauns evolved to live with and among humans, the unseelie evolved to have a taste for human flesh. Unseelie don't blend in. They're monsters, ancient and dark. The unseelie are to us what sharks and alligators are to humans, if the sharks and alligators had human minds and could tell you they planned to suck out your eyeballs before they chomped on your head like it was a cheese ball. They are a leftover race from a barbaric time now relegated to the annals of our history.

Tens of thousands of years ago, a war broke out between the seelie and unseelie fae in the Americas. The seelie fae had evolved to look, sound, and act like the early indigenous humans who lived on these lands. The unseelie had evolved to think of humans as either food or slaves.

Evolution turned them into monsters with sharp teeth and claws and a taste for blood. When the seelie conquered the unseelie, the ancient rulers of our kind erected a wall to contain the unseelie in Shadowvale, a massive fairy realm where they live freely in the wilds, safely separate from the rest of us.

The seelie though were not solely responsible for winning the war against the unseelie. The god Odin sent his *light ones*, elves with an ancient magic foreign to us, to help our people. To this day, a religious order of elves called Guardians maintains the wall. They fortify the magic that keeps the unseelie where they belong and keep watch over the border. In over ten thousand years, there has never been a breach, or at least that's what we're taught in school. As far as I know, Yissevel is the first.

Seven and I arrive at the wall just after sunrise, and an elf dressed in a dark blue hood greets us at the door.

"Godmother told us you were coming," he says in a deep melodious voice that sets me on edge. Like Godmother's, his voice seems to be too big for his body. I've never met an elf before—they never leave their priory, and I've never had a reason to come here. I try to glimpse under the hood. All I can catch is jet-black hair and light blue eyes that seem too big for his head. I've read that elves have pointed ears, but his are covered. He's a bit shorter than Seven and is built slight, more like a pixie, but I know better than to think his narrower stature means he's powerless. Just like Godmother, elves have old magic, true magic not limited to luck. It's the same magic that fuels the wards surrounding Devashire.

"I'm Sophia, and this is Seven," I say, because it seems like the polite thing to do and I'm too nervous to remain silent.

The elf bows at the waist. "I am Elred."

While I'm wondering if I should bow back or maybe curtsy, Seven draws a box from his pack about as long as his hand and half as deep. It looks like it's made of solid gold. "A gift in appreciation for your help today." He bows and holds it out to the elf who accepts it with his own obeisance. He opens the lid. I can't see what's inside, but golden light reflects onto the elf's face.

He closes the top. "By Odin, your offering is found worthy. Welcome to Heimdall's Priory. Come with me."

The elf leads us through a door and down a long, narrow corridor. The structure might be better described as a dam. Now that I'm inside it, I realize our entire house could fit within its width and height. In school they'd made us memorize that the wall was around 600 feet tall, but it's different seeing it up close. From the outside, it's massive and awe-inspiring, carved with symbols that reveal it for the ancient relic it is. Being inside it is something else altogether. The inner world of the wall is bustling with modern activity. Elred explains that Heimdall's Priory is a subsection of the wall, where the guardians live and work. Their living quarters are on the second floor. The first floor is where they monitor the barrier between us and Shadowvale. We pass a glass room, and I notice elves with security equipment similar to what Seven showed me in Dragonfly.

"You have electronic surveillance?" I sputter, flabbergasted.

The elf flashes me an amused grin. "You didn't think it was all prayers and rituals, did you? Even Odin needs a little help these days."

My jaw drops, and I exchange looks with Seven.

The elf keys us into a secured room, and my sense of amazement ratchets up a few more notches. We are standing in front of a mirror—a massive, gilt-framed mirror —that ripples occasionally as if it's formed of liquid silver. My eyes snap to the corner when I think I see the shadow of a fishlike creature swim beneath the surface. The silver swells after the thing and then settles smooth again.

"What is this?" I say under my breath because the sound in here reminds me of a library or a funeral home. Every instinct I have tells me to whisper.

"This is how we go through," Seven whispers against my ear. He's behind me, watching me. I'd been so distracted with the mirror, I hadn't noticed him move in close.

The elf approaches a rack on the wall and selects a gold staff with a bulbous hook on the end. "There's a reason that Seven can't fly you in his helicopter to take you to Shadowvale."

I clear my throat. "I assumed the magic prevented that."

The elf chuckles. "Oh, you can fly over this wall, but you will never reach Shadowvale. You'll pass right into US airspace. The only way to the unseelie kingdom is through this mirror."

"It's a portal?" I narrow my eyes. How in the hell did Yissevel get through this without anyone noticing?

"Yes." Elred approaches the mirror.

"Is this the only one of its kind?" I ask quickly.

"No," Elred says, "but they are rare, and each is heavily guarded."

I open my mouth to ask how many elves work here, but Seven's hand clamps over it. Elred raises his staff, uttering some words in ancient elvish. "Once I stir the silver, you must go through before it settles. Do not stop until you reach the meadow on the other side. I cannot help you if you become trapped."

That sounds ominous.

Seven slides his hand into mine and a fine shiver travels through me. I'm really doing this. I'm going to see a world no one I know has ever seen. Anticipation drives my pulse. Adrenaline floods my system. I should be scared, but I'm not. I'm... excited.

The elf plunges the staff into the silver and grunts as he stirs in giant strokes. His muscles bulge beneath his robes from the effort. A swirl, like a whirlpool, starts at the center of the mirror and then opens into a tunnel.

He draws out the staff. "Now!"

TWENTY-THREE

Seven leaps into the swirling silver, dragging me by the hand behind him. I rush after him, my feet landing on a squishy, wet floor of questionable constitution. I almost stumble. I find my footing but lose my breath at the sheer magnificent beauty that surrounds us.

This tunnel isn't the molten silver I expected it to be from the anteroom. The reflection is fragmented, composed of swirling night. Stars twinkle and jet across the sky above me. They cascade along the sides of the tunnel, sparkle, fizzle, and darken at my feet. I'm inside a galaxy spiraling on fast forward. I feel small but connected, like a very important barnacle clinging to the side of a whale.

I'm tempted, oh so tempted, to dive into that sea of stars. If Seven's hand wasn't gripping mine, I'm not sure I could avoid sticking a finger into the whirl of twinkling energy that pulses around us. It beckons, a universe to be discovered. I can imagine what it would feel like against my skin, the cool hands of a lover, the lap of gentle waves. The velvet darkness between the silver promises the sweet oblivion of deep sleep. Oh, how I long for it. I deserve a rest after all I've been through.

Shadows shift in the beyond. Silhouettes dancing just out of sight, causing ripples in the silver stars. Ghosts reach for me. I lift my hand to reach back.

Seven's warm grasp tugs me forward harder, and I see the field beyond. It looks dull in comparison to the glittering world we are part of. I want to stay here! I want to touch and taste what lies within. I pause, but Seven isn't having it. Luck rushes through the connection of our touch, and then with one last tug, I'm flying out of the mirror and landing on my stomach in a field of bright green clover.

"Breathe, Sophia!" Seven removes my pack, then rolls me over.

I try to pull air into my lungs but can't. Have I forgotten how to? Black spots circle in my vision.

"Sophia! Come on, breathe!" Seven commands, slapping my cheek. Both his hands land on my chest. He works them under the collar of my shirt until his palms are skin to skin against me. A bubbly rush of luck flows into me, seeming to inflate my lungs from within. A loud, eye-popping gasp breaks my lips. Seven removes his hands from my bare skin, leaving two cold spots in their wake.

"That's it," he says, softly brushing the hair from my face. "Deep breaths." He stretches out beside me. I'm seized with chills and shiver hard, my teeth clacking together. Seven pulls me against him, wrapping me in warm limbs and blasting me with another bubbly rush of luck that feels like direct sun on an eighty-degree day.

"Ahhh." I moan at the feel of it.

I feel his lips press into the side of my hair.

"I'm okay. I'm okay." I rotate in his arms to face him. I'm shocked at the level of concern I see on his face. A tear escapes the corner of my eye. I wipe it away with a trembling hand.

"I don't know why I'm crying," I admit, although he never asked me. He strokes my hair, and the feel of his touch and his silence are like a truth serum. "Being in that tunnel, I felt... full. And now I just feel alone." I rub my chest.

"You're not alone," he says softly. "I'm here. I won't leave you."

Warmth returns to my bones, along with an acute awareness of how close he is. The clover under us is soft as a feather bed. It matches his eyes. Sun bakes my skin, its light drawing out the copper and blond highlights in his toffee-colored hair. Gods, he's beautiful. Beautiful and powerful and at the moment entirely focused on me.

"Did you feel it?" I ask. "The draw of it?"

He nods. "But it was different for me."

"What did you feel?"

His brow furrows, his expression going serious. "I felt entirely in control, as if I could command my own fate."

I snort. "So like always then."

He gives a low laugh but doesn't respond to that. Some part of me acknowledges that I should get up, but his fingers are still in my hair, the palm of his hand is now cupping my face. I can't bring myself to move.

"What was that anyway? I saw figures beyond the stars."

"Niflheim. It's the Norse version of the afterlife."

"Would have been nice if someone warned me that the tunnel would try to tempt me to my doom."

"Elred did. He told you not to stop until you reached the meadow."

I groan. "Oh yes, that fully encompasses the danger of walking through eternity," I say sarcastically.

He tucks hair behind my ear. "They say it draws you in with the promise of delivering you from your greatest fear."

I recall the feelings inside the tunnel, like I was surrounded by people who knew me. People I could trust who would never betray me. "So my greatest fear is being alone, and yours is losing control."

"More or less."

"Thank the gods you were strong enough to pull us through."

He gives a roguish grin. "Just lucky I guess."

I lay there, staring into his face for an embarrassingly long time, the smell of the clover beneath my cheek bringing back long-ago memories. The sun shimmers across half our faces, filling me with warmth and contentment. His fingers stroke my hair. My heart remembers this. My heart wants to live here again in this place of intimacy, of sweet words and casual touches.

My heart is stupid.

I climb to my feet and swing my pack onto my shoulders, checking that my bow and quiver are secured to the sides. With a sigh, he dons his own. For a moment, we simply take in our surroundings.

We stand in a field of clover that stretches for miles in every direction. Heimdall's Priory and the symbol-etched marble wall it's a part of stretches behind us, to the east. To the north is the lightly forested base of a rolling mountain range. To the west, a dark, twisted forest, mist curling over knobby roots of densely growing trees. To the south, a river with an ancient looking stone castle beyond. Rumor has it that King Kieran, our former monarch, moved there after Godmother rose to power following the Civil War and cast him out of Devashire, but no one has seen him in decades.

"Thistlebend Castle. Do you think Kieran actually lives there?"

"Where else would he be?"

I shrug. "Maybe she killed him and only says he lives there to keep the people from electing another—someone stronger who might threaten her power."

He laughs. "Seems like something she would do."

I widen my eyes at him, not because I'm surprised—I've heard stories about Godmother—but because he admits it. "Why do you work for her if you know how brutal she can be?"

He cuts off my train of thought with a raised hand, his luck brushing by me as it serpentines around us. "Mountains," he says with certainty.

"What about them?"

"I have a strong feeling Yissevel lives in the valley between the two peaks." He points toward the mountains to the north and the squiggle of green between them.

"Should I even ask how you know that?" It's not as if there exists a celebrity map of unseelie residences. Yissevel is ancient and well known in the lore of fairies, but as far as I know, no one's actually visited his lair.

He winks in my direction. "I don't know for sure, but that's where my luck is telling me to go."

"Great. Here's hoping your luck knows what it's doing."

He laughs. "It hasn't failed me yet."

We start for the mountains. Halfway across the field, a black horse darts out of the dark, twisting forest to the west and races across the clover toward the mountains. The animal turns its head to look at us, and its horn glints in the sunlight. I blink and blink again, but yes, I'm watching a unicorn gallop no more than a hundred yards in front of me. It races off into the trees at the base of the mountains, and I lose sight of it.

I turn toward Seven, my mouth dropping open. For once he looks as awestruck as me. "I've never seen one in the wild before. I mean there was that crippled one they had in the petting zoo at Sunshine Kingdom for a while, but this is entirely different."

He shakes his head, his eyes sparkling with amazement. "I guess we're not in Devashire anymore, Sophead."

"Will you stop calling me that! I'm a grown woman. It sounds like a nickname for a child or a little sister. I doubt you want to think of me as either."

He snorts. "I disagree. I think it's the nickname earned by a woman who was formidable enough at the tender age of fourteen to punch a merman in the nose before her leprechaun boyfriend could even gather enough luck and focus to rescue her from his clutches." His laugh seems to vibrate in the air around me. "It was the first time I realized how different you were. Indomitable."

Warmth blooms in the general region of my heart, and I deny an urge to rub away the ache in my chest. It takes all my willpower to keep my mouth shut. If I say a word, I'm afraid he'll see right through me, right down to that tiny sliver of hope that lingers at my gooey center. I snap my poker face into place.

"I think you should reconsider a relationship with me." He doesn't look at me, just keeps walking toward the mountains.

The problem is that the tiny sliver of hope I cling to when it comes to Seven is locked behind a wall and guarded by a warrior forged in the urban wilds of America where I survived by protecting my heart with a ruthlessness that wasn't there before the Yule Ball. He doesn't know what I resorted to in the early days. He doesn't know the person I've become.

"Why? Because you ripped me a new asshole when I told Godmother I knew who the victim was? Was that meant to sweep me off my feet?"

"No."

"Oh, then I'm supposed to swoon into your arms because you dressed me up like a doll and treated me like an accessory at the club the other night."

"No!" He huffs in exasperation. "I didn't even want you to go! We were on a mission."

"Right, right. Gee, Seven, I'm having trouble making a case for why I should reconsider turning my life into a pretzel to have sex with you on the sly. Am I supposed to be impressed by how you somehow roped Godmother into putting me on this case—"

He stops walking and whirls to face me, grabbing my arm so that I can't ignore him. "How about because of the chemistry? The kiss we shared. The kiss you returned after you said you forgave me. How about because I can't stop thinking about you?"

I bark a laugh. "Teenage me. The me you think you remember."

"No, woman." He gives me a little shake, his eyes sparking with flecks of gold in the sunlight. "You, *now*, the pixie who was clever enough to survive and raise a daughter on her own. The one who has no problem mouthing off to my father even though he's kicked her in the teeth. I can't stop thinking about the woman who's half my size and even less lucky but won't take an ounce of shit from me or anyone else, who's brave enough to stir up answers about a murder that I wasn't able to find even though I run the godsdamned security office! The one who never backs down from a fight and would do anything for her kid. I'm talking about the woman I kissed and the one who kissed me back."

Gods, the fire I've ignited in his soul is such a turn-on, I almost let my feelings slip. But my warrior raises her spear and strokes the head of the tiger that waits by her side, all my luck, all my power, defending what's left of my heart.

"Oh that," I say with a breathy laugh. "I thought we said everything that needed to be said on the subject."

He studies me for a moment, his eyes narrowing, and then the corner of his mouth lifts. He drops my arm, and we begin walking again. "Right. You told me all about it. The world we live in, leprechauns and pixies, dirty little secrets, yada, yada, yada... Thing is, I think that's all talk. I think you want to give this thing a go as much as I do. As I recall, you held *something* against me Friday night, and it wasn't a grudge."

My mind immediately sends me a brilliant memory of my body flush against his. "I guess I let the music and the liquor get the best of me," I blurt.

"You hadn't been drinking. You never had a chance, and we'd left the music behind in the Dragonfly."

"I was tired. Thinking about the past made me nostalgic," I toss out.

"You were wet for me, and your tongue promised things your body longed to deliver."

My cheeks burn at his words, and I can't help but inhale sharply at the truth in them. I can't think of a witty comeback, so I go for the low hanging fruit. "Maybe you just got lucky. There was a lot of it flowing that night."

A deep growl rumbles in his throat, and he scowls at

me. "I did not use luck to get you to kiss me. That was all you, Sophia, and you know it."

"I definitely felt your luck in that room."

"After. After you kissed me back and only for your pleasure."

I scoff mercilessly, my warrior pounding the end of her spear against the floor of my inner cave. "I guess we remember it differently," I say coldly.

"That's it," he says under his breath. Before I can react, he's taken me in his arms and his lips crash against mine.

I try to maintain my cool, try to tamp down my emotions and keep the warrior front and center, but my blood heats. It isn't luck that makes me return the kiss. There's no rush or tingle against my skin. Pure, old-fashioned passion rolls through me. I open for him and welcome a deeper kiss. His hands are in my hair. Mine are on his stomach, pressed flat and skimming the hard planes of his torso. He's hard and lean. I can't get enough. Without breaking the kiss, he finds my hips and tugs me against him. The feel of his cock, long and thick between us, is unmistakable. Gods, he really was born lucky. As I lean in, I feel light, and my left foot lifts behind me, my wings fluttering.

I've all but melted into him when he suddenly pushes me away with both hands. I'm adhered to him so thoroughly, I can almost hear a pop as the kiss breaks and I'm left cold and wanting, the weight of my backpack perceptible again.

I make a noise that sounds like "MMMhuhwah?"

He tips his head and slants me a purely masculine smile. "It's settled. It wasn't luck." He turns and starts strolling toward the mountain again.

[illegible] [illegible]

[illegible] [illegible] I know [illegible]
[illegible]
[illegible]
[illegible]
[illegible]

[illegible]
[illegible]
[illegible]
[illegible]
[illegible]
[illegible]
[illegible]

TWENTY-FOUR

I catch up to him once my legs agree to obey. I'm livid. He's toyed with me one too many times. "Are you saying that kiss was some kind of experiment?"

Now a self-satisfied grin has taken over his face. "You claimed I used luck to get you to kiss me. I simply proved that no luck was required. You *wanted* to kiss me. You enthusiastically kissed me back."

My mouth drops open. "You asshole!"

"An asshole you enjoy kissing." He bounces a little on his toes. Did he just skip? Oh my gods!

I grumble, but I can't deny it. Instead, I just lower my head and shuffle after him, keeping space between us. "Didn't enjoy it," I mumble, but it's so obvious I'm lying that my cheeks burn hotter.

"Don't worry, Sophead, I'll do it again soon. I have every intention of making up for lost time with you and proving to you that we belong together."

Still a little dizzy, I murmur, "This again. Are you kidding me?"

Now he looks in my direction. "No. Not kidding." After a

few more steps, his gaze locks on the horizon and he says, "You asked me why I thought we belonged together."

"Yeah, and I think your answer was something like I'd be a good bang."

If looks could burn, I'd be crispy. "You told me you thought I was living in the past, that my attraction to you wasn't real, but based on how I remembered you as a kid."

"It has to be. We haven't spent enough time together as adults."

"Thing is, it's both."

I glance in his direction, but his eyes are pinned to the horizon. "The day you met me, when we were both six, I was crying. I told you before that I didn't remember why, but I do."

I knew it!

"My mother forgot me."

I wince at the undercurrent of emotion in his voice, even though I'd suspected this piece of information based on what Mom had remembered.

"My father worked constantly, and my mother stayed home. She didn't have anywhere to be or anything to do. We had a housekeeper, a butler, a cook..." He scratched the back of his head. "The only thing she had to do was care for my sister and pick me up from school. She forgot. I stood outside Bailiwick's and watched all our classmates meet their parents and walk away, one after another, until I was alone. That's when I'd gone into the woods."

"That's horrible, Seven. But how could she forget you? Wouldn't your luck make sure she remembered?"

He snorted. "It should have. But the thing about a leprechaun's luck is it's directed based on our will, and another leprechaun's will and luck can counteract it."

I feel breathless as understanding bridges the space

between us. A heavy weight forms in my chest. "Your mom didn't want to remember. She left you on purpose."

He gives a solid nod. "When I was older, I realized that she'd wanted me to have to ask the headmistress to call my father. She abandoned me to get my father's attention. That never happened because you came. Your family was warm and kind to me. She always hated that. Cursed about it after your mom dropped me home."

I catch myself grinding my teeth. Seven's family situation is seriously fucked up. What type of mother tries to use their six-year-old as a pawn? A vision of Seven as a child fills my mind, and tears prick my eyes. All that luck, all that wealth, and his family situation was a steaming pile of bear dung.

"I'm so sorry, Seven. You were a child, and you deserved better."

He grins and focuses that brilliant green gaze on me. "I want to be with you, Sophia, because when I look at you, I not only see the little girl who was there for me that day, but I see a woman who uprooted her entire life for the sake of her daughter. You would never forget Arden. And more, you don't give a fuck about fae society. You are your own person. Being with you is a total escape from the constant pressure to be on all the time. You can't imagine how appealing that is to me."

I open my mouth to respond, but I'm completely speechless. My inner warrior is gone, and in her place is a warm, gooey heart-shaped pat of butter that slides over my rib cage and drops, sizzling, into my lower abdomen. I trudge toward the mountains, my memories and emotions forming a huge knot that I can't untangle.

In some ways, I wish Seven was a pixie and that I'd planted the seeds of humiliation, grief, and betrayal I'd coughed up the night of the ball. The physical manifestation of my emotions would have been a brutal thing, a dark tangle of thorns to rival my parents' feelings about me. But had I planted them, and had they grown in my parents' garden, I could have managed them now. The seeds of Seven's apology and explanation, if he were able to produce them, would choke it out. And I would know—definitively know—exactly how he felt and how strongly. I'd be able to *see* it.

But he's not a pixie, and his feelings will never take physical form like mine. Which means I have to trust what he says is true. I have to trust him. And that's a tall order for a poker player like me who's always prepared for a bluff. A woman like me who knows the sting of betrayal. It's all made more complicated by the societal pressures, including his father's control, that keep us from being together publicly. A secret relationship means no stakes and no accountability to anyone but each other. There's so much that bothers me about that.

The benefit of all this rumination is that it's distracted me from the walking we're doing. By the time I think about how far we've traveled, we are closing in on the sunny wood at the base of the mountain. I haven't felt the distance at all. It's as if my agitation has its own wings.

"You're awfully quiet over there," he finally says. "Have you sworn off speaking to me now?"

"I'm not sure what to say. You're right, I'd never forget my child. But I don't think you should romanticize what I did. There were days I regretted it. In some ways, I think, had I known what I was in for, I would have found another way."

His shoulders sag. "Tell me what it was like for you after you left... out there."

"You've been beyond Devashire. You know what it's like."

"For business. That was temporary and sanctioned. Not like what you did."

I don't want to tell him. It's not pretty. I hook my thumbs in the straps of my backpack and heave a sigh. "I don't think you really want to know."

"Try me."

I haven't told anyone this story, not even Arden. By the time she was old enough to understand our surroundings, I'd done what I'd had to do to make us a home.

"I'll start you off. When I went looking for you, I learned that you disguised yourself as a Ms. Effie Conrad. You used your luck to temporarily trap the real Effie in her hotel room by making the bathroom door handle break off in her hand. Then you used illusion to make yourself look like her, stole her passport, and boarded a bus to Tennessee. That's when you dropped off the face of the earth as far as I could tell."

Wow, he really did look into my disappearance. "I did in a way." I laugh darkly. "If you count sleeping beneath an underpass falling off the face of the earth."

His smile dissolves, but I'm relieved that the nuance in his turn of lip doesn't seem to hold disapproval. Instead, there's pity there, delayed as it may be, and I'm okay with that. It was a pitiful time in my life.

"I couldn't continue to impersonate Effie because she'd be let out of that room as soon as the cleaning crew found her. I shed her illusion in the restroom at the first stop outside the border and abandoned her identification there. Tossed it in the back of a truck."

"We wondered how it ended up in Pennsylvania."

I chew my lip. "Only problem was I couldn't be myself, obviously. So I took on the identity of a woman who was cleaning the bathrooms. Once I looked like her, I was able to take her purse from the employee area. I used her identity to get as far as Nashville, but after paying cash for the bus ticket, I only had enough for one very meager meal. I didn't dare use her credit cards. When we stopped in Lexington, I knew I had to change again and find some food quickly. Between the morning sickness and starvation, I was in danger of running out of luck. The only thing saving me was Kiko."

"Who's Kiko?"

I clam up. I don't want to tell Seven about Dark Stranger. What if he judges me? On some level, he knows what I did, but knowing something in the abstract is different from visualizing the details. I strip the memory down to its most basic components and say, "She's a Japanese lucky cat statue. She's made of jade with a blue-iron arm. I siphon off extra luck into her to store for later. She helped me a lot in the early days when I couldn't produce enough luck at one time to get by."

"Hmm." Something unreadable passes through his expression. Curiosity about the lucky charm?

I glance toward the woods. Almost there. "She was a gift from a friend," I say vaguely.

He grunts.

"Anyway, I used what luck was left in her to pose as a human undocumented worker and take a job as a maid. No one I worked with had papers, and the hotel owner was kind to me. But the pay wasn't enough to cover a place to live, so I bought a sleeping bag and slept along the underpass with other homeless people. Slowly I saved money, and with time and regular meals, I recharged my luck."

I stop speaking when Seven's finger goes to his lips. We've reached the woods, but he's hesitating to step onto the trail in front of us. Luck swirls around him like an anxious dragon. He darts a glance in my direction. "I have a feeling we shouldn't step on the path."

"What sort of feeling?" My bow is in my hand and I've nocked an arrow before I take my next breath.

He swipes a stone from the ground near our feet and throws it as far as he can down the path. As soon as it drops to the trail, a dozen six-inch tall creatures swarm it, teeth and claws flashing. Pebbles fly. The stone is reduced to gravel in seconds.

"Brutal little suckers," I whisper, backing behind Seven and returning my arrow to its quiver. My bow is useless in this situation. There are too many of them.

Seven grabs my elbow and yanks me into the thick of the trees. He holds a finger to his lips, clasping my hand in his. We begin silently picking our way through the woods until the ground ramps up and the walk becomes a climb. Hours later, we break from the trees and find ourselves on an outcropping of stone at the mouth of a cave. Seven motions for me to wait and searches within. When he comes out again, he's smiling.

"Our lucky day," he says with a wink. "It's vacant. We can spend the night here. It should be safe."

"Spend the night? I didn't know we were spending the night," I say, my voice rising in pitch.

Seven looks confused. "You thought we would cross into Shadowvale, find Yissevel's lair, and get him to answer our questions, all before popping back home in time for dinner and bed?"

I shrug. "Honestly, I was too focused on coming here at all to think about that. It sounds obvious now. Hey, there's no tent or bedroll in my pack!"

He chuckles. "That's because your old friend Seven is

carrying it for you. There's only the two of us after all. More efficient to share."

He doffs his pack at the mouth of the cave and starts digging inside it.

Realization dawns. "Wait, is that your way of telling me there's only one tent?"

"It's only one night, Sophia, and I promise to keep my luck to myself, unless you don't want me to." He casts me a crooked smile and then wanders off toward the trees.

"But... but... Where are you going?"

"To collect some firewood. Do us both a favor and find some meals in that pack of yours. I'm starving."

TWENTY-FIVE

I'm going to have to sleep next to Seven tonight, on the same mat, under the same covers, inside the same tent. Anticipation and anxiety war in my gut, flip-flopping my stomach until I can barely taste the reconstituted stew I'm eating or feel the warmth of the fire glowing in front of me. All I can think about is the kiss we shared earlier. I squirm on my log, thinking about the sleeping arrangements. Seven must sense my discomfort because we haven't said anything to each other in over an hour.

"You never finished your story." He breaks the silence, crumpling the remains of his stew bag and stowing it back in his pack to carry out. "You said you'd been... living on the streets, regaining your luck." He swallows heavily and stares down at his feet.

"Right." I'm thankful for the distraction and pick up where I left off. "I was working as a maid and posing as a human undocumented worker when the unthinkable happened." Seven is staring at me now, unblinking, as if I'm the most important person in his world. That unwavering, focused attention is intoxicating. I wonder how many women would kill to be in my position at the moment. I savor the feeling and keep on talking. "My boss figured out I was a fairy. I was so young and incredibly stupid. One day when I thought I was alone in the hotel, I spread my wings. I just needed to stretch. I'd never had them tucked away for so long before. I should have known that he'd have hidden cameras."

Seven pulls two tin cups from his pack and fills them both with boiling water from the kettle. He drops a tea bag in each and offers me a cup. "Let me guess, he threatened to turn you in."

I dunk the tea bag, watching the liquid darken within the mug. "Actually, he made me an offer. Turns out he also owned a strip club, and he was willing to pay handsomely if I could impersonate popular celebrities and show up to strip."

Seven glares at me over his tea, his expression humorless. "You worked as a stripper?"

I can't tell if the sudden tension his body is putting off is from disbelief, judgment, or plain old-fashioned male interest. "I did. It was good money, and it wasn't like I was exposing my own skin. I wasn't even naked under my illusion. All the audience saw was what I wanted them to see. But apparently that illusion was enough to attract the attention of a local pimp. He followed me back to my camp under the bridge. Of course I ditched my illusion right after the show, but this guy had figured out that one woman walked into the locker room and a different woman came out. He suspected what I was."

I've never seen Seven go so still. He isn't drinking. He isn't fidgeting. He's not even blinking. He looks like a statue across the fire, his face carefully impassive, his attention completely fixated on me.

"I'd seen this guy around. There was a prostitute who used to sleep near the spot I did. She died a few weeks after I arrived. Drug overdose. This guy was her pimp, and I guess he figured a pixie would be a stellar replacement for his dead girl. He grabbed me and tried to force me into his truck. Clocked me right in the eye. I drained all the luck I had left in Kiko and landed a knee squarely in his balls. I left him lying in the street, grabbed everything I had that could fit in my pack, and raced directly to the bus stop. I changed my appearance and bought a ticket to Las Vegas."

I look down at my tea. My hands are trembling, sending tiny ripples through the liquid. Seven stands and rounds the fire to take a seat next to me and pull me into his arms. For a long time, he doesn't say anything, just tucks my head under his chin and stares at the fire.

"Why Vegas?" he finally asks.

I sigh. "You. You'd taught me how to play poker, and it dawned on me that playing cards was safer than stripping. I had a plan. If I used luck irregularly and sparingly, I knew I could win. I was four months pregnant by that time. I needed better living arrangements, but I couldn't go to a homeless shelter because I didn't have papers."

"Smart. FIRE monitors those regularly."

"I had enough to make it to Vegas. Started playing in back rooms of bars, cash games, under the table. Sometimes I posed as a white man. Sometimes as a sweet old lady. People fell for it. And after all those games we played together, Seven, I was more than good. I was great. I hardly had to use my luck at all. I won, and I kept winning. Soon, I had enough to pay a man for a fake ID. Then I rented a tiny apartment and used the utility bills to establish a new identity. As my due date grew closer, I purchased better papers. My passport was indistinguishable from a real one. I used it to get an actual driver's license. I even obtained a social security number.

"By the time I went into labor, I had enough cash saved to pay for the delivery. A few more wins, and I'd rented my first house. And then Arden and I, we just lived. I played a half dozen big games each year and tried to avoid as much human interaction beyond the table as possible. Arden enjoyed an almost normal childhood. Oh, I told her what I was when she was old enough to keep our secret, and I eventually showed her my wings, but otherwise, she was a normal, happy little girl who attended public school and who everyone seemed to love the moment they met her."

Seven draws back and looks at me, and there's so much pain in his eyes. It's more than regret. He's tortured. I see guilt and more in his expression, though I can't fully interpret the emotions there, but I sense he blames himself for what happened to me. "It never should have been like this," he says in a voice laden with self-loathing. "You shouldn't have had to be this strong. I looked for you, Sophia. I swear I tried."

"Seven, it wasn't your fault. Your dad poisoned you." Saying the words aloud brings the horror of it to the forefront for me, and I grimace. I wonder at the damage it caused him, the scars inside that no one else can see. I wonder how he gets out of bed every morning and faces a man who cost him... I can't define what I meant to him back then, but if what he tells me is true, his father's cruelty changed everything. "Gods, how do you continue working with him after that kind of abuse?"

Seven sits up straighter and gives a maniacal laugh. "Why do you think I ended up head of security for all Dragonfly? How do you think I came to work for Godmother, Sophia?"

"I don't know. I assumed she asked for your help at some point."

He scoffs and looks away from me, shaking his head. When he speaks again, it's through his teeth. "No one will ever punish my father for what he did. He's too rich and too lucky. But I see everything now. I've made it my mission to cultivate a network that's beyond his control. Yes, he's chairman of Lucky Enterprises and has ultimate control over the Delaney family fortune. But by becoming head of security I'm in the only role in Lucky Enterprises that reports to no one but the board of directors. That position gives me the resources to stay two steps ahead of him. It gives me a feasible reason to keep secrets from him, like when I searched for you. And even his influence can't reach me when it comes to the work I do for Godmother. How do I face him every day? By knowing I've created safe zones where he can't always see me. He can't always reach me. He can't always control me. It's not total freedom, but it's a start." He takes a sip of his tea.

Everything becomes clear in that moment. Seven's path had everything to do with me and everything to do with breaking free of his father's hold. My mother said he started working for Godmother right after I left. He was trying to use his position to find me. He was trying to gain enough power to stand up to his abusive father. I don't know why with all Seven's luck and resources he didn't find me over the years, but I suspect his father had something to do with it. His bigoted, abusive, and vindictive father probably used his own luck and resources to keep me from his son. Maybe that's why I was finally caught. Maybe dear old Dad lost focus on me after all these years.

I end my internal speculation when Seven's hand cups my cheek and his touch interrupts my higher-level thinking. His face is close, our breath mingling. All my concentration is diverted to the heat rushing to my core and the need pulsing in my veins. Seven didn't mean to hurt me. He wanted me. He still wants me.

"Is it too late for us?" he asks, his lips hovering close to mine. "A relationship with me is risky. More risky for you than for me. But I know you, Sophia. You've never said no to a challenge."

"No," I admit.

"There's something here between us, a spark that refuses to go out. And it's not just from before. It's now. It's here."

"There is." Where is my inner warrior? I can't find her, and if I could I'd probably throw a bag over her head and send her packing anyway. I'm breathless from desire, my skin tingling, not from his luck but from mine. All of me wants to reach for him. I know it's a bad idea.

Despite our tangled pasts, we are nothing alike. He's a privileged, filthy-rich leprechaun who's used to getting exactly what he wants when he wants it. A relationship with him would be a constant battle to hold my own with less luck, fewer resources. It's true what he said, I'd be assuming most of the risk. If his father found out about us, the man who poisoned his own son to keep him from me, I don't even want to consider what type of hell he'd make my life to pressure me away from Seven. That possibility aside, there's the social risk. Other women would hate me and try to bring me down for stealing Dragonfly's most eligible bachelor. The social columns would be all atwitter about the scandalous relationship between a pixie and a leprechaun. Arden might be teased about it at school. My parents' shop might suffer.

For all those reasons, I know that Seven will never truly

be mine. Any relationship we might have will exist in the shadows, impermanent and secret. I know this, and I am having trouble remembering why I should care. Whatever the future might bring, this thing between Seven and me has been fated for a long time. Our connection is written in the stars. What would it be like to take Seven as my secret lover?

"Maybe we should leave it up to fate," he says suddenly, standing and crossing to his bag. "Care to make a wager?" He reaches inside and pulls out a deck of cards. "Five-card draw. If I win, we give this thing between us a chance."

"And if I win?"

"You tell me."

"If I win, you owe me a favor to be named later." A favor from a leprechaun is worth far more than any amount of money.

A smile warms his expression. "Deal." He spreads a blanket from his pack on the ground beside the fire and sits cross-legged. He shuffles the cards.

"The use of luck is strictly prohibited," I clarify.

He hands me the cards. "Agreed. You deal."

His gaze holds an edge as I shuffle the cards a few more times and then deal. I place the deck in the space between us.

Everything about this situation reminds me of the poker lessons Seven used to give me. They started when I was around eleven, I think, with him showing me the different poker hands and their rankings. Over the years, our lessons turned into games, and those games turned into dates.

I look at my cards. I'm one short of a straight flush, queen through nine of clubs. He tosses two cards and draws. I toss one and grin when the king of clubs fills my hand. Our eyes lock and I tip my hand. He whistles and shows me his full house.

I've won.

His smile fades as he stares at my winning hand. "All my luck is worthless when it comes to you," he mumbles.

"What?" I heard him well enough, but my mind replays my dream. Hadn't he said something similar? A chill runs along my spine.

"Nothing." He pulls his knees into his chest and turns toward the fire. "You win. I owe you a favor. Joke's on you, I would have given one to you anyway."

He looks vulnerable, so vulnerable I can picture his heart on the ground between us. Was that what my dream was about? On some level, did my subconscious see what's been in front of me all along, since the moment I returned to Dragonfly? The boy who once was my best friend and then my first love, the man with all the luck in the world, was still unable to win against his circumstances.

I stack the cards between us but can't stop looking at him. What happens in Shadowvale stays in Shadowvale. There are no cameras here. No prying eyes. If there's one place I can safely explore my feelings for Seven, it's here and now.

I'm probably going to regret this.

Crawling forward on my hands and knees, I press my lips to his.

TWENTY-SIX

Seven kisses me back without question, and he drags me onto his lap, supporting my back with a firm hand. My eyes close. This feels right. His kiss is soft and warm, a thorough worshipping of my lips within the fire's crackling glow.

My hands move to his face, the prickle of his stubble fascinating me. I trace my fingers behind his ears, drag my nails through the short hair at the back of his neck. The touch seems to ignite something within him. His fingers wrap around my neck, his thumb stroking the front of my throat. I open wider for him, welcoming him in. He growls his pleasure into my mouth.

That's when I feel that dragon he carries within him come to life. Luck rises in the air around us, a hot coiling purr that makes me tremble as it brushes my skin.

"Is this okay?" he asks softly.

"Yes." I can't deny this any longer. His kiss holds the promise of intense pleasure. It's been so long since I've been with anyone. So long since I've been touched. It's time we had the night we were supposed to have all those years ago. "I need you, Seven, please."

When his lips meet mine again, they bring a current of luck like I've never felt before. My blood bubbles in my veins, hot and light. Tingles slide between my breasts and out to the tips of my nipples, tightening the sensitive flesh. Effervescent heat rushes between my legs, teasing the bundle of nerves there until I ache with need for more. I gasp and he moves his kiss to my neck. I can't catch my breath. His hands work under my shirt and find my breasts, rolling their tips between his thumb and forefinger, even as his luck fizzes electric under the skin there.

"Breathe, Sophia," he says, and I realize I'm holding my breath. I blow out a shaky sigh and meld into his chest.

"This won't do." His hands circle my waist, and then I'm being lifted. My legs wrap around his waist of their own accord. Gods, in this position, his hard cock rubs against my center in a way that draws that hot tingle south, eliciting a moan that he captures in his mouth. With a grace no human man could accomplish, he gets to his feet, carries me into the cave and through the mouth of our tent, where he kneels on the pallet he's made there. A small lantern he's hung from the ceiling of the tent casts the space in a dim light.

"Up." I lift my arms. His hands are under my shirt again, and he tugs it over my head and off me. I arch into the heat of his mouth as it finds where his hands left off, teasing my nipple through the lace of my bra. Anticipation shoots through me, the tight grip of his fingers stoking my internal fire. Any attempt my thoughts make to surface are forced down by a primal instinct to give myself over to him.

A firm touch traces along the center of my back, and he unhooks my bra, casting it aside. His eyes are a hot, molten green, as if someone had melted down emeralds and mixed them with moonlight. Luck sizzles against my skin, that invisible, purring dragon winding around my neck, around my arms, between my thighs.

"Show them to me," he commands in a deep voice, all grit, that reverberates at my core, leaving me breathless. My wings unfurl. Ah, the feeling is heavenly, like letting go, like falling. He strokes each wing appreciatively, gentle and teasing at the tips, adjusting to a deep massage when he reaches the sensitive area of my back where they join the rest of my body. I lean into his touch and he sucks one of my nipples hard. Oh gods, my body hums for him like a musical instrument.

He draws back and places a hand between my breasts, pushing gently. I lean back onto my elbows so he can see me, and his fingers trace slowly over my stomach. His luck follows his gaze as he takes me in, luck, like effervescent velvet, teasing my flesh lower and lower until the ache between my legs is an exquisite torture. I tip my head back and pant. If he keeps this up, I'm going to come before he even touches me below the waist.

"Not yet. Not before I taste you." It's a command, and his luck draws back. I desperately want to chase after the feeling, but he casts a wicked grin in my direction. "Have a little patience, Sophia."

He pulls my boots off one by one, then makes short work of my zipper. My pants and everything underneath come off next. He's still fully dressed, and I reach for his fly, but he dodges my touch. "Not yet. Lean back."

"You're not the boss of me." I reach for his fly again, and his luck plows into me like a hot fizzy wave. It fills me from within, pressing against my inner walls. I gasp and fall back on my elbows, arching into the hot purr.

"That's better," he says. His hands land on my knees, stroke down to grip my inner thighs tight enough that it's just on the edge of pain, and he spreads my legs, baring me to him. I'm so exposed in every way. Completely naked, my body thrumming under the influence of his power. He's kneeling between my thighs, fully clothed and watching me hungrily. What must I look like? Mouth swollen from his rough kisses, nipples hard, core slick with need.

"Gods, I've waited a long time for this." His voice is lower, gritty. Luck pounds into me again. I arch and spread my knees wider. I'm beyond words.

"Mmm. Good girl." He presses a kiss at the apex of my thighs. I moan, tension coiling deep within me. His hands find my hips and he pulls back, blowing cool air over my clit. I've only just processed the sensation when he flattens his tongue and licks up my slit from back to front. I almost buck off the mat. I feel his dark laugh rumble against me as his tongue toys with my most sensitive flesh and the rush of his luck fills me from the inside again.

This is what it's like with a leprechaun. When he gets lucky, he gets lucky. He knows exactly where to touch me. Exactly what I need. His tongue is fluttering in just the right spot as his fingers follow the vibration of his luck to massage inside me.

I lose all control. I arch and cry out as an orgasm rips through me. It's intense, all-consuming, but he doesn't let up. He sucks me into his hot mouth as his fingers work deep inside, thrusting in just the right place.

"Seven, it's too much," I say breathlessly.

"Again," he commands, and that hot purr fills me once more.

I haven't even come down completely from my first orgasm when the second one plows into me, more intense than the first. I turn boneless, riding out the aftershocks flat on my back. "Seven!"

This time, he stretches out beside me, a decidedly male and self-satisfied grin on his face, and watches me recover. His hand is splayed across my belly, warm, firm fingers bridging from hip to ribs.

"I've waited a long time to do that," he says. "I wanted it to be memorable."

Memorable? More like life altering. I shudder in his arms as an aftershock of pleasure rocks through me. I stare at him through my lashes, tipping up the corner of my mouth. "Goal achieved. But the game isn't over." I reach for his fly and hear his breath hiss between his teeth.

Things are just getting interesting when a feral growl splits the night. Seven grabs my wrist and tips his ear toward the tent flap. He frowns and leaps to his feet, zipping and buttoning his pants again. "Stay here. This won't take long."

Bullshit. I'm not letting him face whatever unseelie might be out there alone.

He slips out the tent and into the night. I dress, pull on my boots and grab my bow and quiver, following him into the darkness. Light on my feet, I move silently toward the edge of the plateau. I can't see Seven, but I'm so hopped up on his luck, I can sense him. My eyes adjust to the dark and I meld into the woods.

Almost immediately, I spot the beast facing off against Seven. It's cerulean blue with lime green spots that might be beautiful if the creature wasn't obviously deadly. With a mouth lined with three rows of teeth and six sets of nostrils that run from the upper lip to its ridged brow, I'm sure its bite is every bit as deadly as its roar.

Seven stands in its line of sight, about a hundred feet

from it, sweat blooming on his brow. His eyes flare that brilliant emerald green. I can feel the brush of his luck but can't see what he's trying to do. The night sky is clear. None of the trees look as if they might fall. The ground doesn't quake. He might be trying to stop the beast's heart, but if he is, it isn't working.

The beast prowls slowly toward Seven. I raise my bow and nock an arrow. A bird lands on a heavy branch that stretches far up and across the pathway between the beast and Seven. Another bird lands and then another and another. The creature prowls forward. Luck surges off Seven, and the fattest raccoon-like creature I've ever seen bounds out on the same branch.

Crack. The branch drops, smashing onto the beast's head. The birds scatter and the raccoon creature leaps to the tree with a shriek. It's a huge branch and a long drop. The beast's chin slams into the ground and blood dribbles from its nostrils. Seven dusts off his hands and turns back toward camp.

Shit, he's a sweaty mess. He looks... empty. There are dark circles under his eyes, and he's limping a little. His appearance doesn't make sense. That tree branch couldn't have drained a leprechaun's luck. Then it dawns on me that he's drained because of *me*, because of what we did. He was thrumming my body with luck only minutes ago, and damn, he must have pulled out all the stops.

He hasn't seen me yet. I've used my luck to camouflage myself. I'm dark as night and the texture of tree bark. Still, if he had any luck left at all, he'd have noticed me. He must be bone dry.

The branch moves. I look back at the beast and it's rising, shaking its head and snorting angrily. Seven's eyes widen when he sees it. He pulls something from his pocket that flashes gold in the moonlight.

The beast pounces.

My arrow flies, and I focus all my luck on making my aim true. The living arrow enters the creature's ear and slices through the thickest part of its head. Its body seizes in the air, but Seven has to throw himself out of the way to avoid its claws as it crumples to the earth, dead. Now Seven's eyes find me, and I drop my illusion.

"Thanks," he says.

"Don't mention it." I wink. "But I might. I might mention it a lot to as many people as possible. I think the story of how Sophie the pixie saved the ass of Seven the leprechaun would make a great bar ballad." I sling a slow cheeky smile in his direction.

"Sophia Larkspur, was that a joke? Gods, she still has a sense of humor." He swaggers toward me, his confidence outweighing the luck he has left in his arsenal.

"No," I say flatly. "I'm not being funny. I plan to tell everyone who will listen that I saved your life with my badass archery skills."

His eyes narrow. "Will you also tell them what we were doing that caused me to almost drain myself dry?" His gaze rakes lasciviously down my body, and I quell the desire to squirm.

"Eating by the fire?"

"No. After the eating but before the monster. In the tent." He's standing right in front of me. Close. Temptingly close.

I rub my chin. "I'm not sure I remember exactly how you got yourself into this mess, Seven."

He grabs me around the waist and sweeps me against

him, leaving me breathless. "Perhaps I should show you again."

We're both panting now, and all I can think is that Seven is in my arms. He's mine again. It's like something out of a dream.

"I'd like that," I say breathlessly.

He sighs. "Unfortunately, we both need to sleep and recharge in case any of his friends come back." He points his chin at the dead beast.

As a pixie, I can't propel luck into him like he's done to me. It crosses my mind to give him Kiko, but it takes time to siphon off enough luck to fill her. She's for emergencies, and having hot leprechaun sex with Seven hardly fits that description as much as it might seem so at the moment. "You can't have hot leprechaun sex without luck?"

Taking my hand, Seven tugs me toward the tent. He arches a brow and shoots me a look that makes my stomach do a little backflip. "Patience, Sophia. For what I plan to do to you, I need a full tank."

TWENTY-SEVEN

Lucky me, I wake with a leprechaun curled around me. We're both fully dressed, but his arm holds me firmly against his chest and his breath skates along the base of my neck. The corners of my lips curl upward, as a warm, contented feeling fills me.

Warning bells draw me fully awake. It's dangerous to feel this way. This emotion is too close to the blind adoration I felt as a teenager, the same feeling that came before the worst experience of my life. Allowing myself to think Seven is mine, to flirt with loving him again, makes me vulnerable. It's foolish. It's fantasy.

Then I remember that fooling around in Shadowvale means nothing. No one can see us here. Seven doesn't have to face his father's wrath here. It's the ultimate place to keep a secret. Since I've returned to Devashire, our relationship has been all about secrets. He has a professional reason to be near me thanks to Godmother. He's been careful not to show public displays of affection. At the club, he made me change my appearance. He's always kept his distance or used luck to keep anyone from noticing us together.

I'd be an idiot to think this is anything more than exactly what it was, one night of pleasure. Isn't that why I allowed myself to indulge in it in the first place? It was supposed to be a safe way to get this thing with Seven out of my system.

A bone-deep sadness weighs me down at the thought. Last night, I'd convinced myself I'd be okay with becoming Seven's secret lover, at least for one night. This morning, in the light of day, it's oh so clear that my heart—my crazy, vulnerable, traitorous heart—wants more. I know this feeling. I've been here before. I'm falling in love with Seven.

A tear streams down my cheek and I wipe it away.

"Hey, what's going on inside that pretty little head?" He shifts to press a kiss to my temple, and frowns as he wipes away another tear.

"I think... last night was a mistake," I say softly.

He pushes himself up to a seated position, his expression turning stone-cold serious. "No, it wasn't."

I sit up too, pressing both hands to my chest. "Last night was incredible, but we both know that once we leave here, it will be like this never happened. Sure, we could carry on in secret for a while, but at some point, you'd be expected to marry some equally powerful and successful leprechaun to carry on your family's dynasty. Sooner or later, what happened here will be a distant memory. It will be better, less painful for both of us if it's sooner."

"You seem to think you know my future better than I do." He folds his arms in reproach.

"We both know it's inevitable." *And I feel too much for you to taste what it's like to have you, knowing I'll have to give you up.* I wipe another round of tears.

"Because you think I would never take this relationship public."

I tip my head. "You have your father, your company, and your reputation to think about Seven. I don't judge you; I just need... more."

He snorts and points at his chest. "You don't judge me? I don't care about any of that, Sophia. If this were just about me, I'd do it in a heartbeat to have you. I might be able to keep you safe from my father, but the minute people found out about us, they'd gossip and harass you. The things they would say would make your and Arden's life hell. The secrecy is as much for your sake as mine."

"I know," I say, my heart clenching painfully.

He shakes his head. "You don't. Not all of it. Standing up to my father means being prepared to break from Lucky Enterprises. He holds a controlling interest. Honestly, I'd consider it if not for what it would mean for people with fewer choices than me. I wouldn't be there anymore to buffer Evangeline from his bullshit. I've done it since we were small, and she's not ready to handle him herself. And then there are the employees. You know, before I took control, there were no benefits for pixies and satyrs, and the pay hadn't kept up with inflation in twenty years. Oh, and under Dad's control, pixies wouldn't be allowed as customers in the club anymore. He doesn't think they belong."

"More of a reason we should end this here, before it gets more... complicated." *Before I fall in love with you.*

He considers that for a moment. All at once, his eyes go wild, feral, like an animal backed into a corner. "No," he says firmly.

"No?" I wait for him to elaborate.

His jaw clenches and his lips twitch. But he just looks at me and repeats, "No!"

I gape at him, unsure what to say to that. It's just as

well, he slips out of the tent before I have a chance to say anything.

For the time it takes to pack up my things and roll up the blankets and the mat, I consider his "no" and my blood starts to heat. Since when does he get to decide? I haven't made any commitments. I'm a grown woman and I know what's best for me. I burst from the tent in a full huff, throwing the roll at him with an unnecessary amount of force.

"I'm sensing you have something to say." He starts strapping the rolls onto his pack.

I lift my chin. "You don't get to tell me no, Seven."

He slams a cup into his pack. "I've waited too long to get you back. I'm not giving you up that easily. We should have never been apart in the first place. If it wasn't for my father's interference—"

"You know, I thought about that. I asked myself just now, if we'd kept our relationship secret sixteen years ago, would we still be together?"

"Of course we would," he says. "You wouldn't have left Devashire if the Yule Ball never happened."

I shake my head. "I don't think so. Because even if I never left, I would have grown up, Seven, and I would have wanted more. I am *worth* more than being someone's dirty little secret."

"I never suggested you become my *dirty little secret*. I'd never treat you that way."

"You didn't have to suggest it. It's the only option left once going public and staying apart are off the table." Tears blur my vision as I step into him and fist his shirt, bringing our faces close. My voice cracks as I say, "I am a pixie, and I am a woman, and I deserve love and happiness. I've been through too much to settle for less. Arden has been through too much. The fact is, I have lived a lie for the last sixteen years, and I was good at it Seven." I shake my head. "I've perfected the bluff. But I realize now, facing another life of lies, that I just don't want to do it anymore. It's time for me to cut my losses, fold, and leave the table. Last night, I thought I could settle, I thought stolen moments with you would be enough, but I was wrong. I want it all or I want nothing, and in our world, all just isn't possible. I'm sorry." I'm trembling as I release him.

Pain travels through Seven's expression before his face turns impassive and cold. His voice is flat and emotionless as he says, "You're right. You deserve more."

He turns from me and we dismantle the tent in silence.

An hour later, I find myself hiking along a path between two mountains. It's cold, and I've donned every layer of clothing in my pack and tucked my wings inside for warmth. We haven't said a word to each other since we left the campsite. But we're going to have to get over what happened and move beyond our feelings because I see a flash of bone white through the trees up ahead and I think we've reached our destination.

"What's the plan, Seven?" I whisper. The hair on my arms is standing on end, and I find myself touching my bow to reassure myself it's still there.

He grunts. "We walk into Yissevel's lair and ask him what he was doing in Dragonfly. See what he says."

I laugh. "Do you expect him to answer us before or after he tears our teeth and bones from our bodies?"

"Hoping for before," he says a little too seriously. He's scanning our surroundings, likely analyzing how he can leverage luck in this situation.

"Hope isn't a strategy."

He snorts.

"What happened to that gun I saw you wearing the other day?"

"The guardians won't let it through. We're in unseelie territory. It's considered a human weapon and isn't allowed."

"But my bow is?"

He kicks up an eyebrow. "Invented by a pixie."

Hmm. I had no idea. I blow out a deep breath. "Yissevel can't fly," I say. "I'll ask the questions, and you pummel him with luck. If we get into trouble, I'll take off. You'll be okay, right?" He knows what I mean. I want to know if he's recharged the luck he spent on me last night.

A corner of his mouth tips up. "At full power. I'll survive. Don't worry about me."

"It's a plan." Not a very good one but the best I can think of.

I take my bow off my shoulder and nock an arrow. We're close enough now that I start to worry. Yissevel's home is bone white for a reason. Up close, I can make out pyramids of skulls, bleached white from the sun, wedged together to form a foundation for a network of femur bones, some human, some not, that create the entrance. The path to his front door is pebbled with teeth.

I wonder again how this creature could have spawned the human folklore of the Tooth Fairy. It was like people couldn't tolerate the horror, so their minds created a more palatable fiction, a creature who took sacrificial teeth in exchange for money and looked more like a pixie than a monster. What would they do if they knew the truth?

We approach the eight-foot-tall doors made of polished ivory. Seven grabs on to the bone handle and pulls. I guess we're not knocking then. The door swings open.

I have a bad feeling about this.

The crunch of our boots on the millions of teeth lining the entryway sends chills along my skin as I follow Seven inside. It's quiet here. Too quiet. Only now do I miss the strange sounds of birdlike creatures that accompanied us on our journey here. This place is as silent as a tomb and smells like one as well. Not a rotting smell—no fresh dead here—but the scent of ancient things, bleached bone, leather, and dust. I make the mistake of looking up and realize we are in a catacomb of sorts. The room is shaped like a church, the bones narrowing to a point, the gaps between letting in enough daylight to see by.

The teeth in front of my toes rattle although I haven't moved. They settle, then rattle again. "Seven?"

I draw a shaky breath as I whirl toward the hall at the end of the large room we're in. Seven is already turned in that direction. Luck coils around him, and something gold glints in his hand. It distracts me for a second before my eyes snap back to the hall.

Yissevel is there, the floor vibrating with every heavy footstep.

The creature is more horrific than I'd imagined. Seeing him on camera and in sketches hasn't prepared me for this. He's at least eight feet tall and composed entirely of bones held together by sinew and what must be magic. His head is a fleshless skull with tufts of hair growing from the bones, rheumy eyes, a hole where a nose should be, and a lipless smile of narrow teeth. Within his rib cage, a heart must beat because I see the leathery connective tissue pulse beneath his left arm. He stares down in our general direction, wearing nothing but a loose and filthy cloth that circles his waist and ties over one shoulder. Yissevel is a walking, breathing skeleton from my deepest, darkest nightmares, and he's staring at Seven as if he's his next meal.

"Back so soon?" Yissevel sniffs the air.

What? I look between Yissevel and Seven, who is visibly shaken. Yissevel's eyes swivel in his skull and I realize he's not focusing on either of us. His eyesight must not be very good. He tips his head back and sniffs the air again. He can't see us; he smells us.

"What have you brought me this time, leprechaun?" Yissevel takes another step forward. "More meat? More *bones*?"

"We've come to ask for your help," I say in a loud clear voice. My arrow is still anchored between my fingers, the bowstring drawn taut.

Yissevel stops, pivots toward me and sniffs. "A pixie? Not expecting you. You need help? First, you bring Yissevel teeth!" he booms.

"Was a leprechaun here before?" My hands are shaking, and I try in vain to steady my arrow. Beside me, Seven's eyes glow. He's completely focused on the bone fairy.

The creature's head turns right, then left, sniffing the air. "A leprechaun brings me a pixie, and now a pixie brings me a leprechaun? What treachery there is among the seelie."

A leprechaun *was* here before. I glance at Seven, but he doesn't look my way. His luck slithers around the room. Out of the corner of my eye, I see him squat and pick something up from among the carpet of teeth.

"What did the leprechaun who was here before want you to do?" I ask. "You said he brought you a pixie. Was she dead or alive when he gave her to you?"

"Just dead. Yissevel prefers dead. He will not do it again."

"Do what again?"

"Yissevel does not care for the smell in that place. Too sweet." The creature sniffs again. Takes another step toward me. "Pixie hearts are sweet but small. Barely a meal. Not enough payment to cross the silver. Yissevel will only leave for human meat, human bones. He likes them best."

"Who was here before? Who offered you pixie flesh in exchange for your help?"

"You would know, little one. Tell him Yissevel will not go again for only pixie. Man flesh is what I crave." The creature whirls faster than anything that big should move. He sniffs the air in front of Seven. "Although Yissevel wouldn't mind sampling leprechaun. You are different. Younger. Sweeter."

"Was it an *older* leprechaun who visited you before?" I ask.

He snorts and sniffs closer to Seven.

"There's been a mistake," Seven says. He backs for the door, waving a hand at me to do the same. "Sorry to have bothered you."

What's he doing? We can't leave now! We still don't know who killed Phoebe or how Yissevel made it through the silver.

"No bother." The creature takes a step toward us. "Come closer. Let Yissevel look at you."

Seven starts moving in earnest toward the door, motioning for me to go too.

"First taste of leprechaun." Yissevel lunges, faster than I expect. His hand sweeps toward Seven... and misses! The boney fingertips of the creature's fingers brush against his shirt as Seven leans out of reach.

My arrow flies. *Fuck!* I didn't consciously release it, but seeing that thing dive for Seven, my fingers acted of their own accord. I was aiming for that pulse under its left arm, but he's already shifted and the arrow bounces harmlessly off Yissevel's rib cage. The only thing I've accomplished with that shot is to turn its attention from Seven back on me.

Yissevel growls and charges. "Come here pixie treat!"

I jump and lift straight up as his fist closes around the space where I just was. "I thought you liked your meat dead!"

"Hungry," Yissevel bellows. "Exceptions must be made."

I flutter my wings faster but I can only fly so high. The ceilings in this bone dwelling aren't tall enough for me to rise out of his reach.

"Get the fuck out of here!" Seven yells, motioning for me to fly toward the door. True anger rattles his voice.

I try to flee, but Yissevel is on me, sniffing the air and reaching for me. As I drop to fly through the open door, a boney hand closes around me, crushing my wings.

"Let me go!" I scream.

"Pretty teeth. Pretty bones," it says, its rank breath blowing back my hair as it brings me toward its mouth.

"Put her down, Yissevel," Seven warns. His voice is charged with luck, and it rattles the bones over our heads.

Yissevel's milky gray eyes shift, but he doesn't even pause. He holds me as the claws of his opposite hand reach toward my chest. "Heart first. Then spleen. Then the bones in between," he singsongs.

Just like he did to the others, only I'm alive to experience it. *Fuck!* I turn my face away.

Gold flashes through the air and plunks against the bones of the roof. Yissevel has just enough time to swivel his eyes up before the ceiling collapses on his head. I scream as he drops me, my crushed wings unable to recover fast enough to carry my falling weight.

Seven catches me in his arms with an oomph, barely an inch outside the collapse of bones. He sets me on my feet, then holds out his hand. A gold coin falls from the sky into it. I've never seen a coin like this. I watch him flip it over his knuckles and between his fingers. There's a woman on one side, a dragonfly on the other, and it looks positively ancient.

He pushes me toward the exit before I have time to ask him about it, and I don't hesitate to move. He's right behind me... until suddenly he's not. Seven's being dragged across the carpet of teeth. Behind him the pile of bones rattles and falls away from Yissevel who rises, pissed off but otherwise unhurt. Seven dangles by one leg over Yissevel's mouth. The coin flies from his hand, hitting the creature in one eye. Yissevel roars and drops Seven but catches him in his opposite hand. The gold rolls under the pile of bones.

I nock my last arrow and aim it at Yissevel's heart. I don't let it fly, however, because the ground has started to quake. Seven. He's sweating buckets, luck coiling off him and between us like the massive invisible dragon I picture it to be. He has limited options; there's nothing around us but fallen bones. My skin tingles with the intensity of the power flowing off him.

Yissevel sways on his feet. He snaps at Seven with his teeth, but he can't steady himself enough to get the leprechaun into his mouth.

The ground cracks to my left, bringing down one wall of Yissevel's lair. It only serves to enrage him more.

Leprechaun or not, there's no way Seven can keep this up. I take a deep breath and stretch my wings. They're sore, but when I flap them, I lift off the ground. Once in the air, the earthquake can't shake my bones and I level my arrow, aiming at Yissevel's heart.

"Make it count, Sophead. I'm almost out of juice!" Seven yells, his eyes two emerald green spotlights in the dim interior.

I close one eye and release my held breath. The arrow flies. It slips between Yissevel's ribs and pierces the throbbing sinew there. Seven drops like a stone from the creature's hand and crumples into the piles of bones, but my aim was true. Yissevel topples, blows out a breath, and moves no more.

Only after I'm sure the unseelie monster is dead do I land and pull my arrow from his side. I wipe it on the creature's garb before sliding it back into my quiver. I might need it for the journey home. The earth has stopped quaking. *Seven.* I run to him. His shirt is soaked with sweat, and he's lying perfectly still, face pallid.

"Are you hurt?" I ask.

He nods. "Ankle." A shard of bone from the collapsed wall protrudes from the flesh just below his calf. I reach for it, but he stops me, "No!" He swallows hard. "I used too much luck. I'm negative. If you remove that now, I'll bleed out."

"You let yourself go negative?" I say disbelievingly.

"Gods, Sophia. It wasn't intentional. I was trying to save our hides and heal your wings at the same time."

I remember my crushed wings, incapable of flight when Yissevel had dropped me. I was able to carry my weight at just the right time. Not my doing. "Hold still."

He gives me a wary look.

I reach into my bag for Kiko and press her jade belly into his hand. He takes a deep breath. Slowly, color returns to his cheeks. I dig out the first aid kit and find the bandages. He sits up and yanks the bone from his leg. Lucky him, it wasn't in as deep as I'd feared. I press a piece of gauze to the wound to stymie the blood and then start to wrap it.

"Who do you think was using Yissevel? It sounded like it was a leprechaun."

Seven frowns. "I'm not sure, but I intend to find out." His voice sounds funny. I glance in his direction, my mind fighting my heart on what to do next.

"Yissevel thought you were him at first."

"Because a leprechaun was behind this."

"A leprechaun who smells like you."

"It wasn't me, Sophia."

"No." I want to look away from him as I say it, but I force myself to hold his gaze. "But maybe it was someone in your family."

He shakes his head, but I sense it's not in denial but disappointment. "Why would he do this? He already has everything."

"Why would he poison you?" My voice rises in volume. "Why would he say what he said to me? Why does he hate pixies so damn much?"

"Think about what you're accusing him of. This is more than bigotry. This is murder. Murder of humans, inside and outside Devashire."

"But he has a special pass from the US government, doesn't he? He has to as the chairman of Lucky Enterprises. All those slot machines your company sells to US casinos and the Dragonfly merchandise... He has to meet with buyers. That can't all take place in Devashire."

"No," Seven says through his teeth.

"He hates pixies." I frown. "I don't know why he used Yissevel or why he killed those two humans, but he is the most likely to have the means. He must be working with one of the elves or somehow have a mirror."

As soon as I've tied off the bandage, he hands Kiko back to me, clambers to his feet and limps toward the exit. I put her away before hoisting the pack onto my shoulders and following after him.

"I'm not trying to upset you, Seven. I just think we have to consider the most obvious explanation for what just happened. Chance Delaney is our most likely suspect."

"Shut up, Sophia."

I balk, a weight forming in my chest at the harshness in his tone. I'm exhausted. I don't have the energy to fight him on this or to carry the burden of the truth alone.

His eyes spark emerald when he turns back toward me. "I'm not saying you're wrong." His expression softens. "But please, for five minutes, just let me think."

All righty then. I drop back a few feet. I won't let Seven deny this, but I understand why the trauma he's lived through might cause him to avoid the hard truth. I can't be part of that denial. When we get back to Devashire, I'll tell Godmother everything, whether or not Seven is on board with that plan. I don't know why Chance Delaney committed these murders, and I don't care. He's going to finally pay—for this, for what he did to Seven, and for what he did to me. I will take him down with my own boot on his neck if I have to. I'd rather have Seven on board though, so I back off and remain silent.

The journey is thankfully uneventful, and we set up camp on the same plateau we did before. Once the tent is erected and the fire blazes between us, Seven finally looks at me and breaks the silence with four little words.

"I lied to you."

TWENTY-EIGHT

I lower the cup of tea I'm holding and glare at him. "You lied to me? About what?"

"The night my father poisoned me, he didn't lock me in my room."

My blood turns to ice at the admission. There's something about the way he says it that unsettles me, like he's sharing a dark secret, like he's peeling back the curtain on a deep shame. I give him my full attention.

"So you *were* free to leave, but still didn't find help or a way to tell me what happened?" I say the words without judgment. The thought will be hard to live with, but I can forgive him for it. He was just a kid, in a horrible situation. I think of him back then, barely older than Arden. The memory hurts, but I can move beyond it.

He rubs his palms together slowly. "What I mean is, my father didn't hold me in my bedroom. He has... cells under his hunting cabin in the mountains outside Elderflame. He took me there when I was unconscious and locked me up. I'd never been there before. I didn't know how depraved he was until then."

The horror of the revelation makes my skin crawl. "Seven, are you saying that your father has actual prison cells under his hunting cabin where he locked you up?" I lower my voice although there is no one here to overhear us. "Was it like a sex dungeon or something?"

He shakes his head. "I don't know for sure what it is or why it's there, but there was nothing pleasurable in that room." He's silent for a moment, staring down into his tea. "And I wasn't alone."

My hand trembles, and I almost spill my drink. "Seven..."

"There was a woman in the cell next to mine. I never saw her face, but she spoke to me through the wall. She comforted me." He closes his eyes, and I can see the burden this secret has placed on him. Then it dawns on me, this conversation isn't just about then. It's about now.

"Oh my gods, Seven! Do you think he was keeping the woman prisoner there? Was she a pixie?"

A muscle in his jaw twitches, and he rubs it absently. He hasn't shaved since we left Devashire, and I can hear his stubble grate against his fingers. Seven, the leprechaun who always looks fresh and acts smooth, suddenly appears old and worn. I've reached the great and powerful Oz and pulled back the curtain to find the heart of an emotionally exhausted boy.

"Anything is possible." He rubs his eyes. "And then there's this." He holds a button up between his thumb and forefinger.

"What is that?"

"It's a button. A custom-made button with the initials VS on the back."

"Who's VS?"

"Valentine Sullivan. He's a satyr who makes custom

buttons. These things are hundreds of dollars a pop. Whoever was using Yissevel was extremely rich."

I set my tea on the ground beside my feet and round the fire to sit next to him. "Your father has always outwardly hated pixies. What if he abducted those women?"

Seven stares into the fire. "Maybe he didn't have to. Maybe they were there willingly."

"What?"

"The woman who comforted me didn't seem unhappy, Sophia. She didn't ask me to send help once I was freed."

"Oh my gods."

"He's the luckiest creature in Devashire, and every one of them was in that club, looking for... something."

"But... but... if they were his mistresses, why would he use Yissevel to have one of them killed?"

"I don't know that he did. I've been thinking about this, and Yissevel said it was someone who smelled like me. Not necessarily my father. Maybe it was another leprechaun. A jealous rival who wants to embarrass my father by creating enough havoc that his pixie fetish is made public."

I wince. Pixie fetish. *Fuck*. It makes sense. Chance was always extreme in his outward hatred toward me and other pixies. It's like those human homophobes who finally come out as gay. If pixies were his secret passion, it explains why he worked so hard to insulate himself from suspicion.

"It's possible a rival is trying to frame him or perhaps blackmail him." I place my hand on Seven's leg supportively.

He exhales a shaky breath. "If my father was involved, we have to have proof before we go to Godmother. He's too powerful. If he finds out we're on to him, he'll have all his t's crossed and i's dotted before Godmother can even question him or I can call in enough officers to contain him."

"We have to go there," I say. "If you can get us into that cabin, there might still be women there. We can question them, find out what they know. We have two dead humans and one dead pixie. It's possible that your father has no connection at all to Phoebe, but there's only one way to find out for sure."

He nods his head. "Tomorrow is Wednesday. Dad will be meeting with the accountants at the casino to review their weekly breakdown of revenue and expenses. We can go while he's distracted."

⁕⁕⁕

WE WAKE EARLY AND ARRIVE AT THE WALL BEFORE MIDDAY. ONE of the elves spots us from the watchtower, and minutes later the mirror liquefies to allow us to pass. Either I've become resistant to the pull of the swirling stars or it's easier to pass into Devashire from Shadowvale than the other way around. Whatever it is, this time I'm not tempted to dive to my doom.

I lean back against the leather seat of Seven's Mercedes as we zoom through the streets of Elderflame and up into the mountains where only the wealthiest of his kind maintain homes. Ancient forest surrounds us. We gain elevation, and the road becomes narrower until eventually blacktop gives way to stone and Seven has to slow his vehicle to keep from kicking up rubble.

I've never been to this area. To say it is remote would be an understatement. We are over two hours from Dragonfly, and that's with Seven driving at top speed. There is no one out here. I haven't seen a home or driveway in twenty minutes.

No one to hear you scream.

This entire mess is creeping me out. I'd suspected Seven's family was dysfunctional after what I'd learned the past few days, but "dungeon under the hunting cabin" is a step beyond what I ever imagined, even on those nights sleeping under that bridge when Chance became every devil in my nightmares. I comfort myself with the thought that we might be minutes away from the clue that connects us to the killer and solves this murder. If we take Chance down in the process, more reason to celebrate.

Seven pulls into a winding drive and stops before a log cabin that is far bigger than my parents' home. It's grander than any home I've ever lived in. Luxury cabin would be a better descriptor than hunting cabin. It's perfectly landscaped with eastern bluestar, butterfly weed, and cardinal flower, edged in partridgeberry. A walkway of bluestone leads to the door.

"Leave your bow," Seven says.

"What? Why?"

"In case we run into the housekeeper. It'll be hard to explain. I promise I'll protect you from anything we find down there."

Housekeeper or houseguest, if we do find someone in Chance's dungeon who wants to be there, I can see how sticking an arrow in her face would be a poor way to say hello. I leave my bow and quiver with my pack.

Once the car is parked, I open the door and start for the cabin but Seven stops me with a wave of his hand. "Careful."

I look where he's pointing. A circle of red-capped toad-stools lines the property. "A fairy ring. He's warded the place." Not a particularly strong ward but the best he could do with luck alone. He'd need old magic like Godmother's to create something stronger.

"I've got it." Seven focuses his energy, and I feel his power swirl between us. He leans down and digs up one of the mushrooms with his bare hands, breaking the ring. He carries it to the fountain and places the bottom in the water. "I'll replace it on our way out."

We walk together toward the front door, but then he takes my hand and leads me around to the back of the cabin. He stops in front of a subterranean window with a deep well lined in stone. It's dark, dank, and home to one too many spiders.

"You can't be serious." I flash him an incredulous look.

"This is how I got out last time."

I feel my eyes bulge. "Wait, you had to break out? I thought your father let you out!"

He reaches down and jostles the narrow window. The lock gives way, and it slides open. Without another word, he slips through the dark opening.

I can't believe I'm doing this. My skin turns clammy and my heart flutters at the sight of that dark hole. *Sure, drop into my father's dungeon where pixies are being held and maybe tortured and killed.* Pixies like me. Held by a leprechaun who outwardly hates *me*. Why am I doing this?

"Crazy," I mumble to myself. But I know why. There's no other way. If the worst is happening, Seven and I are in a unique position to take Chance down, but only if we can stay ahead of him. If I don't do this, his next victim could be someone I love, someone like Penelope or gods-forbid, Arden. That last thought drives me on. I blow out a breath and drop through the window.

My eyes adjust, and I see Seven at the end of a long

stone hallway. It's too dim for me to read his expression but his body language is grim, his shoulders slumped, his head bowed. I walk toward him but pull up short when I pass the first room. These aren't cells with bars but chambers with glass-paneled doors. I can see inside, but if the pixie caged there can see me, she doesn't show it. She's filthy, dressed in rags and thinner than any pixie should be, sitting cross-legged on a narrow bed.

A primal urge to run sends a tremor through me. I force myself to try the doorknob, but of course it's locked.

"Seven, get her out of there," I say. It will take more luck than I have to find the key or crack the lock.

"There are five of them, Sophia. The other five."

I rush down the hall, counting the women behind the windows. My voice shakes as I say, "I see that. Let's get them out of here and call Godmother for backup. Your father did this. He has to be stopped."

Seven turns to me, and I realize why he isn't moving. A lump forms in my throat at the defeated look in his eyes. He's broken. Damaged. Burning up from the inside. I can see him turning to ash right in front of me.

I take his face in my trembling hands. "This is not your fault. Your father did this. Not you. He's a very sick man. But right now it's up to us to make this right. Help me get these people out of here."

The words are barely out of my mouth when the door that must lead to the rest of the house flies open and Chance Delaney strides in.

TWENTY-NINE

"What are *you* doing here?" Chance growls. He straightens his tie, looking as if he came directly from the boardroom in his carefully tailored suit. Not a hair out of place. No one would suspect the horror show he created here just by looking at him.

My skin crawls thinking about what he's done. Slowly, I inch toward the window. If I can slip out, I can call Godmother for help.

"Why? Why did you do this?" Seven gestures toward the locked rooms, toward the vacant eyes of the women inside them.

"This is where they belong, son," Chance says seriously. "They're a lesser species. They're ours to own. Don't tell me you haven't wanted one for yourself. Dammit, the truth is standing right there." He points at me.

"I want her but not to own. As a partner... to love." He glares bravely at his father.

I stop moving, frozen by the revelation. Seven wants me *to love*. Warmth spreads through my torso, even as the horror around me leaves me cold.

"Don't be a fool. No one will accept it. It just isn't done. Besides, they *want* to be owned."

"Then why kill her? Phoebe?" Seven asks through his teeth.

"That... was an accident. That little bird swore she'd never sullied herself with a human. I caught her with her hands on him. I thought it would be enough to kill the human scum in front of her, but she wasn't content like my other birds. She wanted out. And of course I couldn't allow that to happen. Once something is mine, it's mine. She said she wanted a relationship, then changed her mind. Flighty little bitch. I *had* to punish her. Sadly, she broke under pressure."

My blood turns to ice at his evil grin, and I take another slow step back. Almost there. I can feel a breeze drift through the open window and my heart races, desperately wanting out of this room.

"So you killed her and fed her to Yissevel."

He chuckles. "Brilliant plan on my part. Convenient way to dispose of the body."

"But why leave the remains in the square? You must know how bad it would be for business if humans saw that." Seven's face is distorted in disgust. He steps slowly to his left, drawing Chance's attention away from me.

Chance scoffs. "So much to learn..." He shakes his head. "Dragonfly isn't everything, Seven. Lucky Enterprises is on the verge of something big, far bigger than you could ever imagine. Did you think fae would act as jesters forever? This failed experiment of Godmother's is almost over, and the sooner the humans know their place, the better."

"You're a madman." Seven looks like he might be sick.

It hits me like a ton of bricks then. Seven is doing the thing I thought he'd never do. He's standing up to his father, and he's not backing down. And he's doing it for me, so that I can escape. I take another step back as tears well in my eyes. I know this hurts him, and as proud as I am of him, I'm anxious to call Godmother and relieve him of this torment.

"You only think that because you don't know the truth. Not yet. But I'll teach you. We'll manage this together." Chance's eyes drift to me, and I realize I'm the thing to be managed in this scenario.

I take another step back. The window is right behind and above me. But before I can take off through it, Chance raises his hand. Instantly, my feet slip on a patch of slick flooring, and my legs fly out from under me. All the air is knocked from my lungs when my back slaps the floor. For a moment, I can't draw a breath.

"Leave her alone!" Seven places himself between us, and I feel his luck fill the room, that invisible dragon of energy coiling, fueled by fire and ready to do battle.

Chance laughs, and another kind of energy forces its way into the room. His is also serpentine but cold as ice. I picture it pale blue and slick as a viper's belly. All the oxygen in the space is crowded out by the monsters who've filled it, and I struggle to take tiny sips of air. My ribs ache.

"They're tougher than they look, you know," Chance says through a sneer, pointing his chin at me. "Those delicate bones and gossamer wings are camouflage. They're wildcats underneath." His face spreads into a lecherous grin, and my stomach turns over at the connotation. What did he do to these women? I scuffle to my feet, my ribs aching.

"Stay down!" Chance orders me. "Or I'll take you down. We're not done with you."

Seven's expression turns deadly. "Don't talk to her like

that! Don't look at her. You overbearing, psycho, perverted freak!" His fist shoots out, but it never makes contact. Chance bends backward, body rotating at an unnatural speed and angle, and Seven's strike misses his face by a quarter inch. The older man retaliates, fists jabbing toward Seven's center in rapid succession. Seven easily dodges them, his body contorting just out of reach. His feet barely move, but it's enough. Seven ducks and kicks, his foot skimming past Chance's knee.

Luck matches luck. The fight speeds up. Jab, hook, kick. Nothing lands. Power wraps and tangles as the dragon and the viper clash, becoming too big for the room and rattling the walls.

These two men are not expert fighters. I've seen enough fights firsthand to know that on skill alone, neither would last long in hand-to-hand combat. Both are desk jockeys, not UFC fighters. There's nothing inspired about the moves they use or their athletic ability. This isn't a competition of speed or strength. It's luck vs. luck. Neither will land a punch or kick until their power starts to wane. The one who runs out of luck first will be at the mercy of the other.

Crap, this is bad. Chance is stronger. It's a simple matter of age and experience. He's older and heavier. In the fae world that coincides with a greater ability to store and use luck. This is a fight Seven can't win. Not without my help.

I push through the ache in my ribs and rush for the window, flapping my wings to lift me through the small opening.

"Stop!" I hear Chance yell. I duck as a piece of the ceiling above me collapses, and then the lights go out.

I COME AWAKE TO PAIN AND THE SOUND OF GRUNTS AND FALLING stones. I couldn't have been out long, because the dust hasn't settled, but I'm trapped under pieces of the ceiling and wall. Ironically, the opening above me is bigger now, the window having caved in, but it doesn't matter. I can't move. My ribs ache, and I think my leg might be broken. My left arm is numb and caught under the rubble.

Power twists in the air around me. I tip my head and get a glimpse of Seven. There's a red welt on his face. Chance must have gotten a punch in. We're running out of time.

A gaunt face with two haunting blue eyes appears above me. I almost gasp but she places a finger over her thin lips. I dart a glance to the room beside me and see that when Chance caused the collapse that trapped me, he destroyed part of the wall of the closest cell and freed one of his captives. I don't know her name, only that she's a pixie like me.

Help me, I mouth, my eyes moving to the stones pinning me down.

She glances over her shoulder at the men. They've moved out of my field of vision, and I can't see what she sees, but I can feel it. Seven's power is barely detectable in the room, and the cold viper of Chance's luck slithers against my skin. I sense it going in for the kill, and flash the pixie a panicked look. Together, we're able to shift enough stones to free me.

Silently, I stand. I know Seven sees me, but he doesn't

make eye contact. Instead, he pivots and strikes, intentionally distracting his father. I help the other pixie through the window and then fly out after her where I grab her hand and sprint for the car.

"Can you speak?" I ask.

"Y-yes," she says.

Quickly, I open the car door, grab my cell phone, and dial Godmother's emergency number. She answers on the second ring. I rattle off the address of the cabin and then shove the phone into the pixie's hands.

"Explain to her," I say. "She'll have questions."

The pixie nods.

I retrieve my bow and quiver, slinging them over my shoulder. I have one arrow, the one I pulled from Yissevel's side. I grab Kiko, then realize she's empty. We used her to recharge Seven yesterday when he went negative, and I never refilled her. *Fuck!* The lucky cat has been my salvation time and time again. What am I going to do? Seven is doomed if I don't go back in there.

This is crazy. I need a plan. I'm injured, and I'm low on luck. Think, Sophia. What do you do at the poker table when you're short on chips and don't have the cards? Think. Think. Think. I stare at Kiko again, and an idea sparks.

I'm an excellent liar. There's only one thing to do in a situation like this—bluff.

I grab what I need from my pack and move toward the window. The pixie lowers the phone and whispers, "What are you doing? He'll kill you!"

For a split second I consider that I could stay out of it. I could wait, safely outside the fray, for Godmother to save us. But Seven was right when he'd said I never shied away from a challenge. Seven promised he'd protect me, and he sacrificed himself to live up to that promise. I'm not leaving him. I can't.

"That's a gamble I'm willing to take. I won't let Chance get away with this." I limp back to the window and drop into the dungeon again.

My ribs throb when I land. I can't put weight on my left ankle. It hurts when I breathe, and there's a trickle of something warm and wet running near the corner of my eye. I steady myself, nock my only arrow, and point it at Chance.

"Welcome back, little bird," Chance says through an evil smile. He's straddling Seven's bloody body. My breath quivers in my throat. Seven looks dead, and I can no longer sense even a hint of his luck in the room.

"Back away from him or I'll put an arrow through your heart," I threaten.

He laughs and turns, spreading his arms. "Try it, honey. It won't hurt me. I've still got enough in the tank to take you down and show you what I do to little girls who don't know their place."

Chance is tired, drained, and critically arrogant, but he's the oldest and strongest leprechaun in Devashire. *All in.* I close one eye, aim, and release a deep breath. Every ounce of luck I have left, I pour into my arrow. Will it be enough?

He swaggers another step toward me. My arrow flies and lands in his right pec, under his collarbone. It's a shot that might be painful but certainly isn't deadly.

I school my features into a carefully impassive mask.

Chance scoffs. "You missed."

"Maybe I did, but at least I tried. At least I had the guts to stand up to you. How many people know about what you've done to Seven, what you've done to these women? How many people have done nothing?"

He laughs at me. "Stupid girl. Who do you think you're talking to? I make the rules."

Another step toward me. "Fine. You win. Are you going to kill me now like you did Phoebe?"

Another step and he grabs the end of the arrow and yanks it from his flesh. There's a spurt of blood that blooms like a rose on his white dress shirt. "I'll let you in on a little secret, Sophia." His face contorts into something from my nightmares. He's the devil come to tear off my wings. "I was jealous of Seven the night I poisoned him. The thought of him having you when I couldn't drove me insane."

Eww. I back away, all the way to the wall under the window, but he keeps coming. He reaches me, grabs my throat and squeezes. I'm trembling and in so much pain I can barely remain standing. I don't try to hide it. I notice the remaining four pixies are at their doors. I don't know if they can see or hear anything through that strange glass, but they know something is going on.

"I'll have you now," Chance says darkly. "A little luck and a lot of money and I'll have you in that empty cell. They'll all assume you ran away again. You'll be mine."

"Before you do, can I ask you something?" I wheeze out through his choking grip, meeting his gaze straight on. His expression changes and I know I've surprised him. He expected me to crumble and I'm still standing. "When you poisoned Seven, how long did it take for the blue iron to take effect?"

"Minutes," he says. "Why? Morbid curiosity, little bird?"

"No. I just want to know how long to wait before you fall." My eyes drift to my arrow on the floor and the glint of blue—the remains of Kiko's blue-iron arm—tied to the tip.

I'd pulled a string off the hat Grandma knitted for me and used it to tie the arm to the tip of my living arrow. Then I funneled what remained of my luck into my arrow, to make sure the tip shattered when it entered his body. I was never aiming for his heart. I was aiming for center mass. I knew Chance would use his luck to knock my arrow off course, but also that in his weakness, there was a limit to how much. My shot hit him in a place that would be harmless to him normally. But I didn't care. All I had to do was hit him. Anywhere would do. Several pieces of blue iron are currently lodged within him, poisoning his blood, festering.

He looks down and seems surprised by the amount of blood staining his shirt. His wound isn't healing. He snorts as if he can't quite believe what he's seeing and then sways on his feet.

I have no luck left, but that never stopped me before. I cock my arm back and deliver a very human jab to his nose with the heel of my palm. He staggers, confused by the blood dribbling from his face. It drips onto his palms. His eyes are wild.

I hobble after him.

My voice comes out loud and strong, rage inflating my lungs. "You think you're better than me because you have more money and power. When I was in America, I met guys like you at the poker table, Chance. You have a lucky streak, and you think it means you're superior. You think because you were born with a silver spoon in your mouth that it will always be there. But the problem with relying on luck is eventually it runs out, and then all you have left is your skill to play the game. You've never had to play on empty, and it shows."

I clock him again, and he stumbles away from me, swaying on his feet.

"You're not better than me," I hiss. "You were *never* better than me. You were just luckier and wealthier. And now that's over. I've. Outplayed. You."

The daggers he shoots at me would turn me to swiss cheese if they were real. He swings a bloody paw at me, but I easily move out of the way. No luck necessary.

"No one loves you," I continue, a smile in my voice. "They might fear you, but they don't love you. No one is in your corner. When your luck runs out, people like me who've actually paid our dues move in. People with skill and patience. Good people. Today is not your lucky day."

I raise my bow, wind up, and swing it like a bat, throwing my weight behind it. It smacks into his temple. His head snaps to the side, and then he crumples. He doesn't get up. With everything I have left, I kick him in the ribs. No response. I squat down and take his pulse. Alive but definitely out. *Fucker.*

"Seven." I leave Chance and rush to his side. I'm so tired, but somehow I flip him over. He's beat up bad. One eye is swollen shut, and his T-shirt is soaked in blood.

"Gods, Sophia, run!" he mumbles when his good eye flutters open and he recognizes me.

"Chance is knocked out. I'm okay." I brush back the hair from his face. A gash in his forehead bloodies my hand.

"Tried to distract 'im so you could get away."

"It worked. I got out. I got help. Godmother is on her way."

He takes my hand, and a corner of his mouth twitches. I think it's the only part of his face he can still move. "So sorry..."

"Shhh."

A drop hits our coupled hands, and I realize it came from my face. I wipe away the next tear, and then lean down to press a kiss to that unbruised corner of his mouth. All my adrenaline is gone, and I stretch out beside him on the floor, closing my eyes and pressing my forehead to his temple. "It's over."

I'm not sure when I pass out, but when I wake, I'm no longer touching Seven. He's still there, a few feet away from me but appears to be unconscious.

I hear a snap like a thick branch breaking over a knee and reposition myself so I can see the source. Godmother is there, power swirling around her and filling the room with the scent of violets. Chance hovers in the air in front of her, held within bonds of light that tether him to the walls like he's trapped in a massive spiderweb.

"You stupid fuck," Godmother says, her voice reverberating in the space. "Now you will finally pay for your crimes." There's another snap, and his calf bends at a painful angle, the foot kicking toward her while the rest of the leg remains stationary. My eyes widen as I take in his mangled fingers, his dangling arm. Chase screams, his voice already going hoarse.

Oh my gods. She's breaking his bones one by one!

Godmother's gaze drifts to me. Our eyes lock. I haven't made a sound, and my poker face is firmly in place. I convey no judgment or approval. I make no attempt to move.

Two satyrs arrive with a stretcher through the main door that must lead to the rest of the cabin. They move toward Seven.

"No, not that one." She points at me with her chin.

The satyrs lower the stretcher beside me and lift me onto it. While one straps me in, the other slips a needle into my arm.

"Oww," I say. The pain fades, and a warm, floaty feeling overcomes me. I blink, and Godmother and the dungeon are gone. We're halfway up the stairs I assume lead to the main floor. A moment later, we reach the top. I glimpse a well-appointed living room with a large mirror that covers most of one wall. My head spins. There's something familiar about it. I need to ask Seven...

I blink again, and this time my eyes remain closed.

THIRTY

I wake in a hospital bed. There's only one hospital in Devashire, and I know I'm in it by the buzz happening in my blood. I'm as light as air, and bubbles brush the underside of my skin. They've been feeding me luck along with the fluids dripping into my arm. My chest, arm, and ankle are wrapped, but the pain is gone. I don't know what kind of painkillers are involved, but I'm feeling remarkably better.

Until I meet a pair of reptilian eyes in the face of a dark man in an even darker suit. He hovers over me, too close. I cringe, pushing myself deeper into the bed and wishing the mattress would swallow me.

"Well, well, well, it appears you've slipped through my fingers once more," Agent Donovan says. He's as terrifying as ever, a psychopath in law-enforcement clothing.

"Touch me and I'll scream," I warn.

"Relax." He rolls his eyes. "I'm not here to hurt you."

"What do you want?"

He folds himself into a seat beside the bed. "I came to

say goodbye. It seems you have friends in high places, Sophia. Godmother traded access to Chance Delaney for expunging your record. As far as we're concerned at FIRE, you and that human daughter of yours are free and clear of all wrongdoing."

I breathe a heavy sigh of relief.

He shakes his head. "Sad. You and I could have had so much fun. I doubt Chance will be as... amusing."

I shudder at his tone.

"If you feel the same way, by all means, leave Devashire again. I'd love to bring you back into the fold." He flashes that psycho smile that makes bile rise in my throat.

I'm relieved when Godmother appears in my doorway, her commanding presence reaching into the room. It's the first and only time I've ever been relieved to see Godmother.

"Ah, you're awake." She gives my tormentor a once-over. "Donovan, what the hell are you doing here? I thought we had an understanding."

He smiles his weirdly blue smile. "Just checking in on the woman of the hour. I'm on my way out. I've filled Sophia in on our agreement. She's officially off our roster... unless she decides to cross the border again, and as a law-abiding citizen, her daughter's passport has been reinstated." With one last glance at me, he scurries out the door and hopefully out of my life for good.

"That man is damaged in ways I never knew humans could be," Godmother says with a low grunt. She sits down in the chair Donovan vacated. It's then that I notice a flower arrangement in her hands. She sets the small vase on the end table beside me, and I breathe in the scent of red roses and purple daisies.

"Thank you for visiting," I say, although after watching her torture Chance, I'm ready for her to go. "Is Seven okay?"

"He's fine. Although for security reasons he's opted to recover at home with a private nurse. With the news of his father's arrest going public, Seven is now chairman of Lucky Enterprises and head of the Delaney empire. A lot of responsibility comes with the role and plenty of risk. There are many who would like to disrupt that dynasty."

I can only imagine. I knew Chance's imprisonment would change Seven's life, but I've never lived that lifestyle. I'm sure there's much I don't understand about what he's going through. "So Chance is finally behind bars."

"Our prisons don't have bars." Godmother's dark eyes twinkle.

"That's right." Ashgate, the fairy prison, is a mountain with cells carved into its depths. Criminals are magically sealed inside. "Behind stone."

She gives a dark chuckle. "I owe my thanks to you for taking him down. Brilliant to use his own blue iron against him. I assume you obtained it from his stores. It would be illegal to bring it into Devashire."

"Of course," I say immediately. She doesn't need to know about Kiko. Besides, a human gave her to me at the Dragonfly Club. I simply brought her back again. That's different than bringing something in that originated on the outside. "Did you know Chance once poisoned Seven with blue iron?"

"I am aware," she says, lifting her chin. "Although back then we lacked enough proof to hold him accountable. Now we have five pixies willing to give details of their horrific abduction, not to mention testimony by you and Seven. It's enough to put him away for a very long time. He won't be able to buy his way out of this one."

"He admitted to us what he did," I say. "Yissevel was a convenient way to dispose of the bodies. But he also said there was more, some big plans Seven didn't know about. Do you know what he was talking about?"

Godmother smooths the front of her gown. "Unfortunately, no. But when I interrogated Chance, it was clear to me that he's lost his mind. He's been drunk with power for so long he thinks of himself as a god. Whatever he was up to, you can be sure it stops here. We confiscated the silver he was using to travel to Shadowvale. It's safely with the guardians now."

I remember the mirror I saw when they were hauling me out of the hunting cabin. So it was a portal. I heave a relieved sigh that it's in good hands, although a little voice in the back of my head would love to know how he got it in the first place.

"What he said... It was so disturbing. He made it sound like Lucky Enterprises wanted to destroy Dragonfly. Like he had plans to subjugate humans."

The knowing smile that turns Godmother's full lips creates a dimple in her dark cheek, as if she finds the concept wholly amusing. "Do you know why we named the park Dragonfly Hollow when we established it in 1864?"

I shake my head.

"Dragonflies sparkle, Sophia. Humans are fascinated by their colors and their beauty. But they are also the deadliest predator in existence. In fact, they catch over 95 percent of their prey thanks to their almost supernatural agility and focus. They ambush their quarry, hovering just out of sight, then attacking from below or behind. Their game is torn apart and consumed immediately, and their appetite is insatiable.

"Humans... all they see is a shiny insect, bright with

fragile wings. They assume it is a creature created for their pleasure, when in reality the dragonfly owns their world and their space. Dragonflies have been the apex predator of their environment since before humans existed.

"We are the dragonflies, Sophia. There are fewer of us than there are humans, just as there are fewer dragonflies than mosquitos. But we are the more powerful beings. They think they are in control. They think we are a beautiful dalliance. But we take from them exactly what we want and need, and they bring it to us willingly. We help them, and they help us. Just as the gods intended.

"After the Civil War, there were those who felt we should abandon the old ways, eschew peace, and free the unseelie to conquer our human attackers and take control of the Americas. I was of the mind that no blood need be shed to conquer. The secret to subjugation is finding a person's weakness. That's how you bring them to their knees. We've done that with humans. They worship us with their dollars.

"Thankfully the Guardians agreed, and so together we created this place and the peace we enjoy. Chance is not the first to suggest that the fae could and should have more: more power, more money, more glory. None of them have ever understood the value of peace. Power doesn't always come by the sword. It isn't bought with the shedding of blood. That is a human fallacy us fae have no time for. It comes with the adoration of hearts and minds. It comes with control. What we have now is as good as it gets, Sophia. And as long as I'm in charge, it will remain this way."

I stare at her for a good long moment, her power looming thick in the room. The only thing I can think to say is, "I'm glad it's you in charge."

She smiles and tips her head in my direction. "I'm glad you think so because we have business to discuss."

I blink nervously.

"You solved this case. Dragonfly couldn't have done it without you."

"Then am I right in assuming that I'm officially free of our bargain?" I hold my breath hopefully.

She waves a graceful hand between us, and the air grows thick with her power. Bright white vines appear around me. They snap and recede. I feel light and free.

"It is done. As of now, you are unbound. Although I must say, given the position I found you and Seven in, it seems you rather enjoyed your time together. You have a talent for this kind of work. I hope you'll consider helping me again in the future of your own volition."

Not likely. I glance down at my tangled fingers.

"Regardless, I'm happy things worked out and you've returned to Devashire. It seems your young Arden has already endeared herself to the staff at Bailiwick's. I understand that her passport has been reinstated, and she is once again a US citizen, but we'd all like to see her call Devashire home. She belongs here, surrounded by family."

My stomach clenches, and my eyes flick to the wall where the date is scrawled across a white board with my nurse's name and my care itinerary. I've missed Arden's first day of school. Holding back tears, I say, "Well, at least until she leaves for college."

Godmother spreads her hands. "There are fine universities in Devashire too. Who knows, her talents might change our world. There's never been anyone like her." She stands to leave just as Arden and my parents appear in the doorway, overflowing with flowers and gifts.

I open my arms wide, and Arden rushes into them. I kiss the side of her head, anxious for her to tell me everything.

Over Arden's shoulder, Godmother meets my eyes. "Goodbye, Sophia."

I watch Godmother slip away, the realization that Arden and I are truly free settling over me with the warm, comforting hugs of the people I love.

CHAPTER

THIRTY-ONE

Three days later, I'm discharged from the hospital. My rib is still healing, but the rest of me is back to normal again thanks to plenty of luck and fae attention. The most bothersome part is the ache unrelated to my injuries. Seven didn't come to the hospital. River came, as did Penelope. My family visited daily. But no Seven. He hasn't called or texted. He hasn't sent flowers.

Undeniably, he's healing too, and as Godmother mentioned, he's got a lot on his plate taking over the family business. I could make excuses for him. But I'm not doing that anymore. The truth is that Seven hasn't carved out five minutes to check on my well-being. I wish that didn't hurt, but it does.

Once I'm home, I shower and change into my most comfortable clothes and make myself a giant mug of tea. My parents can see I need rest and alone time, and so they take Arden shopping while Grandma stays with me. But even wrapped in one of Grandma's knitted blankets in front of a roaring fire, I can't seem to take any comfort. All I want to do is cry, but that warrior inside me refuses to let the tears fall. I'm not going to let him do this to me.

"I always knew you would take that bastard down one day," Grandma says. She's come from the kitchen and slides a plate of cookies onto the table beside me.

"Thanks, Grandma. I get it from you, you know."

"Of course you do, honey. Kick-assery runs in our blood." She sits down in the big chair next to the fire and picks up her knitting needles.

"What are you making?" The oddly shaped rectangle she's knitting is bright purple and as wide as her arm.

"Isn't it obvious? A scarf, dear, for Arden. I thought she could use one for school."

I can't hold back a laugh. "Grandma, that thing is wide enough for her to wear it as a cape."

She holds the massive square up to the light and flutters her silver wings. "You're right. I'm making a cape! I've never made a cape before. It's *lovely*."

My new goal is to be as confident as Grandma when I grow up.

"Are we ever going to talk about Seven?" she says, her needles working again. "I'm an old woman, Sophia. I can't wait forever."

"What's there to say? He hasn't called or come to visit. Our job for Godmother is over, so..."

"Oh, but he did! He came to see you at the hospital."

I almost spill my tea. I throw off my covers and scooch to her end of the sofa. "When? I don't ever remember Seven coming to see me." Did he come when I was knocked out on painkillers? Did I forget?

"That's because he never made it to your room." Grandma blinks at me over her knitting and flashes me a gossipy grin.

I grab a cookie from the plate and plug it into my mouth to keep from raising my voice at her. "Please explain," I say around a mouthful.

"Well, he hobbled in the same day Godmother came to see you. We were all waiting in the hall, but I had to go to the restroom. You know when you're my age, you always have to pee. So I went to that restroom by the nurse's station. Did I tell you I knitted a cover for their phone?"

My fingers curl in frustration, and I hold my hands out to her, palms up, eyes to the heavens. "Grandma, when did you see Seven?"

She clears her throat. "My, a person might think you had feelings for the boy considering how excited you've become, Sophia. Should I start knitting something in white?"

I heave a sigh toward her. "Grandma, please!"

"All right. Godmother left your room, and Arden and your parents went in. I'd just come out of the bathroom. Seven stepped off the elevator, looking like he might fall over at any moment. The man wasn't well, honey. Bruises everywhere. Swollen eye. And Godmother was in his face. She told him that if he loved you, he would leave it alone. She said you were free, and he should let you be happy. I thought the poor boy was going to pull his hair out. He took one last look at your room and then turned and left."

My mouth drops open. "Why didn't you tell me this before?"

She raises her shoulders to her ears. "You know me, honey. I don't like to get involved in other people's drama."

I huff incredulously. "Grandma, you literally live for other people's drama! Your nose prints are all over your front window from watching the neighbors so closely!"

"Hmm, well, maybe I was worried you'd try to go after

him, and you were in no shape to leave your bed. *Now*, however, you are in fine shape, and if I were to speculate, he is likely feeling much better as well."

My throat makes a little squeak as I try to respond and find my brain has turned into a jumble of nonsensical impulses. I can't believe my grandmother kept this from me! Then I narrow in on her crooked little smile, and think I can definitely believe it.

"You've been sitting on this for days!"

She slants me a mischievous grin. "It took a righteous amount of stamina, I'll tell you that." She nods her gray head. Our conversation is interrupted by the doorbell. Grandma and I exchange curious looks.

"Who could that be?" I ask.

"Maybe he's feeling better." Grandma bobs her gray brows.

She's insufferable. I hoist myself off the couch and hobble to the door. When I open it, a runway model is standing on the other side, shiny red hair falling over one eye in a wave, svelte body poured into a violet dress with a satin belt above tall black boots with stiletto heels. Radiant emerald eyes find mine, and she smiles. It's like the lights come on.

"Hi Sophia! Just who I came to see." She brushes her hair back behind her shoulder.

"Evangeline? What are you doing here?"

"I came to drop off your key. My assistant was supposed to do it, but we've been so swamped redistributing job responsibilities after what happened with our father that all of us are overwhelmed. I had an appointment in the neighborhood and thought, *What the hell?*" She pulls a large envelope from her purse and hands it to me. I tear it open to see a key and a short stack of papers inside.

"Seven told me to tell you not to go to the room yet because the work crew is still in there. Something with the flooring." She waves a hand. "I don't know. Anyway, it will be a few more days until we can get tables set up. Then I'll want to bring in a photographer for some pictures and video for social media. You should be ready for your first class by the end of the month." Her teeth are so white. What the hell sort of toothpaste does she even use?

I shake my head. "I'm sorry, but I don't know what you're talking about. What room? What class?"

She juts her chin out incredulously. "You're going to give poker lessons to humans at the casino! Why do you look like this is the first time you're hearing about this?"

"Because it's the first time I'm hearing about this!"

"Huh." She looks confused. "Seven's been selling it to the board since the second you two got back from your mission. I'm sure if you tell him you don't want to do it—"

"Oh, I *want* to do it." The thought of playing my favorite game again, legitimately, in Dragonfly, is too good to be true. There has to be a catch. I can't believe Seven pulled this off.

"Good," Evangeline says with a sigh. "All the details are in there. Salary, benefits, hours of operation. It's all negotiable. Let Seven know if something isn't to your satisfaction; he's heading this project. Someone from my team will be in touch about the advertising blitz." She brushes her hands off. "Great to see you again, Sophia. Welcome aboard!" She turns and strides gracefully toward the parking lot.

I slowly close the door, the manila envelope heavy in my hand. Grandma appears by my side. "What in carnations was that all about?"

"Tarnation," I correct.

"Huh?"

"The expression is what in tarnation, not what in carnations."

She rolls her eyes. "You say it your way; I'll say it mine." She tears the envelope from my hands and pulls out the letter inside. She starts to giggle.

"Why are you laughing?"

"You're going to be making more than your mother and father combined!"

I snatch the letter from her hands. Two hundred thousand per year. Full benefits for myself and my dependents. Tuition reimbursement for self and dependents. All in exchange for me teaching two classes a day, five days a week and for my permission to be used as a spokesperson for Dragonfly Casino's upcoming ad campaign.

"There has to be a catch. Don't you think there has to be a catch?"

My grandmother shrugs. "I can't think of one." I stare at her for a moment, and then we both start jumping up and down, squealing. "What are you waiting for? Don't you have somewhere to be?" Grandma asks. "This sort of thing deserves a thank-you, in person."

I stop jumping. A heavy weight descends onto my shoulders. "But if he wanted to see me, wouldn't he have come to me?"

Grandma frowns. "Not if Godmother convinced him that he could only make your life more difficult. Oh, if he cared for you less, he might, but I think we both know how he feels." She touches the letter in my hand.

I think about that for a moment. The last time Seven and I spoke about us, I'd told him that I deserved more and he'd agreed. Was staying away and doing this for me his way of giving me what I wanted?

Every impulse tells me to go to him. The desire is so strong, I know a younger me wouldn't be able to deny it. But I force myself to pause and think. "Godmother is never wrong about these things. He *will* make my life more difficult."

"As if it's been so easy up till now," Grandma says softly. Her blue eyes twinkle above a sad smile. "Life is short, Sophia, and when you're my age, you'll know that regret follows things you did and things you didn't do equally. The real question is, which will you find easier to live with?"

I stuff the letter back into the envelope with the key. "Will you tell Arden, Mom, and Dad where I've gone?"

She grins a conspiratorial grin. "Of course I will."

I take two steps toward the door, then realize what I'm wearing. "I should get changed... and do my hair and makeup."

"He's not going to care about any of that, and you know it."

I kick off my slippers and shove my feet into my sneakers. My hand is on the doorknob before a much bigger problem comes to mind. "I don't have a car, and I can't ride the bus like this. The rules say I have to be in a gown."

Grandma reaches into her giant knitted purse and retrieves her keys. She jingles them. "Maribelle is parked in lot A with a full tank of gas. Use a little illusion to get to her and you're home free."

I swipe the keys from her hand and spend a little luck to transform my appearance into something more appropriate, a purple gown, heels, full makeup and an updo. Then I swoop down to deliver a kiss to Grandma's cheek. "Thank you."

She waves a hand dismissively. "I don't need that car

back tonight, Sophia. I think I'll stay here. I'll see you in the morning."

"Grandma! Just because I go over there doesn't mean I'm going to spend the night!"

The look she gives me over her glasses is full of mirth. She shrugs again. "What do I know? I'm an old woman. I go to bed early." She waves at me, and I'm out the door.

THIRTY-TWO

Seven's building is locked down tighter than Fort Knox, and I don't have the benefit of parking in his private garage. Worse, I had to drop my illusion because it was costing me too much luck and I'm still recovering. It's not strictly necessary here in Elderflame, so it didn't make sense to keep it up. But as I stand in front of the security desk in full view of dozens of passersby through the wall of windows on the ground floor, I'm ashamed of my messy bun, sweats, and T-shirt. I do not fit in here.

"You say you have an appointment with Mr. Delaney?" the security guard behind the desk asks, eyeing me skeptically and clicking his mouse. He's a satyr, big, burly, and perfectly capable of throwing me out on my ass if he so chooses. "I don't have any record of that."

"No, I don't have an appointment. We're friends, and I stopped by to... to... listen, just call up there and tell him I'm here."

His lips draw into a flat line. "Mr. Delaney is in a very important meeting this afternoon. If you'd like to leave a message, I can give it to him tonight and ask him to call you."

I cross my arms and tap my foot, glaring at his nametag. "Eric, is it? Do you know that the last person who kept me from seeing Seven got fired?" A deep groove forms in his brow. "It's true. Seven and I are friends. Very *good* friends. And if he finds out you didn't even tell him I was here, he will be extremely displeased."

I have no idea if this is true or a bald-faced lie. What exactly did my grandmother hear? Could she have been mistaken about Seven wanting to see me? What if he *is* in an important meeting and I disturb him? I don't relish the thought of making him angry at me. Oh, this was a bad idea. Am I really here in my sweats threatening this guy?

Eric reaches for the phone and brings it to his ear. He presses a button and relays that I'm there to someone whom I can only assume is another security guard by the exchange. There's a pause, and then all the color drains from Eric's face. Slowly, he hangs up the phone. Our eyes lock.

"Mr. Delaney is on his way down. He'd like to show you up himself," he says softly.

I can't help the knowing little smile I give him that has "I told you so" written all over it. "Thank you."

A few minutes later, elevator doors to my left open, and Seven, in all his dark-suited glory, walks into the hall along with three other leprechauns in professional attire. He shakes hands with each of them, exchanging pleasantries and apologizing for ending the meeting early. The others are on their way out the door when he turns a focused laser beam of attention on me.

He approaches until we're toe-to-toe. The footsteps of the men stop, and I glance over my shoulder. They're staring, openmouthed, as are a crowd of onlookers who are gathering on the other side of the window. My wings are out. I'm not using illusion. Every one of those people know exactly who I am and exactly who he is, and he's looking at me with the kind of focus that only comes from a lover. My heart rate quickens.

"It's good to see you," he says softly.

"Good to see you too." I shift from foot to foot. "Evangeline brought me a key and an offer today. I thought I'd come by personally to tell you I accept."

Seven beams. "You deserve it. You'll be brilliant. Humans are going to swarm to learn how to play from Soho Lane herself."

"Thank you for this. You have no idea what it means to me."

His eyes crinkle at the corners. "I think I do."

Silence unspools between us. The security guard is staring. Behind me, the other leprechauns are still staring. Outside the window, there is now a crowd of all manner of fae all staring. A flash goes off. Someone just took our picture.

"Um, aren't you going to invite me up?"

"I'd hoped you'd come." He places his hands on my shoulders, his intense focus ratcheting up my pulse another notch.

"I just..." I glance around me again. "Everyone is watching."

He drops his hands, his face falling. "You only came to say thank you."

I stare at him for three long heartbeats. "No. I also came to tell you to forget what I said before about deserving better. There's no one better than you for me, Seven."

"What about the part about wanting it all," he whispers.

"I still do. I probably always will. But I'm willing to take what I can get."

"But you'd prefer no secrets."

I glance over my shoulder at the crowd gathering on the other side of the window. "Yes."

He inhales, looking down at me through his lashes. "You sure about that?"

"Positive."

In the next second, his hands are cradling my face and his lips are on mine in a kiss that could never be mistaken as simply friendly. It's head-spinning, oxygen-depriving madness. I feel that kiss down to my soul. Luck fizzes through me, and I rise up on my toes, meeting the kiss with deliberate passion.

Lights pop. People snap our picture through the window, their murmurs rising. I pull back, panting. "As much as I appreciate this, can we go upstairs?" I allow my eyes to flood with heat. "There are still some things that belong behind closed doors."

Warming me with a dazzling smile, he leads me to the elevator. There's a bob in my step as I enter. I catch a glimpse of Eric's baffled expression as the doors close behind us. As soon as they do, I'm hyperaware of the exact position of Seven's body in the enclosed space, of the bright, citrusy fragrance of his cologne, the way his suit drapes perfectly off his shoulders, the way his eyes haven't left me since they landed on me moments ago.

His face is healed. I can't even tell he was beaten almost to death only days ago. Tension builds between us, a deliciously weighty feeling in my torso turning over as he takes me in, his stare palpable. "You look like you have something to say to me."

"My grandmother told me you stopped by the hospital to see me but that Godmother sent you away."

He nods.

"What were you going to tell me?"

He blinks rapidly, his tongue darting across his lower lip. "I think you know what I came to tell you." He reaches out and hits the red button on the panel. The elevator stops. "What happened downstairs, I might be able to manage the fallout if you change your mind right now, but if you come home with me and we do this, Sophia, there's no going back for me. You said you wanted it all. I do too, and there's no one standing in our way anymore. I want you to be mine. Entirely mine. Do you understand? I can't settle for halfway with you. I can't wait any longer."

"Who says you have to?" The words come out a croak, strangled by the intensity. He moves in until my back hits the far wall and his arms are bracketing my head. His face is close, and it's like someone released a thousand dragonflies in my lower belly. The butterflies have been replaced by something far more thrilling and aggressive. Hot, fluttering, bubbly luck rises in me. My breath hitches.

"This is just the beginning. I will take us public, and it will be the most selfish thing I ever do. You won't have a moment of peace. The press will be all over you, and the gossip pages will enjoy a heyday like you've never experienced. The *Daily Hatter* will have you on the front page, not just the gossip column."

My mind fills with streams of color, and I have to take a deep breath to steady myself. "Let them talk."

He winces. "I can't promise there won't be fallout for your family or Arden. I can help with some of that but...."

"I don't care," I say breathlessly. "We'll manage it. Arden's passport has been restored. She'll be gone in a matter of months. I want you, Seven. Nothing you tell me will change that."

He drops his forehead to mine and releases a shaky breath that skates across my face. "You have no idea how happy it makes me that you feel that way."

"I think I do."

Slowly, his face moves in closer, but just as his lips softly brush mine, a bell chimes. Seven doesn't move, but he reaches an arm out to lift the red phone off the hook. "Hmm? Yes. Fine. Bumped it," he says. He hits the button without breaking eye contact and the elevator starts up again.

When the doors open, he sweeps me into his foyer and kisses me right in front of the security guard waiting outside his door. It is not a chaste kiss. This is a claiming, deep, bend-you-over-backward kiss that instantly turns my knees to water and my blood effervescent. I want to live inside this kiss. When he draws back to unlock his door, I catch a glimpse of the security guard's face, and it almost unsettles me. There's surprise but also something darker, something I might describe as disgust if I wasn't so high on luck and blissfully drawn into the moment. Fuck him. If he wants to be a bigot, he better keep his thoughts to himself, or I imagine he won't be around for long.

I giggle as Seven pulls me inside and closes the door behind us. He tugs the elastic from my hair. "Oh. Sorry about my appearance. I should have cleaned up before I came."

"Why?" he says breathlessly. "I'm just going to mess you up again."

Zing. Holy crap, I've never been this turned on. His

mouth is on mine again, and his hands are hot under my shirt, coursing along my ribs, thumbs grazing the underside of my breasts as he backs me through the large entryway deeper into the apartment. I gasp for breath when he pulls my shirt over my head and giggle as my bra clasp conveniently breaks and the garment all but falls off me.

"I liked that bra," I say.

"I'll buy you another one. I'll buy you the whole fucking store." His hands are on my waist again, and I wrap my arms around his neck and climb up his body, my legs riding his hips. He growls, clutching my ass and driving the kiss deeper.

His knees bump something behind us, and we tip over, my back bouncing on a velvety black comforter. He reaches for my waistband, but I catch his wrists. "Oh, we've already done the thing where I'm the only one naked in the room." I bite my lip. "This time you're coming along with me."

He doesn't miss how I stress the word *coming*. I push him back and reach for his fly. His belt buckle jingles as I unbuckle, unzip, and free his erection. I have him in my mouth before I've pushed his pants and everything else down his legs.

"Gods, Sophia. *Fuck!*" His fingers grip my shoulders as I bask in the taste of him, licking and swirling my tongue before taking him deep into my throat. The closer he gets, the more I feel his excitement fizzing at my core. He's pounding luck into me. It vibrates between my legs, filling me. It dances across my skin, slopes along my breasts, tightening the tips.

Seven moans, and hot liquid jets down my throat at the same moment my own orgasm grips me in its clutches, wringing pleasure from me with both hands.

I swallow him down and turn boneless, flopping onto the big black bed and closing my eyes.

"Look at me, Sophia," he orders and I obey. Fuck, the intensity in his gaze is preternatural. "We're not done."

My eyes widen as he tosses off his jacket and dress shirt, then steps out of his pants. My shoes are next and then my sweats and panties. He's already hard again. *Lucky me.* Gods, the man is a work of art, thick and long, his body a canvas of lean muscle with broad shoulders and a tapered waist that begs to be licked. I open my mouth to do so, but he hoists me back into the center of the velvet spread and stretches out over me, running the head of his cock along my slit.

His eyes meet mine. "No going back," he says. "After this, we leave the past behind and we build something new, together, come what may."

"Come what may," I repeat. I can't form any more complex thoughts than that. I need him in me so bad I can hardly breathe.

I get my wish.

His hands thread into mine on either side of my head as he slides into me, forcing a gasp from my throat. My vision blurs with unshed tears. I try to blink them away, but one falls.

Seven stops immediately. "What's wrong? Am I hurting you? When I said there was no going back, I meant emotionally. If you want me to stop, I will."

I laugh a little. "I don't want you to stop."

"Then what is it?"

With a nudge of my hip, I roll him onto his back and rise above him, spreading my wings. More tears fall against his chest. My throat feels thick as I admit, "This is the first time I've ever had sex truly as myself."

He grimaces as if I've hit him in the stomach, then reaches up to stroke along my upper right wing. His fingers trace along the side of my face, between my breasts. "I'm honored it's me." He lifts his hips and fills me until I moan.

I flutter my wings, sending a vibration down my body that makes him arch under me. "Keep doing that," he growls. His fingers dig into my hips. I ride his thrusts until that delicious, coiled tension builds deep within my core again, deeper than before, bigger.

It unravels all at once, like I've sliced open a ball of elastic bands. I lose myself entirely in the bubbles, snaps, and flares of pleasure. My head tilts back, and I grind myself against Seven in the most brazen way. I feel him come apart beneath me, hear him yell my name. Luck swirls around us, brushing me with its fiery energy and drawing out my pleasure.

When I've finally flopped forward and rolled on my side, Seven reaches for me and tucks me into his chest, his lips brushing the top of my head. "You make me feel lucky, Sophia. Truly lucky."

"Me too."

THIRTY-THREE

Waking in Seven's arms is like a dream. He's warm and beautiful, even with his hair mussed from our lovemaking. I've lost count of how many times he made me come. We've been sleeping and fucking off and on all night long. His arms reach for me again, and I push them away.

"I need water, Seven, and maybe a snack. Sustenance!"

He blinks at me sleepily. "Help yourself to anything in the kitchen. Hurry back." He presses a sleepy kiss to my temple.

I slide out of bed and snatch his shirt from the floor. It's as long as a dress on me, and I roll the sleeves and button the front. There's no one here but us, but the last thing I want is to see my naked reflection in all the polished gold and ebony in this place. I slip out of the room, closing the door quietly behind me.

This penthouse is huge. I stroll down the hall in the direction of the kitchen only to realize that I've gone the wrong way. Where I expect the living room to be with its koi river and floor-to-ceiling windows, I find a library with floor-to-ceiling books. I must be at the back of the building.

A short investigation confirms my hypothesis as the windows in this room have a southern view of the city. Wow. His home takes up the entire top floor.

I whirl, forgetting about my hunger and thirst when I see the books and artifacts lining the shelves. At the very center of the room is a desk with an ink blotter and a reading lamp. Surrounding it are leather volumes and the occasional piece of art. I start walking the first row. Interesting. Most of these are anthropology books. The next row is biology. The next chemistry. Gods, what I would give for a good romance. I had no idea Seven was into such heavy courses of study. If anything, I'd think he'd have business books.

As I turn down the center row, I spot a door in the side of the room. It stands out because it's made of glass and there's a pad to the right with a digital display of the temperature and humidity inside. Interesting. I've seen this before. A friend at the Bellagio once took me on a tour of the museum archives. Seven must have a special collection of rare artifacts to require such a room.

Curiosity fills me, and I attempt to enter. It's locked but there's a keypad. I think for a minute and then spend some luck to come up with my best guess. I type in the date we met. It doesn't work. I try the day I came back. Locked. My mouth twitches. Gods, I could just ask the man. An hour ago, I had my finger in his ass; I'm sure he'd show me around his special collection. But the gambler in me is obsessed now. I want to break the code. Using a bit more luck, I concentrate, and another date pops into my head, one that holds far less enjoyable connotations. It's the date of the Yule Ball. The date Seven ghosted me and I took out my sorrows in the arms of a human man I never saw again.

The door clicks. Lights turn on automatically with my

movement, and what I see on the shelves inside *confuses* me. Seven isn't preserving archaeology or artwork. I'm surrounded by... charms. For a moment, I feel like I'm back in my parents' store, only the items here are preserved like butterflies under glass. Stacks of wide and thin display drawers are stored inside three large shelves. I slide a drawer out. Acorns composed of all different materials and in a variety of sizes are displayed on blue velvet behind the protective panel. I slide it back into the shelf. The next one exhibits evil eyes and hamsas. I return it to its place. My mouth drops open when I inspect the next display. Horse-shoes, and one of them is blue. That is definitely blue iron.

Frost fills my veins, and I all but shove the drawer into place and then back away from it. My ass bumps another shelf, and I whirl. Something gold catches my eye, and I pull out the second drawer down. Rows of maneki-nekos stare up at me through the window of their box. None of them is exactly like Kiko, but they're all similar. I make out the familiar hint of blue on one of the arms.

What the hell is this? Blue iron is forbidden in Devashire, and these objects thrum with their own power. Seven is collecting good luck charms, some of them ancient, some of them newly minted. I glance down to see a display of gold coins on the bottom shelf similar to the one he'd used in Shadowvale.

This is a strange hobby at best. At worst, it's the sign of a man obsessed with amplifying his power. I stare and stare. Something about all this is bothering me, but I can't quite put it together.

And then the door behind me opens, and Seven is standing there in a pair of black silk pajama bottoms and nothing else. "This isn't the kitchen." His eyes wrinkle at the corners.

"I got lost." I swallow. "What is this, Seven? There's blue iron in here." I shake my head.

He leans a shoulder against the inside of the door. "My mother collected lucky artifacts. Some of these were hers. She got me started when I was young. Leprechauns are born with more luck than any creature on the planet, but luck requires focus and experience. After my father drove you away and my mother left him, I started researching magical objects in earnest. Have you ever wondered how Godmother went from lucky to inherently magical? Some say objects like these amplified her power and then changed it altogether. My mother used objects like these to free herself from my father. I thought I might need to use them one day as well."

What? I knew Seven's mother had divorced his father, but I didn't realize she had escaped his clutches using ancient luck magic. "Where is your mother now, Seven?"

He chuckles. "No one knows. Not even me."

A chill courses through me.

"Oh, she's alive. She sent me a letter a few years back to say she was safe but couldn't risk telling me where she lived. She's using luck to protect herself from discovery." He rubs the back of his neck. "Maybe if she hears that Dad's in Ashgate, she'll come out of hiding."

I turn back toward the case. "The coin you used against the beast in Shadowvale and Yissevel..."

"Protects its bearer from harm. Unfortunately, it doesn't protect anyone else. I had to throw it at Yissevel's eye to distract him from you."

I run my fingers along the maneki-nekos and stare at them longingly. "I had to destroy Kiko to take Chance down."

"Take one."

"Where did you find them? I've never seen them in any of the shops. It's always been a mystery to me where Dark Stranger got Kiko."

"Dark Stranger?" He squeezes his eyes shut for a long blink and laughs. "They don't exist anywhere in Devashire but here, not with the properties you want. I obtained these from Koyasan."

I start to reach for one but stop when his words hit home. "If these lucky cats aren't available in Dragonfly, where did Arden's father get the one he gave me?"

Even though I've never told Seven that Kiko came from Arden's father, he doesn't react to the news, and I stiffen when I see the look on his face. He's suddenly distant, like his mind is somewhere else.

"I looked for you, Sophia. I used every bit of extra luck I had to try to find you. I thought you must be dead or under the protection of another leprechaun because nothing I tried worked. I was amplifying myself with every type of charm I could get my hands on. I searched hours of security footage. I hired investigators."

I'm so confused. If that were true, he should have found me. I'm good but not hide-from-a-leprechaun-who-under-stands-technology good. "That doesn't make sense."

"I didn't understand it until you came home and Godmother helped me put things together."

"What are you talking about?"

"The night of the Yule Ball, my father poisoned me and locked me in that dungeon under the cabin."

"What has that got to do with—"

"My father made a mistake. I recovered from the blue iron faster than he expected and escaped through the window well. Once free, I went directly to Godmother, hoping she'd protect me. When I told her what happened and how much I loved you, she said she'd give me what I wanted in exchange for my promise to work for her. I agreed."

"You struck a bargain with Godmother? Over me?"

"I thought she'd make everything right. I ate what she gave me without another thought."

"Seven?" I wasn't sure where he was going with this story, but I didn't like it.

"I saw you sitting at the bar in Dragonfly. You didn't look like you, but I knew it was you. I could always tell. It's the way you hold your shoulders. There were so many men around you that night. All I wanted to do was explain. But when I spoke to you, I couldn't bring myself to—"

"When did you ever speak to me?"

"You didn't know it was me that night because Godmother had changed my appearance."

"What?" None of this makes sense. I want to say more but all breath has left my lungs.

"She also told me exactly where to find you. Once I spoke to you, I knew I couldn't tell you who I really was. You were so angry with me. So I gave you what you asked for. I comforted you. And I planned to tell you. I planned to explain everything, but I didn't even have school as an excuse to crawl out from under his thumb. My mother left, and my father, angered at the circumstances of my escape and hers, locked everything down to keep me from following her. He assigned a security contingent to me twenty-four seven. I was a prisoner in my own home for weeks. By the time I had any way to see you or get a message to you, you were already gone."

A sob seeps out my tight throat. My heart is pounding.

"I didn't know Arden existed until she called your parents and you returned to Dragonfly. Godmother fed her that brownie with the intention of visualizing what part of her heritage was dominant. Was she more human or more pixie? The magic revealed her origins. I couldn't see it, you couldn't see it, but Godmother did. And when she did, she instantly welcomed Arden into the fold.

"I didn't understand why until the hospital. Oh, I suspected. Anyone would have suspected. The timing seemed to prove what my instincts were telling me, but I hadn't thought it was possible, you understand. There's no history of it. You need proof before you allow yourself to believe something like this, and Godmother was the only one who could give it to me."

He scrubs his face with his hands and runs his fingers through his hair.

"And she waited. She held it over my head like she always does. Godmother waited until the hospital to confirm what I already knew. Deep inside I knew."

"Seven?" my voice comes out as a raspy whisper.

"She warned me to stay away. Everything will be harder, especially now." He paces the small space. "I think she knew I wouldn't keep it from you, and once you knew, Arden would know. And there are expectations, Sophia. There are things I won't be able to control. That's why I tried to stay away, but then *you* came to *me*, and I couldn't turn you away. Not after everything. I won't ever turn you away again."

"Just say it! I need to hear the words." I can't breathe. It's like I've been pulled under water, and I can't get to the surface.

"Don't you see? Everything makes sense when you put it together. I couldn't find you all those years because another leprechaun was protecting you. Her luck made you invisible to me until recently when she changed her mind and wished for something else. A tiny leprechaun with ten fingers and ten toes."

"Seven... Oh gods..."

He looks me in the eye, spine straight, jaw hard as steel, and says the thing that changes everything.

"I'm the man who left you Kiko, Sophia. Arden is mine."

THIRTY-FOUR

A steady throb begins between my temples, and for a long moment I can't speak. All the words have become trapped in my throat. At first I want to deny it. I shake my head and try to think of some way it isn't true. But that thought dissolves as fast as I think of Kiko and what I saw in that room. I don't doubt his story. It all makes sense. The little things about Dark Stranger I was drawn to. The way the night unfolded. If I had been older back then, more experienced, I might have detected the signature of magic on his skin, but I was young. I didn't want to see it that night, even if I could have. Now, looking back, it all fits. Oh gods, bargaining with Seven at his most vulnerable fits Godmother's MO to a tee.

But believing him doesn't do a thing to help ease the overwhelming sense I've been deceived. Seven slept with me under false pretenses and kept it a secret all this time! It's a betrayal that stings. A violation. I can't resist the temptation to lash out.

"Arden is not *yours*," I snap, my face hot with rage.

"She is, Sophia. Godmother confirmed it. She's half leprechaun."

I glare at him, and everything I am feeling must come through as clear as day because he takes a large step back. "You might be her father, but she isn't *yours*. Was it you who fed her in the middle of the night and rocked her back to sleep? Picked her up when she fell and kissed her boo-boos? Did you teach her how to ride a bike and how to stand up to the bullies at school?" I hold up a finger between us. "You might be her father, but she is not *yours*."

His throat bobs on a swallow. "You're right. It was a poor choice of words." Tension thickens the air between us. "I'm sorry this is how you found out. I wish there was an easier way. I should have told you... before. Even before Godmother confirmed it. I just... *couldn't*."

I bury my face in my trembling hands, all my cherished memories of Dark Stranger rushing back to me. Those memories and Kiko—oh gods, she came from Seven!— kept me alive the years I was living on the streets. I try to reconcile everything that happened that night with the man standing in front of me and all that's happened over the last weeks. I have to swallow down the emotion rising in my throat and I sob openly from the effort.

I want to kill him. I want to run into his arms.

"Please forgive me," he rasps. "I was so young. I couldn't say no to you." He rubs my shoulders. "What can I do? How can I make this better?"

"Godmother told you not to tell me, didn't she?" I say through my teeth, lowering my hands to look at him. I know it's true, and I know why.

He takes a deep breath. "She refused to confirm Arden was mine until we solved the case, and threatened to not tell me at all if I confessed that I was the one who was with you that night before then. She said it might interfere with our work. Once we solved the case and she finally told me Arden was my daughter, I came to the hospital to tell you, but she convinced me it would ruin your life and Arden's. She told me if I loved you, I'd stay away from you."

My conversation with her in the hospital comes back to me—the way her eyes twinkled when she'd said there had never been anyone like Arden. She knew. She *knew!* And not only did she not tell me, she used her influence to convince Seven not to. "Godmother never does anything out of the goodness of her heart. There's a reason she didn't want you to tell me, and it isn't to save me or Arden from pain."

"Godmother stores up secrets like currency." He runs a hand down his face. "And this is a powerful secret."

My mood darkens further the more I think about it. Exhaustion and hunger combine to stir my stomach, and I brace myself against the wall.

Seven reaches out slowly, cautiously, his eyes meeting mine in silent question. I give him a barely perceptible nod. "Come to the kitchen. I'll make tea."

I allow him to wrap an arm around my shoulders and usher me out the door. He leads me to a surprisingly cozy kitchen in the otherwise modern penthouse and starts a kettle. The sound of the steam building fills the space. All of what he's told me swirls in my brain, and I feel the seed of an intense and prickly emotion forming deep within me. I repress the urge to cough. "Everything changes now. It has to."

He spoons loose tea into a pot and pours in the boiling water. Reaching above his head, he retrieves two mugs from the cupboard and sets them on the counter. When he speaks again, it's with the confidence and authority of a man who fills out every inch of the suits he wears daily.

"In all likelihood, my father will spend the rest of his life in prison. Evangeline has no children. My mother has cut all ties with the family. As my daughter, Arden is the sole heir to my half of the Delaney fortune. It won't matter that she's part pixie, Sophia. The leprechaun elite will want to meet her. She'll become the most eligible bachelorette in Devashire overnight."

I can't keep my face from betraying my feelings. "You say it like it's a good thing, but they won't want her for her. Those elites are a pack of wolves desperate to bite a piece off of her. She can't even wield luck! They'll eat her alive!"

He presses his lips into a thin line. "She can wield luck. That's what I've been trying to tell you. She's been using her luck all along."

I think back to what he said in his secured room. "You think she protected me when I was living in the US?"

"I *know* she did. And when she called your parents and they needed help getting you back, I just happened to be standing right next to Godmother when she got the call."

I can't believe I didn't see the signs. "But if Arden's fae, why couldn't she pass through the moon gate?"

"The ward keeps out anyone foreign to Devashire. Any fairy born outside the boundaries might have had the same problem until Godmother welcomed them in and they became a citizen of Devashire."

Lifting the mug, I take a sip of tea. It's too hot, and it burns my tongue. I stare at the mug as if it's betrayed me. "She got herself into Bailiwick's, didn't she?"

"She did. I was prepared to help her, but I didn't need to." Seven said something like this before but I discounted it. "She doesn't know she's doing it, Sophia. It's as natural to her as breathing."

I bury my face in my hands. "Oh my gods, Seven! What

are we going to do? All she knows is the human world. She's wanted to be a doctor since she was twelve. Her entire life, we've made decisions based on the assumption she was a US citizen, human, and born on US soil. This means she's not. She's one hundred percent fae. If this comes out, she won't be able to leave Devashire. They'll suspend her passport again."

"She seems happy enough here." His expression is controlled, but I glimpse a spark of hope.

"Because she thinks her stay is temporary. This will crush her."

"Maybe not. I hear she's thriving at Bailiwick's."

I stare down into my tea, my thoughts racing. "Who knows about this, other than us?"

"No one. You, me, and Godmother. That's it."

I take a deep breath and brace myself. "She's still human-passing. That gives her options. We need time to break this to her gently and give her a chance to decide for herself without any pressure from the outside. We can't draw any extra attention to her. No one can suspect the truth until we know for sure what she wants."

He cocks his head. "Unlikely we can avoid scrutiny. We're together now. We kissed in front of a dozen cameras. Tomorrow, our pictures are going to be all over the *Daily Hatter*. Arden's life is about to change no matter what she chooses."

My brows squeeze together and I can't meet his eyes as I say, "Can you stop it? What would it take to undo what we did tonight?"

The sharp rasp of his inhale fills the space between us and he braces himself on the counter. His stare turns cold as ice, but there's something more behind the mask he's slid into place. I see it then, *fear*. The dragon rises, his luck flailing as if he's not exactly in control of it. Pure, concentrated power blows back my hair and all the cabinet doors fall off their hinges at once, rattling as they slam into the floor.

What had he said to me before? *You'd never abandon your daughter.* But what he meant when it came to us is I'd never abandon someone I loved. He showed me his vulnerable underbelly and I just slid a dagger into it.

I leap off my stool and round the counter, reaching for him. The tornado of energy in the room is a force to reckon with. It beats against me like a storm, deafening in its intensity. I try my best to push through it, to get to him. "No, Seven, I didn't mean that! I'm here. I'm here! I'm not going anywhere."

The dragon settles, slithering around me and I rush into him, taking his face in my hands. His gaze softens as he looks at me. "What happened tonight with you, I meant it. I'm yours, okay?"

He releases a shaky breath. "You forgive me?"

I hesitate, searching my heart. This is one thing I won't bluff about. Am I angry? Yes. At him, at me, and at Godmother. Shocked? Undeniably. But sad or disappointed? *No.* I check my emotions again, just to be sure. "Yes," I say. "I forgive you, Seven."

He releases a sigh of relief.

"And there's something else." I meet his eyes and touch my forehead to his, tears coming again. "I'm glad it was you. I'm glad you were my first, and I can't think of a better father for Arden."

"Oh Sophia..." He kisses me desperately. I give him what he needs but then put space between us. "Seven... about what I said before... We need to talk about this."

He pulls me harder against him. "It can wait."

"It can't. I need you to cover up what happened tonight."

He stares down at me, jaw clenching.

"I'm just asking for time before we go public," I say quickly, swallowing the lump in my throat. "To see if this is right for Arden, without... complications. If there's a way she can still have the life she wants, I want to give that to her. If we tell no one and get her into college in the US, she can live a normal human life."

Seven tips his head back and stares at the ceiling. "Until people notice she's not aging."

"We can worry about that fifty years from now." I place my hands flat on his chest. "You don't know what it's like being a pixie here. We are second-class citizens, only eligible to work certain jobs, always struggling to make ends meet, used for our bodies because we've got nothing else to sell."

A growl of frustration rips from his throat. "It won't be like that for her or for you. I'll make sure of it."

I shake my head. "You only say that because you've always had privilege. Everyone knows she's mine, Seven, and the things people say and think about pixies will be hurled at her from day one. Her fellow pixies will distrust her because of her leprechaun blood, and your fellow leprechauns will keep her at arm's length because of her pixie blood. It will be a lonely, bitter life."

"You don't know that."

Everything becomes as clear as day in my mind. "If you act right now, you can use your luck to make sure those pictures of us don't turn out. You can have Evangeline spin this as a PR stunt for the casino. If you stay away from me, people will buy it. And most importantly, Arden will have the time and space she needs to decide. You can teach her about what she is in secret, without interference, without risking her options."

"I just got you back." His voice cracks. "I'm so tired of secrets."

I feel a hot, wet tear roll down my cheek. "I know. I am too. But she leaves for school in the fall. Things will be different then. You know I'm right. The publicity we'll draw as a couple if those pictures are published will put too much scrutiny on her."

"So then we manage that, together."

"Seven, you deceived me—"

"I didn't mean—"

"I know you didn't mean to. I remember how you tried to do the right thing that night. I know how Godmother works, and I can only imagine how she tricked you into that situation."

His gaze shifts away from mine but he doesn't say anything.

"The fact of the matter is that because of how things went down, in the eyes of the law, Arden is human, and it's to her advantage to stay human. Unless and until she chooses something different for herself, I feel we have a responsibility to protect her." I sigh. "If there's one thing playing poker has taught me, it's that there are things you can control and things you can't. Some moves are skill. Others are probability. With luck, we can skew the odds in our favor, but we can never focus on everything. We can never know for sure what power the other players bring to the table. Right now, we have a chance to control this. We have a chance to protect what remains of Arden's childhood and give her choices we never had."

He releases me and rubs his head as if it hurts.

"Help me do this. It's only a matter of months before

she goes to college. After she's gone, we can go public, see where this goes." I regret the choice of words the moment they are out of my mouth.

"See where this goes?" Profound disappointment clouds his eyes, and he holds out his hands to me. "I'm already there, Sophia. I love you. I have always loved you."

"I love you too." The words almost shatter me. I want to give him what he wants, but I can't do it at Arden's expense.

"Then let's not waste any more time," he whispers.

Gods, I never thought it would be me begging Seven to keep our relationship hidden. My entire life has been turned on its head.

"It's four months. Please give her this," I beg. "Give her a choice." When he shakes his head, I add, "You owe me a favor."

He freezes, eyes narrowing.

"I won it fair and square."

"The poker game." He scoffs and runs his fingers through his hair, backing away from me.

"Yes."

Hesitating, he stares at me as if he's pondering every other option. "Fine. But for the record, I hate this. If you think it's right for Arden, I'll do it. I'll do it for you, and I'll do it for her."

"I promise, this is temporary."

He pinches the bridge of his nose, looking as tired as I've ever seen him. "I'll take care of the pictures. Anything I can't do with luck, Evangeline will manage with lawyers and spin."

I nod. "I'll get dressed. You should have your driver take me home. Say I was here to discuss my new position with your company."

Reluctantly, he agrees and I move for the bedroom and my clothes. A strong hand lands on my arm and whirls me into his chest. I don't fight it when his lips crash down on mine. The room spins. Heat claims my mouth as luck rushes over my skin, brushes along my collarbones, tightens the tips of my breasts. His hand presses into the space between my wings, and I arch into him, fluttering, aching with need in a heartbeat. The rush of his luck inside me is a delicious, bubbly purr. I moan and grind against him, needing him in me.

He breaks away and looks at me through his lashes. Cool air rushes between us. Seven closes his eyes, his throat bobbing on a swallow. When he opens them again, the unguarded Seven I've glimpsed is gone, replaced by the public façade he shows everyone else—Mr. Delaney, now chairman of the board of Lucky Enterprises, cool and totally professional. He reaches for his phone. "Ready the car," he says to whoever answers. "I'll text you the address."

Our eyes meet one last time. After a long beat, we both turn and walk in opposite directions.

I'm halfway to the bedroom when a fit of coughing overcomes me and a seed pops out of my mouth and into my waiting hand. It's smooth, red, and heart-shaped. Tears form in my eyes as I stare down at *love* in physical form resting in my palm. I picture it again, that fantasy of mine. A house for Seven and me with a fairy garden, the first one ever planted with a leprechaun. This seed has all the potential to become something beautiful and unique. Something as special as our love.

I find my purse and drop it into the zippered compartment before reaching for my clothes.

Not today, but someday.

*Thank you for reading **LUCKY ME**! I hope you've enjoyed Sophia and Seven's love story as much as I do. Continue the story with the second book in the His Dark Charms duet **LUCKY US**.*

Can Seven and Sophia transcend social pressures to finally be together in the way they've always longed to be? Once Arden learns that Seven is her father, will she choose to stay with her fairy family or pursue her dreams in the human world ? Get answers to these questions along with more leprechaun heat in **LUCKY US**!

Visit https://geni.us/luckymebonus for an exclusive bonus scene

LUCKY US

HIS DARK CHARMS
BOOK TWO

USA TODAY BESTSELLING AUTHOR

GENEVIEVE JACK

BOMBSHELL KISS GIVES LESS BANG THAN EXPECTED

Devashire is once again abuzz with rumors about most eligible bachelor, Seven Delaney. In what is being called the bombshell of all kisses, no less than a dozen fairies have come forward to attest that they saw Seven kissing prodigal daughter Sophia Larkspur through the window of the Victory Building in Elderflame on Tuesday. This reporter has it on good authority the two engaged in a bout of tongue wrestling worthy of an Olympic medal.

Despite the purported heat of this public encounter and the enthusiasm their audience had for capturing it, oddly none of the pictures or videos taken are intelligible. If you are equally puzzled at the plausibility that a glare from the glass should occur at every angle in conjunction with simultaneous equipment malfunctions, then you will understand why I sought out Seven for a statement. Clearly luck was at play.

Although yours truly did not score an audience with the leprechaun, PR spokesperson and sister to the man himself, Evangeline Delaney, offered this:

"Do we have your attention, Devashire? The Dragonfly Casino is pleased to announce that for the first time ever, we will be offering poker lessons to human guests with the potential to expand the program to interested fairies in the future. Beginning later this month, Sophia Larkspur, aka Soho Lane, who made a name for herself as a poker pro while living in the United States, will bring her personal expertise to the table for a fee. Specific session dates and times to be announced. And yes, this partnership was sealed with a kiss!"

There you have it, Hatters! We should have suspected, given the circumstances, that this was a publicity stunt. A public relationship between a leprechaun and a pixie would be shocking, but the unconquerable Seven Delaney choosing a pixie is truly preposterous. Far more logical that the Lucky Enterprises mogul knows how to get your attention!

What do you think about opening poker lessons to fae despite the ban on regular play? Your favorite columnist wants to know. Leave me your comments at DailyHatter.com.

Fairly Goodweather
Columnist

CHAPTER

ONE

Everyone thinks they want a fairy-tale life, but those stories always focus on the wrong things. Cinderella rises above her circumstances when she enchants the prince. No one stops to consider that everything the prince knew about her was a deception. None of it was hers. Not the dress, not the shoes, not the pumpkin carriage. She pulled fictional history's greatest bluff. What happened next? After the wedding in the castle, did she rise to the demands of being a princess? Did the townspeople magically set aside their envy and spite and accept her as a regent? Or did happily ever after come with a dark and dangerous edge? It's possible Cinderella found herself in an equally difficult predicament, simply serving a new master.

I think about that story a lot when I ponder my own situation. Seven and I have known each other since we were children and our love is built on more than just a single night's dancing, but the divide between who he is and who I am couldn't be more complete. And I wonder if we will ever close that gap. Will there ever be a time I don't have to bluff? Will my relationship with Seven ever be accepted as real? I don't know. At the moment, I'm still riding in the pumpkin.

"Tip your head back and to the right, Sophia." Evangeline motions for me to adjust my position and I do, arching over the poker table at an angle that I'm sure makes the best of my figure but is terribly uncomfortable. The elbow I'm braced on prickles as if it's fallen asleep, and I'm starving. I missed lunch because the photographer is in a time crunch. My stomach growls a threat that it might start eating me from the inside.

Still, I smile as the camera shutter releases a series of fast clicks and the photographer, an artsy-looking leprechaun with long silver hair, moves around me. At least my outfit is flattering. With me leaning back like this, the floor-length dress splits midthigh, revealing one gold stiletto and the majority of my right leg. The sparkly red number hugs my waist and gives my breasts a marvelous, strapless boost. There's no room for a bra of any kind. The thing is backless—convenient, considering my wings have to be out for this shoot—but that means my upper half is precariously tucked into a stiff panel of fabric that runs from my sacrum to just above my nipples. Honestly, the fact I'm not spilling out of it is a feat of fashion genius. I'd thank luck or magic, but being fae, I'd feel it if there was any involved. We can sense both even if we can't always see them at work. Alas, my skin does not tingle and my own luck is nestled deep within me, snoring peacefully.

"Okay, darling, turn toward me and look directly at the camera, ankles crossed, both hands on the table on either side of your hips." The photographer squats down, adjusting his lens.

I do as he asks, beaming down at him, but he doesn't take the picture.

"Drop the smile. Look at me like I'm a competitor. I'm the player standing between you and a big win." He makes a few more adjustments while I try to dredge up the right look.

I spent the majority of my sixteen years in the United States supporting myself by playing poker. One of the skills that came with the territory was the ability to hide my actual emotions behind a poker face, the ability to either be unreadable or to telegraph an emotion that is inconsistent with what I'm feeling. The look I give the photographer now is one of supreme confidence and determination. It's an expression meant to intimidate. I'm projecting intensity, telling my opponent that I'm holding cards so good they might as well push their chips into the middle of the table right now. My smile dissolves, but not entirely. I close my lips but keep them slightly upturned at one corner, preserving the tightness in my eyes. When I lower my chin, my dark hair falls over one eye.

"Gods, Sophia," Evangeline says in a low voice. "You look like you're holding the secret to the universe behind your back."

"Maybe I am," I say, sending her a wink.

The photographer stands, studying his screen. "That's it. I think we got it. Thanks, darling. You were a wonderful model." He takes a step forward and kisses me on the cheek, his breath skating over my skin. He's a leprechaun, but up until this point, he's kept his luck to himself. Now I feel it beside me like a large, predatory bird. I give him a nod, and he hurriedly collects his things before kissing Evangeline on both cheeks. "You'll have the comps tomorrow by end of day."

"Thanks, Mac." She brushes her shiny red hair over one shoulder as she watches him leave.

Only a few short weeks ago, I thought the Delaneys hated me, especially Evangeline's brother, Seven. He stood me up at the Yule ball when we were teenagers and humiliated me in front of everyone in Dragonfly Hollow. Turns out Seven didn't want to hurt me at all. He was a victim of his psycho father, Chance, who'd poisoned him with blue iron —the only substance in the world capable of draining a fairy's luck—and kept him locked in a dungeon beneath his hunting cabin.

Weirder still, it turns out Seven is Arden's father. That little revelation is thanks to some serious magical interference by Godmother. I still don't completely understand her motives, but I do know this: Seven and I deserve to make up for lost time. Unfortunately, until we have a chance to tell Arden about her unlikely origins, we've decided to keep our relationship a secret. We want to give her choices. We want to give her a chance to control the narrative about her own life.

Seven's responsible for getting me this job teaching poker, and his sister, Evangeline, the head of public relations for Lucky Enterprises, is leaning into the moment. This photo shoot is just the start. I have interviews with all the major news outlets in Devashire scheduled over the next two weeks, at the end of which I'll be teaching my very first class.

"You did a great job today." Evangeline hits me with one of her ten-thousand-watt smiles. Just like her brother, she's supermodel attractive, the kind of person who walks into the room and turns every head. She's tall, thin, and radiates confidence. But then that's what being a leprechaun does for you. Leprechauns are always beautiful. Their luck seeps out of their pores.

"Thanks. I'm not used to being photographed. I hope Mac can get what he needs from what we did today."

She laughs. "Are you kidding me? Sophia, I don't think you realize how lovely you are."

"For a pixie," I add in for her.

"For anyone. If it weren't for the wings, I'd swear you were a leprechaun. I think living among humans was good for you." She shakes her head. "That look in your eyes. I've never seen a pixie look like that. You're a badass. And if people knew what you really did for Devashire, they'd treat you like one."

What I did was help take down her father and prove he was imprisoning pixies in his rural sex dungeon. He also murdered a few people for reasons that only he and maybe Godmother fully understand. Together, Seven and I proved Chance was guilty of murder. He's now serving a life sentence in Ashgate Prison.

I try not to think too much about the night we took him down. It still shakes me. I'm not sure if what Eva says is true—if Devashire society knew, would they respect me more? It's a moot point. Godmother took credit for solving the case, and the only people who know my part in it are Seven, Eva, and my friends River and Penelope, all of whom have been sworn to secrecy. One does not challenge Godmother's narrative of events. Not unless one wants to have one's wings broken.

I glance down at my toes. My stomach growls loud enough that I'm sure Eva hears it. "Uh, thanks. Are we done for the day?"

She laughs. "No, I want to introduce you to some high

rollers. But go ahead and take a break. It sounds like you need one. Eat and get changed into something more comfortable, then meet me in my office."

I open my mouth to say okay, but the word never leaves my lips. My breath hitches when the buzz of Seven's luck skates across the back of my neck, over my shoulder, and between my breasts. My nipples tighten at the feel of it, and I have to draw a breath to steady myself. The tingle of it causes the tiny hairs on my arms to stand on end, and everything inside me takes on an electrical charge.

Evangeline's lips quirk into an impish grin. There is no way she can't sense that. "In my office by four, Sophia," she singsongs before striding out the door without looking back.

I adjust my dress and smooth my hair, suddenly filled with a different type of hunger. My heels click on the hardwood floors of the new poker room as I push my way through the gold-plated doors and into the foyer of the Dragonfly Casino. My steps falter when I see Seven standing in front of a poster advertising the latest Cirque du Soleil production going on in the theater.

My very own personal Prince Charming.

His back is to me, which means I have a moment to observe him as my inner world goes topsy-turvy with attraction. The soft shine of his toffee-colored hair picks up the gold reflected off the shiny surfaces in the room and contrasts perfectly with his dark suit, specially tailored to make the most of his broad shoulders. His jacket skims down to his hips in a perfect taper, both professional and somehow sensual, as if the material loves to touch him as much as I do. His long legs end in polished Italian-leather loafers.

As quietly as I can, I sidle up to him, leaving a few feet of space between us. Nothing to see here. Just two people who happen to be reading the same poster at the same time.

"That dress should be illegal," he whispers, his head still tilted as if he's studying the picture of the aerial act in front of him. "I take that back. It should be perfectly legal in the privacy of my bedroom. Outside of it, I'd prefer you wrapped in a hooded cloak."

I lick my bottom lip. "So sad. This dress, with me in it, is about to be plastered all over social media to promote the new poker classes. Evangeline picked it out."

A growl rumbles from his chest. "Is there no justice in this world? If she must flaunt you for all to see, shouldn't I, at least, be the first to enjoy you in it, to touch you beneath the material, to... help you out of it?"

My lips twitch. "Who are you to claim first dibs?"

Only his eyes move, but I see him glance in my direction, his emerald gaze twinkling with his regard. "The one who loves you."

He's said it to me before, but hearing it now still sends a thrill through me and makes my heart thump in my chest. I know what he wants to hear. There is one thing that Seven needs from me more than anything else, the thing I've learned holds his pieces together.

"Be the first then. I'm *yours*, after all. Do with me as you wish." Aside from his sister, I am the one person in his life who knows him, his true heart, and knowing that I accept him, that I want to be his and want him to be mine is a balm to the wounds his neglectful parents left behind.

His throat bobs on a hard swallow, and his chest rises and falls at a faster rate. "Come."

His luck coils around me, nudging me to follow him as he turns and strides through an unmarked door near the banquet hall. I check over both shoulders. No one is watching. Of course not. Not with him concentrating his luck to make sure we're alone.

I duck inside.

Seven's arm circles my waist, and he pulls me against his chest in the darkness. I hear the lock slide into place, and then the light clicks on. We're in some kind of utility room, surrounded by shelves of tablecloths, aprons, and cloth napkins. At the back is a stack of folding tables.

I pivot in his arms to face him. "Classy digs, Seven, but I was hoping for a gas station bathroom."

He gives one breathy laugh, but the heat in his eyes shows me he isn't in a comedic mood. His expression is ravenous, predatory, *feral*.

"Are you done modeling for photos today?" he asks, deep and low.

"Yes." My voice comes out in a squeak, my throat tight from the intensity he's putting off.

The smile he gives me is positively wolfish. "Good."

Luck slams into me like an ocean wave I didn't see coming. Someone has popped the cork on a bottle of champagne and bubbles rush between my legs, through my torso, and to the tips of my breasts. Electric fizz tingles in my blood. My knees wobble but he has me, one hand between my wings and the other in my hair.

When his lips crash down on mine, it isn't gentle. He's claiming me with a desperation that tells me exactly how Seven feels about our clandestine circumstances. Leprechauns aren't used to being denied what they want, and he wants me. All of me.

I melt into him, opening wider for him, his tongue stroking expertly against mine. His thumb braces under my jaw, his fingers wrapped firmly around the base of my skull. The way he's gripping me is almost painful. Almost.

Instead, it makes me feel secure. Safe. And completely turned on.

He shifts me back to the tables and lifts me as if I weigh nothing, perching my bottom on the top of the stack. My dress shifts. Despite hours of staying in place no matter which way I moved, my breasts spill out of the top. He catches one in his mouth, sucking hard. I have to flutter my wings to stay balanced in this position, and I dig my fingers into his hair to steady myself.

"You are so beautiful." Emerald-green eyes flash in the dim room, and he smiles wickedly at me, breath skating across my nipple. "I saw that photographer kiss you."

"You were watching me?" Not surprising really. Security cameras record every corner of the casino.

"Only at the end. I wanted to check if you were done."

"Did it bother you when he kissed me on the cheek?"

He laughs darkly. "Only because I have no way of marking you as mine. I wanted to throw open the doors to that room and make it clear as day that you're spoken for. Instead, I'll have to settle for reminding you of the same."

"How do you plan to do that?" I ask breathlessly.

His hands work under the skirt of my dress, bunching the shiny material around my hips. Adroit fingers hook into the sides of my panties and slide them down my legs. Once they're off, he brings them to his nose and inhales. My blood heats at the sight, and my breath comes in pants. He slips them into his pocket, then plants his hands on my inner thighs and shoves them apart, exposing me.

"Seven," I gasp.

He lowers himself to his knees in front of me and licks up my center with the flat of his tongue.

My cheeks heat. I arch against his mouth, and he flicks and circles my clit before plunging his tongue inside me.

His luck follows, filling me with a rush of effervescence that presses against my inner walls even as he worships every inch of pleasure-inducing skin between my thighs. I can't form words.

It takes an embarrassingly short amount of time for my head to tip back in a silent scream of overwhelming pleasure. I'm still blinded by the light of the first orgasm when he rises, hooking one of my legs over his shoulder, and enters me fast and hard, sending me over the edge again.

"Oh. Gods. Sev. En." He's thrusting so hard it feels like my teeth might clack together. The only thing I want is for him to thrust harder, to hold me tighter. I want him so close I can smell him on my skin days from now when we have to be apart.

He grips my hips, his face buried in my neck as he pounds into me until he finds his release, tremors of ecstasy rippling through him in my arms. We're as close as two people can get, all my limbs wrapped tight around him, and I hold him to me.

He runs his nose from my jaw to my ear. "I love you, Sophia."

"I love you too."

Drawing back, he returns my panties and helps me fix my dress, which thanks to his luck hasn't ripped or sustained a single wrinkle, then zips his pants and takes a seat next to me on the tables. Leaning against the wall, he pulls me against his side. I make myself comfortable.

"So tonight's the night," he says.

"Yeah. It took some doing, but my grandmother is playing bridge in Sunnyville, my parents have a date planned, and Arden isn't babysitting for Penelope. We'll have the house and her all to ourselves for at least two hours."

It's taken a few days for me to arrange everything, but it's important to both of us that Arden be the first to know that Seven is her father and that she is the only pixie/leprechaun hybrid in existence. What a heavy hammer to be dropped on her. She's lived her entire life believing she's half-human. She believes it because I believed it, thanks to Godmother's trickery. But it's time she knows the truth. She deserves to know.

"When should I come?"

"Six should be safe."

He nods.

I tip my head back until it clunks against the wall behind me. "I hope she doesn't hate me."

"If she hates anyone, it will be me. You couldn't tell Arden what you didn't know, and I'm going to make sure she understands that."

"You're putting a lot of trust in a teenager to have a logical response to this situation."

He frowns. "Admittedly, I don't have much experience with teenagers. When Evangeline was her age, I was just two years older and still a teenager myself."

I groan. "Let me fill you in on raising teenagers. Arden is an exceptionally responsible, levelheaded, and remarkable young woman with the potential to turn into a hormonal, irrational beast when pushed beyond her limits. It doesn't happen often, but it does happen."

He strokes the back of my head. "Whatever happens, however she reacts, it will be okay." His voice is soft. "We're in this together. I'll do whatever it takes to protect both of you. I promise."

Is that my heart or a warm pat of butter sliding down my ribs? "I know you will."

A shadow passes through his expression, and he

glances away from me. "You know it's a lie though. If I was willing to do anything, I'd stay away from both of you. You'd be safer and happier."

I grab his chin and turn his face toward me. "Safe is overrated, and I couldn't be any happier than this."

He sighs and kisses me before glancing at his watch. "I'm fifteen minutes late for a meeting."

"You'd better get going then." I scamper off the stack of tables.

"Before I do, there's something I want you to have."

"Hmm?" I straighten my dress.

He reaches into his pocket and pulls out a necklace with a coin dangling from the end. I recognize it as one from his collection of charms, the magical objects he keeps in a hermetically sealed room in his office. He once brought a coin just like this with us to Shadowvale and used it to distract Yissevel the bone fairy so that I could escape the unseelie's clutches. It's gold with the imprint of a goddess on one side and a dragonfly on the other, and he's mounted it on a matching chain.

"I want you to wear this."

"Why?" I ask hesitantly.

"Because it protects its wearer from harm and because it will make the man who loves you happy you're wearing his gift," he says around a half smile.

"Who could say no to that?" I pivot, moving my hair aside so he can fasten the chain around my neck. The coin rests just below the hollow of my throat. "Thank you."

In response, he kisses me just below my ear. "One day this will all be easier."

I smooth my hair and check my makeup in the bottom of a silver tray, but like everything else, it's fine. Seven's luck has kept every one of my hairs in place.

I replace the tray and turn in his arms. "I'm not sure it will ever be easier exactly." He frowns, and I continue. "But it will be worth it. I know it will be worth it."

His usual lopsided grin comes back in full force. "See you tonight."

Acknowledgments

What makes us lucky? Is it love? Family? Privilege? Can we ever know how lucky we are until we lose everything? Is it possible we are luckier than we believe ourselves to be?

LUCKY ME has been brewing in my story cauldron for a number of years. I'd never read a leprechaun romance or one with a magic system based on luck. In fact, the idea for this book was ridiculous for many reasons. But I couldn't leave it alone. Sophia and Seven kept nagging at me, demanding their story be told.

As this story comes to a close, I feel very lucky to be surrounded by people who helped make this book possible. First, authors Sloane Caldwell and Kate Bateman, you both helped me with a few particularly difficult scenes in ways that would make me choose you first in any escape room situation. I am seriously indebted to both of you for your help and honest critique. Authors Sara Whitney and Nadine Mutas, thank you as well for your guidance and support with this story in its early stages. Your encouragement kept me going.

Editor Angela James, thank you for the developmental and line editing you contributed to this manuscript. Your insight is much appreciated, and I hope your care with this story shows. And finally, a big thank you to Linda and Crystalle from Victory Editing for proofreading . These days, it takes a village to bring a book into the world, and this one was no exception.

And finally, thank you to all the readers who gave this one a chance. It might not be what you're used to, but I hope you enjoyed the journey. Lucky you, it's not over!

MEET GENEVIEVE JACK

USA Today bestselling and multi-award winning author Genevieve Jack writes wild, witty, and wicked-hot paranormal romance and romantic fantasy. She believes there's magic in every breath we take and probably something supernatural living in most dark basements. You can summon her with coffee, wine, and books, but she sticks around for dogs and chocolate. Her novels feature badass heroines, fiercely loyal heroes, and fantasy elements that will fill you with wonder. Learn more at Genevieve Jack.com.

Do you know Jack? Keep in touch to stay in the know about new releases, sales, and giveaways.

Join my VIP reader group
Sign up for my newsletter

facebook.com/AuthorGenevieveJack

instagram.com/authorgenevievejack

bookbub.com/authors/genevieve-jack

tiktok.com/@Genevievejackbooks

x.com/genevieve_jack

MORE FROM GENEVIEVE JACK!

His Dark Charms Duet

Lucky Me

Lucky Us

The Treasure of Paragon

The Dragon of New Orleans, Book 1

Windy City Dragon, Book 2,

Manhattan Dragon, Book 3

The Dragon of Sedona, Book 4

The Dragon of Cecil Court, Book 5

Highland Dragon, Book 6

Hidden Dragon, Book 7

The Dragons of Paragon, Book 8

The Last Dragon, Book 9

The Angel of Paragon, Book 10

The Three Sisters Trilogy

The Tanglewood Witches

Tanglewood Magic

Tanglewood Legacy

Knight Games

The Ghost and The Graveyard, Book 1

Kick the Candle, Book 2

Queen of the Hill, Book 3

Mother May I, Book 4

A Game of Hearts

The Wolves of Fireborn Pack Trilogy

Fated Bonds

Feral Instincts

Forever Mated